Things I Couldn't Explain

Things We Couldn't Explain

Betsy Tobin

Published by Accent Press Ltd 2014

ISBN: 9781783753086

By The Same Author

Novels
Bone House
The Bounce
Ice Land
Crimson China

Short Fiction
The Clockmaster
Joyride

This book is dedicated to Mickey Tobin,
whose history at least partially inspired it.

And to the Bexley High School Class of '79.

'You have hidden these things from the wise and learned,
and revealed them to little children.'

Matthew 11:25

Ethan

I used to think this was just an ordinary town. That was before strange things started happening here, things we couldn't explain. This is my home now, even though I've only spent a tiny portion of my life here. Sometimes a place works on you – it creeps inside and takes root and won't let go. And I guess that's what happened to me in Jericho. Because the stranger things get here, the more I want to stay.

According to my Latin teacher the city we're named after is one of the oldest in the world. He said that in ancient times Jericho was an oasis in the middle of the desert: a place of swaying palm trees and natural springs and fragrant orange groves, where people worshipped the moon. Mark Antony gave the oasis to Cleopatra, who claimed that the perfume from its persimmons drove men wild. But in the end the city was doomed. Mark Antony and Cleopatra both committed suicide, and Jericho was sold to Herod, a madman who murdered his own family. Later, it became the scene of one of the bloodiest battles in the Old Testament. When Joshua marched his army into Jericho, he told his men that nothing should be spared, not even the livestock. I've always wondered how a goat could be implicated in a holy war. Didn't anyone stop to question the wisdom of slaughtering animals? But faith is blind. I know that now, even if I didn't before.

The people who settled this town in the early eighteenth century were German Lutherans who came across the Allegheny Mountains by horse and cart. Later they were followed by Methodists, Baptists, Episcopalians, Catholics, Congregationalists, Presbyterians, and, last but not least, Jehovah's Witnesses. You wouldn't think a small town like this one could stretch to hold so many branches of one faith. You'd also be forgiven for wondering why each group insisted on worshipping their own version of the same God, but then Christians have never been much for compromise. I guess the first settlers chose the name because it was holy, or maybe they thought it was poetic – either way they decided to ignore its history. Maybe my family should have realised that a town with such an illustrious namesake might mean trouble. But if I hadn't moved to Jericho, I never would have met Annemarie. So I guess I have God to thank for that miracle. Or maybe I should thank the moon.

Annemarie

I was born sighted. In fact, the world was mine for more than five years. Sometimes I think I stored up a lifetime of pictures over that time, an endlessly revolving kaleidoscope of images that I will never get through, no matter how many times I turn them round and round in my mind. Ethan is convinced my world is brighter than his. He's decided that the world in my head is like some kind of pop-up greeting card: bigger, better, and more vibrant. But at the same time, not quite real.

Are my colours more dazzling than his? Maybe. I guess we'll never know. That suits me fine though. I have a new plan for living, especially after the events of the past few months – sort of my own personal gospel. The idea I live by now is ambiguity. I love the sound of this word, the way all five syllables come crashing together to form a kind of vague suggestion. But even more I like what it means. 'Cause we'll never really know for certain what happened to me – whether it was God or the Virgin Mary or a crazy dance of my chromosomes. I can live with ambiguity, because it doesn't try to trap me with conviction. These days, what I really can't deal with is other people's certainty. I guess, when it comes down to it, I choose darkness over light.

The world's been dark since I was five. I remember listening to Dr Paulson tell my mother that children adapt more easily to blindness than adults do. He said I was lucky to have been sighted for so long – that my mind would quickly learn to fill in the gaps. Looking back, I think it took me two years. By the time I was seven, I was rewired. It's true what they say about your senses: that when one is switched off, the others glow more brightly. Though I couldn't see, I grew more observant. I sensed things others didn't, and asked questions. People were tolerant – after all, I was an unlucky child whose genes had been blighted by some mysterious force before my birth. So they indulged me, and told me things they shouldn't. I learned to listen carefully, and to remember. Often it was the silences that told me most.

When I was ten I asked Dr Paulson to explain the reasons for my blindness. He hesitated, breathing hard through his nostrils, and I could sense his mind groping towards an answer. Finally he said that vision was like a lightning storm behind the eyes; except in my case, he explained, the storm was misfiring. Instead of sending millions of flashes from my eye to my brain, the nerves were flaring off into darkness, like tiny shooting stars that fade before they land. But when I asked him why my nerves had lost their way, he paused uneasily then told me that God had deemed it so.

'God wants me to be blind?' I asked.

'God had a purpose when he took away your sight,' he said evasively.

'What purpose?'

He coughed, and I had the sudden image of a small mongrel dog crouched nervously at his feet. 'That's for you to discover. In time.' He rose, anxious to be free of me, and I listened as both he and the dog left the room.

Dr Paulson's words stayed with me. After that day I saw my blindness not as a punishment, nor as an affliction, but as a mystery that could be solved in an infinite number of ways. I still haven't discovered why God made me blind, but I've found out other things. Maybe that's why I don't mind going to church and listening to sermons. Even though they claim to preach the truth, we all know that, deep down inside, religion is just one big leap of faith. Cora Lynn says God made me blind because He knew I wouldn't fail at it, like it was some sort of test of endurance or flexibility. I reckon she would know, since she's the closest thing I've got to a sister, on account of the fact that her mama helped look after me when I was small, and we've played together since we were babies. After I lost my sight, Cora Lynn made me tie a bandana around her eyes every time she came round to play, so that we could be even. But it wasn't because she felt sorry for me, it was because she was jealous: blindness made me special, and Cora Lynn wanted a piece of it. It was her idea when we were eight years old that we should stuff our ears with Ada's cotton balls and pretend we were Helen Keller, until one day Mama found us groping our way around the neighbourhood, completely deaf and blind, and went ballistic. These days when she comes around to visit, Cora Lynn sometimes puts the blindfold on again for old time's sake. 'Blindness is gonna be your ticket out of this town, Annemarie,' she always says. ''Cause it's what makes you divine.'

Apart from Cora Lynn, I spend most of my time with Ethan. He moved in next door a few years ago and after about six months started tutoring me in math. Ethan is in love with me – I don't need vision to see that. His longing has got so powerful I can taste it when he stands too close. Which he does a lot, lately. Sometimes we're like two magnets, pulling towards each other. Then just at the last moment, one of us flips and suddenly we're repelled. Just like that. I keep wondering why that happens. Is it God doing that? And what does He care about two seventeen year olds anyway? Even if one of them is blind.

And pregnant. I can't believe I'm saying those words. But they did the tests and I am well and truly with child. Which is pretty peculiar, considering I'm a virgin. Spiteful even. I wonder if the Virgin Mary felt this way? Dr Paulson says it could be possible. Sort of. He says that, medically, a woman might be able to conceive without a man. But it doesn't happen very often. 'Like every few millennia?' I asked. He didn't answer. In fact, he seemed a bit hazy on the details. Not to put too fine a point on it, Dr Paulson isn't exactly a rocket scientist. I reckon he scraped through some Podunk medical school, then came back to practise in Jericho because it's the only place that would have him. When I asked him for specifics he mumbled something about X chromosomes and cystic tumours and said he'd get back to me. In the meantime, there's a team of geneticists from Park Shore Hospital who've decided that I'm some sort of medical phenomenon. And the local parish has launched its own investigation. If there's going to be a miracle around here, you can be sure the Church wants a piece of it.

That's why I decided to make this recording. Ethan calls it a diary, but I'm calling it my official version of events. Because I can already tell this story is going to spin like a pinwheel in a hurricane, with me right at the centre, stuck fast. Anyway, I feel more comfortable saying things out loud than committing them to paper. The State of Ohio bought me a Braille typewriter last year, but there isn't much point in using it as no one can read what I've written afterwards. Most of the time it just sits in the corner of my bedroom watching me. Ethan gave me this tape recorder for Christmas. It's got four buttons: start, stop, rewind, and play, a microphone in

6

one end and a tiny speaker in the other. So I can listen to what I've said and redo it if I haven't got it right. I know he's desperate to hear what's on the tapes. But there's got to be a part of me he doesn't see. I mean, he's got all the advantages, being sighted. He can come and go when he pleases, can watch me from his house whenever he likes. I know he does that, can sense it somehow. Sometimes I go to my window at night and wave at him. The first time he rang me up afterwards and asked me how I knew. Now he doesn't bother.

I don't know how I know, but I do – that and a whole lot of other things I shouldn't. Cora Lynn says that when God took away my vision he replaced it with second sight. But I think maybe it's in my blood. My grandmother used to talk to dead people, only she called them angels. When I was a little girl, she used to say, 'Move over, your angel wants to sit beside you.' I did as I was told, scooted over to make room, because I loved her and wanted to believe. But it wasn't easy, because her angels were quick to judge. When I'd ask for another slice of cake she'd frown and say, 'Your angel's shaking her head.' Towards the end she lost her marbles and Mama had to put her in a home. She died when I was six – about a year after I became blind. I don't think she ever realised I'd lost my sight. Though maybe her angels did.

But the real story started almost four weeks ago, back in early June. One night a big storm rolled in, about an hour after I'd gone to bed. It was what Deacon Joe calls a humdinger – which is to say, the worst we'd had in years. There was no way I could sleep through it. The storm must have passed right through Jericho, because I could see the lightning flash behind my eyes and feel the thunderclaps deep inside my chest. I lay there and listened to it rage around us, until it eventually moved off and became nothing more than a grumble on the horizon. When it was finally over the silence was eerie, as if the lightning had swept away everything in its path. I was nearly asleep when suddenly I felt a presence in my room, as if someone was standing at the foot of my bed, and a small stir of air. I sat up, my heart racing, and instinctively pulled the covers up to my neck. 'Who's there?' I called out. My voice seemed to flit around the room like a sparrow. I waited, hardly daring to breathe, but after a few moments the presence faded and disappeared. Afterwards, I wondered if I'd dreamed it.

I fell asleep, but when I woke the next morning I knew that something wasn't right. My belly felt like it was on fire – like someone had literally lit a torch in my womb. At first I thought maybe it was heartburn, and I remember crying out, then reaching for the bottle of water I always keep beside my bed and knocking it to the floor. I scrambled around on my hands and knees, and when I finally found it I drank the whole thing in one go – just trying to douse the flames. Eventually I calmed down, took some deep breaths, and the heat started to subside. I got up feeling rattled and decided the lightning must have touched my head. I dressed and forced down some toast, though my stomach was sliding around. Ethan was meant to be working at the gas station that day and, since I didn't have much else to do, I decided to walk round. In truth, I just wanted to hear his voice. But God had other ideas.

When I got to the garage, I could hear someone in the back of the workshop banging on metal, so I wandered over to the doorway and stopped. All at once, the smell of oil made me woozy. I put a hand out to steady myself on the doorframe. 'Gabe, is that you?' I called out.

'Hey Annemarie.' His voice floated over from the far side of the garage.

'Where are you? Sounds like you're inside a box.'

'I'm over here under this chassis. Just trying to fix an oil leak. Boss reckons it's the carburettor, but I got a hunch it's back here somewhere.' I heard him fiddle with some tools for a moment. 'Yep, found it,' he said. 'Just where I thought it would be.'

'Gabe, is Ethan working today?'

'He went over to Youngstown to pick up some spare parts. He should be back soon.'

'OK. Mind if I wait?'

'Sure. Nice to have some human company for a change.'

I smiled. I'd always had a soft spot for Gabe. I listened to him fiddle with the engine for another minute. 'Gabe, how'd you ever learn so much about cars?'

'I don't know. It's in my blood, I guess. I've always been good at fixing stuff.' I heard him slide out from under the car and rummage around in a box of tools, before disappearing beneath the car again. 'Engines aren't so hard, Annemarie. If you listen close enough, they'll tell you what's wrong.'

'I guess so.'

'Gabe Junior used to talk to 'em. He reckoned cars had feelings, just like we do. And that you had to sweet-talk 'em if you wanted them to behave.'

Gabe Junior died in a car accident when he was nine. One day he chased a ball into the road and got hit by a speeding BMW driven by a lawyer from Shaker Heights. The lawyer had been doing 50 in a 35mph zone, but he still managed to argue that Gabe Junior shouldn't have been playing with a ball so close to the road. The lawyer ended up with a fine and a suspended sentence, while Gabe and his wife Shona lost their only child. It could have happened to anyone, I guess, but it struck me as especially sad that it was Gabe Junior.

'Did you ever think about giving up cars and doing something different?' I asked.

'Yeah, I thought about it. Especially after the accident.

But cars are what I know best.' He was silent for a minute. 'Besides, it's not the cars that are to blame, it's the people who drive them.'

'Yeah, I guess you're right.'

'Anyways Gabe Junior loved cars. I reckon he would have made a fine mechanic one day. Every night I stop by his grave on the way home from work and tell him so.'

'Gabe, did you and Shona ever think about having another child?' I asked. 'You know, after Gabe Junior died?' I heard him fiddle around in the toolbox some more, and for a moment I thought he wasn't going to answer.

'When Gabe Junior was born, Shona got a bad infection,' he said finally. 'Afterwards, the doctors said she couldn't conceive again.'

'Oh. I'm sorry.'

'That's OK. It was a long time ago now. Shona and I still count our blessings that we had nine years with Gabe Junior. That's more than some folks get.'

'Yeah, I guess so,' I said.

He came out from under the car again and walked over to me. 'You feeling all right, Annemarie? You look a little peaky.'

'Guess I woke up on the wrong side of bed. And the oil smell isn't helping, I gotta admit.'

'You wanna sit down?' He pulled up a chair and helped me into it. As soon as I did, I felt nauseous and tipped my head between my knees.

'Gabe? I might need a bucket,' I said, upside-down.

'Oh, jeez.' He grabbed a bucket and thrust it into my hands, and I retched into it. After a moment, I sat back and lowered the bucket. I heard him take it and rinse it out at the tap in the corner.

'I'm really sorry,' I said weakly.

'You OK now? Here, take this.' He handed me a wad of

wet paper towel and I wiped my face with it.

'Yeah. I'm a bit better.'

'You want a glass of water?'

'Actually I think I need to eat something. You got any food?'

'I got some peanut butter crackers.'

'They'll do.' I heard him rustle in a drawer and after a minute he put a packet of peanut butter crackers in my hands. I tore it open and stuffed one in my mouth. It tasted of heaven.

'Wow, Annemarie. Looks like you needed that.'

'Sorry,' I said, my mouth full.

'No problem. When Shona was pregnant, she couldn't get enough of those. Better watch it though. Shona put on thirty pounds during her first trimester. She looked like a warehouse by the end. But I doubt that'll happen to you, being so slight and all.'

I stopped chewing and swallowed a lump of cracker. 'Gabe, I'm not pregnant,' I said, my heart starting to rev like one of his engines.

'Oh.' He hesitated, and I could sense his confusion. 'Sorry, Annemarie. I just assumed ...' His voice trailed off.

'That's OK.'

'It's just that you got that *look*.'

'What look?'

'Kind of shiny-haired and big-eyed, like you're sucking up air for two. Horses get it. And cows too. You know, in the spring.'

It isn't possible, I thought desperately. But a part of me already knew.

I didn't tell anyone at first. Not Cora Lynn, or even Ethan. I waited, and the following week I missed a period. By that point I wasn't exactly reconciled, but a part of me wasn't completely surprised. My life had never conformed to the rules, and this struck me as another instance of it veering off on a crazy detour that no one else was required to take. I figured I would have to tell someone soon, but I wasn't quite sure who to tell or even what to say. It wasn't a straightforward story – everyone except Ethan would assume he was the father. And I suppose I could have let them. But the thing is, I was raised on the Ten Commandments – they're part of who I am and lying isn't. So the problem was how to tell the truth. But truth's a slippery thing sometimes. And I had a feeling it might wriggle away from me if I wasn't careful. The truth is I was, and still am, a virgin. I realise that sounds suspicious, but you'll have to take my word for it. And Ethan's. Lord knows, we wanted to change that. We've been hovering round each other these past six months like flies to a cowpat. But something kept us apart. Ethan always said it was guilt, but now I think it was something else: some sort of intervention.

I decided to tell him first, but of course he got angry and accused me of two-timing. 'With who?' I asked. 'Deacon Joe?!' Deacon Joe is my step-uncle and he's the last person on the planet I would sleep with. Ethan knows this, but I could still feel him frowning – like a stubborn child who refuses to come out to play. 'Ethan,' I said, taking his hand, 'outside of school times, I am with you nearly every waking moment. When could I possibly sleep with someone else?'

'Annemarie, you can't conceive a baby without sex.'

'We don't *know* that,' I said. 'It might be possible. And anyway it's a bit of a moot point. 'Cause it's happened.'

'Have you been to a doctor?'

'You're the first person I've told.'

'Then how can you be sure?'

'I can't explain how. I just am.'

Ethan sighed. 'Look, even if I believe you, no one else will,' he said.

'Maybe not, but I guess we'll find out.'

'We should have done it months ago,' he said glumly.

'Don't you see?' I said. 'We weren't meant to. This is what has kept us apart. I don't know how, but it did. It was there all the time, waiting inside me.'

'Like a time bomb,' he said miserably.

'I think you're confusing creation with destruction.'

'If you say so.'

'Look, this might make things difficult for a while.'

'Like decades?' he asked.

'I'm just saying, things will probably get worse before they get better,' I warned, thinking of Mama and Deacon Joe. Ethan hesitated for a long moment.

'Annemarie,' he said finally. 'How could things possibly get worse?'

But once again, I knew. When I was a little girl I always identified with Miriam, child prophetess and rebellious older sister of Moses. When Miriam was seven she dreamed that her mother would give birth to a son who would one day lead the Jews out of Egypt. She persuaded her parents to defy the Pharoah's orders, and when the infant Moses was born they did not throw him in the river as commanded, but kept him hidden until the day his desperate mother placed him in a basket and left him in the bulrushes by the Nile. But it was Miriam who hid nearby to ensure that her prophecy would come true, and when the Pharoah's daughter stumbled upon the basket, it was Miriam who leaped out of the reeds and offered to find her a Hebrew wet nurse – thus contriving to reunite Moses with his mother. Even though Miriam was blessed with the power of a seer, she knew when to take matters into her own hands. She was stubborn, cunning, and resourceful, and I decided that in the coming months I would have to be the same.

So the following Sunday evening I gathered them all together to break the news. We sat at the kitchen table – Ethan and I on one side, Mama, Ada and Deacon Joe on the other – and I felt like I was guest of honour at a war council. When I told them I thought I was pregnant, for an instant the room went eerily silent. Then I heard Deacon Joe's chair creak ominously as he leaned forward. 'You!' he snarled in Ethan's direction. 'Math, my ass!'

'Joe!' cried Ada.

'Ethan's not the father,' I said quickly.

'Honey, what are you saying?' Ada asked tentatively.

'If Ethan isn't the father, then who is?' demanded Deacon Joe.

'No one.'

'Annemarie, you are beginning to try our patience,' he said irritably. 'May I remind you of the ninth commandment?'

'Thou shalt not bear false witness,' I said.

'Precisely,' he said. 'Satan is the father of all lies.'

'This is not a falsehood,' I said. 'I swear it.' Deacon Joe took a deep breath and exhaled through his nostrils, and I could almost see them flaring. I turned towards Mama, desperate to know what she was thinking. So far she hadn't said a word, and I knew from experience that Mama's silence could be far worse than Deacon Joe's spoken condemnation.

'Annemarie,' Mama finally said in a flat voice, 'do you honestly think we're that stupid?' The air between us almost crackled with hostility.

'Mama, I do not think you're stupid. I swear to you, it's the truth.'

'Honey, lies are like snakes,' said Ada anxiously. 'They'll turn and bite you at the first opportunity.'

'I'm not lying,' I insisted. 'I don't know how it happened, but it did.'

'Annemarie, what exactly are you saying? That you conceived a baby all by yourself?' asked Deacon Joe.

'Yes,' I said. For a long moment no one said a word.

'I think we're done here,' said Mama.

Ethan was right. Despite all my protestations, they refused to believe me. In the end we had to call an arbitrary halt to the discussion, with the resolution that Mama would ring the doctor's office first thing in the morning. Before we got up Deacon Joe insisted on leading a prayer, so we sat around the table, all five of us, hands clasped, listening to him recite the prayer of the penitent. He carried on so long my bladder was nearly fit to burst, and when he finally finished I heard him rise, his chair groaning from the strain of it. Deacon Joe's not fat but he's what the clothing stores call 'plus size' on account of all those chicken buckets he's so fond of. Ethan says his hair is like a shiny metal helmet, as if someone buffs him up each night while he's asleep.

Later, long after Ethan had been sent home, and Mama and Ada had gone to bed, Deacon Joe came to see me in my bedroom. I heard him lumber heavily up the stairs. When he reached my door he didn't knock, just opened it and stood there for an eternal moment, his anger expanding like a balloon until it filled the room – by which time it felt like he was looming over me like one of those giant Thanksgiving Day Parade characters. In that instant I had a vision of him as Underdog, with sneaky eyebrows, floppy ears and a long blue cape flowing out behind him. Except he wasn't Underdog. He was Deacon Joe and he was hopping mad. He stood there for a long moment, radiating fury, then finally turned and clomped away down the hall. I wondered about the source of his anger:

whether it was righteousness or jealousy, 'cause ever since Deacon Joe came into our lives he's been unhealthily fixated on me. He may be Ada's fourth husband (and therefore technically only my step-uncle) but he has involved himself in nearly every aspect of my upbringing. Mama and Ada look to him for advice on just about everything – I swear they'd let him choose what brand of menstrual pads to buy if they could.

It was Deacon Joe's idea that I be homeschooled. Up until he married Ada three years ago, I was mainstreamed at the local high school, though I only attended mornings. I guess I was relieved when Mama took his advice and withdrew me. Being at school with sighted kids was like throwing a man dying of thirst into the ocean. So much went on around me that my senses were on permanent overload. But I was never a partaker. Once I was back home, Deacon Joe took it on himself to oversee my education, which means that now I'm an expert on all things ecclesiastical. The first thing he did was mail-order a copy of The Talking Bible, all ninety-seven hours of it. Deacon Joe says the Bible has enough stories in it to last a lifetime and I've certainly heard them all, though I prefer the Old Testament for sheer entertainment value. Mama likes the classics, so I've listened to my fair share of those too: Nathaniel Hawthorne, Mark Twain, Louisa May Alcott, Ernest Hemingway and F. Scott Fitzgerald. Anything she could lay her hands on from the Ohio Blind Library. Ethan tutors me three times a week in math 'cause neither Mama nor Deacon Joe has a head for figures, owing largely to the fact that they never learned their times tables, though it's one of my best subjects. And Deacon Joe does history with me, which consists mainly of readings on his two favourite topics: World War Two and the Bible. Ask me something about the Luftwaffe or the Corinthians and most likely I'll know the answer. But that's about it. Deacon Joe doesn't set much stock in science, which is hardly surprising. Though I think he's beginning to realise that there's more to biology than just the birds and the bees.

In the evenings, Ethan reads me poetry. I like Emily Dickinson best, even if she was just a lonely old spinster scribbling away in the attic. I've always thought that she and I had something vital and romantic in common, 'cause up until now we both led an imagined life. According to Emily, *exhilaration is the breeze that lifts us from the ground, and leaves us in another place whose statement is not found.* I wondered how she knew what exhilaration felt like; or whether she only dreamed of being lifted from the ground. Now I feel as if I've reached that other place she writes about, because reality has finally got more interesting than my wonderings. Lord only knows what Emily Dickinson would make of my life.

The day after the war council, I went to see Dr Paulson. Mama wanted to come with me but I told her that if I was old enough to gestate, I was old enough to have a conversation about gestation. Besides, I didn't exactly want her peering over his shoulder when he did the examination. After Dr Paulson had taken some blood and urine samples, I sat in silence while he fiddled with the results for a few minutes. Then he came over and sat down heavily in a chair. 'Well, Annemarie,' he said with a sigh, 'normally I would offer my congratulations. But in your case, I guess it better be condolences. It would appear that you are indeed pregnant.' He took a deep breath and exhaled. 'In order to accurately date your pregnancy, it would be helpful to know exactly when intercourse took place.'

I hesitated. 'Didn't Mama speak to you?'

'Your mama briefly outlined the situation, yes.'

'Then you'll know there was no date,' I said. He hesitated.

'Annemarie, are you completely sure you understand the question?' he asked. 'Your mama suggested I might need to explain a little more fully.'

'I know what intercourse is,' I said, mortified. Though in truth, it wasn't a word I'd ever spoken aloud. Deacon Joe referred to it as fornication, as in: *After midnight, only fornication happens*. 'And I would definitely remember if it took place!' I added.

'You know,' Dr Paulson said carefully, 'saying something didn't happen, won't alter what did.'

'I can't tell you what I don't know.'

'Ah. Well, that's a different proposition altogether. And you don't know because ... it happened more than once?' he asked.

'No! Lord, no! I already told you. It didn't happen!'

'Fine,' he said curtly. I heard him open a drawer and take out some papers. 'When was the date of your last period?' he asked.

'The tenth of May,' I said.

'You're certain about that?'

'Yes.'

'Yet you don't know the date when relations took place?'

I sighed. 'No,' I said. Any further denial seemed pointless.

'Blind or not, a girl with your smarts ought to know better,' he said summarily, standing up. 'Guess it's time for us to take a look.'

I undressed and stretched out on his examination table while he poked and prodded my abdomen with his hands. And I couldn't help but think how funny it was that doctors always fall back on touch to tell them what they need to know.

'As far as I can tell,' he said, 'you seem to be about six weeks pregnant. Which would suggest intercourse took place in late May. Would that be about right?'

'If you say so,' I said.

'You ever had an internal examination before?' he asked.

'Internal?'

'Gynaecological.' He pronounced it *guy-knee-co-logical*.

'No, sir.'

'Well, we should probably do one now,' he said a little unwillingly. I had the feeling he didn't warm to this part of the job. The idea of an internal exam made me feel queasy, but if I was going to give birth I reckoned I'd have to get used to other people's heads stuck between my thighs. And anyway, I was hardly in a position to argue. He placed my feet in two cold metal brackets at the base of the bed, then instructed me to take a deep breath and relax. It was the first time I'd ever had what Mama calls my 'sacred parts' on display, and I was terrified. As I felt him gently probe, I squeezed my eyes closed and tried to picture angels flying overhead. Small cherubic faces floating in the clouds. And then I felt his fingers cease, and there was a long moment of silence.

'So the two of you did *not* have relations?' he asked carefully.

'That is correct.'

'There was definitely no ...?' He stopped himself.

'Definitely not.'

'And yet ... you do seem to be pregnant.' He sounded genuinely confused at this point, as if thinking aloud.

'You mean, I may *not* be?'

'I didn't say that. It's just ... unusual, given the presentation.' He made me sound like a layer cake.

'So is it possible?' I asked cautiously.

'Is what possible?'

'Is it possible to get pregnant without having sex?'

'Well, theoretically, there has to be an egg. And there has to be sperm. And the two have to come together.' He paused.

'Did you all even *have* sex education at school when you were younger?' he asked, clearly irritated.

'Sort of.'

'Then I guess you weren't paying attention that day,' he said.

'I guess not.'

He cleared his throat, and I heard the snap of latex as he pulled off his gloves. 'Why don't you haul your clothes back on and I'll see you outside,' he said coldly. And before I could climb out of the stirrups, I heard the door open and close, leaving me alone in the silence, splayed like a frog.

Not surprisingly, I was intact. Or, in the words of the Bible, undefiled. My mind floated back to *Deuteronomy*, and the fate of the wife whose token of virginity was not in evidence on her wedding night. *And the men of her city shall stone her with stones that she may die.* But I was not such a transgressor. And the proof was there for him to see. So why did I feel the stain of Dr Paulson's disapproval all over me? Both for being pregnant in the first place, and for the peculiar failures of my anatomy now that I was with child.

I knew at once from Mama's tone of voice when I came through the front door that there'd been a telephone conversation. He must have called her as soon as I left his office. Lord only knows what he said to her while I was tap-tap-tapping my way home. 'Well?' she asked.

'Well what?'

'What did he say?'

'He said that I'm pregnant. Which I already knew.'

'What else did he say?'

'He said the presentation was unusual.'

She hesitated. 'He told *me* it was peculiar,' she admitted.

'Well, that is what I have been trying to explain.'

'Annemarie, you need to be straight with me. Did you or did you not have sex with that boy?'

'I did not.' I felt her eyes on me as she digested my words.

'Well, you must've done *something*,' she said finally. ''Cause babies don't just fall from the sky.' She sounded defeated, which was the way I felt too. We stood there in pained silence for a minute, ringed by her dismay.

'I'm tired,' I said. 'They say early pregnancy does that to you. But maybe you don't remember.'

'I remember it all, Annemarie. Especially the ring on my finger.'

'You are not exactly a poster queen for marriage, Mama.'

'That may be, but it's not me we're speaking of,' she said.

There was nothing more I could say. I turned away from her and started up the stairs, retreating to the holy sanctity of my bedroom.

And the truth shall set you free, I thought wearily.

Ethan

It wasn't me. They think it was, but it wasn't. If only. These last six months I've barely laid a hand on her. I've wanted to so bad it almost made me sick. Lately I've been thinking that desire is like a mad dog, 'cause of the way it sinks its teeth into you and won't let go. Not to mention the way it twists you inside out. Deacon Joe says desire is nothing more than lust in disguise, and lust is a capital sin because it leads you on a carnal path to others – the ones he calls 'crimes of the flesh against the spirit'. God knows, the Church is no stranger to crimes of the flesh – after two years in Jericho, I've learned that much. Deacon Joe says the only way to deal with lust is to temper it with prayer. I reckon he's an expert on the subject, 'cause he's been lusting after Annemarie for as long as I can remember. No wonder he spends so much time in what he calls 'silent contemplation'.

Sometimes, when I'm with her, I close my eyes and lean in close, so that my lips are only a breath away from hers, just trying to *inhale* her without her knowing. The last time she gave a little laugh, and asked me why my eyes were closed. I don't know how she knew. I used to think she had a sixth sense or something. Now I think she's hotwired directly into heaven. Because if anyone is full of grace around here, it's Annemarie. The people in this town think they are holier than thou, but I reckon they don't know the first thing about divinity. The truth is, I've barely even kissed her. Though it feels like in other ways we've gone much further. Not physical ways, but ways of the mind, and of the heart. Christ, I sound like an idiot! She's just a girl. A beautiful, seventeen-year-old girl. Who happens to be blind. At least, that's what I used to think. Now I wish that was the whole story. Above all, I wish that she was normal. Which is to say, sighted, and untouched by the hand of God. But the Holy Spirit had bigger plans for Annemarie.

She was the one who decided I should make this tape, to accompany the one she was making. She said the record wouldn't be complete if I didn't tell my side of things. Annemarie wasn't there when the visions started, and though I've tried to describe them to her, I don't know exactly what she sees in her mind, so she's probably right that you should hear about them from me. She usually is. To be honest, I don't know why I'm a part of this story at all – I mean, why God chose me and not someone else in the parish. Maybe He thought I needed some extra persuasion, but Annemarie says it's because I'm one of the innocents. I told her that she was the innocent one, and she just smiled and shook her head. *Unto the pure all things are pure*, she said. Annemarie knows I hate it when she quotes scripture; she does it just to rile me. Anyway, I don't believe in innocence any more. And it's not exactly something I aspire to, especially with respect to her.

But if I'm going to tell my side of things I'll have to go right back to the beginning, almost two years ago now, though it feels like aeons. My story starts here in

Jericho – and Annemarie, her pregnancy, the visions, even Father O'Shea – they're all wrapped up together in it. Now, when I look back on my life before I moved here, the past seems like nothing more than a tiny speck on my memory. My family moved here from Arizona in the fall of '77, the year I turned fifteen. My mom more or less picked the town at random off the map, mainly because she liked the sound of it. My dad's an actuary with a big insurance company. That summer he'd been promoted to manager of the tri-state region, so in September we loaded all our earthly possessions into a moving van and drove out here – a journey that lasted an eternity as far as I was concerned. When we got here I think we were all a little disappointed, because Jericho doesn't really live up to its name. It's not much more than a crossroads really, with three churches (Catholic, Lutheran and Baptist), a pizza parlour, a gas station, a post office, and a 7-Eleven. Not a wall in sight. Even the high school is in the next township, half a mile down the road, though they still call themselves the Buglers.

It took me a while to realise that Jericho is one of those towns that thinks highly of itself, without anyone ever really knowing why. When I first told kids at Jericho High that I'd moved here from Arizona, I might as well have said I'd come from Mars, or maybe Russia. They looked at me with glazed eyes, then shrugged and turned away. I got the impression that my family was unusual, because Jericho isn't really a place people come to: they're born here and they stay until they die. The town sits in fairly flat farmland and looks pretty ordinary, with modest wooden shingled houses, neat picket fences, and tidy front lawns. You can't help but drive right through it, as the county highway splits it down the middle, but most of the other roads lead nowhere. Nearly everyone lives on the dead-end roads, and they have names like Serenity Lane and Broad Vista Avenue, or Island View Boulevard, even when there isn't an island or vista in sight – almost as if the town is trying to convince itself that it's more than the sum of its parts. The street we moved into is called Church Road, which gets points for accuracy if not for style, and it sits just off Township Highway 37. Our house is supposedly built in the Colonial Style, which means that it has two storeys and is made of brick, with white shutters and a gable in the attic where my bedroom is.

The day my family first drove into town, I remember my mom getting out of the car before my father had even shut off the engine. She turned a full circle, taking it all in – what little there was to see. Then she looked at my dad behind the wheel and shrugged. 'Could be worse,' she called out.

'Yup,' agreed Dad, nodding.

And that was it. They decided to stay. I don't think there are two more passive people on the face of this planet. But I guess I should be grateful, 'cause if we hadn't settled in Jericho, I'd never have met Annemarie.

I didn't speak to her for the first three months. Deacon Joe had already taken her out of school, and back then she was pretty well kept under lock and key most of the time, like Rapunzel or something. But my bedroom window looked directly down on to hers. And it didn't take long for me to notice her. Even at fifteen, Annemarie was uncommonly beautiful, with thick maple-coloured hair that fell almost to her waist, and eyes that were large and round and disconcertingly pale. At night she used to stand in the window looking out at the darkness, but it was a few months before I discovered she was blind.

It was Moose who told me. He was the first person I met at Jericho High, and is still the guy I hang out with when I'm not with Annemarie. We both do AP Math and play horn in the band, though in other ways we're totally different. Moose is a jock, for one thing. He plays centre forward for the basketball team (six foot two and rising, with dark brown hair, huge woolly eyebrows, and ears that look like jug handles) and I'm not much for sports, though the school tried hard to recruit me to do cross-country – something I regard as completely masochistic. (What's the point of running until you throw up?) When I asked Moose who the girl next door was and why she didn't go to school, he threw me a look of total contempt. 'Don't go there, dude,' he said. 'She's way out of bounds. Trust me, others have tried and failed before you. Her uncle is one bad-ass gatekeeper. Anyway forget it, 'cause she's blind.'

'You mean *blind* blind, or just blind to guys like you?'

'She's blind, Ethan. As in sightless,' he said flatly.

'Oh.'

I had never known anyone blind before and the information silenced me. No doubt Moose thought that would be the end of it. But if anything it made Annemarie even more appealing in my eyes. By then, if I had any hopes of leading a normal life in Jericho, it was too late, because Annemarie had already worked her silent magic on me. I told her once, much later, that I thought she'd bewitched me, standing in the window all those months.

'*Thou shall not suffer a witch to live,*' she said with a smile.

'But here you are,' I replied. 'And anyway, it's me who's suffering.'

'If I was a witch, why wouldn't I cure my blindness?'

'Maybe you don't want to,' I offered. 'Maybe you ... prefer it this way.' My heart skipped a beat when I said this, and I wondered whether she'd be angry, even though I suspected it was the truth. She frowned for a moment.

'Maybe I do,' she finally agreed. 'But just so you know,

I'm not a witch, or a sorcerer, or even an enchantress.' I reached out and took her hand, and pulled her closer to me, lowering my voice.

'You are *definitely* an enchantress,' I said. She laughed and let go, stepping lightly away, and I felt a sudden wave of relief that I'd not angered her.

'OK,' she admitted. 'Well, maybe *that* I am.'

So the first problem was how to meet her. I began to ingratiate myself with the neighbours. I raked leaves on the whole street that autumn, and when the first snow fell in early December I was out at dawn, shovelling the sidewalks and even Annemarie's driveway. That morning, Deacon Joe came out of the house and appeared from behind the hedge that shielded it from the driveway. He was wearing an enormous black-and-red checked wool jacket, a camouflage hat with earflaps, and carried a shovel in his hand. He stopped short when he saw me, his heavy features collapsing into a frown that somehow seemed to double the size of his neck. He stood watching me for a moment, his breath rising in wispy clouds of white, then cleared his throat a little too loudly.

'You're doing mighty fine work there, son,' he called out.

'Thank you, sir,' I said, pausing in my efforts.

'Are you expecting to be paid?'

'No, sir. It's my pleasure.' He came towards me, halting about six feet from where I stood.

'You got a name?'

'Ethan.'

'Good Christian name. It means strong, I believe.'

'Yes, sir.'

'It also means impetuous,' he added with a smile. He looked around at his newly cleared driveway. 'Maybe you're a little bit of both.'

'I couldn't say,' I replied uneasily, though I had the sudden sense that the conversation was headed in a bad direction.

'Expect you're fixing to meet up with my niece,' he said, looking straight at me. My insides sort of deflated; I felt my hands start to sweat inside my thermal gloves.

'Sorry?'

'Annemarie. She's a rare flower of a girl. Unfortunately, she's also blind.'

'Yes, sir. I heard that. I'm very sorry.'

'Your people church-goers?' he asked, nodding towards my house.

'We're new here. We ... haven't joined one yet,' I offered lamely. We'd lived in Jericho nearly three months.

'Well, see that you do,' he said with a nod. 'I'm the deacon over at St Paul's. You and your family would be welcome there if you'd care to attend.'

'Yes, sir. Thank you. I'll be sure to tell them,' I mumbled.

'Well, I should be thanking *you* for all your fine labours,' he said, gesturing towards the driveway. He turned to go, then paused and turned back to me.

'Annemarie'll be at church on Sunday,' he said, snagging my gaze. I nodded, a lump forming in my throat. Then I watched his great lumbering frame disappear behind the front door.

So that's how I found God. The following Sunday I put on my best pair of corduroys and a collared shirt. When I appeared at breakfast, my parents were seated at the table wearing checked pyjamas and matching flannel bathrobes that they'd ordered from the Sears catalogue. They looked like grown-up versions of the Bobbsey Twins, except my dad boycotted shaving on weekends, so by Sunday his face always looked a bit gravelly. He was buried in the headlines while Mom was doing the crossword, her forehead scrunched with concentration. When she saw me, she smiled with surprise. 'You're up early,' she said.

'Off to church.'

My father poked his head out from behind the newspaper. 'Church? *Which* church?'

'St Paul's.'

He and Mom exchanged a look. 'The Catholic one?'

'Is it?' I asked innocently, reaching for a box of Pop-Tarts on the counter. 'You guys wanna come along? Might do you good. Might meet some of the neighbours.'

'I've met the neighbours,' said Mom lightly. 'And anyway we're Unitarian.'

'We are?' asked my father, looking at her with vague surprise.

'Sort of,' she said with a shrug. 'Or at least, I always thought we *would* be ...'

'If you could be bothered,' I said. 'But you can't.'

'Because I don't choose to,' she said, a little defensively.

'Well, I do,' I replied, grabbing my coat and making for the door.

'Have fun,' mumbled my father from behind his newspaper. 'Or whatever it is you do in church.'

Needless to say it was pretty much my first experience. Except for the odd wedding or funeral, I had no real history with organised religion. When I got there the church was already nearly full, with people sitting silently in the pews, while an organist in the balcony played something solemn and repetitive. I slid into the back row, my eyes scanning the church for Annemarie. I finally found her, right up front, flanked by her mama and aunt, like female sentries set to guard her chastity. Deacon Joe was busy lighting candles along the back of the altar, and when he was finished he took a seat in a chair to the right of the pulpit while the rest of us waited for the service to start.

For the next hour I tried to fake it, leaping up when others stood, sitting or kneeling a second too late, and slurring the words to prayers and hymns that everyone else seemed to know by heart. The sermon was about fidelity, not so much the marital kind as the religious kind. I listened for the first few minutes, but after that my mind strayed, and I occupied myself by solving quadratic equations in my head. I was relieved when it was finally over, and the priest came walking down the aisle, followed by Deacon Joe at a respectable distance, his shiny hair glowing with reverence. As he walked past I saw him clock me, and he raised an eyebrow in mild surprise. I knew then that he'd underestimated me, not to mention my devotion to Annemarie. Some might have even called it my fidelity.

But afterwards he kept his bargain and waved me over. Annemarie listened with her head tilted slightly, her pale eyes looking just left of mine, as Deacon Joe told her how I'd cleared the driveway of snow without being asked. An old woman approached him and he turned away, leaving Annemarie and me alone for a second. 'When did you move in?' she asked.

'Early September.'

'And you haven't come to call?'

'I've been kind of busy,' I mumbled. Too late, I realised she was teasing me, as the corners of her mouth twitched upwards ever so slightly.

'So what do you think of Jericho?'

'It's OK.'

30

'Liar.'

'OK, it's less than OK. Much less.'

'You're not really Catholic, are you?' She was smiling now, but it wasn't a question.

'How'd you know?'

'Lucky guess.'

'I'm ... experimenting with new faiths,' I ventured.

'And your bedroom window looks right at mine,' she said. I hesitated, colouring, and saw that Deacon Joe was watching me over the shoulder of his parishioner.

'Um. Yeah. How'd you know *that*?'

'I didn't,' she said. 'But now I do.' At that moment Deacon Joe walked over and took her arm, saying it was time to go. As he led her away, she turned back towards me.

'See you around, Ethan,' she said with a half-smile.

'See ya,' I repeated dumbly, realising once again that she was mocking me with her words. As they walked out together, Deacon Joe threw me one last steely gaze, as if to say: *She may be blind, but she's way out of your league!*

Fortunately for me, God didn't agree. Early the following spring I placed first in the Ohio All-State Mathematics Championship, just a few days after Deacon Joe had pinned a notice on the Church Hall bulletin board seeking a math tutor for Annemarie. I like to think that the Lord had a hand in the timing: that He was rewarding me for my fidelity, since by then I'd become a fixture at Sunday Mass. Once or twice I'd been allowed to accompany Annemarie on the walk home, although on those occasions we were never alone, but shepherded by her mother, Deacon Joe and Ada. As far as I could make out Annemarie was never allowed out of the house on her own. So I knew I'd have to find a way into the castle. Luckily, God had given me the formula.

Eva

I was never much good at history. I'm not even a fan of my own. In forty-three years, I've never once felt compelled to set down the events of my life for posterity's sake. And I always thought the urge to do so was a little self-important, not to mention unreliable, because who could resist tidying things up after the fact? But so much has happened these last few weeks that I'm worried it will all get tangled up like old rope in my mind. So I guess if writing things down was good enough for the Apostles, then it's good enough for me – though I'm beginning to realise that the truth is something most of us will never get at. And maybe we aren't meant to.

The night Annemarie confessed that she was pregnant, it was like some part of me got torn open and flayed. The news that she'd forsaken her chastity was bad enough, but her refusal to admit it seemed a thousand times worse. All her life I'd pressed upon her the need for honesty, and her sudden decision to abandon it was baffling. I could sense that Ada and Joe were as mystified as I was, and I was sorry Annemarie hadn't chosen to face me with her sins in private. I'd shared the province of motherhood with Ada from the start, but now that things had gone awry I resented my sister's presence in the room more than she will ever know. I expect it was because I only had myself to blame.

I sat there in dazed silence and wondered whether somewhere in the universe an entirely different life had been set out for us, like a party still waiting for its guests to arrive, and whether we could still find our way there, or whether it was closed to us forever. In the end I decided that if God wanted us to live that life, He would have shown us the path. God wanted us here in Jericho, in the life He'd ordained. And even though we prayed to Him that night and begged His forgiveness, I couldn't help but wonder what part He'd played in Annemarie's undoing.

Another part of me wondered if Jericho itself wasn't to blame. Ada and I had moved up here from West Virginia when Annemarie was barely out of diapers, but though we'd made a place for ourselves, I'd never felt entirely at home. Our grandfather had passed on, leaving us a small inheritance, and Ada had persuaded me that we needed a clean start someplace folks wouldn't pass judgment on our history. At the time we were both fresh out of failed marriages: mine had ended abruptly the year before, and Ada's second husband had hot-footed it back to Texas after she'd caught him in bed with the local sheriff's wife. I hadn't known it but Ada had already set her sights on a new man, a property developer she'd met who was busy buying up vacant lots across Northeastern Ohio. She chose Jericho because she liked the name, and because it was within striking distance of both Youngstown and Akron; I guess she figured if she couldn't find a new husband in one thriving metropolis, she'd turn one up in the other. We bought a ramshackle house beside the town's only Catholic church and quickly joined the congregation, where Ada breezily introduced us both as widows. 'Who's to say we aren't?' she said, when I confronted her. 'And anyway, they might as well be dead, for all the good they've done us,' she scoffed. The year was 1963, and even though I didn't technically approve of her deceit, a part of me was grateful.

So we planted ourselves in Jericho, and with the help of the church, eventually built a life. Ada lost the trail of the property developer but within a few years had hitched herself to a telephone engineer, a marriage that lasted longer than either of the first two (and might have carried on, had he not succumbed prematurely to a heart attack, making her a bona fide widow after all). After his death she had a series of disastrous affairs, followed by a fallow spell, before eventually setting her cap at Deacon Joe, a used-car salesman and pillar of the congregation. Deacon Joe was already married, but that didn't discourage Ada. His wife had a chronic illness that kept her bed-ridden, leaving Ada free to work her mischief round the edges at every available opportunity. After two years Deacon Joe's ailing wife was gracious enough to pass over, leaving Ada a clear shot at him. Even then, Deacon Joe insisted on a six-month period of mourning, though Ada broke him down after about four.

By then, we'd had several years on our own in the house without a man, and a part of me was relieved to hand over the near-constant maintenance issues to someone who was predisposed to deal with them. Deacon Joe was old-fashioned enough to believe that women were incapable of changing a light bulb, much less fixing a leaky faucet or a crack in the windowpane, and who was I to argue? Ada liked a man with strong convictions and he certainly fit the bill in that respect. Plus he'd lived in Jericho all his life, which lent our household a new legitimacy. He was also generous-spirited when it came to Annemarie: from the start he took a strong interest in her welfare, recognising that her disability shouldn't hold her back from leading a normal life – a sentiment I was grateful for, even if we didn't always see eye-to-eye.

But I was never tempted to follow Ada's lead. I knew I couldn't raise a blind child with one hand and bind myself to a husband with the other, so I didn't try, even though that meant I was marginalised within the small community of Jericho. Over the years I'd sidestepped a few offers from local bachelors, and the town had never quite forgiven me. In the eyes of Jericho's residents, a woman who remained single by choice was little better than a recovered alcoholic or an ex-con: we lived under a permanent cloud of suspicion. So Annemarie and I were seen as something less than half a family, made all the more pitiable by her disability. No wonder she'd been led astray, or so the town would think.

In the days that followed her confession, I found myself watching out for Ethan's mother. Though I couldn't count her as a friend (in two years we'd barely exchanged more than a dozen words), I reckoned she was one of the few people who wasn't in a position to judge. I knew that Ethan had told her about the pregnancy, and I wondered what she thought. She was friendly enough but kept to herself, though I often caught sight of her unloading groceries or weeding the flowerbeds outside her front door. For most of the past two years we'd operated on a nod-and-wave basis, with the occasional *how-'bout-that-storm-last-night-thought-it-was-gonna-tear-the-roof-off* remark that passed between us like a hockey puck.

She and her husband hadn't exactly courted the community. For starters, they'd never set foot inside a church, even after Ethan joined the congregation at St Paul's. Ironically, my own parents had done the same: packed Ada and me off to Catechism every Sunday morning, then gone back to bed to sleep off the dregs of Saturday night. Once, early on, I'd asked Ethan whether he might care to invite his parents to a parish supper. He smiled and shook his head, and I saw in his young eyes the embarrassment I'd felt each time I came out of Mass and spotted my daddy's pale blue Thunderbird waiting at the corner. By contrast, when we were growing up, Ada had paid no heed to our parents' godlessness. She shimmied her way round God and the Church and made up her own rules as she went along. By the time we graduated from high school she'd worked her way through most of the altar boys and had even had a casual fling with a young seminary student that nearly got him excommunicated. Ada's always been susceptible to men of the cloth – four husbands later and she is still not above flirting with a visiting priest.

I didn't want to face an ambush of questions from Ada and Joe, so I waited for a day when they'd gone out, then baked a molasses cake and carried it round to Ethan's house, telling myself that it was a kind of penance. But as I walked up the front path, my stomach started turning little flips. I'd seen enough of Ethan's mother to know she wasn't unreasonable – she wasn't ornery or hot-tempered or even proud. But even so, I had to force myself to climb the steps and ring the doorbell, the still-warm cake clutched tightly in my hands. As I waited nervously for her to answer, my mind leaped about, conjuring the worst. She would instantly see me for what I was: a failed wife and the mother of an unchaste daughter.

The house was quiet, but the station wagon was in the driveway so I knew someone was at home. After a minute I heard steps in the hallway and the door opened. Ethan's mother stood there in a sleeveless denim shirt and beige culottes, her brown hair swept hastily back in a clip, and a pair of gardening gloves stuffed under one arm. She had a smudge of dirt across her forehead, but even so she was still what my grandma used to call *kitchen pretty*, which meant that she had a kind of homespun beauty. When she saw me, her eyebrows lifted with surprise. 'Sorry, I was out back,' she said with a smile. There wasn't a hint of blame or malice in her face. Reassured, I offered up the plate.

'I baked you a cake. I hope you like molasses.'

She looked down at it with a confused expression. 'That is so kind ...' she said, her voice trailing off. She looked back up at me and I could see that was genuinely bewildered. I took a deep breath. Had she forgotten?

'I just felt it was right,' I said quickly. 'Given our ... predicament.' My voice landed with a thump on this last word, and I felt the heat rise in my face. She drew a deep breath, then nodded her understanding and opened the door wider.

'Would you like to come in for a cup of coffee?' she asked. I hesitated, and something held me back. I don't know if it was fear or shame or just a prickly sense of discomfort, but I shook my head.

'I just wanted to see if you were OK,' I said. We both stood there for an awkward moment.

'Ethan and Annemarie aren't the first teenagers on the planet to find themselves in this situation,' she said kindly. 'I wish they'd been more prudent, but it doesn't make them bad people, any more than it makes you and me bad mothers.'

I nodded, a lump forming in the back of my throat. Hers was a very Christian view: tolerant and understanding. But I wondered if I agreed with it. I turned to stare at the mulberry tree in the front yard. Planted by the previous owner, it would soon be heavy with fruit that would burst in your fingers the second you tried to pick it. 'The berries stain,' I said, turning back to her and nodding towards the tree. 'But I expect you know that by now.'

She looked at it, her brown eyes thoughtful. 'Yes, I do. But they're still one of my favourites.'

'Enjoy the cake,' I said, turning to go.

'Are you *sure* you won't come in?' she asked, peering at me. I shook my head.

'Some other time.'

'I hope so,' she said. And she honestly seemed to mean it.

Back home, I made a mug of tea and curled my hands around it until the heat turned my palms red. My life had been a series of trials, and up to now I'd met them head on, believing that each time I overcame one I grew stronger as a result. But this time I just felt tired, exhausted by the latest twist in our fortunes, and by the particular demands of our faith. Once, years ago, Father O'Shea had preached an entire sermon based on the notion that faith begins where reason ends. It was an idea I'd always struggled with: why had God given us the ability to reason if we couldn't call upon it to shore up our faith? Surely reason and faith should be joined forever, like man and wife? Together, they were what made us human.

I hadn't been the only one who'd struggled with the sermon that day. Standing way up high in his pulpit, Father O'Shea had looked down upon us and proclaimed that faith was the conviction of all things unseen. Annemarie had been especially restless up until that point in the Mass, shifting uncomfortably in the pew and fiddling with the pages of a hymnal, but when he said those words she suddenly grew still. I looked down and saw the creases in her forehead knit tightly together. For the next few minutes she scarcely drew a breath, so hard was her mind at work turning his words over and over in her head. After Mass she was still subdued, and as we walked home she stopped at one point and asked me if my faith was the same as hers. 'I expect so,' I replied.

'But ... *you* can see.'

'Faith doesn't need eyes to see,' I said.

Annemarie frowned. 'But Father O'Shea says that faith is believing in what you can't see. So my faith has to be bigger than yours. 'Cause I don't see anything.'

We walked on in silence. As usual, she had a point. Her entire world was based on a gigantic leap of faith: on moving forward into the darkness, and trusting that she wouldn't fall into the abyss. 'Mama?' she asked after a minute.

'You're right, Annemarie. Your faith is bigger than mine,' I said.

She gave my hand a little satisfied squeeze. 'I thought so,' she said with a smile. 'But don't worry. If you run out, I'll give you some of mine.'

Now, more than six years later, I wonder if her faith is big enough to carry us both.

Annemarie

After my visit to Dr Paulson, the house seemed to simmer with suspicion. In spite of his report, they still believed I'd brought the pregnancy on myself, and there was nothing I could say to dissuade them. After a few days I stopped trying, and poor Ethan was more frustrated than ever. But it wasn't until a few weeks later that things went into free fall. By then it was late July and the air outside was so sticky I could taste it. I sat in front of the fan in my bedroom, listening to Mama's old records (Joni Mitchell and Cat Stevens) and learning how to knit. It was the social worker who first suggested knitting. I discovered that teenage pregnancy immediately lands you on the social services register, and within a week I'd been assigned my own caseworker, a woman named Cassandra. She stopped by one afternoon, and after chatting briefly to Mama downstairs she knocked on my bedroom door.

From the moment I opened it I sensed that Cassandra was unlike anyone I'd ever met: her presence felt different. She introduced herself in a friendly way and asked if she could have a look around my room. I tracked her closely as she floated about, casually perusing my books, tapes and record albums. It's difficult to explain, but I have always catalogued people by the aura they give off when I first meet them: nervous, agitated, angry, depressed, upbeat. It took me a few minutes to pinpoint Cassandra's, because it was completely unfamiliar to me. But her aura could only be described as serene.

I formed an instant picture of her in my mind. Tall and thin, with creamy pale skin and hair that was almost white, like an elegant Siamese cat with startling blue eyes the colour of aquamarines. After she'd flicked through my album collection (I'd marked the covers with Braille stickers so as to tell them apart, a detail which delighted Cassandra), I couldn't help asking her what she looked like. She laughed. 'Unremarkable,' she said.

'You don't seem unremarkable.'

'Don't I? Well, that's good, I guess. Do you always ask people what they look like?'

'Not usually.'

'Then I suppose I should be flattered.'

'What did you and Mama talk about downstairs?' I asked.

'Oh, this and that. Your due date. How you were coping. What your expectations were.'

'Probably should have asked how *she* was coping,' I said.

'OK. How's she coping?'

'Not very well.'

'Well, that's hardly surprising, is it?' Cassandra said gently.

'I guess not.'

'Anyway, she's not my concern. You are.'

'So you're here to ask me questions?'

'If you don't mind.'

'Yeah, OK.'

'Good,' said Cassandra, settling herself on the end of my bed. 'Now the first thing is: do you know how to knit?'

I didn't, so she taught me, right then and there. She'd brought a large bag full of different-coloured yarn and lots of needles of every size, and we settled down to work side-by-side. She wanted to know whether I saw colours in my mind and, if so, which was my favourite? After some dithering on my part, I finally decided on blue. Though I explained that my blue was probably different from hers.

'Different how?'

I shrugged.

'Is it celestial?' she asked.

'Sort of.' I wondered how she knew.

'Celestial it is then,' she said, and I could hear her rummaging around in her bag, where she apparently kept all the colours of the rainbow. She taught me how to cast on, how to form both the knit and purl stitches, and how to probe with my fingertips afterwards to make sure I hadn't dropped one. It might seem strange, but no one had ever taught me to do anything with my hands before, and at once I found it oddly satisfying: both soothing and rhythmic. Once I'd got the hang of it, she pulled out her own knitting and we worked in silence for a few minutes.

'Why knitting?' I asked.

'Why not? Knitting is very therapeutic. It calms the soul. And if there's one thing teenage mothers need, it's calm. On top of that, knitting's practical. You could be making a blanket for your baby right now.'

A blanket for my baby. The words seeped into my mind. Until that moment I'd only thought about the pregnancy. I hadn't really considered that there would be a baby at the end of it. At once the idea filled me with alarm. As if sensing my unease, Cassandra stopped knitting and laid a hand on my arm. 'Everything's going to be fine,' she said in a reassuring voice. I felt a pulse of warmth jump from her arm to mine and then travel round my body, right to my toes. Then I took a deep breath and tried to conjure an image of myself knitting in a year's time, a baby in a basket by my side. But for some reason, I couldn't complete the picture in my mind. It was all there: me, the knitting and the basket, but inside the basket all I saw was an empty patch of white.

We carried on for a while, and Cassandra asked me about my taste in music, the books I liked, who my friends were. I explained that Ethan came by most evenings, and that he tutored me in math and read me poetry. 'Sounds like a nice boy,' she remarked. 'Is he the baby's father?'

I hesitated. Mama had warned me not to discuss the finer points of the pregnancy with Cassandra.

'Sort of,' I said.

I braced myself for more questions, but they didn't come. Cassandra remained quiet, and the only sound in the room was the steady click-click of her needles. Perversely, her refusal to press me made me wonder whether I should tell her the truth. But I figured I was already in enough hot water with Mama, so I sat there, my needles poised in the air like two tiny sabres, until she eventually asked me why I'd stopped knitting. When she left, Cassandra dug out two large balls of wool, placing them in my hands.

'Celestial blue,' she said. 'May I come again next week?'

'Will we knit?' I asked.

'If you wish.'

'All right.'

I liked Cassandra. But Mama was more wary. When she found out that we'd spent the hour knitting she practically blew steam out of her nostrils. Then she had a bit of a rant about wasting taxpayers' money. For the past week Mama had been pressing me about my plans regarding the pregnancy, but so far I'd refused to discuss it, mostly because I didn't have a clue. That same evening, she came to my room and hovered in the doorway like an angry wasp. 'What is it?' I asked.

'Did that woman even *mention* adoption?'

'She didn't. But you have.'

'There is no shame in adoption, Annemarie. The Bible itself has plenty of stories of adoption. Moses. Esther. Jesus himself was adopted by Joseph.'

'Yes, Mama,' I sighed. 'I've heard those stories.'

'But adoption isn't good enough for you.'

'Mama, it's not me we're speaking of.'

She was silent then. She'd never once talked about the baby – at least, not as a living, breathing thing. It was almost as if she couldn't picture it either. Or maybe she just didn't want to. Right then I could hear her mentally tussling with herself, because any further discussion would take us deep into baby territory. And she didn't want to go there. After a long pause I heard her turn and retreat down the stairs.

Seeing as how I hadn't got beyond the idea of pregnancy, I wasn't ready to think about adoption just yet. There's a reason it takes nine months to grow a baby, I decided. Both the baby and I needed time. Later that evening Ethan stopped by, flopping down beside me on the floor in front of the fan. 'What you knitting?' he asked. I didn't have the courage to say it was a baby blanket, so instead I told him about Cassandra's visit.

'She sounds crazy.'

'No! Really, she was comforting. When she laid her hand on mine it was like being bathed in warm light. She took away all my fears.'

'Well, that's good. I guess,' he said doubtfully.

'You should meet her.'

'Will she make me knit?'

44

'She thought you sounded nice.'

'You told her about me?'

'Why wouldn't I?'

'So she thinks I'm the father.'

'Ethan, *everyone* thinks you're the father.'

'Yeah, I'm having trouble with that part.'

I heard him take a deep breath, then slowly let it out. I knew he wasn't exactly thrilled about the state we'd got ourselves into. The state I had got us into. But he was doing his best to be supportive. Even if it left him frustrated in just about every way.

Just then Deacon Joe knocked on the door. 'Annemarie, time for Ethan to go on home,' his voice boomed out. Ethan leaned into me.

'It's only eight-thirty,' he whispered. 'What's his problem?'

'I'm knocked up,' I whispered back.

'Oh, yeah. I almost forgot.'

'And as far as he's concerned, you're responsible.'

'I should be so lucky,' said Ethan, standing up.

I listened as he left the room and did a little do-si-do on the landing to get past Deacon Joe. When he was gone I could feel Deacon Joe staring at me through the open doorway. I looked directly at the place where he stood.

'What?' I said.

For once he was speechless. He stood there for a long moment, his frustration coming at me in waves, and it struck me that for all their differences, he and Ethan were both men. Then I heard his great lumbering form disappear down the stairs, leaving me alone with my celestial blue.

That was our last night of normality. The next morning I woke in a tangled sweat of sheets, the heat of the sun screaming through my bedroom window. Ohio in July can be as hot as Hades, and as I crawled out of bed the heat snagged in my chest. Ethan was working all day, and Mama and Ada had been planning a trip to the new mall just north of Youngstown, which beckoned with the promise of central air conditioning, if nothing else. That left me and Deacon Joe to swelter on our own – a prospect I was dreading.

I took a cold shower then put on a bikini top and cut-offs, the sort of outfit Deacon Joe calls *harlot's get-up*. I'd slept late and it was running towards noon by the time I got downstairs. Mama and Ada were long gone, and there was cold coffee in the machine. I filled the biggest glass I could find with ice and poured in coffee, topping it up with cream and three spoons of sugar. Mama had been on to me about cutting back on caffeine for the baby's sake, but seeing as how I didn't drink, smoke or do drugs, I'd decided the baby could clear at least one hurdle. The house was quiet and I was hoping Deacon Joe was down at the car dealership when I heard the screen door open behind me.

'Tarnation!' Deacon Joe came inside and within a second the kitchen smelled like an armpit.

'Hot enough?'

'You said it. Kind of day that melts the tarmac. Fan belt's bust on the Chrysler. I was just out there trying to fix it.'

'Mama and Ada gone?'

'Yep. Just you and me today.' The way he said it made me cringe. 'Thought maybe we should look through those college applications.'

'It's Saturday.'

'All the more reason.' Deacon Joe was fixated on me going to a good Christian college, preferably one close to home. So far he hadn't seemed to take on board that a baby might complicate things. He disappeared and then returned a minute later, dropping a file folder heavily on to the kitchen table. 'Your mama and I had a look through the catalogues. These are all good colleges within an hour or two's drive. And your grades should get you into any of them. But you'll need to write an essay for the application.'

'Yep.'

'Reckon I could help you out with that.'

'I can manage.'

'Well, you'll need some help filling out the forms.'

'Ethan can help me. He's already done his.'

Deacon Joe paused and I could feel him eyeing me. 'That boy has not exactly been a boon so far,' he said hotly.

'He got me an A in math.'

'He got you an F in morality.'

I decided to let that one slide by.

'You may not be overly concerned with salvation, but your mama and I are,' Deacon Joe continued.

'I reckon God has bigger fish to fry than me and Ethan.'

'Sin can't be wiped clean like a chalkboard, Annemarie.'

I got up and crossed over to the fridge to grab some more ice cubes. It was too hot for lectures and Deacon Joe was getting on my nerves. I filled my glass to the brim and turned back to him. '*Though your sins are as scarlet, they will be as white as snow,*' I said.

'Mocking the scriptures won't help. You *will* be called to account.'

'Expect you'll have a few of your own sins to account for one day.'

'Expect I will,' he said. 'But that doesn't lessen yours.'

I told him I had a headache and grabbed the folder, retreating to my bedroom for the rest of the afternoon. If I ever got to college, I thought crossly, it wouldn't be within striking distance of Deacon Joe. I shoved the file deep under my bed, where I hoped that it would languish for eternity.

College wasn't exactly top of my list at the moment, anyway. I was having enough trouble just getting through the day.

I called up Cora Lynn and invited her round to break the tedium of heat and Deacon Joe. I'd told her the truth about the pregnancy not long after I'd told Ethan, otherwise she would have teased me without mercy about my failure to use contraception. (Cora Lynn is nothing if not practical.) When she arrived she kicked off her flip-flops and launched herself on to my bed, smelling of Dubble Bubble and Prell shampoo, and cracking her gum loudly. 'Mama told me if I got knocked up like you, she'd throw me out of the house,' she said.

I sighed and threw myself down next to her.

'She must think I'm a scarlet woman.'

'Nah, she just thinks you're a stupid white girl who didn't know any better.'

'That's worse,' I groaned. 'I feel like Bathsheba.'

'Bath-who?'

'The wife of Uriah. While Uriah was away at war, King David looked out from his rooftop and saw Bathsheba bathing. He seduced her and afterwards she fell pregnant.'

'But you aren't anybody's wife. And you weren't seduced.'

'OK, so I'm not *exactly* like Bathsheba. But in the Bible she's a fallen woman. Like me.'

'The Bible says *every* woman's fallen,' said Cora Lynn dismissively.

'Except the Virgin Mary,' I pointed out.

'Exactly. And what fun did *she* have?'

Cora Lynn and I whiled away the afternoon eating peanut M&Ms, reading *National Enquirer* and listening to records. She's a huge fan of a new singer called Prince, and spent most of the afternoon trying to persuade me to name the baby after him.

'Why would I name my baby after someone who doesn't have a last name?'

'He's royalty. He doesn't need a last name.'

'What if it's a girl?' I asked.

'Princette,' she said, rolling over and placing a palm across my belly.

'Come on, Princette, give us a little kick.'

'I don't think she can do that yet,' I said. 'Seeing as how she's only about the size of an M&M.'

'Well, tell her to hurry up,' said Cora Lynn, climbing off the bed. ''Cause I wanna see what colour she'll be.'

'She'll be white, you idiot. Like me.'

'How do you know? She's a miracle baby. She can be any damn colour she pleases. And she might just come out brown like me.'

After Cora Lynn had gone, I lay there for a while imagining the baby as a peanut M&M. I worked my way through all the colours in the bag, and decided in the end that Cora Lynn had a point. Brown might be the best, after all.

Ethan had promised to come by after work, but when he eventually turned up, I knew at once something was wrong. As soon as he stepped into the room I sensed it, because he smelled different. It took me a moment to work out it was the scent of fear. I pulled him inside and shut the door. 'What's wrong?' I said.

'Nothing.' His voice came out strangely, sort of hoarse, as if it had been squeezed.

'Ethan, something's happened. Are you all right?'

'No, nothing's ...' He stopped short. Ethan had never lied to me before and I knew he couldn't then. 'I saw something, that's all. Someone. On my way here.'

'Who?'

'I don't know. A stranger. I don't know what she was. Maybe it was a dream.' He sat down heavily on the bed. 'Damn, it's hot,' he muttered. I pulled the fan closer to us and sat down beside him.

'Tell me what you saw.'

'A woman. As I was crossing the churchyard. She was standing right beside the wayside shrine.

'OK. What sort of woman?'

'I don't know. She wasn't from around here. She was ... different.'

'Different how?'

'It's hard to explain. Everything. Her hair, her clothes, the way she spoke.'

'You talked to her?'

'Yeah.'

'And? What did she say?'

'She said that you were blessed. Except she said it in a weird way. With two syllables. Like *bless-ed*.'

'She talked about me?'

'She *only* talked about you.'

'Oh.' I frowned. 'What else did she say?'

'She said the baby was a gift.'

I paused, and suddenly my insides twisted with alarm. 'What baby? *My* baby?' I asked tentatively.

'*The* baby, Annemarie.'

'A gift from who?' It came out like a whisper, and even as I asked the question, I knew I didn't want the answer. All at once I felt myself sort of falling through the air.

'She said it was a gift from the Holy Spirit.'

Ethan's voice had dropped so low I barely heard him. *Oh Lord*, I thought. Suddenly it all made sense. A terrible, sickening sense. For a long moment I couldn't speak. 'Do you think ... she might be right?' I finally asked.

'Maybe. Anything's possible.'

'But ... why?'

'I don't know why. But at least it explains *how*.'

'Ethan, maybe this is some sort of practical joke.'

'No one's laughing, Annemarie,' he said.

'Or ... or maybe she was crazy. Some crazy person who found out I was pregnant and –'

'No. She wasn't crazy.'

'How do you know?'

Ethan paused then, and I could sense that he was wrestling with himself. 'Because she disappeared. Right in front of my eyes.'

'What do you mean?' I asked.

'I swear to God, Annemarie, she just vanished. Right into thin air.'

We both sat there, shocked into silence. I had never heard Ethan speak so seriously about anything. And for once I had no reply. Instead I listened, aware at once of a myriad of sounds: the quiet whirr of the fan blades, the noise of a passing car, the buzz of a lawnmower down the street. And the thunderous beat of my heart. 'Are you OK?' Ethan eventually asked.

'Should I be?'

He took a deep breath and exhaled heavily. 'Who knows? Until today, I wasn't even a believer.'

'Well, I was. But if God thinks he can make us more devout simply by knocking me up, He's got another thing coming,' I said crossly, jumping up and crossing over to the stereo. 'Let's listen to some music.' I punched the cassette recorder, skipping it forward until it reached 'Moonshadow', then turned the volume up as high as it would go. We lay side-by-side on the bed, and I felt as if the Cat had penned the song just for me.

I was leapin' and hoppin' all right. How was it that I hadn't known? I thought my pregnancy was a biological accident, not some random act of divinity. And my response was an unholy torrent of anger. Why had God picked me? Hadn't my life already been torn apart by blindness? And couldn't He have settled His bless-ed sights on someone else?

All at once I felt like a hostage, both to my blindness and to the foetus lurking deep inside me. Because there was nowhere for me to hide from God in that moment. What little control I'd managed to have over my life had suddenly been snatched away. I felt like Jonah in the belly of the whale, being toyed with by the waves. And like Jonah, my first instinct was to defy God and rebel. I lay there next to Ethan on the bed and wondered what I could do that would anger God the most, and the solution hit me like a slap. Baby or no baby, maybe it was time to put an end to my precious chastity, I thought hotly. I knew that Ethan wouldn't object.

'Ethan.' I turned to him and reached a hand out towards him, first stroking his hair, then trailing a finger from his forehead down the bridge of his nose to his lips, where I let it rest. I felt him part his lips slightly, then take a deep breath.

'Annemarie,' he murmured. 'What are you doing?'

'What we should have done a long time ago,' I whispered, inching forward so that my body was pressed up against his. Ethan exhaled and took my hand in his, gently pulling it down to my side. Then he leaned forward until his lips rested by my ear.

'Not like this,' he whispered. 'Not when you're angry. And not out of spite. When we do it, I want it to be because you don't want anything else, any*one* else, in the whole world but me.' I felt his lips just brush my cheek, and it sent a warm curl right down my spine. I sighed. He was right. Anger and lust don't make good bedfellows. I pulled away from him, my mind flying to the strange woman in the churchyard. Maybe she was one of Grandma's angels – which is to say, maybe Ethan had dreamed her up. The pregnancy had put him under a lot of stress, and that, coupled with the ungodly summer heat, meant that his mind might have conjured the entire scene. As if sensing my doubt, his hand reached out and found mine again, and this time he gave it a gentle squeeze.

'I'm sorry,' he said. 'But it happened, I swear. She was there. And then she wasn't.' His voice trailed off. I lay there in stunned silence, and let the song swallow me. Just like the Cat, I had no tears to give to God that night. I didn't feel that He deserved them, after all He'd done to me. Ethan and I lay side-by-side until the late-summer night devoured the room, and the moon threw its vengeful shadow down upon us.

Ethan

There was a moment that first spring, right after I'd started tutoring Annemarie, when I knew I should have kissed her. It was our third session, and we were sitting side-by-side at the desk in her bedroom. It had been raining most of the afternoon, and for an hour or so we'd been struggling through logarithms. But all at once the clouds cleared and a shaft of golden light came through the window. It settled right on her, and I swear in that moment she looked like a goddess. The equation flew out of my head, and all I could think of was how unbelievably lucky I was to be sitting there with such a beautiful girl. She must have sensed something, because she turned to me with a strange half-smile.

'You're not concentrating,' she said.

'No, I am,' I protested. 'It's just ... the sunlight. I wish you could see it. It's incredible.'

She took a deep breath and closed her eyes. 'I *can* see it. It's amazing.'

She was inches away; I could practically taste the softness of her lips on mine. I knew that she was waiting for me, knew that the moment I'd longed for had finally arrived, but something held me back. I don't know if it was fear or shyness or God or the Devil, but in that instant I froze, my heart thumping so hard I thought for sure she'd hear it.

Eventually she opened her eyes and looked straight at me, and I saw that they were full of regret. At the same time the clouds outside returned and suddenly both the golden light and my window of opportunity were gone. Even now I wonder whether if I'd acted on my instincts that day, none of this would have ever happened: the pregnancy, the visions, even the stuff with Father O'Shea. Because if I'd gone ahead and kissed her, one thing might have led to another, and Annemarie would have been a sinner. Then maybe God would have bestowed His terrible blessing on someone else. So I guess I have only myself to blame.

It hadn't been easy to persuade Deacon Joe to take me on as her tutor in the first place. From the start, he seemed pretty certain that I was the left hand of Satan, and it was only because Annemarie's mama and Aunt Ada intervened on my behalf that he felt obliged to hire me. I think it was Ada who swung it for me in the end. In truth I'd always found Annemarie's aunt pretty terrifying. She wore tight-fitting skirts and tops that plunged so low her cleavage made me dizzy. She also decked herself out from head to toe in loud jewellery, which made her look as if she'd just robbed the five and dime. Annemarie said she'd been married four times altogether, and that her first husband was in prison, the second had absconded, and the last one had died. I guess she set her sights on Deacon Joe because she thought that he was flush, even though he only part-owned a used-car dealership. It sure wasn't because of his hair.

Ada and Annemarie's mama had both been sent to a strict Catholic girls' school in West Virginia, even though their parents almost never set foot inside a church. But their education had affected them in different ways: Ada had grown up wild and rebellious, while Annemarie said her mama had been a pillar of the community – singing in the church choir, volunteering at the old folks' home, and marrying a nice young man from the congregation who later turned out to be gay. Three months after Annemarie was born, he'd run off to California with the parish accountant and the only thing her mama had to show for it was a faded postcard from Tijuana saying he was sorry.

So when I first approached Deacon Joe about tutoring Annemarie he brushed me off, saying that only a bona fide math teacher would do. 'This isn't totting up sums, Ethan,' he said. 'We need a mature, knowledgeable individual. Preferably a *female*.' Fortunately, the small town of Jericho did not contain such a person, or at least no one else presented themself within the right time frame. Three weeks after I won the math contest, I overheard Ada tell Deacon Joe that providence had put me on their doorstep, and that he'd be a fool not to recognise it. Deacon Joe relented and offered me a 'probationary period', but warned me not to take liberties with Annemarie. Mathematics was the priority and we were to stick to the curriculum he'd give me with no deviation allowed. Later, when I thanked Ada for her intervention, she gave me a wink that made my throat tighten like a boa constrictor.

When I told Moose I was going to tutor Annemarie, he shook his head and whistled. 'Better you than me. That house gives me the creeps. It looks like Notre Dame.' Annemarie's house *was* a bit imposing. It was a mix of strange styles, like someone had changed their mind several times while it was being built, and was in a bad state of repair. It was tall and dark and covered with ivy, and there was a small round tower on the left side of the top floor that was strictly off-limits owing to the fact that it was structurally unsound. A thick, chest-high hedge ran down the side of the driveway. All in all, the place wasn't exactly welcoming.

But I didn't mind: I would have three hours a week alone with Annemarie. Three hours to gaze at her without the evil eye of Deacon Joe bearing down upon me in return. I couldn't believe my luck. Even so, the first lesson didn't go all that smoothly. When I got to her house, Annemarie's mom told me I'd find her upstairs in her bedroom. I'd never set foot inside the house, let alone in her room, so as I climbed the dark stairway my head was crowded with all kinds of visions. My heart was slamming inside my chest like a caged animal by the time I knocked on the door. Annemarie opened it wearing Levi's jeans and a long-sleeved turquoise T-shirt that clung tightly to her body. Her frame was long and slender and neatly matched mine for height, and her light brown hair hung loose in wispy ringlets that tumbled almost to her waist. For a moment I couldn't breathe. She pulled the door open and took a step back, and all I could think of in that instant was that Annemarie was the human equivalent of a perfect number: one that is equal to the sum of its quotients. I knew four perfect numbers (6, 28, 496 and 8,128) and right then they all popped into my head. Perfection.

'Are you coming in?' she asked me, the corners of her mouth twitching upwards slightly. 'Or are we gonna do math in the hallway?'

That day I taught her what a perfect number was, even though it wasn't on the syllabus, and explained that in ancient times mathematicians regarded perfect numbers as both virtuous and beautiful. 'God made the world in six days,' Annemarie mused. 'So maybe He expected it to be full of virtue and beauty.'

'It is,' I said, looking straight at her and thinking that God must have had Annemarie in mind. She blushed then, a delicate pink tinge that made her even more gorgeous.

'Not always,' she said, in a slightly reproving tone.

At the end of the hour there was a rap on the door and, before we could answer, it opened and Deacon Joe was standing there. He cleared his throat and stood with his hands on his hips. Annemarie and I shifted a few inches apart.

'Hour's up,' he said tersely.

'We'll just finish up this problem set,' I replied.

'Fine. But just so you know, I won't be paying extra if you work overtime.'

'It's my pleasure.'

Deacon Joe's eyes flashed back, as if to say: *Don't even consider your pleasure in all of this!* 'I'll see you downstairs,' he said, turning away. When I looked back at Annemarie, she was smiling.

'Is it really?' she asked.

'What?'

'Your pleasure?' She said it in such a provocative way that I felt a baseball-sized lump form in my throat.

'Um ... well ...' I stammered uneasily. She laughed, cutting me off.

'I'm only joking, Ethan!'

I exhaled with relief. 'Yeah, I know.'

'But just for the record, it pleases me too,' she said.

I like to think that was our first date, because we never really had a proper one. For the next several months we stuck more or less to the scheduled times. After awhile Deacon Joe stopped lurking around the doorway when we were due to finish, and we began to stray further and further from logarithms. The day Annemarie turned seventeen I brought her a book of poems by Emily Dickinson, and she insisted that we lie side-by-side on the floor while I read them out loud. Annemarie thought you had to be looking at the sky when you read poetry, even though we were stuck inside and she was blind. 'It's the principle,' she insisted. 'Poetry doesn't grow out of the ground, it comes down from the clouds.' After I'd read the poems, I kind of understood what she meant.

Eventually I stopped coming round at the regular times, and just turned up on the doorstep most evenings after school. About the same time, Deacon Joe stopped paying me. It was one of those unspoken things, sort of a tit for tat. He was granting me unlimited access in exchange for making sure Annemarie got the grades she needed. Deacon Joe was always tight with cash, so I guess he recognised an opportunity to cut corners when he saw it. But I think it still rankled because every time he opened the front door to me, he'd suck in his breath as if he was swallowing his pride. Moose thought I was an idiot for carrying on without pay, especially when I confessed to him I still hadn't even got to first base, but I would have done anything just to be around Annemarie, frankly. I was that far gone.

But visiting the house posed another problem for me. Apart from Deacon Joe, I also had Ada to contend with. Deacon Joe and Annemarie's mom helped out at church clubs on Tuesday and Thursday evenings, and on those nights Ada used to waylay me in the hallway. One night, as I started to climb the stairs, she asked if I could help her change a light bulb in the bedroom. When we got to her room it was dark and she suggested I stand on her bed to reach the fitting. I took off my sneakers and climbed on to the bed, which was a huge king-size affair strewn with little square cushions. I took the new bulb from her and stretched my arm up to the ceiling, but the mattress was so soft I lost my balance, and in a flash Ada had leaned forward, her hands gripping my hips so tight I could feel her fingernails digging into my skin.

'Here, honey, let me steady you,' she said, a little breathlessly. I could smell her perfume in the darkness, mixed with the aroma of something else I didn't even want to contemplate. I reached up again, this time on to my toes, and the mattress gave way like a marshmallow, toppling me forward. Ada was still holding on to my waist and we both fell flat on the bed, her body sprawled across my legs. I leaped out from under her so fast it was like someone had lit a match beneath me, but Ada just cackled and said, 'Land sakes, you're a jumpy one!'

'I don't think I'm tall enough to reach,' I said quickly.

'Oh, you're *plenty* tall enough,' she insisted.

Annemarie must have heard the commotion because just then she came to the doorway. 'Ethan?' she called.

'He's just here helping me change the light bulb,' Ada said, but there was a slight hitch to her tone, as if she was throwing down the gauntlet. Annemarie reached out and felt along the wall until she found the light switch, then flicked it on. The bulb came on just fine, and I turned back to Ada with surprise. 'Well, what do you know?' she said, her pencilled eyebrows shooting up. 'Joe must have changed it while I was out.'

Annemarie was a bit sulky that evening, and though I was embarrassed to be caught out with Ada, I reckoned it was a good sign that Annemarie was jealous. After that she made a point of answering the door herself on Tuesday and Thursday evenings, and even though we never spoke about Ada directly, I could tell Annemarie wasn't gonna let her aunt loose on me again. The next day, when I told Moose what had happened, he snorted and said, 'What'd I tell you about that house? It's like the Christians and the lions! Except you're the Christian.'

The next Sunday Annemarie insisted on waiting outside the church alone until I arrived. When I did she took my arm and asked me to walk her to the family's pew, but when we got there she pulled me in with her, forcing me to sit down beside her. 'What are you doing?' I hissed.

'You belong up here. With me.'

'Deacon Joe will skin me alive!'

'Let him try.'

'I'd rather he didn't!' Just then Ada, who was sitting on the other side of Annemarie, leaned over and shushed me.

'Sorry,' I mouthed. I felt totally exposed sitting next to Annemarie at the front of the church, and far preferred the anonymity of the back row, where I could daydream as I liked. Now she'd made me a pawn in some private battle she was waging with Deacon Joe. It wasn't a fight I would have chosen, and I wondered what had brought it on. Just then Deacon Joe caught my eye and I saw his nose flare ever so slightly. He settled his gaze on me for what seemed like an eternity, until I was forced to look down at the hymn book in my lap.

After church Deacon Joe made the rounds of the congregation, seemingly ignoring us. Eventually, when it was almost time to go, Annemarie excused herself to go to the bathroom and he suddenly appeared from nowhere. 'I see you've moved up in the world,' he said quietly.

'It wasn't my idea,' I protested.

'Annemarie can be as foolish as any young girl her age,' he said, eyeing the crowd. 'But I assume you know better.'

I nodded, uncertain what I was agreeing to.

'Glad we're on the same page,' he said, turning to go.

Later, when I explained what had transpired, Annemarie was furious. 'And you agreed?'

'Well. Sort of. I'm not really sure ...'

'Ethan, you are weak!'

'It's not worth it, Annemarie. I don't really care.'

'You'd rather sit alone than with me?'

'I didn't say that. I just meant ... there are other things that are more important in the scheme of things.'

'Like what?!' she demanded.

'Like ... being able to see you whenever I want,' I stammered.

'But not in church.'

'What do you mean?'

'You want to be with me, but not in church.'

'Annemarie, it's not exactly quality time.'

'Then why do you come?'

She kind of had me on that one. *'Cause it's part of the package*, I thought to myself. Annemarie, church, Deacon Joe, Ada, her mother ... they were all lumped together in my mind.

'I come because I want to be near you,' I said finally.

'Near, but not with.'

'Not if it causes problems.'

'Well, near but not with is a problem for *me*,' she said then. 'So what's it gonna be? Near or with?'

I hesitated. What she meant, of course, was *who's* it gonna be? Would I let her win this particular battle, or Deacon Joe?

'With,' I said. 'Of course, with.'

'Good.'

That was our first fight. Afterwards, I went round to see Moose for consolation. His mom was baking brownies when

I arrived – real ones, which is to say not from a box (the only sort my mom ever made). Moose's mom wore checked aprons, made meals in a crockpot, and occasionally answered the door wearing curlers in her hair, a sight that vaguely alarmed me when I first encountered it. Moose was still in bed, so I went upstairs to his room. He had recently painted it black, only to decide that black was a bit of a downer, so he'd redone it in white, only to lose interest after one coat, which meant that it now looked like sludge. When I told him about my fight with Annemarie, he rolled over and threw a pillow at me.

'You woke me up to tell me that?'

'I woke you up because it's nearly two.'

'You are such a loser,' he moaned. 'I can't believe you'd choose Joan of Arc over Sophie Strater.' Sophie Strater was a cheerleader he'd been trying to get me to go out with for months. She was loud, blonde and had big breasts, which did little to distinguish her from the rest of the squad, as far as I was concerned. She was also the best friend of Moose's girlfriend, Shelly.

'Joan of Arc is way more interesting than Sophie Strater,' I said.

'Interesting. Oh, man. Not top of the list,' he mumbled face down to the mattress.

'Well, maybe not on yours, but it's definitely on mine.'

'Along with frustration, misery and humiliation. Not to mention blindness.'

'Hey, I told you. No blind jokes.' I threw the pillow back at him. Moose rolled over again and looked at me.

'Who's joking? Seriously, Ethan. You're in purgatory, man.'

OK, so he was right. Maybe I was in purgatory, for now. But that didn't mean I was condemned to eternal damnation.

Even Deacon Joe said that purgatory was just a temporary stop on the way to heaven, a place for spiritual purification, whatever that is. So there was hope for me yet. I was determined that Annemarie and I would find our own way to paradise, either here in Jericho or somewhere else. So right now I was happy to be cleansed. After all, I decided, being clean wasn't so bad. Just so long as it wasn't everlasting.

But I was still troubled about what had happened at church, so the next night I cornered Annemarie. 'What was all that about yesterday? With you and Deacon Joe?' Annemarie sighed and tilted her head right back, as if she was looking at the ceiling. But of course she wasn't.

'Yesterday was just a little sparring match,' she said.

'What do you mean?' I asked suspiciously.

'Deacon Joe wants me to go to blind camp next summer, and I told him flat out at breakfast yesterday that I wasn't going.'

'Blind camp?'

'You know. A camp for teens. Who happen to be blind.'

'And?'

'I'm not really used to hanging out with blind kids, Ethan.'

That was true. In all the time I'd known her, Annemarie had only ever hung out with me and Cora Lynn.

'But ... would it be so bad? I mean, it might be good to meet some other blind kids.'

'Look, that's not the point. I'm sure blind camp is fine.'

'Then why not go?'

'Because he's trying to define me through my blindness. He wants to put me in the blind box and keep me there.'

'Really? You think that's what he wants? Why?'

'Because it makes me more dependent on him.'

Huh. I thought about it for a moment. Maybe she was

right. Annemarie might be blind, but she also had a knack for seeing into other people's minds.

'So I need to assert myself against him, to remind him that he's not my father, or my boss. Or anything else, for that matter.'

Definitely not anything else! I thought.

'So yesterday was my first act of defiance. And I intend there to be more.'

Oh, jeez. If she wasn't careful, Annemarie was going to turn our relatively peaceful purgatory into a living hell. It had always been my role to defy Deacon Joe, not hers. And I wasn't sure I trusted her with it.

'Look, Annemarie, he could make things really difficult for us.'

'Let him.'

'For *me*.'

'You can take it,' she said staunchly, lifting her chin.

I wasn't sure her faith in me was justified.

Eva

I dreaded the day when Annemarie's pregnancy would become public knowledge. Folks in Jericho were quick to condemn and slow to forgive. My mama used to say that small towns bred narrow minds and pinched hearts, but I'd always thought that people bent their minds together because they felt safer that way. The downside to all that security was that folks in Jericho could be almost wilfully ignorant. In the months after Annemarie lost her sight, people were surprised and vaguely alarmed to bump into us at the supermarket, or on a trip to the post office, as if blindness should condemn a child to a life inside a darkened room. After she went blind, Annemarie never received party invitations or offers to play: no mother wanted the responsibility of a blind child in their home, and even fewer wanted to expose their own children to the misfortune of her disability. By the time she was six, Annemarie could empty a playground in minutes. No one was prepared to see a blind child fall from a jungle gym, or step in front of a moving swing. The other mothers would offer anxious smiles, check their watches, then nod to each other and quickly gather their things, calling briskly to their offspring. They'd turn to me with a shrug of apology, rolling their eyes. 'We've been here for *hours*,' they would say.

Luckily Annemarie saw none of this, though I sometimes wondered if she sensed the effect her blindness had on those around us. The shrinking away of humanity, I called it in my darker moments. Ada was more blunt: the *stinking array* of humanity, she would say with a snort. For all her faults, Ada stood by me through it all. Though she veered and swerved through her own life, she never shirked the ups and downs of mine. And having successfully dodged children, she positively doted on Annemarie. 'That child fell straight from heaven,' she used to say when Annemarie was little. 'Anybody who can't see that is more blind than she is.' But over the years, folks in Jericho did start to see. As she moved through adolescence, Annemarie went about her life as if being blind was no worse than having a nagging cough or a trick knee. And without realising it, she earned the respect of those around her, and eventually their admiration.

Which is why I was so worried. On the face of it, there was something tragic and grubby about a seventeen-year-old blind girl getting knocked up by the boy next-door. Annemarie had worked hard to earn her dignity; I couldn't stand to see her lose it so easily. Deacon Joe must have felt the same way, because for the next few weeks he went around in a funk, refusing to speak to anyone. But Ada remained unfazed. 'For heaven's sake, it's the seventies, not the fifties,' she hissed at me one night after dinner. 'No one's gonna make her wear a scarlet letter!'

'People will talk.'

'Let them. It doesn't mean we have to listen.'

'What about the Church?'

'What about it? If the Church weren't so backward in its notions, Annemarie wouldn't be in this predicament in the first place,' she retorted. Ada had always been disdainful of the Church's position on contraception, saying that asking married couples to abstain from sex was like putting bunnies in a hutch and expecting them to stay in different corners.

'Well, at some point she'll have to go to Confession,' I said. Ada picked up her coffee cup and shrugged.

'Not before the last trimester.'

Privately, Ada's nonchalance about Annemarie's situation irritated me. With her cavalier attitude towards marriage and relationships, Ada hadn't exactly been the best role model all these years. Though she and I had long ago agreed to differ on the subject, Ada had no trouble reconciling her chequered marital history with her faith. 'Jesus went into the desert for forty days, not forty years,' she used to say dismissively. 'He didn't intend for me to die an old maid.' And even Deacon Joe, who was far more conservative about such matters, had always been willing to suspend the rules when it came to Ada's past.

'Catholicism isn't some kind of smorgasbord,' I'd said to her when she told me she was getting married for the fourth time. 'You don't just get to pick and choose.'

'God will punish me for my sins, not my mistakes,' she replied staunchly. And she believed it. In Ada's judgment, men were mistakes not sins, and marriage was a holy union until you deemed it otherwise. At which point it became an inconvenience. So I guess it was no surprise that she found it easier to reconcile herself to the loss of Annemarie's chastity, relegating it in her mind to the category of jumbo-sized slip-up rather than cardinal sin.

Deacon Joe, on the other hand, was far more censorious. But it gradually became clear that he wasn't just angry for Annemarie's sake: he was angry for his own. He seemed to take it personally, as if she had deliberately set out to sabotage his efforts to provide her with a sound moral and religious education. And he was determined to make her pay: snapping at her every time she came into the room, and refusing to let her accompany him on his regular visits to the elderly. He behaved as if she'd done it just to spite him, which was nothing short of ridiculous. Any idiot could see that sparks flew like crossfire between Annemarie and Ethan; it was plainly evident to everyone but Deacon Joe that they'd simply fallen prey to teenage lust.

One night after dinner, Deacon Joe waited until Annemarie had gone up to her bedroom then produced a pamphlet from his briefcase, throwing it down on the table between us. On the front was an emblem of a pink heart with a stork flying overhead. 'What's this?' asked Ada suspiciously. She picked up the pamphlet and opened it.

'Convent of the Sacred Heart. Just over the Kentucky border,' he said.

'It's a home for unwed mothers,' she said, her eyes flicking up to him. 'What's all this about, Joe?'

'I took the liberty of making a few enquiries over the past week. And this looks like our best option. It's out of state, so no chance of anyone down there recognising her. And they'll handle everything, start to finish. It's a one-stop shop.'

'You want to send Annemarie away?' I asked, astonished. I might have been embarrassed and humiliated by our situation, but never in my wildest dreams had I envisaged sending her away.

'It's a time-honoured solution,' he said defensively. 'And the only *obvious* one available to us. Annemarie's life will be ruined forever if she stays here in Jericho. Not to mention the impact it will have on the rest of us.'

I turned to Ada. 'Were *you* in on this?' She shook her head.

'Joe, you never said anything to me about a home,' she said.

'We agreed that I should look into a solution,' he said to her.

'We agreed that you'd investigate adoption,' said Ada threateningly. She turned to me and shrugged. 'Just in case, you know?'

'I gave the convent a call first thing this morning,' said Deacon Joe. 'They took a little persuading on account of Annemarie being blind and all, but in the end they agreed to take her for the last three months of her confinement. We'll have to keep her off the streets until then, and hope for the best.'

'Annemarie is not gonna be shipped off to some pregnancy prison in Kentucky!' I said.

'Of course she isn't,' said Ada quickly, reaching for my hand and giving it a squeeze.

'Sixteen weeks. Start to finish. That's all it'll take,' said Joe. 'If Annemarie wants to find a decent God-fearing husband, it's her best shot. You know as well as I do that no one wants to buy the cow once the milk's been given away for free.'

'Annemarie is not a farm animal. And we are *not* casting her out!' I said.

'No, we are endeavouring to save her. Afterwards, she'll be able to resume her old life. She can go to college, find a good husband, maybe even raise a *real* family one day,' he added pointedly.

I frowned. So if Annemarie stuck to Deacon Joe's rules then one day she could have a *real* family! What in God's name did that make us? I picked up the leaflet, tore it in half, tore it again, then put it in the trash. Then I turned back to face him.

'Annemarie stays here – in Jericho – with us,' I said. 'And we take what comes.'

Annemarie

The day after Ethan's encounter with the woman in the graveyard, the sunsets started. It was a Sunday in mid-July and we were on our way to a church supper. At my suggestion, Deacon Joe and Ada and Mama had gone ahead to help set up, and Ethan and I were due to walk round later. The weather was still viciously hot, though by the time we left it had shifted from unbearable to uncomfortable. Even so, I was relieved to be outside again, as I'd spent almost the entire week in the relative cool of my bedroom. As we crossed the yard, I was reminded of how much I loved the sounds of an Ohio summer evening. It was like a choral requiem for everything that had lived and died during the day. When I was young I'd spent hours sitting outside in the darkness, isolating and cataloguing the sounds of insects in my mind. I learned to recognise them all: the high soprano chirrup of the crickets, the slightly lower screech of the grasshoppers, the steady tenor buzz of the cicadas, and the occasional bass dive bomb of a junebug. But my favourite was the katydid: elusive, faint and girlishly high, fitting for its name.

As Ethan and I crossed the meadow that lay between our

house and the churchyard, I felt the heat of the low evening sun on my face. The night-time insects had yet to appear, but I could hear the alto buzz of honey bees as we made our way through the dry summer grass. That morning we'd discussed whether we should tell anyone about his conversation with the Virgin Mary, but Ethan had argued that no one would believe us, and for once I'd agreed. Although I was anxious to prove my innocence to Mama and Deacon Joe, I knew that without proof I would only heap more scorn and anger upon us both. All at once Ethan stopped and laid a hand on my arm, and I could tell by the firmness of his grip that something was wrong. 'What is it?' I asked.

'I'm not sure,' he said doubtfully. He didn't move, nor did he release his grip on my arm.

'Is she back?'

'No. It's not that,' he said quickly. Then he paused. 'Well. Not exactly.'

'What is it then? What are you looking at?'

'The sky,' he murmured. 'Oh, God,' he added, his voice barely audible.

'Ethan, what is it? You have to tell me!'

He was silent for a long moment, and when he spoke his voice was incredulous. 'Her face, Annemarie. Her face is in the sky!'

It was the first time in years that I truly wished I could see. I asked him to describe it for me, and slowly, almost unwillingly, Ethan explained how the sun had slipped behind a hazy bank of clouds on the horizon, and as it did her features suddenly appeared, picked out in hues of orange and gold. 'Is it beautiful?' I asked.

'Yes.' He seemed mesmerised by the sight of her. Or drugged. I couldn't tell which, but I could barely get his attention. Fortunately, no one but us was around. We stood there for the next few minutes until the image began to fade in the dying light, then it disappeared altogether. When it was over, I turned to him.

'Is she gone?'

'Yes.'

'It's the Virgin Mary, isn't it?'

He was silent.

'Ethan?'

'I guess so,' he said. 'It must be.'

'What do we do now?'

'I don't know. Wait 'til she comes back?'

'What is it that she wants?'

'Maybe she wants to tell us something.'

'She already told us something, Ethan.'

'Maybe there's something else.'

Lord Almighty, I thought. What else could there possibly be?

We went to the church supper but everything around me seemed muffled, as if I was listening to it from underwater. Ethan stayed with me but was pretty quiet; for once I had no idea what was going through his head. When it was over, he suggested that I walk home with Ada and Deacon Joe instead of him.

'Are you all right?' I asked.

'Just tired. Think I'll head home,' he said.

'OK.'

I surrendered myself to Deacon Joe and Ada. Walking home across the churchyard, I listened for the night-time sounds that I'd missed earlier. But instead of taking comfort from them, I felt an intense pang of longing. I realised that I wanted things to be as they'd been before – before the pregnancy and the visions. I wanted it to be just Ethan and me and the bugs again.

Cassandra came the next day. I showed her what I'd done over the past week, which amounted to barely more than an inch of baby blanket. I told her I could see why knitting had gone out of fashion.

'The thing about knitting,' she said, settling down beside me on the bed, 'is that it's all about the process. People think it's about the product, but it's not. The product is just a means to an end.'

'So what's the end?'

'The process is the end.'

'Huh.' I wasn't sure I followed, but I was prepared to take her word for it. I did find it soothing.

'Has Ethan been around?' she asked casually.

'Sure. He's here pretty much every day.'

'And what does he think about the pregnancy?' I felt my gut clench slightly.

'Well, he's not exactly thrilled, I guess.'

'So he's not really on board? For being a parent.'

'Um ... I'm not sure he's thought that far ahead yet.'

'I see.' She let a few moments go by, during which I could hear her needles clicking away at great speed, next to the dull rhythmic plod of my own.

'What about you?' she asked then. 'Have you thought that far ahead?'

I hesitated. The truth was I hadn't thought about being a parent. Whenever I tried, I failed. For whatever reason, the image of me as a mother simply wouldn't come.

'Well,' I said finally, 'so far, it's been more about the process. Rather than the product.'

'Ah,' she said knowingly.

'But I assume I'll get there,' I added.

'I assume you will, too.'

When Ethan came by after supper that evening, I told him what I'd said to Cassandra. 'Being pregnant makes me feel so inadequate,' I complained.

'You're not inadequate, Annemarie. Not yet anyway. You're doing everything you need to do.'

'Well, I'm basically just an incubator. It's not like I actually have to *do* anything.'

'It'll get harder.'

'Do you think so?'

'Yes.'

He was silent for a moment, and I wondered how he knew. I felt like he was withholding something, and I realised that I'd been talking pretty much non-stop since he came in, so I waited for him to speak. Outside I could hear the sound of a sprinkler; Deacon Joe was obsessive about the lawn and often watered it in the evening. Ethan got up from the bed and went over to the side of the room where the window was, almost as if he was trying to distance himself from me. 'I saw her again,' he said then.

'You did? When?'

'Last night. On the way home. She was by the shrine again.'

'Did she speak to you?'

'Sort of.'

'What did she say?'

'Well, it was a little difficult to follow. I think it was some kind of prayer. She started by saying her soul magnified the Lord. And that she was his handmaiden. But I kind of lost the thread after that.'

'The Magnificat,' I said. 'It's her canticle.'

'That doesn't really help me, Annemarie.'

'It's like her song.'

'Oh. Well, she didn't really sing it. She spoke it.'

'And when it was finished?'

'She smiled. And then she disappeared.'

'She smiled at you?'

'I guess so. I mean, I was the only one there.'

I didn't understand. Why was she appearing to Ethan and not to me, if I was the blessed one? Was it because I was blind? There were other ways to communicate apart from sight, I thought with irritation. The Virgin Mary, of all people, should know that.

'So,' I said a little awkwardly. 'What do we do now?'

'We wait and see, I guess.'

'Whether she comes again?'

'Yeah.'

She'll come again, I thought. But not to me.

We didn't have to wait long. Less than an hour, in fact. As the sun began to sink on the horizon, her face appeared once again in the sky. But this time it was Deacon Joe who saw it first. He'd gone outside to move the sprinkler, and when he'd finished he turned round and there she was. Up in my room, we heard him hollering for Ada and Mama in a tone of complete astonishment. It took us only an instant to realise why.

'It's her,' said Ethan urgently. And he shot out of the room at warp speed. I followed as closely as I could. I could hear Mama and Ada coming down the hallway from the kitchen.

'What is it, Joe?' Ada called out. We all fell out of the front door on to the lawn.

'Look there, in the sky!' shouted Deacon Joe from the far end of the yard.

There was a long pause, and once again I was practically choking with frustration

'Land sakes!' cried Ada.

'Holy Mother of Jesus,' murmured Mama.

'Ethan?' I said. He reached over and took my hand in a gesture of comfort.

'It's the same,' he said quietly. 'The same as last night.'

Suddenly Deacon Joe was at my shoulder. 'You saw this before?' he demanded.

'Sort of,' said Ethan.

'What do you mean, sort of! When?'

'Last night. On the way to supper.'

'And you didn't say anything?'

Ethan hesitated for a split-second. 'I thought I'd imagined it,' he stammered. 'I mean, it was difficult. No one else was around.'

Except me, I thought crossly. I waited, wondering if he was going to say anything about the other, more intimate, encounters he'd had. But he must have decided right then to keep them to himself. We all stood there for a moment, watching.

'She's beautiful,' murmured Ada.

'She surely is,' agreed Deacon Joe, a note of wonder in his voice. 'I wonder why she's come to us?'

I felt Ethan squeeze my hand slightly, uncertain whether he was urging me to speak or stay silent. And just like the night before, the Virgin went as quickly as she came, leaving everyone slightly giddy, and wavering with uncertainty.

'You don't suppose that was just a ... trick of the eye, do you?' said Deacon Joe after we'd gone back inside.

'Or some sort of strange cloud formation?' said Mama.

'But we all saw it!' said Ada.

'Of course we did. It's just ... we don't know what it was exactly that we saw,' said Deacon Joe. 'Could've been some sort of hoax.' His words had an immediate effect: I could feel their doubt take root, and as it did the elation of the previous minutes began to drain from the room. Ethan gave my hand another squeeze, as if to caution me to remain silent. I knew what he was thinking: it would take more than one sunset to convince them.

'Well, if Ethan saw it last night, then maybe it'll happen again tomorrow,' said Ada tentatively. Deacon Joe grunted.

'I wouldn't bet on it,' he said, turning away.

But the rest of the town didn't agree. A couple of other locals had seen the display and by lunchtime the next day the whole of Jericho was practically heaving with excitement. By about seven o'clock that night, the commotion started. I was in my room when I heard the sound of cars pulling up and parking on the street outside. Word had got round that the vision was clearest from the churchyard across from our house. The sun wasn't due to set until eight-thirty, but people weren't taking any chances. I could hear more and more of them arriving, and after a few minutes I called down to Mama.

'What's happening outside?'

'Looks like the Fourth of July Parade,' she said. 'There must be a hundred people out there sitting on blankets and plastic chairs. Some of them have even brought coolers and picnic baskets – they're making a party out of it.' Just then I heard someone turn on a boom box, only to be shouted down by a chorus of disapproval. It seemed that picnic baskets were OK, but the Top 40 might put the Virgin Mary off. Mama went and rounded up Deacon Joe and Ada and we carried some lawn chairs across the road to the churchyard.

'Hey Annemarie,' a voice called out as soon as I'd settled down in my chair. It was a girl called Saskia who had befriended me briefly in the ninth grade, when she decided I might be her ticket to the honour roll. For about six weeks Saskia used to come round in the evenings for homework sessions that consisted of her reading the questions aloud and me dictating the answers. She was obsessed with a boy called Shane Maddox, whose father taught driver's education and also coached the track team, of which Shane was a rising star. Earlier this year I'd heard that Shane had broken his neck in a pole vault accident, by which time Saskia had ditched her academic aspirations to focus her energies exclusively on him. Shane was laid up in traction for three months and rumour had it that Coach Maddox walked into Shane's bedroom one night and discovered Saskia naked on top of him. I had to give her credit; Saskia wasn't about to let traction or a broken neck get in her way.

'Hey Saskia,' I replied.

'Isn't this crazy?' she said breathlessly. 'Who would have thought that something like this would happen in Jericho?!'

'Who would have thought,' I repeated. 'How's Shane?'

'He's doing real good. Coach says he should be back in school by September.'

'No more pole vault though, huh?'

'Nah. Shane's a bit bummed by that.'

'Poor Shane.'

'He says it was like flying with the angels,' said Saskia. 'But I told him he doesn't need to fly with the angels any more, 'cause he's got me.' She giggled.

He surely does, I thought. Just then I felt Ethan's presence like a cool breeze, and in another second he touched my shoulder lightly.

'Hey,' he said, dropping down beside me in the grass.

'Hey. I wasn't sure you were coming,' I replied.

'Sorry. Something came up.'

Something bigger than Mary? I thought. I waited to see if he would elaborate, but he said nothing more. Perhaps he'd already seen her today.

The crowd settled into a mood of nervous anticipation,

though Ethan seemed subdued again. I wanted to ask him if he'd had another encounter, but there were too many people around, and I wasn't sure how truthful he'd be. After half an hour the crowd grew restless, and some people wandered off. I could hear a group of younger kids playing Frisbee in the field behind me, and someone had turned the radio on again, this time with no opposition.

'Maybe she won't show,' I said.

'She'll show,' said Ethan quietly. Almost as if he knew. Ten seconds later I heard a shout go up, followed by a general stirring of the crowd.

'What's happening?' I asked, sitting forward.

'She's there. But it's ... harder to see. The cloud cover's too heavy, I think. All you can make out is an outline, not her features.'

'What's all the fuss about?' a man shouted from behind us. 'It's just a goddamn' bit of haze!'

'Wait for it, idiot,' muttered Ethan under his breath.

In a few more seconds the crowd gasped, a collective intake of breath that made the hair rise on the back of my neck.

'Told you,' said Ethan quietly.

'Oh my God! Is this for real?' I heard Saskia exclaim behind us.

'She's more real than you are,' murmured Ethan. I could feel him growing more agitated every second, his anger at the crowd radiating off him in hostile waves. By now people were cheering and clapping and going crazy with excitement. Someone at the back started chanting 'Mary, Mary', and within seconds the crowd had taken it up, making it sound like we were at a prize fight.

'Christ, I'm out of here,' said Ethan under his breath. I heard him spring to his feet and move off, leaving me alone with the Virgin Mary and a hundred frenzied followers.

Ethan

I spent the entire spring and summer that first year trying to morph from Annemarie's tutor into her boyfriend. But looking back on it, I was really just a pawn in her ongoing power struggles with Deacon Joe. She may have won the battle over blind camp that first summer, but as far as I could make out, she was losing the war with him at home. Under the guise of education, Deacon Joe started carving out more and more of her daily (or rather, evening) schedule for a random assortment of stupid hobbies. He decided that her keen hearing meant that she was musically gifted, so he introduced her to the German woman who played organ at church. He was too cheap to shell out for a piano (let alone an organ), so Annemarie was forced to have her lessons on a tiny electric keyboard, which sounded like a tinny cartoon version of the real thing.

Frau Beaver (actually her name was Bieber, but after I learned that it meant 'beaver' in German the name kind of stuck) was in her late sixties and had fled Berlin before the war. Somehow she'd ended up as the organist at St Paul's, even though she was the only Jewish person living in Jericho.

Actually she lived about a mile down the road in the small town of Berlin, a place that shared precisely nothing with its namesake, though it hadn't stopped her from settling there for sentimental reasons forty years earlier. Annemarie thought she was exotic and spent hours quizzing her about life under Hitler, not to mention her views on the Old Testament. Though the Beaver had lived in America for decades, her accent was still so thick I struggled to understand her. (She said *sunder* for thunder and *surfife* for survive.) Annemarie had lessons with her three mornings a week and (at Deacon Joe's suggestion, I was certain) was given masses of practice, which meant that she was forever plonking out scales when I came by. Some nights we barely had time to get through our math homework, let alone anything else, before the arpeggios took over.

At the same time Deacon Joe suggested that Annemarie should become fluent in another language, a notion that instantly caught her fancy. After a few false starts (Japanese, Russian – she wouldn't even *consider* something as boring as French or Spanish) she settled on Italian as her preferred choice. Instead of a tutor, Deacon Joe came across a set of second-hand Berlitz language tapes at a garage sale and Annemarie dutifully ploughed her way through them. Soon she was saying stuff like *ciao bello* and *arrivederci* all the time, which drove me crazy, so eventually I banned her from speaking Italian when I was around. The problem was that Annemarie *liked* her new hobbies, so it was hard to argue that they were tools of Deacon Joe's oppression. But I knew that he was secretly trying to run her ragged, so she wouldn't have time for *amore*.

So our second fight was about extra-curricular activities. 'Look, he's just trying to make sure I get into a good college,' she told me one night after I'd complained for the hundredth time.

'He's trying to make sure you don't have a social life.'

'But I don't have a social life.'

I didn't really like the implication. What did that make me? 'Look, Annemarie, I want to hang out with you. But every time I come round, you're up to your eyeballs in scales and *italiano*.'

'OK, let's compromise. I'll see you on Monday, Wednesday and Friday evenings, and do my organ and Italian on Tuesdays and Thursdays.' Somehow, without her even realising, Deacon Joe had got us back on to a timetable. And I was further than ever before from being Annemarie's boyfriend.

Moose wasn't impressed. 'Oh, man, she is *sooo* not into you,' he said.

'Thanks, Moose. I really appreciate your support.'

'Why don't you at least come out with me and Shelly and Sophie on Friday night?'

'No, thanks. I'm tied up.' Friday was one of Annemarie's nights, and even as I said the words, I knew I was being truly pathetic.

'Fine. You snooze, you lose, bro.'

'Guess I'll snooze.' But over the next few days I started to wonder if I was losing my perspective. I'd been fixated on Annemarie for most of the past year, and she was so different from anyone else I'd ever known that I'd almost forgotten what real girls were like. Sure I saw normal girls at school, but that wasn't the same as going out with one, or even having a conversation. Let alone making out. So I decided a date with Sophie Strater might be the answer. A date would help me understand whether I was on the right track chasing Annemarie, or missing out altogether.

So I called Moose and told him I'd do the double date. But being a total loser, I asked if we could move it to Saturday night instead. I might have been anticipating making out with Sophie, but I wasn't prepared to give up a night with Annemarie in the meantime. Moose sounded pleased on the phone, if a little surprised. 'So what changed your mind?' he asked.

'Her breasts.'

'Good reason.'

We went to the movies, which was pretty much the only thing to do on a Saturday night in Jericho. Except the cinema was in a mall three towns east, just outside Youngstown. Moose drove his Trans Am, which was a piece-of-shit car really, but it seemed to impress Sophie, who sat in the back with Shelly, whispering and lapsing into occasional fits of giggles. We stopped at a convenience store and Moose bought a couple of six-packs with his brother's ID and by the time we got to the mall the mood had lifted and Moose suggested we skip the film and drive to Wilson Creek Park instead.

Although it was mid-October, we were having a late burst of Indian summer and the weather was still pretty warm. We drove over to the western side of the park, not far from the old suspension bridge. Moose parked in a remote lot and got a couple of blankets out of the trunk. I had to admire him; he was nothing if not prepared. We carried the beers and blankets out on to the hundred-year-old bridge, a fanciful construction of lacy arches and thirty-foot-tall wrought-iron spires that looked like something straight out of Disney. Sophie and Shelly immediately began waltzing up and down the bridge pretending they were Cinderella, and Moose and I decided we'd be the Hunchbacks of Notre Dame, so we climbed up to the top of the spires and swung from one hand until the girls started screaming that we would die and made us come down. We laid the blankets out on a grassy bank and Moose and Shelly planted themselves on one and Sophie

84

settled herself on the other and looked up at me expectantly.

She was wearing tight designer jeans and a pale pink, wrap-around cardigan with a plunging neckline and a bow at the waist that practically screamed *Untie me!* Every time I looked in her direction my eyes flew straight to her cleavage, where a tiny but alluring birthmark nestled deep inside. I sat down beside her on the blanket and Moose tossed us a couple of cans of beer. I popped the lid on one and handed it to her, forcing myself to look straight into her eyes.

'Thanks,' she said, smiling.

'My pleasure.'

'Is it?' Sophie raised an eyebrow suggestively.

I realised that I'd heard those words before in completely different circumstances, and looked away in embarrassment. I lifted my beer and drank half of it, drowning my deceit. Sophie watched me, then took a long drink of her own. 'So ... it took you long enough to ask me out,' she said teasingly. I looked over at her. She was nice enough looking, with shoulder-length dark blonde hair that curled in feathered layers away from her face, and a slightly upturned nose. She was wearing a bit of eye shadow and lip gloss, something I was unused to, and I instantly found myself wondering what Annemarie would look like if she did the same. And just as I had that thought, Sophie leaned over and kissed me, banishing thoughts of Annemarie in an instant.

I'd forgotten what being with a girl was like, and over the course of the next hour it all came flooding back. *This* was what I had been missing, and, like a man dying of thirst, I drank deeply. Every now and then a tiny current of guilt would run through the back of my mind, but each time I closed my eyes and forced myself to concentrate only on Sophie: her smell, her taste, the feel of her skin beneath my hands, the sound of her breath as it came in little sighs. And in that way, for an hour or so, I too became blind. Eventually Moose and I went to take a leak in the woods. He positioned himself at one tree and I at another. 'You didn't waste any time,' he called over.

'She was kind of up for it.'

'Bro, she was desperate for it.'

'Yeah. I guess so.' So was I, I thought silently. But I wasn't going to admit that to Moose

'Man, you are whipped.'

I frowned. Was I? I mean, what exactly had changed? I would still lust nightly after Annemarie. And I would still, most likely, get nowhere. And Sophie Strater would still be willing and available. 'I don't think so,' I said, buttoning my jeans.

'What do you mean?'

'Well. Just that ... nothing has changed, really.'

'Oh, man. You're not going back to Joan of Arc, are you?'

'Look, Moose. I still like Annemarie. I'm sorry.'

'You are gonna be dead meat with Sophie, you know that?'

I knew that. As we walked through the woods I felt a crushing sense of guilt: not towards Annemarie for what I'd done, but towards Sophie for what I was going to do.

At the end of the night, when we dropped her off, she leaned over and gave me a kiss on the cheek, allowing her lips to stray near my ear. 'Call me,' she whispered.

I froze, unable to respond, unwilling to lie, incapable of telling the truth – and the look in Sophie's eyes was unbearable. She hesitated, and in her wise, female way, knew exactly what was in my head. I watched as confusion turned to pain and then anger, then she got out of the car and slammed the door without another word. Moose turned back to me from the driver's seat, his massive eyebrows raised

86

with alarm, and silently mouthed the words: *Dead meat*. I swallowed and looked out the window, watching Sophie disappear into her house and out of my pathetic teenage life for good.

Except she didn't disappear. She was at school, every day, and each time she passed me in the hallway she'd sort of swell with indignation, then whisper something derogatory to whichever girl was nearest. Within a week a flood of rumours began to circulate in quick succession: I had terrible breath, was a shitty kisser, ejaculated prematurely, and eventually, was gay. I bore each rumour like a penance, and in a way it made it easier to go back to Annemarie. Who on account of being blind and homeschooled, heard none of them. Praise the Lord indeed.

I thought that was the end of it. But a few weeks later Annemarie and I were doing math one evening when she turned to me and said, 'So you never told me: how was your date with Sophie Strater?' I nearly fell off the chair with surprise. Annemarie was wearing this little half-smile, like she'd been sitting on this nugget of information for far too long.

'My what?' I stammered.

'Your date. To the movies.' I was staring at her open-mouthed, and thinking she really *was* some sort of genie, when she gave a little laugh. 'Cora Lynn saw you guys. Outside the mall.' At once I was flooded with relief. Annemarie didn't have superpowers after all – she'd just heard a bit of gossip. But then I thought: *Christ!* What else had she heard? She was facing me, her head tilted with interest, waiting for me to speak.

'Well, it wasn't exactly a date. I was just hanging out with Moose and Shelly that night. And Sophie decided to come along.'

'Mmm,' said Annemarie, nodding. 'What film did you see?'

'Nothing in the end. We couldn't decide.'

'That's feeble! So what'd you end up doing?'

'Nothing much … just kind of … hung around. Went to the park and stuff.'

'Which park?'

'Wilson Creek. Near the suspension bridge.'

'The Cinderella Bridge,' she said in a dreamy tone. 'Mama used to take me there when I was a little girl. I haven't been in years.' She turned to me eagerly, her pale eyes shining with excitement. 'Can we go there sometime? You and me?'

'Yeah. Sure. I guess so,' I said reluctantly. Wilson Creek Park was, at that exact moment, the last place on earth I wanted to go with Annemarie. But I could hardly say no.

'Tomorrow. Let's go tomorrow. When you get done with school.'

So that is how, twice in the same fortnight, I came to be sitting on a blanket in the grass with a girl by the suspension bridge in Wilson Creek Park. Only this time the girl was Annemarie, and I was so nervous (not to mention wracked with guilt) that I could hardly speak, let alone make a move on her. We sat in the gathering dusk on a cool autumn evening and Annemarie listened intently to the sounds around us, pointing out the calls of birds she knew, and the way the water in the river rippled when a gust of wind stirred it, and all I could think was: *I made out here with Sophie Strater*. It was awful – truly the worst night of my life. And after awhile even Annemarie sensed that the evening was not heading in a good direction, so we gathered up the blanket and the cans of Coke (not beer) we'd brought and made our way back across the bridge to the car.

That was our first official date. It had gone so badly that, for days afterwards, the memory of it hung around like a bad smell. Maybe I was being paranoid, but I thought I could feel her sliding even further away from me, so a few weeks later I suggested a second outing to a Friday night basketball game at Jericho High. It was the first game of the season and Moose was the team's star player. We were playing one of our biggest rivals, the Lutheran Longhorns, so the atmosphere was bound to be exciting, even if Annemarie couldn't see. Anyway I could give her a blow-by-blow of what was happening, which would mean sitting close and speaking into her ear for two hours while the crowd went wild around us. The idea appealed to me, and I decided that maybe Moose was right – maybe the prison-like atmosphere of Annemarie's house *was* stifling us somehow. When I asked her whether she'd like to go, her face lit up excitedly. 'Really?' she asked.

'Sure. Moose is playing. He's their big star.'

'Deacon Joe used to play basketball for Jericho High,' she said.

'Well, then, he can't exactly object to you going.'

'I guess not.' She frowned. 'At least, I don't think so.' But we'd forgotten how ornery Deacon Joe could be.

'Crowds. Screaming fans. Pandemonium. Sweat. Why would Annemarie wish to take part in all that hubbub?' he asked grumpily.

'I like hubbub,' she said quickly.

'Since when?' he asked.

'Oh, Joe, for heaven's sake, let her go,' called out Ada from the kitchen. She stuck her head through the doorway. 'She's seventeen. Just because she's blind doesn't mean she can't go out like other kids her age. I used to love high school basketball games.'

'That is precisely what I'm worried about,' said Deacon

Joe loudly. 'From what I know of your misspent youth, she would do well not to follow in your footsteps.'

'Don't be such an old spoilsport,' Ada retorted, wiping her hands on a dishtowel.

'I am not old,' he snapped back. 'I am merely being cautious.'

'Stubborn, more like,' said Ada. 'Annemarie will be just fine with Ethan as a chaperone.' Ada turned and winked at me, and I felt my throat tighten in response.

'She better be.' Deacon Joe turned to me. 'You will seat yourselves right beside the exit,' he said, waggling a finger. 'On the bottom bleacher. If there's a fire, or an explosion, or a stampede, she is your first and only responsibility. You will save her before you save yourself. Is that clear?'

'Yes, sir,' I said.

'For heaven's sake, it's only a basketball game,' interjected Ada.

'And no alcohol or cigarettes. Not to mention any wacky tobaccy.'

'No, sir,' I assured him.

'And you will bring her straight home after the game finishes.'

'Actually, we were hoping to go for pizza afterwards,' Annemarie spoke up quickly. Deacon Joe frowned and shook his head.

'I don't believe that's strictly necessary.'

'Joe, it's pizza! Not the Last Supper,' said Ada, rolling her eyes. 'They're teenagers! They need to eat!' Deacon Joe gave me a look of pure condescension.

'I suppose you youngsters might require some sustenance,' he said, drawing out the syllables of the last word. 'A quick trip for pizza afterwards,' he conceded. 'But home by eleven-thirty.'

We took my dad's station wagon, and from the moment we got into the front seat, the atmosphere was way better than the last time. Annemarie was practically fizzing with excitement and I could tell she'd taken extra care with her hair (shiny, clean, and smelling of peach conditioner) and clothes (brown corduroy jeans, clogs, and a slinky cream top I'd never seen before). I hadn't realised how much she wanted this: the normal stuff of teenage life that I took for granted. She had always seemed above it all, but in fact she wasn't above – just outside. We parked the car in the school lot and I took her hand to lead her in. When we got inside the lobby she could hear the noise from the gymnasium and gave my hand a little squeeze. But at the door to the gym, her feet suddenly froze and her face went white as Crisco.

'Hey,' I whispered into her ear. 'You OK?'

Annemarie didn't reply. I saw her take a deep breath and hold it, like she was trying not to explode. I looked around. For once Deacon Joe may have been right: this was definitely a *hubbub*. The two teams were warming up so there were about twenty players out on the court with at least a dozen balls bouncing at any one time. AC/DC were playing 'Shoot To Thrill' over the PA and the cheerleaders were doing a line dance just past the entrance. The clamour of the crowds, the noise of feet stamping on the bleachers in time to AC/DC, and yes, even the smell of sweat, was pretty overwhelming. For a moment I tried to imagine what the scene must feel like to Annemarie. 'Oh man, this was a bad idea,' I said. 'We should go.' I started to tug on her arm.

'No,' she said quickly. She didn't budge. Instead she took a deep breath, her nostrils flaring slightly. 'I want to stay.'

'Are you sure?'

She didn't answer but she nodded, her pale eyes wide, and I felt her hand tighten on mine. I led her carefully past the cheerleaders, my head turned towards the crowd so I wouldn't have to make eye contact with Sophie Strater, who seemed to be throwing herself into the dance routine with extra enthusiasm just for my sake. I remembered my promise to Deacon Joe, and pulled Annemarie down on to the lowest bleacher about fifteen feet past the cheerleaders. We were a fair ways from the entrance, but there was no way I was going to sit in front of Sophie Strater's bouncing breasts all night.

Once I got Annemarie seated she relaxed and I started to breathe a little more easily. All around us people were staring. I guess it looked strange, a blind girl coming to a basketball game, but I tried to ignore them, and once the play began everybody's attention shifted to the game. I started describing what was happening to Annemarie, who listened carefully to every word and responded like she'd been a fan all her life. When Moose sank a basket she'd yip with delight, and when one of our guys missed she'd frown and furrow her brow. If the referee stopped play she'd grab my arm and make me explain what was happening, sometimes even before I'd worked it out myself. It was a little tiring, but in a funny way, I enjoyed the game way more than I ever had in the past.

At half-time I thought about taking Annemarie outside for some air, but it wasn't easy to negotiate the crowd with her on my arm, so I decided to stay put. Then the cheerleading squad ran out on to the middle of the court, and I felt my insides lurch. 'What's happening now?' asked Annemarie tentatively, almost as if she already knew. For a split-second, I thought about lying.

'I'm not sure,' I said. 'Think it's some sort of cheer thing.'

'Oh.' We sat silently while the cheerleaders took their places.

'Sophie Strater's a cheerleader, isn't she?' asked Annemarie. The music started and it was one of the hit songs from

Grease. The squad pranced about, pointing to the crowd and mouthing the words to 'You're The One That I Want', while Annemarie and I watched in silence. For the first time, she did not ask me to describe what was happening, and I was grateful. At one point Sophie Strater ended up in front of us, so close that I could see the beads of sweat forming on her forehead, and the look in her eye was more or less the biblical definition of wrath. After several excruciating minutes, the routine finally ended. Annemarie turned to me.

'So. Was she any good?'

'Um ... she was OK.' There was an awkward silence. 'Nothing special,' I added. Annemarie tilted her head to one side thoughtfully.

'It could be fun – cheerleading,' she said.

'Actually, I think it's pretty overrated.'

The final quarter of the game was so close it quickly eclipsed the memory of the half-time show. In the end the Buglers edged out the Longhorns 94 to 92 with only a few seconds left on the clock. Moose made the winning basket, and when he did the crowd went berserk. (Had he been there, Deacon Joe would have definitely called it pandemonium.) Annemarie loved it; she stamped her feet and clamped her arms around my neck like a crazed banshee. Across the floor, I watched as the Longhorns' ridiculously dressed mascot tore off his huge headdress (complete with long horns) and blinked at the scoreboard in red-faced disbelief.

'That was great!' Annemarie said breathlessly. 'Can we come again?'

We waited awhile for the gym to clear, then drove over to Fat Ruby's Pizza. When we arrived the place was already mobbed, the way it always was after a big game. Fat Ruby was behind the counter, wearing a dirty white apron and shouting orders to the crowd in a throaty baritone. She was in her late fifties and got fatter every year, but she could still throw pizza dough better than anyone I'd ever seen. We had to fight our way through the crowd, and as we did I spotted Moose and Shelly at a booth near the back. He stood up and waved, raising his enormous eyebrows and motioning for us to join them. I wasn't sure this was such a good idea but there weren't any free tables so I steered Annemarie over to where they were sitting. Moose leaped up to help her into the booth.

'Good game, bro,' I said as we sat down.

'You were awesome,' added Annemarie.

'She's your number one fan,' I explained.

'Hear that, Shelly?' said Moose with a grin. 'Shelly thinks b-ball's overrated.'

'No, I don't,' said Shelly. 'It's just a bit ... samey, that's all.'

'Really? I thought it was so exciting,' said Annemarie. 'What sport do you like?'

'Um ... well, they're all kind of samey, aren't they?' Shelly smiled and shrugged a little sheepishly, and Moose put his arm around her shoulders.

'That's my girl,' he said, winking at me. I left them debating the merits of football and soccer and went to the counter to order. By the time I'd finished, Moose's pizza was up so I carried it back to the booth. True to his style he'd ordered a large with double everything – it looked like someone had tipped the contents of their fridge on it. As I made my way back to the table Shelly passed me on her way to the bathroom, looking a little peeved. I nodded to the pizza and she jerked a thumb back towards the table, where Annemarie and Moose appeared to be having a heated debate.

'They're talking about whether it's better to be deaf or blind,' Shelly said, rolling her eyes. 'I swear Moose can argue about anything.' How they'd got to that particular topic from high school sports I had no idea, but as I took my seat, neither of them seemed to notice me.

'Look, sight is way more important to communication than hearing,' said Moose emphatically, leaning forward across the table. 'And without communication, you can't function.'

'Sight is more important to communication than hearing?!' said Annemarie. 'Are you crazy? I couldn't be having this conversation with you if I couldn't hear!'

'Sure you could. You could be lip-reading,' he countered.

'And missing every other word! Helen Keller said that blindness cuts us off from things, but deafness cuts us off from people.'

'Excuse me, but Helen Keller wasn't exactly in a position to judge. So much of communication is about visual clues. You might understand the words but you can't tell what my expression is.'

'Yes, I can,' Annemarie said smugly. 'I can hear it in your voice.'

'You can *hear* my expression?' he asked sarcastically.

'Yep.'

'OK. What is it now?'

'You're smiling. And raising your eyebrows.'

Moose was indeed smiling, and the second she said it, he raised his eyebrows. He laughed and threw me a glance. 'Man, you're good,' he said admiringly.

Annemarie smiled and tilted her head to one side with obvious pleasure. I felt the first stirrings of jealousy rise up inside me like a cobra. Annemarie and I had only ever talked about her blindness once or twice, and then only in the most cautious way. I'd never really had the courage to ask her outright about it, and all of a sudden I wondered why. I watched in silence as Moose fell upon his pizza. As if sensing my dismay, Annemarie reached down and gave my hand a light squeeze, but the fact that she did this only made me feel worse.

The evening spiralled downwards from there. Moose was funny and annoying and charming all at once. He seemed to light a spark in Annemarie that I'd never seen before. Certainly I'd never had that effect on her. Even Shelly couldn't fail to notice the chemistry between them, and by the end of the meal she and I sat like two sullen children whose parents had ignored them all night long. I was relieved when Annemarie's curfew drew near, as it gave me an excuse to pry her away. But on the drive home she was quieter than she'd ever been – she seemed tired suddenly and distracted, and I sat there like a moron with nothing to say. When we got to her house I leaped out and raced round to her side, reaching down to help her out of the car.

'Ethan, I'm not an invalid,' she said with a laugh. I dropped her arm at once and stepped back.

'Sorry,' I said. We stood there in the cold for an awkward moment.

'No, I'm the one who should be sorry,' she said finally. 'That was the best night ever. Really. Thank you so much for taking me.'

Before I could respond she leaned forward and gave me a kiss on the cheek, then turned and tapped her way up the driveway, oblivious to the darkness of the night. I stood beside the car thinking that I'd just had my first mercy kiss. I wasn't sure what had transpired between her and Moose, but my instincts told me it wasn't good.

Eva

Things really started to unravel after the sunsets began. When I climbed into bed that first night, I kept thinking I should feel something close to elation, or at the very least, a vague sense of joy. But the whole thing just made me feel queasy. As I struggled to get to sleep, I secretly prayed the Virgin Mary wouldn't return. We had enough on our plate without her popping up at random moments in Jericho. And anyway, my own faith had never been rooted in miracles. As far as I was concerned, miracles were like fickle husbands: here one day and gone the next. In other words, they couldn't be trusted.

It wasn't the first time the Virgin Mary had loomed too large in my life. Having been sent to a Catholic girls' school, it had been hard to avoid her. On feast days, we marched in ceremonial parades holding her image, sang hymns in her honour, said rosaries to her and made offerings in her name. In Catechism we were taught the four dogmas: that Mary was the mother of God, that despite giving birth to Jesus she remained a virgin all her life (a neat trick, if ever there was one), that she was free from sin, and that upon her death she was taken bodily into heaven. All of this we were told to accept without question. Which might have been fine, but we were also urged to be just like her. And over time, it dawned on me that the Virgin Mary set too high a bar. She was an unfairly demanding role model for any girl: beautiful, humble, chaste, pure, gentle, kind and good-at-suffering. She was better than we could ever possibly be, and I came to resent her for it. On top of that she cried a lot. She was a perpetual victim, unable to control events happening around her, and dictated to by men: Gabriel, Joseph, God and even Jesus, her own son. In the end she was left with only grief to console her. Not much of a life to aspire to, really. Or so it seemed to me at seventeen.

But I was a good Catholic girl, so I took part in Mary-worship at school, even while I secretly doubted its purpose. I did this partly out of loyalty and partly out of fear. The nuns terrified me: they were fanatically devoted to her, and their anger at anyone who questioned that devotion was equally fierce. Never in my wildest dreams would I have gone against them. So I made my peace with it: if I wanted to lead a good Catholic life, Mary was part of the package, and I would have to put up with her. Up until now, that hadn't posed too big a problem.

Not surprisingly, Deacon Joe and I were on opposite sides of the fence. The minute the sunsets started it was like he'd been virgin-whipped. He bounded around like an oversized toddler and could hardly speak of anything else. He spent most of the next day on the telephone calling up various members of the Youngstown and Cleveland Dioceses, urging them to come to Jericho to see the miraculous appearance of Mary for themselves. And he immediately decided to launch a campaign to raise funds to enlarge the wayside shrine, saying that it was unworthy of the apparitions. 'Jericho could be the next Lourdes,' he declared excitedly. 'If we play our cards right, we might even get a new church out of this. Maybe even a basilica! The Pope himself might come to consecrate it.'

'Don't we need a spring?' asked Ada. 'You know, a holy one that cures people? The Virgin Mother alone won't bring pilgrims to Jericho. People want to be healed.'

'Who says she can't heal?' said Deacon Joe.

'With what?' said Ada sceptically. 'Holy air?'

The only silver lining for me was that the apparitions temporarily distracted Deacon Joe from Annemarie's pregnancy, which gave us all a little bit of breathing space.

My prayers to the Virgin Mary to leave us in peace went unanswered. When she reappeared the next evening, I decided she must have come to Jericho for a reason. Most of the town seemed to think it was pure good fortune, but my own feeling was that she was here to admonish us for our wrongdoings. I couldn't help but think of Annemarie and her pregnancy, but the idea that the Mother of Jesus had come here simply to reprimand a wayward seventeen-year-old girl seemed ridiculous. If teenage sex bothered the Virgin Mary, she'd be cropping up in every town across the Midwest, I told myself. Maybe there was something more sinister happening in Jericho. When I shared this theory with Ada over breakfast, she gave me a withering look. 'Jericho isn't interesting enough to be sinister,' she said dismissively.

'It is now,' I replied.

'What could possibly go on here that would trouble the Virgin Mother?'

'Who knows?' I shrugged. 'Maybe there's a murderer on the prowl.'

'But no one's died.'

'No one we know of.'

'That's ridiculous, Eva.'

'Maybe.' The truth was I had no idea why the Virgin Mary had chosen us. But it didn't stop me wondering. At that moment Deacon Joe wandered into the room and looked at us.

'What's ridiculous?' he asked.

'Eva thinks the Virgin Mother's here to punish us for our sins.'

Joe frowned. 'That's a load of hogwash. The Virgin Mary has come to Jericho to reward us for our devotion. Pure and simple.'

'But there are faithful communities everywhere. Why come here?' I asked.

He shrugged. 'Why not come here?'

'Maybe because of the town's name,' Ada offered.

'Or maybe it's because we are truly exemplary,' said Deacon Joe, emphasising the last word. Annemarie came into the kitchen a minute later and crossed over to the refrigerator, pulling out a carton of orange juice.

'So what do *you* think, Annemarie?' asked Ada. 'Why has the Virgin Mother decided to grace us with her presence?'

Annemarie stopped short, the orange juice carton suspended in mid-air. For an instant she stared in our direction. 'Maybe she's trying to tell us something,' she said pensively.

'Something good or something bad?' I asked.

'Maybe just ... something we need to know.'

'Such as?' I asked.

Annemarie swallowed. 'I think we'll have to wait and see.'

'Well, whatever it is, it must be pretty important for her to come all this way,' said Ada. Annemarie poured herself a glass of juice, then put the carton back and quickly left the room. After she'd gone, Ada shot me a glance, her eyebrows raised.

'What's up with her?'

'Apart from the obvious?' I asked. 'She's a pregnant teenager. With armies of hormones to match.' Ada gave a conciliatory shrug.

But the truth was, Annemarie was more of a mystery to me than ever.

Annemarie

A few days after the whole town turned out to see the Virgin Mary, Ethan moved into the wayside shrine. He didn't tell me beforehand; he just pitched a tent and made camp. That afternoon I was coming down the stairs when I heard Deacon Joe complaining to Ada in the kitchen: 'That boy's come unhinged, if you ask me.'

'He's not unhinged. He's just … confused. Or bewildered or something,' said Ada.

'Well, he'll bewilder Annemarie if we're not careful.'

'In case you've forgotten, he already *has*.'

'Next thing you know, she'll move in with him.'

'Annemarie's way too smart to set up house in a tent,' snapped Ada.

'Well, the sooner we get him out of there, the better.'

'Do you reckon it's legal?' asked Ada.

'To pitch a tent? Why wouldn't it be?'

'But the Church owns the land, doesn't it?'

'The Church owns the land behind the site and to the west.'

'Well, who owns the shrine?'

'I don't know. The city, I guess. Seeing as how it's by the road. But the Church has always maintained it on behalf of the community.'

'Well, then the Church should be the one to kick him out.'

'The Church doesn't have the authority.'

'That's never stopped the Church before.'

'Kick who out?' I asked, pausing in the doorway. They both hesitated. No doubt they were weighing up the odds of me hearing it from someone else.

'That boyfriend of yours has set up a tent by the wayside shrine,' said Deacon Joe. 'Told me he was fixing to move in there for a spell.'

'Ethan said that?'

'He did, honey,' said Ada.

'Well, he does love camping,' I said half-heartedly. 'He used to be a boy scout back in Arizona.'

'Setting up a tent in a churchyard is hardly what I'd call camping,' said Deacon Joe.

'Maybe he wants to be closer to God.'

'Well, he's going about it the wrong way.'

I slipped away from them and went to find Ethan in his tent. I knew the church was ninety-seven paces from our front door, and I remembered the wayside shrine was just beyond it, maybe another thirty paces or so. Ethan must have heard me tapping with the stick because when I reached twenty-five paces, I heard the rustle of nylon somewhere ahead of me.

'Annemarie?'

'Hey.' I came to a stop just in front of him. I reached a hand out, and sure enough, felt the fabric of his tent. 'So this is your new digs, huh?'

'Um ... yeah. For now.' He sounded embarrassed.

'How come you didn't tell me?'

'I wasn't sure you'd understand.'

'I don't. But that's because you've haven't explained it to me yet.'

There was an awkward silence. Ethan didn't seem to want to explain.

'You got somewhere to sit?' I asked.

'Yeah, sure.' He took my hand and pulled me over to a folding plastic lawn chair. As I sat down it creaked and listed heavily to one side. I heard Ethan unfold a second chair, which he set down next to mine.

'You want anything? Some water or something?' he asked.

'No, thanks, I'm good.' We sat for a moment in the heat of the afternoon sun.

'Look, I was going to come by and talk to you this evening.'

'OK. Pretend it's this evening.'

He took a deep breath and let it out slowly. 'The other night, when the whole town was staring at her, I felt this ... intense rush of anger. I swear to God, Annemarie, it felt like a forest fire raging inside me. That's why I left. I went home and took a cold shower, and tried to wash it away, but I just couldn't get rid of it. So around midnight, after everyone had gone home, I came back. And as soon as I got here, the anger just disappeared. Then I felt this amazing sense of calm, and I knew that I should stay. And just wait.'

'Wait for what?'

'I don't know.'

'For her?'

'Maybe. I don't know, Annemarie. I just know that she wants me here.'

'Why?'

'I guess I'll find out.'

'And what about me?'

He hesitated. 'What do you mean?'

'Do you think she wants *me* here?'

'Um. I don't know. Why wouldn't she?'

'You tell me.'

'Annemarie, I don't know what you're talking about.'

'I'm talking about you. And her.'

He hesitated for a long moment. 'It isn't like that,' he said flatly.

'Then what *is* it like?'

'It's ... holy.' He half-swallowed the last word.

So that's it, I thought. I'd introduced Ethan to God, and God had swallowed him. Wholly. 'But you said you were finished with religion,' I argued.

'I thought I was,' he sighed. 'But this is different. Don't you see? This isn't about religion. It's about ... faith.'

'Faith *is* religion, Ethan.'

'Not always.'

He had a point. I couldn't exactly disagree. 'Listen, Ethan,' I said. 'I think it's time we told Mama and Deacon Joe about the visions.'

'You mean my visions?' he asked tentatively. I nodded. 'Yeah.'

'They won't believe you, Annemarie.'

'Why not? They've seen the sunsets.'

'Because it involves me.'

Later that afternoon, Cora Lynn came by and I told her about Ethan and the visions. I figured that if she believed me, then I stood a fighting chance with the others. 'You mean he actually talks to the Virgin Mary?' said Cora Lynn, her voice laced with scepticism. 'Look, Annemarie, it's one thing to see weird shit in the sunset, but it's another thing altogether when the shit starts talking to you.'

'Well, that's what he says anyway.'

'And you believe him?'

'I don't think Ethan would lie. Even though he is starting to seem ...'

'Crazy?'

'Not crazy. Just confused or something. Ada says he's bewildered.'

'She's one to talk!' Cora Lynn's always been scathing about Ada and her marriages; she says Ada's obsessed with the highway of love, but only likes to use the on and off ramps.

'I don't know,' I sighed. 'Maybe it's the heat.'

'Don't go blaming your crazy boyfriend on the Ohio summer!'

'Well, what is it then?'

'The boy needs sex, that's what,' she said with a snort. Cora Lynn was raised Baptist, but she has a broad interpretation of chastity, believing it has more to do with virtue (which she defines as goodness and constancy) than celibacy. Cora Lynn says that if you're in a steady relationship and not having sex, it's like overcharging batteries: sooner or later, you'll both explode. As a result, she's been sleeping with her boyfriend Kelvin for the last six months. When she first confessed to me they'd done it, I laughed and told her she was my Song of Solomon Girl. Cora Lynn had smacked her lips and said, *Get thee to the mountain of myrrh!*

'Look,' I said flatly, 'I don't think Ethan would have sex with me now even if I wanted to.'

'Then he's definitely crazy.'

'It's like she's turned his head.'

'What are you saying?'

'That he's not interested in me any more.'

'Are you telling me you're competing with the Virgin Mary? Over Ethan?'

'Not by choice.'

'Now it's you who's crazy.'

I sighed. 'Yeah, maybe.'

'Have you told anyone else about his visions?'

'Not yet. But I'm planning to. Soon.'

'Good luck with that.'

I decided it might be easier without Ethan present, so that night after supper I gathered Mama, Ada and Deacon Joe around the kitchen table. 'It's about the pregnancy,' I said tentatively. I heard them shift uncomfortably in their seats, and even though I couldn't see them, I knew their faces were set like stone. 'I know you don't believe that I've been chaste, in spite of what Dr Paulson said,' I began slowly. I heard Deacon Joe inhale deeply, as if he could somehow sniff out the truth. 'But now that the sunsets have started, I think the pregnancy might have something to do with them.'

There. I'd said it. For a long moment there was silence. Then I heard Deacon Joe lean forward, his chair creaking ominously, and when he spoke, his voice was low and menacing. 'How *dare* you involve the Virgin Mary in your sordid little pregnancy!' he said.

His tone shocked me, and I wondered whether my decision to reveal the truth had been a bad one. But I'd gone too far to stop now. 'Ethan spoke to her,' I said quickly.

'To who?' said Ada.

'The Virgin Mary.'

'That boy!' Deacon Joe slapped his thigh. 'I do not want to hear another word about that … miscreant any longer! That boy is deranged.'

'Ethan saw her twice. By the wayside shrine. She told him the baby was a gift from the Holy Spirit,' I said.

'What?! And you expect us to believe that?' Deacon Joe practically shouted. 'That some crazed juvenile delinquent you have befriended is communicating directly with the Virgin Mary!'

'Joe! There's no need to be so harsh,' said Ada. 'The poor girl's been through enough.'

I sighed. 'I don't know what I expect any more. I never expected any of this.'

Suddenly, Mama's voice cut through the air. 'Why *you*?' she asked.

I turned to face her, but remained silent.

'Really, Annemarie, why would it be you?' Her tone was full of disbelief. 'I have more ... piety in my little finger than you have in your entire body. I have spent my whole life in worshipful duty, and you have done nothing but ... squander your faith. So why in heaven's name would He choose *you*?'

Mama and I faced each other across a vast ocean of dismay, and I wanted to take her hand but I could not. Certainly, she did not take mine. 'He wouldn't, that's why,' she said with a sigh. 'I don't know what you're playing at.'

'Mama,' I started to protest. But it was like talking to a solid wall of animosity. There was nothing I could do or say that would convince her I was telling the truth.

'We need to get some expert medical advice,' said Ada. 'Maybe there's a logical explanation for all this. Jeremiah Paulson isn't fit to diagnose a common cold, let alone a miracle pregnancy.'

'Amen to that,' muttered Deacon Joe. 'Ada's right. We'll get you to a specialist up in Cleveland, Annemarie, and find out what all this is about.'

'OK,' I said quietly, still facing Mama's direction. I was no longer in charge, and a part of me was relieved.

'OK,' repeated Mama after a moment. But I could tell from her voice that it wasn't.

The next morning I went to see Ethan in his tent and told him what I'd done. No more secrets, I decided. I had fastened the belt of truth around my waist and I was going to wear it, even if it dragged me down to hell in the process. At first Ethan seemed relieved that I'd told them about his visions. But when I explained that I was due to see a team of specialists at Lake Haven Hospital the next day, he suddenly grew angry.

'But we know why you're pregnant, Annemarie.'

'We might. Or we might not. It won't hurt to investigate.'

'What about your faith?' He asked. 'Have you just given up on God?'

'No. I still have my faith, Ethan.'

'The Virgin Mary said that you were blessed. That the baby was a gift.'

'Maybe I don't want to be blessed!'

'Maybe she didn't want to be, either. But we don't always get what we want, do we?'

'No, we don't,' I agreed. 'But I'm still going to Cleveland.'

'And what if they interfere? What if they hurt the baby?'

'How? By doing tests?'

'Yes. I don't know. It's possible.'

'Have a little faith in science, Ethan. You used to.'

'I used to have a lot of things,' he mumbled.

Yeah, I thought. You used to have me.

Ethan

Even though our date last winter to the basketball game hadn't gone perfectly, at the time I still thought it might signal the start of something new in our relationship. The next day I stopped by Annemarie's house in the late afternoon, hoping to rekindle some of the excitement from the previous evening. Her mom told me she was up in her room listening to music, and as I climbed the stairs I recognised 'Doctor My Eyes' come drifting down. Jackson Browne was an old favourite of Moose's, though he freely admitted it was chick music, and I'd never heard Annemarie listen to it before. I stopped dead for a moment, a queasy feeling in the pit of my stomach. I stood there uncertainly until the song ended. Then Annemarie opened her bedroom door.

'Ethan? Is that you?'

'Hey,' I said.

'Are you coming up or are you gonna just hang out on the stairs?'

She sounded a little peeved. I wasn't sure why until I entered the room and saw Moose stretched out on the floor. He looked up and gave me a little wave. 'Hey, man,' he said.

'Moose came by with a Jackson Browne tape he made,' said Annemarie. 'He wanted me to hear 'Doctor My Eyes'. Moose saw him play at the Dome last summer.'

'Yeah, I remember,' I mumbled, unsure whether to sit down or make my excuses and go.

'Ethan hates Jackson Browne,' said Moose, rolling over on to his side and propping his head up one hand.

'You do? Why?'

'I don't hate him,' I said. 'He's just not my favourite.'

'Ethan's more of a Springsteen man,' said Moose.

'Are you? I didn't know that,' said Annemarie with a frown.

That was because we always listened to *her* music when I came round. It hadn't really occurred to me to introduce her to any of mine, though now I wondered why. Annemarie sat down on the floor by Moose and reached over and pressed the play button on the tape deck. After a second, 'Running On Empty' came on. I sat down awkwardly on the floor a little distance from both of them, but as I listened to the song it felt as if all the air in the room was slowly being sucked out, and pretty soon I would suffocate. When it ended, I stood up. 'Hey, sorry. I forgot I promised my mom I'd help her out with some stuff at home,' I said.

Moose gave a little wave. 'Later, bro.'

'See ya,' said Annemarie.

As I left the room, I saw them both turn away. I knew I was being lame, but once I got home I watched from my bedroom window to see how long he stayed. Moose was there for another couple of hours, and when he left I saw him shake hands with Deacon Joe on the doorstep, like they'd entered into some sort of guy pact. I couldn't remember ever shaking hands with Deacon Joe like that – and he and I were way past the stage where it might happen now. But what worried me more was the fact that Moose and Annemarie had been alone in her bedroom for more than two hours.

I couldn't stand it, so I waited a while after Moose left then went round to his house. When he opened the door, his bushy eyebrows shot up with surprise. 'Hey, dude, thought you were helping your mom.'

'We finished.'

'Cool.' He pushed open the door and nodded for me to come in. He was carrying a spatula. 'Just making a burger. You want one?'

'No, thanks.'

'Come out back.' We went through the kitchen into the backyard, where, even though it was November, a giant gas barbecue blazed. Moose's burger sizzled on top. A picnic table sat beside the barbecue, and Moose straddled one of the benches with his long legs and motioned for me to sit down opposite. 'Oh, man, I almost forgot the cheese,' he said, leaping up. He disappeared back into the kitchen, emerging a minute later with half a dozen slices of American cheese, which he proceeded to unwrap and drape across the burger in a tall orange stack.

'So what you doing tonight?' I asked.

'Nothing much.'

'Not seeing Shelly?'

'Nah.'

That wasn't a good sign, I decided. I watched as Moose leaned over and scooped some cheese back onto his burger. The stuff looked like shiny molten plastic.

'How was Annemarie?' I asked.

'She's cool,' he said with a nod, squirting industrial quantities of ketchup and mustard on to a bun. 'You were right about her. Definitely worth pursuing. Even with the vision thing. Or without,' he added with a sideways grin.

Worth *who* pursuing? I wondered. Me or him?

'So what'd you guys talk about?' I asked. Moose shrugged.

'I don't know, just stuff.' He leaned over again and expertly manoeuvred the burger from the grill on to the bun, then closed it and flattened the whole thing with the heel of his palm, the ketchup oozing sideways on to the plate. 'Actually we talked about you,' he said, picking up the burger and taking a massive bite.

'Me?'

Moose nodded, chewing slowly, his Adam's apple bobbing up and down. I waited for him to elaborate, but it was a minute before his mouth was empty. 'She says you put her up on a pedestal,' he said, swallowing. I frowned.

'Is that bad?' I asked.

'It's not where she wants to be, dude.'

'Where does she want to be?'

'I don't know. But not up high, out of reach. She wants to be normal. Like everybody else. But you don't treat her that way.'

He was right. I'd never treated Annemarie like she was normal. Because to me, she wasn't. I decided to come clean with Moose, because I needed to know one way or the other. 'So are you gonna ask her out?' I asked, glancing sideways at him.

'Me!' He looked at me askance. A small spot of ketchup had lodged at the corner of his mouth. 'Dude, I've already got a girlfriend, remember?'

'Yeah, but ...' I hesitated.

'But what? I can't hang out with other girls now?'

'It just seemed like ... maybe you were interested,' I said with a shrug.

'Look, don't be such a *putz*. I'm not trying to steal your girlfriend. But she isn't gonna *be* your girlfriend if you don't get your shit together. Annemarie is desperate for you to make a move on her, you know that?'

'She told you that?'

'No, she didn't tell me that. She didn't *need* to tell me that.'

'Then how do you know?'

'Trust me, I know,' said Moose taking another massive bite of burger. 'Any idiot would know,' he added, his mouth filled with food.

So I was an idiot. Which by then I'd pretty much worked out, even without Moose's help. But what if the signals Annemarie sent Moose were different from the ones she sent me? Maybe she was desperate for *him* to make a move. I figured the only way I could find out was to ask her. But the prospect terrified me. The next day was Sunday, so I decided to confront her after church. On the way home Deacon Joe, Ada and her mama walked behind us, and maybe it was my imagination but our conversation seemed a little forced. When we reached her house Annemarie invited me in, but once in her room the first thing she did was put on the Jackson Browne tape. I waited until the song finished, then leaned over and turned down the volume.

'Hey! I love the next song,' she said. My heart sank. She already knew the tape by heart.

'Can we talk?'

'We already are, aren't we?'

'Well, mostly we're listening.'

'OK. So talk.'

'It's about Moose.' Annemarie tilted her head to one side with interest. At least I'd got her attention.

'What about him?'

'Well, I kind of thought that maybe ... you liked him.'

'I do like him.'

'I mean... really liked him.'

'Oh.' She frowned and turned away from me so that I couldn't see her face.

'Do you?' I waited, but she didn't answer for an eternity. I think I actually stopped breathing.

'Not the way you think,' she said.

'Are you sure?' I asked. She didn't sound sure.

'Yeah, I'm sure. Why?' There was a note of defiance in her voice that made me panic. I knew Moose was right – that I needed to act – but Annemarie didn't seem keen.

'I just don't want you to get hurt, that's all,' I mumbled. Lame!

'Moose wouldn't hurt me.' Annemarie seemed more certain about this than anything she'd said yet. Any response I made would damn me either way, so I said nothing. We sat there in silence, and after a minute Annemarie reached over and turned the volume back up. Later, just as I was leaving, she asked if I would take her to the basketball game on Friday. For an instant I hesitated as I pictured Annemarie, breathless with excitement, waiting for me to tell her that Moose had scored another point. But I couldn't exactly say no.

It was an away game. We were playing the Darville Devils, which meant a longer drive, but from Annemarie's perspective that was about the only difference: one crowded high school gymnasium smelled and sounded pretty much like any other. I'd never been to an away game before, and when we got there I could see why, because as we took our seats the vibes coming off the stands from the home side weren't exactly friendly. The crowd across the gym looked like rednecks: the women all wore polyester and the men had sideburns, baseball caps and beer bellies. Our side wasn't very full, parents and grandparents mostly, and a few loyal girlfriends. As we took a seat on the bottom bleacher, I scanned the crowd behind us and didn't see Shelly. Moose was warming up with the others, and immediately moved across the court towards us to say hello.

'There's Moose,' I said as he drew near.

'Hey, you guys get prizes for loyalty,' he said, dribbling the ball and glancing back at the coach. He lowered his voice then. 'Their team sucks, by the way, so don't expect much of a contest.'

'Does that mean you'll score lots?' asked Annemarie, smiling.

'With you here? Definitely.'

'Well, don't knock yourself out just for my sake,' she laughed.

'Why not?' Moose turned and took an extra long shot at the basket. It hit the rim and bounced off. I saw him glance round at Annemarie as he ran forward to get the ball, and then catch himself when he realised that of course she hadn't seen. He made his way back to us again, still dribbling.

'Hey, what are you guys doing after this?' he asked.

'We were gonna drive back to Jericho and get a pizza,' I said.

'Forget that. There's a keg party at Zeke's. His parents are out of town.'

I hesitated. I didn't want to take Annemarie to a party, but when I turned back to her I could see the same hopeful look on her face that had been there before. She wants this, I thought. Basketball games, keg parties, the whole high school shebang. 'Yeah, OK,' I said. 'If Annemarie wants to.'

'Yes, please!' said Annemarie enthusiastically.

'That's my girl,' said Moose, moving away once again. The phrase was jarring: I realised the last time he'd used it he was talking about Shelly.

116

Moose was right about the other team. We slaughtered them 103 to 67. It was almost too embarrassing to watch, let alone narrate. After awhile I stopped reporting our team's baskets, and Annemarie didn't seem to mind. It was pretty obvious what was going on, anyway. It wasn't as much fun as the last game, and when it ended we slowly made our way back to the car. The parking lot was crowded with home fans still milling about, and the air was sour with disappointment. We moved past a group of hoods, leaning up against a car smoking. My dad's station wagon was parked just behind it, and as I unlocked the passenger door for Annemarie one of them lifted himself off the car and walked over to stand just behind us.

'Hey,' he said. Annemarie stiffened at the sound of his voice, and I turned around to face him, stepping slightly in front of her. The kid was about my age and a fraction shorter, but what he lacked in height he made up for in bravado. His hair was long and dark and cut across his forehead in a slash, and he wore a faded dark green army jacket. He exhaled some smoke, then gestured with his cigarette towards the car.

'This your car?' he asked.

'It's my dad's,' I said.

He nodded. 'Tell your dad his son's an asshole, will you?' He leaned forward and stubbed the cigarette out on the windscreen, smearing the remnants across the glass. His friends laughed and one of them clapped slowly. The guy smiled and turned back to them, taking a bow, then he glanced at Annemarie to see her reaction. Annemarie wasn't carrying a white stick, and I could tell he hadn't realised she was blind.

'Ethan?' she said tentatively. 'Is everything OK?'

'Yeah,' I said, holding his gaze and trying to keep my voice steady. 'Everything's fine.' He glanced over at her and frowned.

'What's with her?' he asked with a nod.

'She's blind,' I said. He hesitated for a moment, weighing up my words.

'Well, I guess that explains why she's with you.' He turned and walked back past his friends, and they all moved off across the parking lot. I turned around and opened the car door for Annemarie.

'What was all that about?' she asked.

'Nothing. Just some jerks.'

'You OK?'

'Yeah, I'm fine.'

But I wasn't. It was humiliating, even if she hadn't seen.

It took me a while to find the party. I'd been to Zeke's house once before but only had a vague memory of where it was, so we drove around searching for the right street. We knew when we'd found it as there were loads of cars outside, including one that had pulled right up on to the lawn. The front door to the house was wide open, in spite of the cold, and I could see a lot of people inside. I pulled the car over by the curb and put it in park.

'This is it,' I said. 'Looks pretty crowded. Sure you want to go in?'

'Yeah,' said Annemarie. 'I'll be OK.'

Moose and the rest of the basketball team were already there. He saw us from across the room and came over. 'You made it. Good man.'

'She was keen, so we're here,' I said half-heartedly.

'Course she was, 'cause she's cool,' said Moose. 'Hey, Annemarie. Come on back to the kitchen. Let's get you guys a beer.'

'OK.'

Moose grabbed her hand and pulled her behind him

towards the kitchen while I looked on. I thought fleetingly of my promise of no alcohol to Deacon Joe, then followed them, feeling the night slide out of my control once again.

'Where's Shelly?' I asked as Moose filled two large plastic cups from the keg.

'She's grounded. I kept her out too late the other night.' He looked at me and grinned.

'So you're a bad influence,' said Annemarie teasingly.

'I try to be,' he replied.

Well, don't try with her! I thought.

We moved away from the keg towards the sitting room, where two guys from the football team were sitting on a fat brown sofa, surrounded by a crowd of onlookers. Zeke was standing on the coffee table in front of them brandishing a can opener. 'Gentlemen, position your beers,' he shouted.

'What's happening?' asked Annemarie.

'They're gonna shotgun the beer,' said Moose. 'You make a hole in the side of the can near the bottom, then put your mouth on the hole and pop the lid.'

'Why?'

''Cause the rush of air forces the beer down your throat in, like, three seconds.' We watched as Zeke punctured each of their cans, then gave the signal for them to pop the lids. They drained the cans in a few seconds, then crunched them flat in their hands, shouting and high-fiving each other.

'So how exciting was that?' Annemarie asked Moose in a low voice.

'Right up there with cow-tipping.'

'People don't really do that, do they?'

'Only when they're young and stupid.'

'Did you?'

'I was young but never stupid,' he said.

She turned to me. 'Did *you* ever tip a cow?'

'I grew up in Arizona. We didn't have cows.'

'Nah, they had coyotes, which don't take kindly to tipping,' said Moose.

Just then a kid from my physics class came through the front door. His eyes were bloodshot and he looked a little ashen.

'Who's got a dark green station wagon?' he shouted to the room.

'Oh, man,' I mumbled, stepping forward. 'I do. Why?'

'Sorry, dude,' he said. 'I kind of backed into the side.'

'Is it bad?'

He looked at me and shrugged, so I followed him outside. When we got there I discovered that it *was* bad. He'd smashed in the driver's door so far that you couldn't open it, and the wheel was at a strange angle.

'Fuck.'

'Dude. I'm real sorry.' He was standing in the road just behind me, weaving slightly.

'Asshole.'

I went back into the house and rang my dad, then started to go outside to wait for him. Moose stopped me by the front door. 'What's the story?'

'Front door's completely fucked. So's the wheel.'

'Oh, man. Not good. Really sorry, dude.'

'My dad's coming. Might have to get a tow.' I hesitated, remembering Annemarie. The idea of leaving her with Moose didn't thrill me, but neither did the alternative of taking her home with my dad in a tow truck.

'Look, don't worry about Annemarie,' he said, reading my mind. 'I'll make sure she gets home.' I looked over at Annemarie, who was laughing at something Zeke was saying.

'She's gotta be back by eleven-thirty,' I said, a little reluctantly.

'No problem.'

But it *was* a problem. Dad and I got home at about a quarter-past and I heard Moose's car pull up ten minutes later. The porch light came on and Deacon Joe stepped outside; he must have been waiting for her. Moose and Annemarie walked up to the front door and I saw Moose step forward and shake hands easily with him. They talked for a minute, but then, instead of leaving, Moose followed them inside.

A few minutes later, Annemarie's bedroom light came on. I was sitting in my room in complete darkness, so there was no way they could have seen me, but the first thing Moose did was walk over to her window and draw the blind. As he did he looked straight at me, and I could have sworn he winked.

Eva

After Annemarie told us about Ethan's encounter by the wayside shrine, I didn't know *what* to think. On the one hand, it certainly explained a few things. But on the other, it opened up a can of worms so large they threatened to devour us. That night I couldn't sleep. It was deathly hot and I had thrown my bedroom windows wide open to catch the breeze, but the air was so still I could hear the tireless whine of mosquitoes against the screen, desperately searching for a way in. As I lay there in the darkness I felt a storm gathering inside me, and I realised that I was angry with just about everyone: with Annemarie for behaving as if she was the chosen one, with Deacon Joe for his mean-spirited righteousness, with Ada for her inability to grasp the seriousness of our predicament, and with the Virgin Mary for interfering with my daughter's innocence.

That is, if I believed Annemarie's story. I desperately wanted to know that she was being honest with us (not to mention that she and Ethan had shown a lick of sense). But at the same time, I didn't want her story to be true: I didn't want her to be singled out for God's blessing, nor did I want her to be venerated for all time. I wanted us to lead a normal life in a normal town where normal things happened to normal people. And as I tossed and turned, I couldn't help but wonder, *why us?* I'd believed in God through thick and thin, and only now was it beginning to dawn on me that there'd been way too much of thin. At every stage of my life I'd done what God and the Church had asked of me, but time and again I'd been rewarded with heartache. Now my past stretched behind me like a winding path strewn with thorns. I'd blindly followed it, never once stopping to consider that there might be an alternative.

My husband Daryl had said as much when he left. 'It was the Church that brought us together and the Church that drove us apart,' he wrote in his final postcard. This had been true, in a way. Certainly, as two young, devout, single parishioners, Daryl and I had been propelled towards each other by powerful forces within the congregation. Over the course of eighteen months we were constantly and deliberately thrown together: at prayer meetings, parish suppers, charity fundraisers, Christmas bazaars and church picnics. It seemed somehow inevitable that we'd wind up together. So we allowed ourselves to be nudged and chivvied, and when it finally happened, it wasn't so much sparks that flew as a quiet reorganisation of our lives.

Our first year of marriage was cautious and respectful. We were both so anxious not to give offence, or force the other's hand, that we failed to grasp just how muted our union was. One day, after several months of married life, it occurred to me that Daryl had never once looked at me naked. Whenever I came out of the shower he always contrived to be facing the other direction, and on the rare nights when we had sex he insisted that we undress beneath the covers. Our lovemaking, when it happened, was silent, hasty and cloaked in darkness. The realisation jarred me, but I was too naïve to fully grasp its implications. It was Ada who unwittingly gave me the wake-up call. By the time I married Daryl, she'd already lapped me and was on her second husband, a Texas oilman called Clayton. He was voracious in his appetites, and Ada used to joke that on weekends he would scarcely let her out of bed. I knew that all men were different, but clearly something was amiss with my husband.

After I fell pregnant with Annemarie, things took a turn for the worse: Daryl simply refused to touch me. At night in bed he inched away; when I took his hand he gently pulled free. It was as if he felt we had fulfilled our religious duty by procreating, and now his task was done. For my part, I guess I was too tired and overwhelmed with pregnancy and the prospect of motherhood to confront him. And maybe some part of me was afraid to discover the worst. Once the baby was born we were both elated for the first few months, but then Daryl decided to train as a deacon. He spent more and more time away from home with his church duties, leaving Annemarie and me to fend for ourselves. It was during this time, I later learned, that he began an affair with the parish accountant, a young Cuban named Antonio whose family had fled Castro's revolution a few years earlier. It was also during this time that Daryl began to question his faith.

One night he came to me in tears, telling me that he could no longer deceive himself, me or the Church. He and Antonio had no choice but to flee. 'I have to trust in my own goodness,' he wrote to me later. 'The Church has no place for me in its heart, but I will always have a place for God in mine.' Daryl wasn't willing to give up his faith or his sexuality, but reconciling the two in Ohio in 1962 was out of the question. We divorced and I lost contact with him a few years later.

I wrote to him when Annemarie lost her sight, to the only address I ever had, but the letter was returned unopened. I never knew whether it hadn't reached him, or whether he simply chose not to read it. Maybe I should have looked for him harder, but I don't think he wanted to be found.

Eventually I slept, but when I woke the next morning I was still in turmoil. I decided that maybe it was time to confront God with my anger, so I rose as quietly as I could and slipped out of the house, walking across the damp morning grass to the church. The heat had broken a little during the night, and for once the sun felt pleasantly warm on my shoulders. It was Wednesday and I knew that the new curate would be taking the mid-week service. I wasn't in the habit of going to church during the middle of the week, but I hadn't realised the same was true of the rest of the congregation. When I entered the church my heart sank when I saw that it was empty. Where were all the faithful followers from last night's sunset? I wondered. Had ordinary Mass paled in comparison with heavenly displays of the Virgin? I felt suddenly embarrassed by the congregation, and wondered what the new curate would make of our hypocrisy. He stood with his back to me in front of the altar, preparing the sacraments, seemingly oblivious to the fact that I was the only soul in attendance.

I slipped into the front pew. As I waited for Mass to begin I looked around, and felt a sense of calm creep back in. St Paul's was a beautiful church, if a little unconventional, but it had taken me years to think so. It had been built shortly before we moved to Jericho, at the start of the sixties, before the free-for-all architecture ushered in by Vatican II, but after the art deco influence of the twenties and thirties. So I guess it was a child of its time, which is to say, the materials and design were modern, but the layout was traditional.

From the outside it looked like it belonged to someplace far more exotic: a series of cubes built in desert-coloured stone, with a square tower on one side that rose straight up like a skyscraper. Inside it had a black slate floor, blonde wooden pews, jade green marble pillars framing the altar, and a tiled mosaic ceiling in blue, yellow and red, laid out in a neat geometric design. Everything had been constructed along straight lines and right angles, so the building looked solid and boxy. But inside it felt spacious and lofty, the way a church should, and it yanked you right out of yourself, which I'd always thought was the point of worship. Along the walls hung a series of small wooden carvings depicting the Stations of the Cross, and above these were tall, rectangular stained-glass windows that rose magnificently to the ceiling, each with a portrait of a saint.

The new curate had joined the parish only a few weeks before – a temporary replacement for Father O'Shea, after an interlude during which we'd been served by a series of locum priests. And while I'd been introduced to him very briefly at a welcome gathering, I'd not yet heard him preach. I felt conspicuous being the only worshipper, but I needn't have worried because when the curate eventually turned round his eyes went straight to the back of the church, as if it was full. One worshipper or a hundred, I decided – maybe it was all the same to a priest. The Mass was shorter than usual, and the liturgy was brief. He spoke about the importance of conscience and the power of reflection. At the end of the service, he spread his hands and looked straight at me, before uttering the words, 'Go in peace, to love and serve the Lord.' Then he walked down the altar and came to a halt just in front of me.

'Father O'Shea warned me that mid-week attendance could be poor,' he said with a smile. 'Thank you for coming.

It's good to see there are some devout members of the congregation here in Jericho.'

I shifted uncomfortably in the pew, feeling like an imposter. 'You should know I'm not feeling especially devout today, Father,' I confessed.

He nodded. 'We all have days like that,' he said kindly.

I frowned. 'Even priests?'

'Especially priests. If they're being honest.'

I peered at him, a little surprised by his tone. I felt certain Father O'Shea would never have admitted so easily to a lapse in faith. 'God expects us to have doubts,' the new curate explained, seeing my reaction. 'Doubt and faith go hand in hand.'

I nodded. The new curate didn't really look like the priests I was used to: he was longer-haired than most, and younger, and he'd clearly forgotten to shave as there was a dark shadow of stubble on his cheeks. Father O'Shea had been the priest at St Paul's for more than two decades, so we were used to an older, more conventional model. But I was aware that priests came in all shapes and sizes.

'May I ask what brings you here today, since you're not feeling so devout?'

I hesitated. I wasn't sure whether I wanted to share my doubts with him. 'I've been wondering why God doesn't always seem to reward the faithful,' I said finally.

'Ah,' he said, nodding his head thoughtfully. 'In what way?'

'It often seems like He punishes them instead.'

'Suffering brings us closer to God. Even in our anger we seek Him out.'

That was true enough, I thought. Otherwise I wouldn't be here.

'And pain brings us closer to each other, for it's something we must all face at one time or another in our lives.'

A predictable enough answer, I thought. Though I couldn't help but wonder what pain he'd endured in his whiskered, priestly life.

'But there are certainly times when God seems absent from our lives,' he conceded.

'And is He really absent?'

The curate took a deep breath and held it for a moment. 'I've never been sure,' he admitted.

'So what do you do during those times?'

'I pray,' he said.

'For what?'

'His return. And for His help. And for His guidance.'

'And does it work?'

'Usually.' He laughed. 'Most of the time, anyway.'

I smiled, in spite of myself. 'Well, prayer it is then, Father.'

He nodded politely. 'I'll leave you to it.'

I watched as he turned and walked away, disappearing into the Sacristy. Already I felt less angry, but I wasn't sure if that was God's doing or the curate's. But I took his advice and I prayed, asking God to leave Annemarie and me alone.

Annemarie

Three days after I confessed, Mama and I made a pilgrimage
to the hospital in Cleveland, which if you're a crow is about
forty-five miles north-west of Jericho. Deacon Joe made a
last-minute bid to come with us, but even Mama balked at
the thought of him discussing my *sacreds* with the doctors.
We hadn't spoken again about Ethan or the pregnancy, but
I could tell it was all festering inside her like a boil. She
was tetchy over breakfast and insisted on leaving straight
afterwards, even though the appointment wasn't until
lunchtime. But it was just as well as the drive took us nearly
two hours, owing to the fact that Mama drives like a nitwit.
She goes so slow that all the other cars rev their engines and
blast their horns as they try to squeeze by. On top of that she
has an aversion to the freeway, so we had to go the whole way
on twisty shunpikes, which nearly made me carsick.

But once we'd set off, her mood lifted. Mama always
seems to change for the better when she gets out of the house,
as if it (or maybe Deacon Joe) oppresses her somehow. She
turned the radio up and hummed along, and would tell me
when we passed something interesting, like a fresh road kill

or a funny sign. At one point she slowed right down and said, 'Hey, Annemarie! We're at the Centre of the World!' I had no idea what she was talking about until she dragged me out of the car and made me stand next to the town sign while she asked a passerby to take our photograph.

The weather was still hot enough to make you perish. Thank God the car had air-conditioning, as I swear we would not have survived the journey otherwise. Even so, I had a thumping headache by the time we got to the city limits. Mama took about fifty wrong turns trying to find the hospital, and when we finally pulled into the parking lot I nearly hugged her out of gratitude.

She took my arm and steered me through the main reception area, in and out of elevators and down endless squeaky corridors, until we finally landed in the OB/GYN outpatient department, where we sat in scratchy upholstered chairs surrounded (according to Mama) by a roomful of women *in the family way*. I could just tell she was searching them all for signs of matrimony. That morning over breakfast she'd suggested I borrow her wedding ring – an offer I politely declined, much to her consternation.

We waited half an hour until a soft-spoken nurse asked us to follow her to an examination room. I had a crazed swarm of butterflies in my stomach by this point, since I was not exactly relishing the idea of being examined by a complete stranger. So a sneeze could have knocked me over when the nurse explained that there was not one doctor waiting to see us, but three. 'Three?' asked Mama. 'Is that ... customary?'

'I believe they all have different specialties,' the nurse explained. 'But I really don't know the particulars.' She opened the door and I heard a rustling of lab coats as all three jumped to their feet. Somehow I just knew they'd all be men. There was a confusing exchange of names and titles:

Dr Barratt was head of Obstetrics, Dr Marshall was head of Genetic Medicine and Dr Hermann was a senior researcher in something beginning with the letter 'C' that I'd never heard of and couldn't really pronounce. I had a sudden image of them as the Magi: thin-faced men wearing saffron-coloured robes and turbans, with greying beards and thoughtful expressions, who would nod wisely when given the details of my case and press their fingertips together. The reality was a little different.

Dr Barratt explained that he'd had a lengthy consultation over the phone with Dr Paulson back in Jericho and had asked his two colleagues to attend my appointment because of the unusual nature of my condition.

'There is nothing unusual about this pregnancy,' countered Mama. For an instant no one said a word. I heard Dr Hermann inhale, and Dr Marshall shift a little uncomfortably in his chair.

'Perhaps not,' Dr Barratt replied in measured tones. 'But that is what we're hoping to establish.'

So they went about establishing that I was, indeed, unusual. This involved a battery of tests, examinations, pinpricks with needles, scans with strange machines, and innumerable bouts of poking and prodding by all three wise men. They tested every fluid in my body, scraped bits off me to peer at under microscopes and did just about everything except dissect me like a frog. They persuaded Mama and me to spend the night in the hospital, so they could complete all their tests in one go, and they even wired up my brain while I slept, which made me feel like some sort of pregnant Bride of Frankenstein. To pass the time, Mama sat flicking through women's magazines in the corner, while I tried to isolate the particular characteristics of each of my Magi. I decided that Dr Barratt was competent and coldly professional, but his home life had suffered over the course of his career (Mama confirmed the pale absence of a ring). Dr Marshall was far more genial, but had a chronic sinus condition and a weight problem (too many doughnuts from the hospital cafeteria). And Dr Hermann was more comfortable with chromosomes than people, which meant he never touched you unless absolutely necessary and rarely looked you in the eye (a diagnosis Mama also confirmed). All three seemed wrong-footed by my blindness, which given that they were doctors was pretty feeble. I decided they could learn a trick or two from Cassandra, my social worker.

The tests took until lunchtime on the second day. They let us out that afternoon and asked us to return for another consultation at four, once the lab results had come back. It was a relief to finally escape the squeaky corridors and stale air-con of the hospital, but when we walked out into the glaring summer sun we nearly turned round and went straight back in. Instead we headed for the car, which after two days sitting in the parking lot was like a furnace. We opened the windows and blasted warm air around, and as we drove through the downtown traffic I could pretty well chew on the smog. Cleveland's been the butt of pollution jokes for the last ten years, ever since the Cuyahoga River caught fire in 1969. Last year, the city hit the headlines again when the mayor's brother tried to rob a bank.

'So where we headed?' I asked Mama.

'Someplace cool.'

'Like the Arctic?'

'I was thinking church.'

For the next forty minutes she drove round and round in circles, muttering to herself. She told me we were headed for a Russian Orthodox church she'd visited many years before as a child, though she had only the vaguest idea of where it was. At last she gave a little shriek of delight. 'Look! There they are!'

'Mama, that's not helpful.'

'The onion church! When I was a little girl we came here on a school trip. We called it the onion church, because it's got these domes on top that look like big fat onions. I wish you could see it, Annemarie, 'cause it's like something out of fairyland.'

Mama may have her faults but she's never lost her sense of wonder. Now she was so excited she was hopping up and down in the driver's seat. We pulled in and parked and she took my hand and led me across the concrete parking lot to the fairy onion church. Inside it was blissfully cool and I decided at once that we should move in, though I figured we'd have to learn Russian. Mama led me all around and described everything in detail: the huge floor-to-ceiling screen of gilded Russian icons that stretched across the entire front of the altar, the most enormous glass chandelier you could imagine, and dozens of stained-glass windows reflecting shafts of coloured light on to the tile floor. Not to mention the murals – there wasn't a single patch of wall or ceiling that hadn't been decorated with pictures from the gospels, said Mama, so you felt like you were stepping right inside the Bible.

When we got tired of wandering round, we sat down on a wooden pew. It was calm and cool and around us we heard only the soft tap of footsteps and the odd hushed murmurings of other visitors. Mama prayed and I sat and contemplated the fact that, whatever views you had about God or religion, churches were definitely sacred in some mysterious way, and everybody should have one – to escape from the chaos of life. Mostly I tried not to think about the test results, or Ethan, or any of the other problems I faced back home. For a moment, it was a blessed relief to be safe inside the fairy onions.

We only left when our stomachs started to rumble. By then it was way past lunchtime, so we gobbled some burgers at a fast-food place and headed back to the hospital. We arrived a few minutes early but the nurse took us straight to the examination room, where the Magi were already busily conferring over my test results. When we came through the door they stopped speaking and jumped to their feet, and once again there was a confusing shuffle of places and chairs, until we were all finally settled.

'So,' said Mama once we were in our seats. 'No need to keep us in suspense. Is my daughter's pregnancy normal?'

'Annemarie's pregnancy does appear to be normal,' said Dr Barratt slowly.

'Which is just as I expected,' said Mama, a little triumphantly.

'But the conception was not,' he added.

'What are you saying?'

'We believe your daughter's pregnancy came about spontaneously.'

'With all due respect, Doctor, sex is almost *always* spontaneous. At least it was in my day.' Mama gave an embarrassed laugh.

'What I mean is, that in Annemarie's case, conception occurred of its own accord.'

There was a long pause while Mama took in what he was saying.

'Of its own accord? Are you saying that a baby just implanted itself in my daughter's womb because it *felt* like it?'

'Not exactly. We're saying that Annemarie has a unique set of physical attributes that may have enabled her to

134

conceive a pregnancy without a partner.'

'To put it more clearly,' explained Dr Marshall, 'we think that Annemarie's eggs may have the capability to develop successfully without sperm.'

'But ... why?'

'She appears to have a highly unusual condition that means her chromosome makeup is different from the rest of her sex.'

'Different how?'

'Well, instead of carrying two X chromosomes like most females, women with this condition have an X and a Y chromosome like a man, but their X chromosome carries a mutation that makes their bodies insensitive to testosterone. Which is why they develop as a female.'

Again there was a silence so cavernous you could have dropped a skyscraper into it. I was so worried about what Mama was thinking that it took me a moment to realise the implication of what he was saying. And when I did my stomach did a little flip.

'Are you saying Annemarie's a *boy*?' asked Mama incredulously.

'Not exactly. For all intents and purposes, Annemarie is female. But her genetic makeup is male. Sometimes, in cases like hers, the patient's genitalia are ambiguous. But Annemarie appears to be anatomically female in every way.'

'Which makes her even *more* unusual,' chipped in Dr Marshall.

'Indeed, we've never seen a case quite like hers,' added Dr Hermann. 'Or even read of one in the literature. Which is why we're so interested.'

'You're interested,' Mama repeated the words in a vaguely wary tone. I could see that she was struggling to judge the motives of the Magi. So was I.

'You must appreciate how significant your daughter's case is to the field of genetic medicine,' continued Dr Hermann, leaning forward. 'This represents an enormous opportunity for us.'

'Not to mention obstetrics,' chipped in Dr Marshall.

'Very significant, I expect,' said Mama cautiously.

'Exactly,' said Dr Barratt, taking charge of the discussion once again. 'It's important to us that you understand. Our proposal is to form a research team to follow Annemarie's pregnancy right through to the baby's birth and beyond, with the intention of publishing the results. The announcement of your daughter's spontaneous conception will have huge consequences for both obstetrics and genetics, I can promise you. Imagine a world where men are no longer needed for procreation, and you start to get a sense of what the long-term implications are.'

A world where men are no longer needed for procreation, I thought to myself. It was not a world I cared to live in, really. Nor one I wanted to bring about. Suddenly the room began to feel unbearably close, and I needed to escape. At that moment the men in front of me seemed more like the Three Musketeers than the Magi, and the thought of them using me for their genetic escapades made me queasy. I could tell Mama felt the same way, because on my right she was positively radiating scorn.

'Gentlemen, I appreciate your time, but I think we're finished for today,' she said, rising to her feet suddenly.

'Please,' said Dr Barratt urgently. 'I understand what a shock this must be.'

'No, I don't think you do,' said Mama matter-of-factly. 'Come on, Annemarie.'

'You do see how vital it is that we have access to Annemarie throughout this pregnancy?'

'I'm afraid it is even more vital that we go home right now,' said Mama, reaching for my hand and pulling me to my feet.

'But you'll return?' Dr Barratt said hopefully.

'We'll think about it,' said Mama, pulling me towards the door. 'But don't hold your breath.'

I wasn't sure what to expect on the ride home. For the first half hour Mama was silent, though once or twice she cursed the rush-hour traffic as we left the city. She was breathing hard through her nose, which meant that she was angry, but I wasn't sure whether it was me or the Magi she was cross with. Finally she pulled over and put the car into park, shutting off the engine.

'Where are we?' I asked.

'Rest stop,' she said.

'Oh. You tired?'

'No, I am simply bewildered.'

'Are we lost?'

'I don't know, Annemarie. Are we?'

That was when I realised she wasn't speaking about the road.

'Annemarie, you need to tell me the truth now. How did all this *really* come about?'

'Mama, I swear you know as much as I do.'

'Well, I know precious little.'

'That makes two of us.'

'This kind of thing doesn't just happen of its own accord. In spite of what those crackpot doctors said.'

'But it has.'

She took a deep breath and let it out slowly. 'You swear that you were never with that boy? In the biblical sense?'

'No. I swear it.'

'And as for you somehow being both a boy *and* a girl,' she mused, 'well, I just can't wrap my head around that one. It strikes me as a load of hogwash.' She was silent for a long moment. 'So that leaves just one more option,' she said finally. 'But I don't hold much truck with that either.'

'But it's possible, isn't it? Miracles happen, don't they? That's what the Bible says.'

'I know what the Bible says,' she sighed. 'But what I *don't* know is whether it's true.'

I sat in stunned silence, listening to the ticking of the clock on the dashboard. It was the first time I had ever heard Mama question her faith. All my life she had been a tower of conviction. And now, when it appeared to matter most, her faith seemed like a flimsy cardboard imitation of the real thing. God truly does work in mysterious ways, I decided, and He was confounding me at every turn. Suddenly a passage from the gospels came into my head. *The wind blows where it chooses, and you hear the sound of it, but you do not know where it comes from or where it goes.* Mama put the car in gear and pulled back on to the road, but it struck me that we had no idea where we were going.

Ethan

After Zeke's keg party in December, things with Annemarie started to unravel. Later that same weekend, Moose broke up with Shelly. I didn't find out about it until I went to school on Monday, but somehow I knew anyway. I spent Saturday in a frenzy of despair imagining what had gone on between Moose and Annemarie after I'd left them on Friday night. And the more I thought about it, the more crazy it made me. By lunchtime I decided that being in close proximity to my bedroom window (and therefore within sight of Annemarie's) was a bad idea, so I locked myself away in the basement for the afternoon and struggled to revise for a calculus exam. By nightfall I'd failed to complete any problem sets, but had successfully conjured Moose and Annemarie into a hundred different stages of undress and a thousand different sexual positions. By the time I went to bed, they were practically divorced.

The next morning I decided to skip church. I couldn't face Annemarie, especially if she was going to be happily post-coital. When I came downstairs my parents looked up from the kitchen table in amazement. 'We thought you'd gone,' my mom said, blinking.

'Just slept late.'

'No church this morning?' asked my dad.

'Nope.'

'Well, I think that calls for a little celebration,' said Mom, leaping to her feet. She decided to cook breakfast, something she rarely did. I didn't know if I was being rewarded for my lack of piety or my decision to stay home with them. As I took my place at the table, my father absent-mindedly handed me the comics section of the Sunday paper. I had been reading the comics since I was five, but had abandoned them over the past year. As I stared down at Blondie and Dagwood, it occurred to me that they had never really been funny. The thought unsettled me, and made me wonder about other aspects of my history. My life in Arizona, my life *pre*-Annemarie, had seemed relatively straightforward. I'd sailed along through the early stages of adolescence without a care, and when puberty arrived, I'd greeted it like an older male cousin I'd heard thrilling tales of and secretly admired. But here in Jericho, things were not what they seemed. Circumstances turned against you without warning, and people let you down. I looked around the kitchen. The only thing that hadn't changed since moving here were my parents. But now even that seemed suspicious.

Behind me, my mother whisked eggs and sizzled butter in a pan. I glanced over at my father. When he came to collect me at Zeke's party, my father had been disconcertingly laid-back. He'd looked over the car and whistled with mock appreciation at the damage. 'Nice one,' he'd said, squatting down and laying a hand on the twisted wheel. 'Better than I could do.' Then he'd glanced up at me with a grin.

'I'm really sorry,' I mumbled. I guess he could tell I was upset because he stood up and patted me on the back then.

'Look, it's not as if you wrapped it around a tree, for

God's sake. This could have happened to anyone, anywhere. It could have happened to your mother at the grocery store.'

I shrugged. Except that it had happened outside a high school keg party where everyone was hammered, I thought. But I decided not to go there. The tow truck turned up a few minutes later, and while the guy set about hooking up the car, my dad and I stood patiently to one side. We declined his offer of a lift home and watched as the truck pulled away from the curb in the darkness, tugging my father's green station wagon behind it like a battered Tonka toy. Afterwards we walked home in silence.

I overheard him the next day speaking to the garage about repairs, but he said nothing more to me about the accident. Now I glanced over at him; he seemed pretty engrossed in whatever story he was reading. Still, I wondered whether he was secretly waiting for me to make amends. 'Dad, if you want me to help pay for the damage to the car, I will,' I offered out of the blue. He peeked at me from behind the headlines, his forehead creased with surprise.

'Ethan, I'm in the insurance business. Stuff happens. If stuff didn't happen, I'd be out of a job.' He disappeared behind his paper once again. 'That's a very kind offer, though,' he added.

'Besides,' said my mom lightly behind me, 'crashing your car is a rite of passage.' She scooped a slice of French toast out of the pan then stepped over to me, tossing it on to my plate like a horseshoe, where it landed with a dull thud. '*Voilà*,' she said.

'Mom, I didn't crash the car. Someone ran into it.'

'Well, it's your first insurance claim,' chipped in my dad. '*That's* definitely a rite of passage.'

'Apparently the boy who ran into you had been drinking,' said Mom, like she was revealing some sort of state secret.

Until that moment, I hadn't realised they'd known. But word gets around in a small town.

'Mom, pretty much everyone at the party was drinking.'

'Well, not everyone crashed their car,' she said pointedly. 'Anyway, there's a difference between drinking and driving, and *drunk* driving.' My dad lowered the newspaper and looked at her askance.

'And the difference is?' he asked.

'That you crash your car,' she said with a shrug, as if this was self-evident. He frowned for a moment, then gave a little nod, as if to say, *yep, that's about the size of it*. Perversely, I felt a flare of irritation at their refusal to be angry with me. Though really it was me who was angry, and it had nothing to do with them.

The next day I was in first period English when I got the news about Moose and Shelly. I overheard Tammy Spears and Missy Carpenter, two of Shelly's closest friends, a few rows behind me. 'Poor Shell,' said Tammy.

'Yeah. He dumped her over the phone.'

'Asshole!'

'He knew her cat had just been diagnosed with cancer, too.'

'What a scumbag.'

'I don't know. I always kind of liked Moose,' said Missy. 'But Shelly said he'd been acting really weird lately.'

'Like how?'

Just then Mrs Jarrell, the teacher, strode into the room and asked everyone to take out their books. We were studying *The Crucible* and I suddenly felt like John Proctor – which is to say weak, and manipulated by forces beyond my control. Not to mention doomed. I kept an eye out all morning but didn't see Moose until lunchtime. He was walking towards his car in the parking lot when I finally found him. 'Hey,' I said, running to catch up with him. 'Where you headed?'

'Out for lunch. Bit too much aggression in the hallways. Shelly's turned the cheerleaders against me. It's like facing a fucking firing squad every time I change classes.'

'Yeah, I heard. What happened?'

'With Shelly?' He shrugged. 'Dunno. Just decided I wasn't into it any more.'

'You mean *her*.'

He stopped walking and looked at me, his bushy eyebrows shooting up in a question.

'You weren't into *her*,' I repeated.

'Whatever.' Moose shook his head and carried on walking. We reached his car and he turned to me. 'You coming?

'Nah. I gotta finish some homework.'

Moose shrugged then climbed into his car, rolling down the window, while I stood to one side. I watched him start the car, but just before he reversed, I stepped forward and put a hand on the door, leaning down to speak to him.

'Hey. Does this have anything to do with Annemarie?'

Moose looked up at me. 'Not really,' he said. But there was a hitch in his tone that alarmed me.

'Look, Moose. Just tell me straight: did anything happen with Annemarie on Friday night?'

'I took her home, if that's what you mean.'

'No. That isn't what I mean.'

Moose took a deep breath and looked away. 'Maybe you should ask her,' he said finally.

I hadn't seen Annemarie since Friday night, and she hadn't called to ask me why I'd missed church, which wasn't exactly a good sign. But I needed to know where things stood, so I went round to her house as soon as school finished. Ada let me in and I got a whiff of lilac-scented perfume as she closed the door behind me. She was wearing a pale pink blouse with pearl buttons (the top three of which were undone in a way that seemed reckless) and flared beige pants that clung tightly to her bottom.

'Hey, stranger,' she said with a smile. 'We all missed you at church yesterday.'

'Yeah, I wasn't feeling too good.'

'Poor lamb.' She gave me a worried look and stepped forward, laying a manicured hand across my forehead. As she looked into my eyes, she took a deep breath and her breasts seemed to move towards me like two torpedoes. My eyes dipped down and back up again. Ada smiled.

'I'm better now,' I said finally, pulling backwards from her touch. She too stepped back, and tilted her head to regard me.

'Well, you sure look fine.' Her eyes widened deliberately.

'Um ... Is Annemarie here?'

Ada crossed her arms and gave me a look, as if to say: *You still prefer her after all this time?* But then she nodded and pointed upstairs. 'Where she always is,' she sighed.

As I climbed the stairs I heard the sound of a male voice drifting down. I stopped short, wondering why Ada hadn't warned me. But in another instant I realised it was the man from Berlitz. Just then I heard him say: *Vuole qualcosa da mangiare?* Annemarie repeated the sentence, exaggerating her pronunciation so much that the last word sounded as if she was accusing someone of murder. Halfway through his next phrase I knocked on the door. I heard her fumbling to turn off the tape machine, and then the door opened. Annemarie stood there uncertainly, wearing jeans and a tie-dyed T-shirt.

'It's me,' I said.

'Hey.' She sounded relieved. And maybe a little sad. I wondered why.

'You're doing your Italian.'

'Yeah, I know. It's not Tuesday.' She shrugged. 'Just thought I'd do a bit extra.'

'It's sounding good.'

'*Mille grazie.*'

'Yeah, whatever.'

Annemarie laughed and stepped aside, and I walked into the room. 'How come you weren't at church yesterday?' she asked.

I hesitated. I could tell her what I'd told Ada. But I hadn't come to exchange lies. What I really wanted, what I desperately needed, was the truth. 'I didn't want to see you,' I admitted.

'Why?'

'I had a bad feeling after Friday night. I saw Moose come back here after the party. He pulled the shade down when he came into your bedroom, like he knew I'd be watching.'

'And were you?'

I took a deep breath and held on to it for a moment. 'Yeah,' I admitted.

'You don't trust me?'

'It isn't that.'

'What is it then?'

'Look, Annemarie, I don't own you. We're not even … we haven't even …'

I broke off. I couldn't say it out loud. Even after all these months, we weren't really boyfriend and girlfriend. I was her *math tutor*, for Christ's sake. And maybe her friend. But nothing more. What right did I have to make any claims? She stood silently for a long moment. I decided that I'd said enough. I would wait for her to speak. Sooner or later, she would tell me what was on her mind. She took a deep breath and let it out slowly.

'I kissed him,' she said finally.

'You kissed him?'

'Yeah, well. We sorta ... made out.'

'Oh, man.' Suddenly I *did* feel sick, like I'd been punched in the gut. I walked over to the window and stared out at my house, imagining myself cowering inside my bedroom, while Moose and Annemarie made out in hers.

'It's not what you think,' she said tentatively.

'Whatever. Look, I think you should find another tutor. This isn't gonna work for me any more.'

'Ethan, it was a mistake. A giant, colossal mistake.'

'Which bit exactly was the mistake?'

'All of it. Moose and me. Kissing. Friday night. It was all wrong.'

'Wrong or right, you did it. That's what matters.'

'No, you don't understand. I'm not talking about guilt. I'm saying that it didn't *feel* the way it's supposed to.'

I hesitated, unsure what she was getting at. 'What do you mean?'

'I didn't really ... enjoy it,' she said.

I stared at her, thinking I'd misheard. And then I thought: *Praise the Lord.* In the space of an instant, I'd died and been resurrected. 'You didn't?' I asked cautiously. 'Why not?'

'I don't know. It just didn't make me ... tingle.'

'Tingle?'

'Yeah, you know. *Tingle.*'

Actually I did know. I knew exactly. When I was kissing Sophie Strater, I may have smouldered slightly, but I never tingled. I'd always imagined that Annemarie and I would, though. Maybe she had too.

'So Moose doesn't make girls tingle,' I said, smiling

broadly. 'I'd always imagined he was such a stud.'

Annemarie burst out laughing. 'Not really. No. At least not with me. Maybe with other girls ...'

'I don't really care about other girls,' I said, cutting her off.

Annemarie stopped laughing and grew very still, like a deer in a meadow when it lifts its head from grazing, sensing that something dangerous is about to happen. I stepped towards her, knowing that if I was ever going to escape purgatory, my time had come. I stopped in front of her, only an inch away, until I could feel the heat radiating off her. She licked her lips and parted them ever so slightly, and I reached down to her waist and pulled her tightly to me, bringing my lips right to hers, and losing myself, finally, in their unbelievable softness. We kissed for a long moment, and I could feel her heart racing under the thin cotton of her T-shirt. I was boiling inside, and I could sense that she was too, as her hands were already pulling at my shirt, reaching under to my skin. I pulled her against me until our bodies were tightly meshed together, her lean frame pressed right into mine, and I felt a current of desire run right through her, causing her to gasp. Suddenly we both stopped, breathing heavily, our faces flushed with heat. She pulled back a little, resting her face against my neck.

'Oh my God,' she said breathlessly. 'Tingling isn't the right word.'

'Not really,' I said.

'It's more like being on fire.'

'Yeah.'

'I didn't know.'

'Well, now you do,' I said, guiding her backwards towards the bed. She put her hands on my chest.

'Wait.'

'What's wrong?'

'Nothing.'

We stood there uncertainly for a minute, me holding her, wanting her more than I'd ever wanted anything, hoping desperately that she wanted me too.

'I'm afraid.'

'Of what?'

'I'm not sure.' She hesitated. 'God maybe.'

'We don't have to do anything.' I heard myself say these words and wondered where they'd come from.

'We don't?'

'Not if you don't want to.' Christ! I hated myself. She took a deep breath and let it out slowly

'Maybe we could just … tingle for a bit?'

'Um … OK.' I wasn't sure what that would involve. She took my hand and pulled me down to sit beside her on the bed. We leaned back against the headboard, and she curled my arm around her shoulder so that she nestled in the crook. I took a deep breath of resignation.

'I've wanted to kiss you forever,' she said after a moment, in a musing tone.

'Me too.'

She turned her face to mine. 'Why didn't you?'

'I don't know,' I said. This was true, in a way. 'I guess I was afraid,' I added. She took my hand and squeezed it.

'Then we're both afraid.'

We sat side-by-side in the gathering dusk with me holding her. I think she even dozed off for a bit. I did not undress her, nor did I press my lips against all the different parts of her body that I'd dreamed of. But it was more than I had hoped for that day. And for once it was enough.

Eva

On the drive back from Cleveland, I nearly hit rock bottom. As I passed the signs for the interstate heading west, all at once the road opened up for me. In a flash it occurred to me that maybe we should follow Daryl's example: leave Jericho, drive to California, and find a quiet place where we could raise the baby on our own. I'd always wanted to see the desert, and for an instant my mind formed a tidy picture of us living in a trailer in the middle of a dusty plain. We could plant a garden, grow vegetables in old tyres, and learn to play the fiddle. Even the Bible says that when you are persecuted in one place, you should flee to another. And at that exact moment I wanted to flee them all: the doctors and their crackpot genetics, Deacon Joe and his censure, and the Virgin Mary and her baffling appearances, not to mention her strange obsession with my daughter. But when I thought about it, the Bible was also full of stories of those who tried to run but could not hide. Jonah, Elijah, Jacob – all of them had failed to outrun their own destiny. Ultimately, I reckoned, Annemarie and I couldn't escape God *or* science. Whatever mysterious force lay behind her pregnancy, we would have to face it head on.

But I was beginning to wonder if we might have to do it without the help of religion. For me, this was almost inconceivable. It was like saying: *walk, but don't use your feet*. All my life the Church had served as both my guiding light and my safety net. When Annemarie was first diagnosed with the illness that would eventually render her blind, I naturally turned to the Church for comfort and solace. I went to see Father O'Shea and confessed to him that I was both heart-broken and terrified at the prospect of raising a blind child. 'God will give you no more pain than you can bear,' he reassured me calmly.

'It's not the prospect of my own pain, Father,' I told him. 'But that of my daughter. She's only a child. She can't be expected to understand or endure pain. It's the prospect of *her* pain that I find unbearable.'

'God understands all this.'

'Then why has He chosen to inflict pain upon her when He could have picked me instead?'

'God has a plan for all of us. You mustn't put your love for your daughter above your love for God,' he admonished.

His words silenced me. I'd never before positioned God and my daughter in the same place at the starting block. If you had asked me to choose God over any other person in my life – my mother or father, my husband or my sister – I would have gladly done so. But I had always held the bond between mother and child to be a sacred one. Isn't that what the Bible teaches us? I wondered.

I returned home confused, and over the next few weeks I scoured the scriptures for tales of mothers and their children. The results made me uneasy. In the first place, the Bible seemed far more fixated on the role of women as wives than as mothers. While it exhorted children to love, honour and obey their parents, parents were urged to discipline, teach and be a model to their offspring. Nowhere was the sacred bond between a mother and her child openly acknowledged, much less celebrated. Indeed, many of the most revered women in the Bible – Hannah, mother of Samuel; Elizabeth, mother of John the Baptist; and even the Virgin Mary – had all repaid God's generosity by giving up their children to his service. At the time I couldn't help but wonder: is this what's being asked of me? Am I being asked to sacrifice my only child to God?

Now, as I drove down the Ohio shunpike, I had an eerie feeling of déjà vu. A sudden image of the Virgin Mary came into my head, whereupon she looked me in the eye and said: *If it was good enough for Jesus and me* ... I glanced over at Annemarie and felt a wave of motherly longing. She'd not spoken for several minutes, and as usual, I had no idea what thoughts were chasing themselves round in her head. Rational or not, the idea of taking her away from Jericho occurred to me again. But Annemarie was no longer a child – what if she refused to come with me? For one thing, I wasn't at all certain I'd be able to pry her away from Ethan. I had to admit that there was something strange and powerful about their union: it had become clear to me over the course of the summer that their feelings for each other were deep and true. What I was only just beginning to realise was how much I envied them. Nothing Daryl and I had ever shared in our brief married life even began to rival what my seventeen-year-old daughter had already kindled with this boy.

So that was the thing: Annemarie and I were living *her* life, but I'd somehow failed to cultivate my own. And for the first time in forever, a part of me longed for something more. In a few years Annemarie would leave home and I would be left alone. The thought of spending the rest of my days in Jericho with only Ada, Deacon Joe and the church for company made me wince. It had been easy enough to hide behind

Annemarie's disability when she was growing up, but I could see that, pregnant or not, my teenage daughter's horizons already outstripped my own. But if Ada and Annemarie had found romance in Jericho, then why couldn't I? Was there something wrong with *my* genetic makeup? Some crucial missing love gene? Nothing in the town had ever inspired me in that direction, it had to be said. There were a handful of eligible men in our congregation: two widowers who were both practically old enough to be Annemarie's grandfather, and an elementary teacher who I strongly suspected was gay (or at the very least, asexual). Apart from that I was acquainted with only a few other single men around town: Fat Ruby had a son in his late thirties who'd been married twice but was currently on the outs; she often complained that he drank too much, so he was hardly what I'd call a catch. And Deacon Joe had hinted once or twice that the wrestling coach at the high school was on the prowl for a wife, though he was overweight and Methodist, and anyway I hated wrestling.

A year ago, Ada had urged me to join a Singles Bible study group that operated out of Youngstown, but I couldn't bring myself to attend. The thought of sitting around with a group of complete strangers in a draughty church basement eyeing each other up behind the covers of the New Testament made me feel depressed. And anyway, being Christian didn't seem a good enough starting point to me now, I'd told her. Wasn't that how things had gone so badly for me the first time? Ada had sighed.

'I just want you to be happy,' she'd said, patting my hand.

'I *am* happy,' I reassured her. And at the time, I fooled myself into thinking it was true. It had taken the appearance of the Virgin Mary in the skies over Jericho to make me realise I was wrong. Maybe I should have been grateful, but frankly it only made me resent God more.

Annemarie

By the time Mama and I got back from Cleveland, all hell had broken loose in Jericho. As soon as we turned on to our street, Mama slowed the car right down to a crawl, and I heard her draw a breath. 'Holy Mother of God,' she said.

'What's wrong?'

'You would not believe this.'

'I might if you told me.'

Just then she slammed on the brakes and hit the horn. I went flying forward, only to be jerked back by the seatbelt, banging my head against the headrest. 'Sorry about that,' said Mama. I heard her roll down her window. 'Excuse me, but I need to get through here!' she shouted.

I rolled down my window and shut off the air conditioning. It sounded like we'd driven straight into an enormous herd of buffalo. People were laughing and chatting all around us, and seemed completely oblivious to the presence of our car. I could have touched them if I'd stuck my arm out. Mama hit the horn again and this time let it blast until I heard the voices start to recede. I had an image of the crowd dividing before us, like Moses at the parting of the Red Sea.

'That's more like it,' Mama said with satisfaction. The car crept slowly forward and eventually came to a halt. 'This is as close as I can get. Road's completely blocked ahead. Looks like some sort of TV crew has set up camp.'

'OK,' I said. Mama turned off the engine and we got out. She came round to my side and I took hold of her arm. 'What time is it?' I asked.

'Nearly sunset, if that's what you mean. She should appear in about fifteen minutes. If she's on time.'

A quarter to Mary, I thought. But I didn't say it out loud, as Mama seemed kind of twitchy.

'I think we better get into the house,' she said.

'Don't you want to watch?'

'I've had my fill of miracles today.' Her voice had definitely taken on an edge.

'Excuse me! Ma'am?' It was a male voice, coming at us from about twenty feet away, and sounding urgent.

'Let's pick up the pace, Annemarie,' Mama murmured in my ear.

'Ma'am! Can I speak with you for a moment?'

'Is he talking to us?' I said.

'It would appear so,' she said tersely. 'But we do not have to oblige him.'

'Ma'am! I just wanted a quick word.' The man was upon us now, and Mama pulled me sharply to one side. His voice was preachy and authoritative, as if he was used to getting his way.

'Not right now,' she said crisply.

'It won't take a second. I only have a couple of brief questions.' Now his voice sounded oily, as if he might try to slither his way into our good graces.

'Which I do not feel like answering right at this time,' Mama countered. I smiled at her resolve.

'Is it true that your daughter has become pregnant through some sort of divine intervention?' the man asked outright. My insides lurched sickeningly. Mama stopped dead.

'Excuse me?'

'There are rumours circulating that your daughter's pregnancy is somehow connected to the mysterious appearance of the Virgin Mary in the sky.'

'I'm sorry, but my daughter's pregnancy is a private family matter,' she said in steely tones.

'Pardon me, Ma'am. I understand you've had a shock. But there are more than four hundred people assembled here this evening. I'd hardly call that a private matter.'

I felt Mama's anger gathering with the force of a hurricane. 'Why does everyone keep saying that I'm in shock? Do I look like I'm in shock? No, I do not! What I am is irate that people keep telling me how I feel! So if you don't mind, we'll be on our way.'

'Is everything all right?' a male voice suddenly intervened at my elbow. For a split-second no one said a word.

'I was just having a word with these good people, Father,' said the reporter unctuously.

'Everything is fine, Father,' said Mama. 'Annemarie and I were just making our way home.'

'Easier said than done, with this crowd. Perhaps I can be of help,' he offered. I realised it was the new curate.

'That would be grand,' said Mama.

'Here, take my arm,' he said, stepping in beside me and folding my hand over his elbow. He smelled of Dial soap and his voice was low and velvety. I decided at once that his aura was benevolent, and it struck me that it couldn't have been more different from Father O'Shea's. Mama stayed on my other side and together they shepherded me through the jostling onlookers. Large crowds make me uneasy, so when we reached the front steps of the house I let out a sigh of relief at the familiar feel of them beneath my feet.

'Thank you so much, Father,' Mama said.

'It was my pleasure. Have a good evening.' I let go of his arm and listened as his footsteps retreated across the grass.

'Was that the new curate?' I asked.

'Yes.'

'He seems nice.'

'He is,' Mama agreed with a weary sigh.

'How did that reporter find out about the pregnancy?' I asked.

'It's a small town, Annemarie,' she said irritably. 'The minute you get a bunion the whole neighbourhood knows about it.' She pushed open the front door and we fell inside. 'Joe? Ada?' she called out to the silence. We stood there for a moment. 'They must be outside in all that hullaballoo,' she said. 'Well, they're welcome to it. I don't know about you, but I need a shower.'

We both felt slightly bruised after our encounters with the Magi and the reporter. I retreated to my bedroom and the comforting voice of Joni, and Mama to her shower. Some time later, when the crowd outside erupted in cheers, I turned the volume up as high as it would go. The song was 'Big Yellow Taxi', and as always, Joni's words seemed infinitely wiser than those I heard around me. Even though Jericho was little more than a crossroads, I realised now that it had been a quiet slice of heaven before things started to go wrong. Certainly life here had been remarkably easy: safe, comfortable and predictable. But a part of me had always yearned for something more, some form of interference, divine or otherwise, that would take me beyond the realm of the ordinary. I had always assumed this would mean escaping the confines of the town. It had never occurred to me that Jericho itself might become extraordinary, and me with it.

It took a few hours for the crowd to finally disperse that night. Hunger eventually drove me downstairs to the kitchen, where Mama sat having coffee at the table with Deacon Joe and Ada. As soon as I appeared in the doorway, a hush fell across the room.

'Don't stop on my account,' I said. 'Is there any dinner?'

'There's chilli on the stove,' said Ada.

'Fine.' I got a bowl down from the cupboard and made my way over to the stove. 'How was the Virgin tonight?'

'We didn't see her,' said Deacon Joe. 'We had a meeting over in Youngstown.' The way he said it made me pause, the ladle hovering halfway between the pot and the bowl.

'What sort of meeting? With who?'

'The Bishop.'

'Was it about the sunsets?' I asked cautiously. Deacon Joe shifted in his chair.

'It was about everything.'

'Everything meaning me?'

'Everything meaning *everything*, Annemarie.'

'There's nothing to fret about,' said Ada. 'We were just covering our bases, that's all. Your mama told us about the doctors up in Cleveland. And we're inclined to believe that you were right in the first place. So it's just as well that we prepared the ground with the diocese.'

'Prepared the ground for what exactly?' I asked cautiously. There was an awkward silence. Deacon Joe cleared his throat.

'Well, the diocese will want to undertake its own investigation, of course.'

'I don't understand.'

'Anytime a miracle is brought to the Church's attention, the Bishop appoints a committee to investigate. They need to verify that what's occurred is genuine. By which they mean: inexplicable. But your case is unusual, because it doesn't involve an illness, much less a cure. And anyway, no one is suggesting canonisation.'

'Canonisation!' I nearly fell over. 'You mean sainthood, don't you? I don't want to be a saint!'

'Calm down! Like Joe said, no one is suggesting sainthood,' Ada rushed to add. 'Anyway, that only happens after you're dead and buried. Not to mention exhumed.' She gave a cackle, and suddenly I wasn't hungry any more. I dropped the ladle in the pan and turned away.

'Honey, you should eat,' said Ada. 'Even baby Jesus needed food.'

'I've got heartburn,' I lied. I'd heard somewhere that it was a common complaint in pregnancy, and I thought the term sort of summed up how I was feeling: *scorched*. All of a sudden I was starting to prefer the Magi and my loopy chromosomes to the diocese and their miracles. 'Maybe the doctors up in Cleveland were right,' I suggested tentatively.

'And maybe the moon is made of green cheese,' said Deacon Joe with a snort of derision. 'Besides, it sounds to us like their motives are suspect. Like they're looking to get a building named after them, or at the very least, a disease.'

'But maybe my chromosomes *aren't* normal,' I said.

'Neither is your eyesight, but that doesn't change who you are,' said Ada.

'The important thing is we need to keep ahold of the situation,' said Deacon Joe fervently. ''Cause if we don't, somebody will snatch it out from under us.' I wasn't sure what he meant by the situation: me, the baby, or something else

158

altogether? What, exactly, was going to be snatched away?

'Is Ethan still out there in his tent?' I asked.

'Last time I checked,' said Deacon Joe. 'Must've earned a good few dozen boy scout badges by now.'

'Apparently he led a prayer this evening for the crowd,' said Ada.

'Ethan led a prayer?' I asked, astonished. He was sounding less and less like the Ethan I knew. So I decided I'd better mosey over to the campsite and find out whether he was an imposter.

'Look,' said Ethan a few minutes later when I'd confronted him, 'if I hadn't led a prayer, the whole thing would have descended into a freak show! You don't know what it's been like these past few days.' He exhaled heavily through his nostrils. 'Do you realise I've had people stopping by here all day long asking for my autograph?'

I hadn't realised. Things seemed quiet enough now, though. The nocturnal bugs were out, and I was enjoying the blanket of hot summer's night that had wrapped itself around me. I was even starting to wonder what it might be like to spend the night with Ethan in his tent. 'So what prayer did you lead?' I asked.

'The Magnificat. It was the only one I could think of,' he mumbled. 'Actually the new curate suggested it,' he confessed a little sheepishly. 'He lent me a Bible too, because I didn't really know the words.'

'I didn't realise you were friends with the new curate.'

'I wasn't really. But he's been bringing me coffee these last few mornings,' Ethan admitted.

'Well anyway, it was a good choice,' I said, trying to sound encouraging; it seemed like Ethan needed reassurance.

'People have short memories, Annemarie. Pea-sized

memories. They get here, and they need to be reminded why they've come.'

'Why *do* they come?' I asked. I needed reminding too.

'To brush up against divinity,' he said. 'Or at least get closer to it. Anyway, the prayer was just a way of keeping a grip on things.'

Wasn't that more or less exactly what Deacon Joe had just said to me in the kitchen at home? Keeping a grip on things seemed to be everybody's top priority at the moment. Why wasn't it mine?

'So how was Cleveland?' Ethan asked.

'Long. Tiring. Confusing.'

'What did they do?'

'Pretty much everything, apart from turn me inside out.'

'Did it hurt?'

'Only psychologically.'

'What?'

'No, it didn't hurt.'

'And is the baby still OK?'

'Yes, Ethan, the baby's fine.' I sighed. It was sweet that he was concerned about the baby, but at the same time, I found it irritating somehow. We sat there in silence for a moment.

'So what did they say about the pregnancy?' He asked reluctantly, like he didn't really want to know.

'They said I conceived the baby by myself.'

'We knew that.'

'Actually, what they said was I'm a boy.'

'What?'

'Well, they said I have the chromosomes of a boy. And the body of a girl.'

He hesitated. 'I could have told you that second bit anyway.'

'Yeah, well. I'm not sure which matters more. My chromosomes or my anatomy.'

'Your anatomy!' he said emphatically. 'Who cares about your chromosomes? No one's ever gonna see your chromosomes, Annemarie. No one's ever gonna undress them, or have sex with them either,' he added. I smiled. This was more like the Ethan I knew. No questions about *his* gender identity. But still, the whole chromosome thing was gnawing at me.

'Ethan, do you think it's really possible that I'm a boy?' He drew in a breath and held on to it for a long moment, like he needed extra oxygen just to consider the question. I felt my stomach do a sour little turn of dismay. He shouldn't have had to think. What I wanted, what I needed, was an emphatic no.

'Does it matter, Annemarie?' he said finally. 'It doesn't change who you are. It doesn't change anything at all, really.'

'No. I guess not.'

But the next morning, when the heat of the sun came screaming through my bedroom window again, I lay in bed and found myself wondering what a boy would feel like when he woke up. And, more importantly, what would he want for breakfast? I decided that the only person who would be honest with me about the whole boy/girl thing was Cora Lynn. So I rolled out of bed, took a cold shower and ate some gender-neutral Corn Flakes, then called her and asked her to meet me at the 7-Eleven in an hour. 'OK. But why the 7-Eleven?' she asked over the phone.

'The baby needs a Slushie.'

I didn't have much else to do so I tapped my way over to the 7-Eleven early. When I got there I sat down on the curb in front of the store, and stretched my legs out in the sun. The front door was open and inside I heard the cash register ring up a sale. After a moment, someone wearing rubber flip-flops and musky aftershave came out of the shop and walked by me, then got in a car and drove off. Must have been a stranger, because anyone who lived in town would have said hello.

'Hey Annemarie,' called out a woman's voice from inside the shop.

'Hey Kelly.' Kelly had worked at the 7-Eleven forever. In fact, she'd been there so long that I remembered what she looked like. Kelly had been plus-plus-plus size twelve years ago, and I was pretty certain that she hadn't changed. But who knows? Maybe she'd dyed her hair in the meantime.

'Hey Kelly,' I called out. 'Is your hair still the same colour?' She came to the door of the shop.

'Pretty much. Why?'

'No reason. Just wondered.'

'It's shorter now. I got it cut in a shag a few years ago.' Cora Lynn had told me about shag haircuts when they first came into fashion. She said they looked like someone had washed a rat, blown it dry, then stuck it on their head. What about the tail? I'd asked her.

'You wanna come inside? It's cooler in here. I just put the air-con on.'

'No, thanks. I'm waiting on Cora Lynn.'

'OK.'

Cora Lynn turned up twenty minutes later, by which time I'd said hello to seven different people, and chatted about the heat seven different times. I swear five people uttered the exact same greeting when they walked past, which amounted to: *Hey Annemarie, hot enough for you?* By the last time, I just gave a little wave of boredom and despair.

'Been waiting long?' Cora Lynn asked, sitting down next to me on the curb with a sigh.

'Long enough to know that conversation is a dying art in

this town.'

'Dead, more like. Folks round here only know how to gossip.'

'And you don't?'

'Course I do. I can gossip with the best of them. I am completely fluent in gossip.'

'That is true.'

'Thank you,' she said in a satisfied tone. 'Is it Slushie time?'

We made our way inside. I knew the layout by heart: doughnuts and Twinkies at the front to the left of the cash register, potato chips and salty stuff all down the centre aisle. Chilled drinks in a refrigerated unit against the far wall, and the Slushie machine in the far corner of the front, to the right of the counter and next to the coffee machine. Once, years before, Kelly had moved the doughnut rack to a completely different wall and when I complained she moved it straight back, saying that the customer always comes first, and that blind customers deserve to be ahead of everybody else.

We made our way over to the Slushie machine. I chose grape and Cora Lynn chose cherry, because she said the red dye suited her lips better than purple, which made her look like a banshee. 'Thanks,' I said. 'I always wanted the banshee look.'

'It's all the same chemicals, Annemarie. They just trick you with the colour into thinking it's different.'

'Let's walk,' I said, once we'd got back outside. Much as I liked Kelly, I didn't really want her privy to my chromosomal secrets. I told Cora Lynn all about the trip to Cleveland, and when I got to the punch line she just about killed herself laughing.

'You mean, I been hanging out all these years with a guy? Hang on a minute. Turn around. I wanna get a look at your Adam's apple.' She took my chin in her hand and pushed it up so she could look at my neck.

'Why my Adam's apple? Why not my breasts?' I asked.

''Cause breasts can be faked!'

'Cora Lynn, I am not faking being a girl!' I pulled away.

'You're right, 'cause you sure as hell don't have an Adam's apple.'

'Anyway, they said I was *anatomically* female. It's just my wiring that's male.'

'So you're wired up like a boy, but running like a girl?'

'I guess so.'

'Kinda like a pink sports car?'

'Um. Not exactly.'

'So what does guy-wiring feel like?'

'That's the thing. I don't really know.'

'Well, do you have guy impulses?'

'What kind of impulses?'

'Um. Like drinking a whole can of Coke in one go so you can burp really loud?'

'No.'

'What about writing your name in the snow with pee?'

'Gross.'

'Do you change your underwear every day?'

'Yes.'

'Then you're definitely a girl.'

'But that's the thing. All of a sudden I'm not sure I feel like a girl.'

'Since when?'

'Since they told me I was a boy.'

'Well, now you're just being gullible.'

'I don't know. When I was little, I went from sighted to being blind practically overnight. It feels a little like that.'

'Yeah, but that was *real*.'

'Who says this isn't real?'

'I do.' She put her hands on my shoulders. 'Listen, Annemarie. Those chromosomes ain't nothing but tiny little specks of dust floatin' around inside your brain. You're the boss. You need to tell 'em what's what.'

'You're saying I need to decide,' I said. She sighed, and I caught the faint scent of cherry on her breath.

'Yeah. That's just what I'm saying.'

Ethan

That first kiss with Annemarie last December should have been the turning point, but the very next day she came down with a terrible case of chicken pox. It had nothing to do with me, but when I turned up at the door the following evening, Deacon Joe glowered at me like I'd somehow personally infected her.

'Annemarie is not receiving visitors,' he said sternly. 'She's unwell and in quarantine.'

Ada came to the door behind him.

'Joe, don't be such a worry-wart. It's just chicken pox. She'll be right as rain in a few days' time.'

'She better be,' he said, grudgingly, before closing the door on me. Later that night, I called Annemarie on the phone. She sounded tired.

'Are you OK?'

'I've been better,' she said.

'Does it hurt?'

'It's more uncomfortable. Like there's something stuck inside me that's dying to get out. Mama keeps coming in every half hour to count the spots. I'm up to thirty-three and more are appearing all the time. They're everywhere, Ethan. On my scalp and in my armpits and in places I don't even want to think about, let alone say out loud. It's almost medieval. I feel like I've got the plague.'

'Everyone gets chicken pox. I know it seems bad now, but trust me, it'll pass.'

'Not everyone gets it as bad as this,' she said doubtfully. A few days later I stopped by with a small bouquet of pink roses I'd bought at the 7-Eleven. Ada opened the door this time and when she saw the flowers her painted eyebrows shot up with surprise.

'Will you look at this? It's a knight in shining armour!' She reached out for the flowers but I held tightly to them.

'Um. They're for Annemarie,' I said.

'I know that, silly. I was just gonna put 'em in some water for you.'

'I was kind of hoping to give them to her first,' I said.

'All right, Romeo. She's upstairs in bed. I better holler up first though, to make sure she's decent.' Ada pushed the door open and I followed her into the hallway. She paused at the foot of the stairs.

'Annemarie? You got clothes on, honey? Ethan's here.'

I heard a rustling, then the door open, followed by Annemarie's voice, sounding like it came from inside a bottle. 'Ethan?'

'You go on up,' said Ada, waving me past. 'But I warn you: she's not a pretty sight.' She gave me a wink and I climbed the stairs. I thought Ada was exaggerating, but I honestly hadn't prepared myself for the shock of seeing Annemarie covered in chicken pox. She was standing in the doorway wearing a pale pink nightgown, and I swear she looked like something out of a cheap horror movie. Her face was covered in angry red welts that distorted her features so much she was barely recognisable. Her lower lip was distended like something you'd see in *National Geographic* and one eye was almost swollen shut due to a massive blister right on the lid.

'Hey,' she said, giving me a weak, lopsided smile.

'Oh, God, I'm sorry,' I said, taken aback.

'Yeah. It's not good. I probably shouldn't let you see me like this,' she said. I was thinking the exact same thing, my feet frozen to the floor. She looked so bad in that instant that I couldn't imagine her ever looking normal again. I had to force myself to speak.

'No, it's OK,' I stammered. Though it wasn't, really. Inside I was reeling. 'I brought you some flowers. Some roses. They smell nice. I thought they might cheer you up.'

'Oh, roses.' She reached out and I put them in her hand, wrapping her fingers round the stems, but not before I counted seven pox scattered across her arm and hand. She raised the flowers to her nose, inhaling deeply.

'They smell lovely, Ethan, thank you so much. What colour are they?'

'Pink.' I was already easing backwards towards the stairs.

'Um ... do you want to stay for a bit?'

'No, I probably shouldn't.'

'I guess you're right. I might infect you.' I didn't tell her I'd already had chicken pox when I was five.

'You should rest,' I said instead.

'Yeah. Mama says she reckons they've stopped coming out now. So I guess I'm past the worst of it. But I think they're gonna take some time to clear up.'

Years, I thought. Maybe decades. And who knew what the scarring would be like? 'You take care of yourself,' I said. 'I'll come see you soon,' I lied.

I didn't. I couldn't bear to. Maybe I was being a dick, but I consoled myself with the thought that if Annemarie could see herself, she wouldn't want me around. So I called her on the phone every night and forced myself to imagine that it was the old Annemarie I was speaking to. Which was difficult when she talked mostly about her illness.

'Dr Paulson said he'd never seen a case as bad as mine,' she told me a few days later. 'Maybe I'm being punished.'

'For what?'

'*You* know.'

'No, I don't.' I honestly had no idea what she was talking about.

'Because we got carried away the other night. In my room.'

'What? The kissing? Are you crazy?'

'Look, Ethan, I got sick straight after. I woke up the next morning with them, for God's sake. Maybe *He* was trying to tell me something.'

'Annemarie, that's the stupidest thing I've ever heard. Besides, you made out with Moose a few days before. And *that* didn't make you ill.'

'Yeah, but with Moose it was different. I didn't want to ...' Again her voice trailed off.

'To what?' I asked, pressing her. She lowered her voice slightly.

'You know. Take it further.'

I took a deep breath. So she'd wanted to take it further. How much further? I wondered. 'So you wanted to take it further?' I asked cautiously.

'Yes. Didn't you?'

'Of course I did.'

We were both silent then, and for a moment all I could hear was the sound of her breathing. 'So maybe this is my punishment,' she said. 'Or maybe it's a warning.'

'Oh my God, this is not a warning! Trust me, Annemarie.

Millions of kids get chicken pox every year. And God is not trying to tell them to be abstinent!'

'How do you know, Ethan? How can you be sure?'

I sighed. I was sure. But persuading her was another matter.

I might have succeeded if it hadn't been for the infestation that Deacon Joe discovered six days later. By then Annemarie's chicken pox had begun to fade, leaving only a scattering of small brown scabs across her face, limbs and torso, like someone had thrown dark, wet confetti on her and it had dried and stuck. The swelling in her face had gone down by then too. I stopped by one evening and was relieved to see that she was starting to resemble her normal self, even though I suspected she might carry a few scars from the worst ones. We were hanging out in her room when we heard Deacon Joe bellowing from the basement, followed by Ada's footsteps hurrying down the stairs.

'What is it, Joe?' she yelled. 'You'll wake the dead!'

Annemarie and I decided to see what was up, so we went down to the kitchen and stood in the basement doorway. We could hear them speaking down below.

'They're everywhere!' he said. 'Look here! And here!'

Annemarie fingered my arm.

'What is it?' she murmured.

'No idea.' We stood silently for a moment, listening.

'Relax, Joe. We'll get pest control in,' said Ada.

'The entire foundation is shot! It'll cost a fortune!'

Ada came up the stairs then, rolling her eyes, with Deacon Joe's lumbering frame just behind. 'What's wrong?' asked Annemarie.

'Termites,' said Ada.

'Worst case I've ever seen,' said Deacon Joe, mopping

his brow with a handkerchief. 'I don't know how they moved in so fast. I was down there not three weeks ago and there wasn't a single sign of them then. But now they're everywhere. They've eaten right through the foundations. We're lucky the house is still standing.'

'Joe, don't be ridiculous. The house isn't gonna keel over. We'll call someone out in the morning.'

'It'll take an army,' he said.

'Then we'll get an army,' Ada replied evenly. 'Let's have a drink and forget about it. There isn't anything we can do tonight.'

'Pray,' he said. 'We can pray.'

'Fine. You go ahead and pray. I'm gonna fix a drink.'

The exterminators came the next day, and the infestation was so bad that the four of them had to evacuate for two nights while the house was napalmed. I offered to let Annemarie stay with me but Deacon Joe rejected that idea, insisting they all go down the road to a motel in Berlin. On the second night I stopped by to see how she was getting on, and we went for a walk down into the centre of town. We had a piece of pie at a diner, and although the weather was nice when we'd set off, by the time we finished and came out of the restaurant the temperature had plummeted and an enormous dark cloud was amassing overhead.

'We'd better get back, it looks like it's about to rain,' I said, conscious that Deacon Joe would freak out if Annemarie got caught outside in a storm. We walked as quickly as we could, but we were still a few minutes from the motel when the bad weather overtook us. Suddenly it felt freezing, and as the storm hit the rain immediately turned to hail. At first it wasn't so bad, just tiny balls of ice pinging down on us, but as we picked up our pace the hail got bigger and bigger, until it was crashing down like frozen golf balls. We both got struck several times and the sound of it bouncing off cars and the sidewalk was truly terrifying. Annemarie tightened her grip on my arm. 'Ethan?' she said, her voice sounding panicked.

'It's OK. We're nearly there.'

'It's hail, isn't it?'

'Yeah. Big ones.' I didn't want to frighten her but it was the biggest hail I'd ever seen, by far. I looked around for someplace to hide but there wasn't anywhere, so I tried to shelter her beneath my arm and carry on. By the time we reached the hotel a minute later we were both frozen and felt like we'd been attacked by aliens from outer space. Deacon Joe was waiting for us just inside the lobby.

'What in God's name were you doing bringing her out in a storm like that?' he shouted.

'It came up out of nowhere. We didn't know it was gonna be so bad,' I said.

'You should've stayed put and waited it out!'

'We're fine,' said Annemarie, her face as white as plaster. She didn't look fine. Deacon Joe took her from me and led her to her room, throwing me a dark look over his shoulder.

I didn't see Annemarie until two days later, after they'd moved back into the house. Ada let me in and when Annemarie opened her bedroom door I saw that she was clutching a small black rosary; I'd never seen her with one before. 'Hey,' I said.

'Hey.' She stood there fingering the rosary, and I could sense that something was wrong.

'What are you doing?'

'Nothing, just ...' Her voice trailed off uncertainly. 'Actually, I was just praying.'

'Oh.' I didn't really know what to say. She wasn't in the habit of praying in her bedroom at night, as far as I was aware, so I wasn't sure what to make of it. She pushed open the door and stood to one side.

'You better come in. We need to talk.' I walked into the room and sat down on the end of her bed.

'What's up?'

'Look, the things that happened these last few weeks. They weren't an accident. I'm certain of it.'

'What are you talking about?' I asked cautiously.

'First the chicken pox, then the termites, and finally that storm.'

'Annemarie, those were all isolated incidents.'

'Maybe to you,' she said. 'But I've been doing a lot of thinking, and I'm certain they were a sign.'

'A sign,' I repeated dumbly.

'Boils, locusts, hail. Does that mean anything to you?'

'Um, no. Should it?'

'*Exodus*, chapters nine and ten. When Moses came out of Egypt? *Let my people go*?'

'Rings a vague bell.'

'The Ten Plagues. They were a warning to Pharoah. Boils, locusts and hail were the sixth, seventh and eighth.'

I took a deep breath and let it out slowly. When Annemarie got an idea in her head there was no stopping her, so I knew I had to respond carefully. 'So you think it's a sign,' I said.

'Yes.'

'Of what?'

'I'm not sure. But like I said before, it might be a warning. To me.'

'Annemarie, I don't mean to be rude but why would God even care that much about you? I mean, He has way bigger things to worry about.'

'I know, I know. I keep telling myself that. And yet ... all three things happened. And they happened to *me*.'

'The hail happened to all of us.'

'Maybe. But I was talking to Cora Lynn and she said it didn't hail in Jericho at all. It only hailed in Berlin. Where we were.'

This was true. That night when I'd got home I'd told my parents we'd been caught in the hailstorm, and they'd looked at me with vague surprise. 'That storm must've passed us right on by,' my mom had said. 'Didn't even rain here.'

'OK,' I said to Annemarie. 'Let's assume God wanted to send you a message. Don't you think He might choose some other means of communicating? I mean, it's not very sophisticated, is it? Chicken pox and wood termites? In fact, it's pretty crude.'

'Yeah, I know. But God works in mysterious ways.'

'So what's next?'

'What do you mean?'

'Which plague comes next?'

'Um ... I can't remember. Frogs maybe?'

'And what about all the other ones? The ones that came before?'

'I don't know, Ethan! It's just a hunch, OK?'

'OK,' I sighed. It didn't look like we'd be going any further in the near future. If we were going anywhere at all.

Somehow after that we just slipped back into purgatory. It was strange how easy it was; like sleeping in your favourite T-shirt, or not showering for days on end. I suppose it was just the path of least resistance. We carried on more or less the way we'd always done, and after a while I stopped daring to hope for more. Christmas and New Year's came and went, and as January rolled into February I began to think of the night I kissed her as some sort of vivid dream, rather than a memory. Eventually, I decided it never happened at all.

Throughout this time Deacon Joe wreaked havoc on our relationship by insisting that Annemarie become more actively involved in the church community. Her new duties took up even more of her time. Two evenings a week he insisted she accompany him to Bible study sessions and on Saturdays there was charity work to be done with the elderly. Deacon Joe made it clear to me that I would not be welcome at either, even though I attended Sunday Mass and was therefore (technically) a member of the congregation. Clearly, he didn't see me as one of the flock. But the more worrying thing was: Annemarie didn't either. When I asked her whether I could come along one night to Bible class, she frowned and said, 'Ethan, you're not *seriously* interested in studying the Bible, are you?'

'I might be,' I offered.

'Go hang out with Moose,' she said dismissively.

Actually I hadn't told her, but Moose and I had fallen out over the kissing incident. After my conversation with him in the parking lot, he started avoiding me in the hallways at school, and we quickly went from being friends to being almost invisible to each other. Sometimes he would give me the barest hint of a nod when I passed him on the way to class, but that was about it. Maybe it's because we're guys, but it all happened so fast that I didn't really know how to stop it. Or even if I wanted to. But it was that chance remark from Annemarie that finally made me realise how much I missed him. So the next Saturday, when she was busy visiting old folks, I went round to his house unannounced. When Moose opened the front door, his bushy eyebrows shot up with surprise.

'I guess you weren't expecting me,' I said.

'You guessed right.'

'Can we talk?'

'Sure,' he said pushing the door wide.

We sat at the picnic table in the garden, even though it was late February and cold enough to see your breath. There was a dried-out splotch of ketchup on the table in front of where I sat. He didn't offer me a burger this time, which I figured wasn't a good sign. But I plunged in anyway, telling him that I was sorry we'd fallen out, and that I was OK with what had happened between him and Annemarie back in December. At once he relaxed, his whole body sort of deflating. I guess he'd been pretty stressed about the whole thing.

'Look, Ethan, I never planned it,' he admitted.

'Yeah, I know.'

'And it was never going to go anywhere,' he added.

'Yeah, I know that too.'

'You do? How?' He sounded a little unsettled by this, and I hesitated before answering. I couldn't exactly tell him that he didn't make her tingle.

''Cause she's in purgatory, man,' I said finally, with a shrug of my shoulders.

'Oh. Yeah. I guess so.' His relief was evident. But then he frowned and leaned forward. 'Dude, does that mean you *still* haven't done anything with her?'

'Well, not really. Not much, anyway.'

Moose shook his head in dismay, as if I was somehow letting down the entire male population by my failure. 'So what's the problem?'

'God's the problem,' I said with a shrug. 'Not to mention Deacon Joe. He thinks I'm the devil incarnate.'

'Dude, I don't know about God. But you can definitely take on Deacon Joe.'

'How?'

'You gotta beat him at his own game.'

'Meaning?'

'Hoop tactics. You need an early offence, to force the defence to react rather than act. Get the ball down the court before he can disrupt your play.'

'Moose, there isn't a ball.'

'Don't be an idiot. It's the same principle. You're being too passive. Letting him call all the shots. You gotta go on the offensive, man.'

'And do what?'

Moose shrugged. 'Embrace the whole church thing.'

'Embrace the church,' I repeated.

'You know what I mean. Somehow you gotta out-church him. And show Annemarie that you're committed.'

'Out-*church* him?'

'Yeah.'

'Like how?'

Moose crossed his arms like an umpire, his eyebrows knit tightly. For an instant I saw the same determination in his eyes that he displayed on court. 'Infiltrate the community,' he said earnestly. 'Ingratiate yourself. Find a secure position. And consolidate your power base.'

I frowned. He'd gone from basketball to guerrilla warfare, and I still didn't have a clue what he was talking about. 'What sort of secure position?' I asked.

Moose grinned, a little too gleefully. 'I was thinking maybe altar boy.'

Eva

The more excited Deacon Joe became over the sunsets, the more irritated they made me. After several days of sightings, our peaceful little town had turned into a heaving tourist trap, so much so that I began to wonder if the Virgin Mary might be on the payroll of the regional tourist board. There was trash everywhere and overflowing garbage cans on the road that stank to high heaven in the heat. And Christian pilgrims, it seemed, could be as noisy and offensive as anyone. They drove huge Cadillacs and unwieldy RVs that clogged up our roads, and they raided the convenience stores, cleaning out pretty much everything that was edible. But what really annoyed me was that the Virgin Mary refused to make her purpose here clear. She did not rain scorn upon us for our abuses, nor did she lavish praise upon us for our devotion. Most importantly, she did not communicate directly with Annemarie, which might have backed up Ethan's story. Frankly, it was all a little too ethereal for my liking.

But unlike me, the press was in heaven. Three days after we got back from Cleveland the six o'clock news featured a special report on Annemarie and the sunsets, fronted by the same oily reporter who'd accosted us that night. He'd managed to speak to just about everyone in town, from her kindergarten teacher to Dr Paulson and even Kelly over at the 7-Eleven, and the picture he painted was of a saintly child whose life had been marked out first by tragedy, then by a miracle. Ada and I watched with horror as the reporter concluded that Annemarie's pregnancy may well be an act of God. When the report was finished, I punched the button on the TV set and turned to her.

'Perfect! Now the entire world knows Annemarie is pregnant,' I said angrily.

'Well, at least he didn't cast doubts on her chastity,' Ada said nervously.

'Frankly, that would have been preferable,' I said. 'How is she ever going to lead a normal life now?'

Within a few hours we got our answer. I'd gone to bed early with a headache when I heard a cry from Ada's bedroom. Deacon Joe was out at a parish meeting so I rushed down the hallway to find Ada standing at her bedroom window, the curtains drawn to one side. I looked down to see a small crowd of people standing in the dark on our front lawn holding lit candles. They stood quietly, staring up at the house with reverent hopeful faces, and when I saw them I wanted to be sick. I stepped back from the window.

'Holy Mother of God,' I said to Ada in a loud whisper. 'Tell me this is not happening!'

'Must have been that damn news report,' she whispered back. 'What do we do?'

Just then Annemarie appeared in the doorway, having heard Ada's cry. 'Mama? Ada? What is it?' Ada looked at me, her eyes widening.

'It's nothing, Annemarie,' I said in a steady voice. 'Just

some rubber-necker tourists left over from the sunsets. You go on back to bed.'

She hesitated, then turned and went back into her bedroom and shut the door.

'We need to call the sheriff,' I whispered. 'This is out of control!' Ada hurried downstairs to Deacon Joe's study to telephone, while I kept watch from behind the curtain. After a few minutes I saw Deacon Joe's car pull up in the driveway and I breathed a sigh of relief. I watched as he got out of the car and stood facing the crowd, his hands on his hips.

'What in tarnation are you people doing on my front lawn?' I heard him say. 'Folks, the show's over! This is private property and you are trespassing!' Deacon Joe moved toward them waving his arms and the crowd shuffled towards the sidewalk, but once there they stopped and refused to disperse. They stood together like a flock of mute sheep, spilling out on to the road. He shook his head and walked into the house, slamming the screen door. I went downstairs just as Ada came out of the study.

'Damn pilgrims!' said Deacon Joe.

'The sheriff's on his way,' said Ada.

'Not a minute too soon,' said Deacon Joe, shaking his head. 'They're gonna ruin my grass!'

After Sheriff Dawson turned up and persuaded the crowd to go home, I was too agitated to sleep. The house felt stifling, so I decided to go for a walk. I crossed the churchyard and made my way over to a wooden bench on the far side of the church. Someone had planted the bare bones of a rose garden there a few years before, which consisted of a six-foot-square patch of dug-up earth and four spindly roses on stakes, their blossoms long since withered by the merciless heat.

I sat down on the bench and fanned myself. Ethan's tent

was about a hundred yards away, but it was closed up and I couldn't tell whether anyone was inside. After a minute I heard a noise behind me and the new curate came walking across the churchyard carrying a green watering can. He was dressed in flip-flops, a faded blue T-shirt and jeans, and as before, he was unshaven. I couldn't help but stare at his feet as he approached, and realised that I'd never before seen a priest's toes. His were long, with neatly trimmed nails and little tufts of dark hair on each knuckle, like a hobbit. I stole a sideways glance at him and saw that his eyelashes, too, were long, and unusually thick for a man's. Truly this man has hair everywhere, I thought.

He nodded to me in greeting and I watched as he carefully poured water on each of the roses, emptying the can, before turning around. 'It looks a little futile, doesn't it? I think they're already dead,' he said in an apologetic tone.

'God is grateful, I'm sure.'

'Well, I got to them a little late. They were fighting for their lives by the time I arrived in Jericho. Think they'd been forgotten.'

'So the blame lies elsewhere.'

'Ah. But we're not in the business of blame, are we? At least, I hope we're not.' He smiled. 'May I join you?' he asked. I nodded, and he sat down beside me.

'Thanks for rescuing us the other evening,' I said.

'Glad I could help.'

'We could have used you tonight, actually.'

'I'm sorry,' he said, turning to me. 'I've only just got back from a meeting over in Youngstown. Did something happen tonight?'

I hesitated, already regretting my remark. The last thing I wanted was to draw attention to our predicament. If he'd missed the news report, not to mention the candlelit vigil, no doubt he'd hear about it soon enough. 'There were a few issues with crowd control,' I said. 'No more than usual.'

He frowned. 'To be perfectly honest, I'm struggling with the sunsets,' he said.

'You're not the only one.'

'I've come to the conclusion that I don't want my faith to be extraordinary. I prefer the everyday garden-bench variety.'

'I couldn't agree more with you.'

'But it appears that you and I are in the minority. So I think the best thing we can do is bide our time, and wait until it all blows over.'

'She,' I reminded him.

He looked at me quizzically.

'Wait until *she* blows over.'

He laughed, the sound ringing out across the church-yard. We sat in conspiratorial silence for a minute, listening to the steady hum of the grasshoppers. He breathed in deeply and stretched out his legs. 'This weather is truly unrelenting,' he said.

'Do you think it's a test?'

'If it is, then I'm failing.'

I smiled, though a part of me found his manner disconcerting. Priests who made jokes were few and far between, and you never really knew where you stood with them. 'I've been sitting here wondering what it is that she wants,' I said.

'We may never find out.'

'My teenage daughter thinks the Virgin Mary has come to Jericho to bless her with a child,' I said. 'She's pregnant, in case you haven't heard,' I added.

He hesitated. 'I've heard whisperings. Generally, I pay them no heed. But I'm sorry if you or your daughter has fallen victim to any sort of maliciousness.' He paused and gave me a wan smile. *'Forgive them, they know not what they do,'* he added.

'Well, it's probably no more than we deserve.'

'Sounds like you're being hard on yourself.'

'Honestly, Father? I don't know *who* to blame. Myself? Annemarie? Her boyfriend? God?'

'Perhaps no one.'

'Maybe. But a part of me still thinks someone's getting off too lightly.'

'The birth of a child is never a matter for blame,' he said gently. 'It's a cause for celebration.'

'I know that,' I sighed. 'But you have to understand, I had thirteen years of Catholic schooling. Chastity was more important to us than air.'

'God wants us to be virtuous, of course. But virtue goes way beyond chastity. And I'm not sure God is terribly interested in chastity for its own sake these days. He has far bigger priorities.'

I turned and peered at him in the darkness. I was starting to wonder if he was a bona fide priest or some sort of imposter. 'What seminary did you say you went to?' I asked, only half in jest. He laughed.

'I didn't. But it was up north, in Michigan. And they were very broad-minded.'

'Apparently. So what would you say is God's top priority?'

He frowned at the roses for a moment. 'Compassion,' he said then.

'Really?' I turned to him with surprise. Compassion hadn't exactly been high on my list of late, though it probably should have been.

'Really,' he nodded. 'The Golden Rule.'

'Do unto others...' I said.

'Yep. Every religion is based on compassion. It's the only

rule you'll ever need.'

His words chastened me. We sat in silence and watched as lightning bugs flickered aimlessly across the darkened churchyard like lost souls. And I couldn't help but wonder when compassion had slipped off the horizon of our lives.

Annemarie

It was a big responsibility. Most people were never given the choice of which gender to be, so I didn't take it lightly. Of course I identified way more with girls, but when pushed, I could certainly see there were advantages to becoming a boy. Men had better opportunities in life and more freedom to behave as they pleased. They didn't have to bother with periods, housework, the pain of childbirth, or even grooming if they didn't want to. And they rarely had to wait in line to pee, not to mention squat in the woods. On top of that, guys never had to worry about their reputation when it came to sex. Girls were sluts if they slept around, frigid if they didn't, and dykes if they didn't care – while guys pretty much just got to be guys, come what may.

But I didn't really feel like a guy. For the next few days I took a vow of silence and retreated to my room to mull it over. I locked the door, drew the blind, turned the fan on high and lay on my bed listening to a carefully balanced selection of male and female artists, while I considered the relative merits of each sex. I thought about the people around me, and wondered whether the qualities that I appreciated in them were ones that owed a debt to gender or had nothing to do with it. I decided that I admired Mama's spontaneity, Ada's warmth, Deacon Joe's commitment to his faith, Cora Lynn's confidence, Ethan's generosity and Cassandra's wisdom. But when it came down to it, these traits all seemed just part of who they were, rather than something society or their gender had enabled them to be.

But I also thought about my own qualities, and where they'd come from. On the second night I broke my vow of silence and rang up Cora Lynn to ask her why she liked me. 'Because you're gonna have a cute little brown baby,' she said, laughing. 'A cute little brown miracle baby!'

'OK, forget about the damn baby,' I said. 'Why'd you like me before?'

She thought about it for a second. 'Because you're fearless. And you don't take any shit.'

'Anything else?' I asked. I'd never thought of myself as fearless, though it pleased me that she did.

'Um. Let's see. You speak better than anybody else I know.'

'I do?'

'Uh-huh. Must be all them tapes you listen to.'

'Must be,' I mused.

'And you're open-minded. In fact, I'd go so far as to say you were tolerant.'

Well, that was true. You couldn't live in my household and not be tolerant, I decided. Not with Mama and Ada and Deacon Joe and all their quirks and foibles to put up with.

'But you're also stubborn,' she went on. 'And obsessed with being blind.'

'That's not fair,' I argued. 'Being blind is as much a part of me as being black is to you.'

'No, it isn't. Folks don't even know you're blind, unless you tell them.'

'But blindness still holds me back.'

'Blindness holds some people back. But not you.'

I decided not to argue, since I knew she was probably right.

Open-mindedness must have come from my father's side. His mind was so open it ran away with him to California, leaving Mama and me to fend for ourselves. Since I'd never met him, I wasn't exactly sure what I'd missed out on. But even as a tiny child I was aware that fathers were something other children had, and possibly benefited from. When I was four, I decided that Father O'Shea was my father, and Mama let me think this far longer than she should have – I guess because she was ashamed that my real father had gone to ground. But then one day after church, I ran up to Father O'Shea and asked if he could get me a bike for my fifth birthday and teach me how to ride it, the way I'd seen other fathers do on our street. Father O'Shea had looked down at me with complete bewilderment, then his gaze had travelled up to Mama, who was standing just behind me, twisting her white gloves with embarrassment. Father O'Shea had cleared his throat and turned away without so much as a word, and I knew then that my bid for a bicycle (much less a father) was doomed, though I didn't know why.

When we got home Mama sat me down and confessed that Father O'Shea was not *my* father, but the father of the parish. I considered this for a moment, then immediately asked who the parish's mother was? Mama explained that the Church did not need mothers, only fathers. 'But Jesus had a mother,' I insisted.

'True,' admitted Mama.

'And I don't have a father,' I persisted.

'Also true,' said Mama.

'If the parish needs a father, then why don't I?'

'Because you have me.' Mama leaned forward and kissed the top of my head, as if to compensate me for something. I wondered then who was being short-changed: me or the parish? As I grew older I realised that Mama was the only single mother in our congregation; no wonder she'd been mortified the day I ran up to Father O'Shea and asked him to be my dad.

By the time I hit puberty, I'd also realised that the Church was uncompromisingly male. When I was fourteen the Pope issued a new doctrine emphatically stating that women could not be ordained as priests. Father O'Shea's sermon was especially full of righteousness that week. It seemed that in the Church's eyes tradition was more important than equality, and masculinity was integral to the priesthood. Deacon Joe had only just come to live with us and I remember arguing with him over dinner that evening. 'Look, Annemarie, it was no accident that Jesus chose twelve *men* to be his Apostles,' pointed out Deacon Joe. 'God made men and women different, and he did it for a reason.'

'What reason?'

'According to *Genesis*, women were created to help men. To assist and enable them to do God's work.'

'So we're kind of like ... secretaries.'

'Well, that's not how I would choose to put it. But in a manner of speaking.' His tone seemed uneasy, as if even he knew he was on shaky ground.

'If men are so important, how come the Church is always referred to as a woman?' I asked.

'I beg your pardon?'

'The Church is always *She* or *Her*.'

'That's because, according to the scriptures, the Church is the bride of Christ.'

'Huh. So kind of like his secretary then.'

I heard Deacon Joe sigh with exasperation. Ada cleared her throat and stood up.

'Time for pie,' she said brightly.

Deacon Joe always had a rebuttal, and often used the Bible to back up his claims. But it seemed to me that the Bible contained so many stories that one could justify almost any position if one looked hard enough within its pages. As a child I'd been drawn to the women in the scriptures, especially the bad ones. I was fascinated by those whose actions brought about the death or ruin of the men around them, such as Delilah and Salome. Or those who wreaked havoc upon entire civilisations, such as Jezebel and Eve. I sympathized with Eve who, just because she showed a little initiative and tried to improve her mind, ended up bringing sin and death into the world, which seemed both drastic and unfair. (When I was five I named my favourite doll Eve and took her everywhere, feeding her bits of apple when Mama wasn't looking.) I also felt sorry for the women who remained unnamed, such as the wives of Lot and Potiphar; God had deemed them so insignificant that He had stripped them of their identity for all time – a fate that seemed unnecessarily cruel, not to mention lacking in imagination. To be fair, there were plenty of good women portrayed in the scriptures, such as Ruth and Rachel. But they seemed boring by comparison, and the qualities they were remembered for, such as loyalty and virtue, struck me as inherently weak.

It occurred to me that my obsession with Biblical women was a strong indicator of my loyalty to the gender I'd been raised with. Such loyalty wouldn't be easy to shed, I reckoned. But how much did I really need my gender anyway? I wondered. If I could live blind, maybe I could live gender-blind. The more I thought about gender and identity, the more my mind turned somersaults. After three days of ruminating on the subject in my room, I decided that I should try a different tack altogether. Maybe if I acted like a boy, it would give me a better sense of whether or not I wanted to be one. So I rang up Cora Lynn again.

'You need to get me some guy clothes,' I told her.

'Say what?'

'I want to try dressing like a boy for a few days. Just to see what it's like.'

'You mean cross-dressing?'

'I guess so.'

'Sweet Lord in heaven. What kind of clothes did you have in mind?'

'I don't know. Maybe I could borrow some of Lewis's stuff?' Lewis was Cora Lynn's younger brother. He was fifteen and nearly six foot tall.

'Like what? Some shirts? Some sweat pants?'

'All of it.'

'*All* of it? You mean like Y-fronts and tube socks and jock straps and shit?'

'If I'm going to act like a boy then I need to feel like one. So, yes. All of it.'

'Remind me why exactly I have to do this?'

''Cause I'm gonna have a cute little brown baby.'

She came round with the clothes the next day. And true to her word, she brought them all. We sat on my bed and I unpacked the paper grocery bag she'd used to carry them in, feeling each item one by one and asking her to describe them to me.

'What's this?'

'Football shirt. Cleveland Browns.'

'What colour?'

'Brown, you idiot. With a bit of orange and white.'

'What's the number?'

'Forty-four. Leroy Kelly.'

'Who's he?'

'Leroy Kelly? He was the best! Think he played running back. But he's retired now.'

'OK. I think I can guess what this is,' I said, taking the next item out of the bag. My fingers felt an elastic strap and a hard cup-shaped bit.

'You asked for it.'

'Yeah, I know. Is it clean?'

'Don't be disgusting. Of course it's clean. And he will mince me into little pieces if he finds out I showed it to you. Much less let you put it on.'

'He won't find out.' I took the next few things out. 'Tube socks?'

'Yep. Yellow stripe.'

'And Y-fronts. And what are these ... shorts? Thought you were gonna bring me sweat pants?'

'Look, his pants are about eight feet long. So I thought these might at least fit you. They've got elastic at the waist.'

'Guess they'll do.' I stood up and started to strip.

'You gonna put it all on now?'

'Yep. Close your eyes. Otherwise it'll ruin the effect.'

Cora Lynn flung herself back on to the pillow. 'Fine. My eyes are shut.'

Quickly I stripped off all my clothes and pulled on Lewis's things. I wasn't sure whether the jock strap went under or over the Y-fronts but in the end I put them on over, positioning the cup where I thought it should go. The shorts and shirt were huge but she was right, at least they more or less fit. I pulled the socks on last, then tied my hair back in a ponytail and tucked it up under an old baseball cap of Deacon Joe's.

'OK. You can look.'

Cora Lynn sat up. 'Huh. Maybe we should've given this a bit more thought,' she said after a moment.

'Why?'

"Cause you look like a dick.'

'That's the point, isn't it?'

'Not that kind of dick.'

'Well, which bits are wrong?'

'All of them.'

'Did you know that there were women all through history who dressed as men and got away with it?'

'Trust me, it wouldn't work.'

'But it did!'

'Wouldn't work for *you*.'

'Look, it can't be that bad. I was hoping to go out somewhere. Like to the 7-Eleven or something. You know, test the water a little.'

'Not with me you aren't.'

'Pleaaassse?'

Cora Lynn sighed and got to her feet. 'Cute little brown baby ain't worth it,' she muttered as we headed out the door.

We walked into town, and truth be told, it was pretty uneventful. Cars did not honk or pull over at the sight of me, and no one we passed said a word. 'See? This isn't so bad,' I said. 'No one can even tell.'

'Trust me, they can tell. They're just being polite.'

We got to the 7-Eleven and went in. I could hear Kelly chatting to a customer at the till, so I headed over to the salty aisle. 'Hey Annemarie. Hey Cora Lynn,' she called out.

'Hey Kelly.' I couldn't hide the disappointment in my voice.

'Something wrong?' she asked.

'Nope,' replied Cora Lynn. 'We're just fine and dandy. Aren't we, Annemarie?'

'I didn't know you were a Browns fan,' said Kelly.

'Neither did she,' said Cora Lynn.

'Let's go,' I said under my breath.

'Don't we even get a Slushie?'

So cross-dressing wasn't the way forward. As soon as we got home I changed into my own clothes and gave Cora Lynn her stuff back. She had a job at the Burger King over in the mall outside Youngstown and was due to work the afternoon shift, so she left. And as soon as she'd gone, I suddenly felt fed up: with blindness, babies, chromosomes, jock straps, sunsets, all of it. For the first time in years, I just wanted to be a normal teenage girl with normal teenage problems, like bad hair, acne and not enough clothes. I lay on my bed, not even wanting music, and let despair take me where it would.

And then the doorbell rang. I thought about ignoring it. But it rang again and again and eventually I went to answer it. Instead of asking who it was, I opened the door. 'I could swear I saw you not half an hour ago dressed in completely different clothes,' said a woman's voice. It was Cassandra, and a part of me thought: *Of course it is.*

'Yeah,' I admitted.

'I don't usually give fashion advice, but this is a much better look for you,' she said. 'May I come in?'

I pushed the door open wider. 'Sure. But can we skip the knitting today? I'm not really in the mood.'

'Of course. What *are* you in the mood for?'

'Iced coffee.' I led her to the kitchen and made us both an iced coffee with extra sugar and cream.

'Where's your mom?' she asked.

'Out with my aunt. Helping some elderly parishioners move house.'

'So how are things?'

'They've been better.'

'I've heard a rumour or two. Thought I ought to come by and hear it from the horse's mouth,' said Cassandra. I considered all the things she might have heard.

'Whatever it was, it's probably true.'

'Tell me about that,' she said.

So I did. I started at the beginning and brought her more or less bang up to date, leaving almost nothing out. It took a long time and I could tell she was listening intently, but she didn't utter a word until I'd finished, when I heard her take a deep breath and exhale.

'My, my,' she said. 'You *have* been busy.'

'So you believe me?'

'Why wouldn't I?' Her faith in me was touching. I thought about all of the doubts I'd encountered in recent weeks: both from my family and from Ethan. No wonder I'd been depressed. I wanted to reach out and take her hand in gratitude, but I didn't.

'Have you seen the sunsets?' I asked instead.

'Oh, yes. Who hasn't? Actually I don't even notice them now. Funny how even the most extraordinary things can seem normal after a time.'

'I don't feel normal.'

'No. I expect you don't,' she said. 'But I reckon you're about the most normal teenager I know.'

'Really? Me?'

'Yep. If being normal means knowing who you are, and what you want out of life, and how you should behave, then I think you qualify.'

'But that's the thing. I don't know any of those things.'

'Don't you?'

I was silent for a moment. I could hear the hum of the refrigerator and the ticking of the clock on the stove. They were familiar sounds, ones I'd heard since I was a tiny child – and I didn't know if it was down to Cassandra's presence, but suddenly I found them oddly comforting. Maybe she was right. Maybe I was trying too hard.

'What should I do?' I asked.

Cassandra hesitated for a moment, and I could almost hear her mind working. 'I think you should talk to Ethan,' she said.

'And say what? He feels like a stranger to me now.'

'You'll think of something.'

So after Cassandra had gone I left the prison of my bedroom and went to see Ethan in his tent. The weather was muggy but overcast, so it wasn't as hot as the previous days had been. I brought my stick and Ethan must have heard me tapping, because as I drew near I heard the zipper on his tent open. 'Annemarie?' he called out.

'Hey,' I said, stopping just in front of the tent.

'Hey.'

There was an awkward moment of silence. 'Do you think we could take a walk or something?' I asked. I heard him come out of the tent and close it up.

'OK.'

I took his arm and we walked, away from his tent and the church and both our houses, and away from the centre of the town. I had an instinct that the further we got from home and the wayside shrine, the better off we'd be, and Ethan must have felt the same because neither of us said a word and we just kept walking for I don't know how long.

Eventually we came to a park on the far outskirts of town that had once belonged to a wealthy industrialist who had bequeathed it to the city many years before. I'd come here often as a child, both before and after I'd lost my sight, so I knew it well. The long driveway was flanked by towering oak trees and led to a vast red-brick mansion surrounded in its entirety by a terrace built of smooth white stone. Beyond the house there were acres of lawn leading down to a thick grove of fir trees and a creek. I led Ethan on a path through a rose garden around to the back of the house. Off to one side, hidden behind a thick clump of vast magnolia bushes, was a tiny grotto built of rough-hewn stone.

'Wow,' he said. 'I've never seen this.'

'This is my favourite bit of the park.'

'If you didn't know it was here, you'd never find it.'

'That's true of all the best places.'

We had to duck our heads to get through the arched opening. Inside was a marble bench and I led him straight to it. We sat down, the stone cool beneath our thighs, the air inside the grotto faintly damp and smelling of past lives. 'It feels a little like a tomb,' he said nervously, his voice echoing off the stone. 'But I like it.'

'I haven't been here in a long time.' I turned to him and he was so close I could hear him swallow. 'I miss you,' I said.

'I miss you too.'

He leaned in towards me and I felt his lips come to rest against my forehead. I could feel the heat of him against my skin, like a fiery hunger that threatened to devour us both. I wanted desperately to kiss him, to lose myself inside that heat, and I knew he felt the same. But if we did that, we would still have the pregnancy and the sunsets to contend with. Not to mention Deacon Joe, the Church, the Magi, and the Virgin Mary herself.

So I pulled back and faced him. 'What are we going to do?' I asked quietly. Ethan seemed to understand. He took a deep breath and let it out slowly.

'I don't know,' he said. 'But whatever we do, we should do it together.'

Ethan

I told Moose that hell would freeze over before I became an altar boy. But in the days that followed, I started to reconsider. I'd never really understood the nature of Annemarie's faith. I knew that it came from somewhere deep inside her, and that it helped to orient her in the world. But I'd always assumed that because of her blindness, Annemarie needed God more than the rest of us. And now I began to wonder if maybe the opposite was true. Annemarie once told me that belief in God wasn't some sort of internal switch that you could just throw. It was something you had to create space for inside yourself, and nurture. 'You have to *grow* God, Ethan,' she said. 'It takes time. And it isn't always easy.'

'But isn't that like saying you're making him up?'

'No. It's more like learning to ride a bike. God is there, but you have to find your way to him. You have to learn how to love him, and how to be loved by him.'

'But how can you be *sure* he's there?'

'I can't,' she said with a smile. Faith meant embracing life's mysteries, and even celebrating them, she explained. She didn't fear the unknown, but, like Emily Dickinson, found beauty in it. 'Religion shouldn't try to give us all the answers, Ethan,' she said. 'It should encourage us to ask the questions. And it should listen, and it should comfort.'

So maybe Annemarie's blindness meant that she was better able to tolerate the mystery of faith than I was. And I had to admit that, in spite of going through the motions, I'd never really given God much of a chance. On top of that, when it came to wooing Deacon Joe, Moose was probably right. I needed to demonstrate that I was committed to Annemarie and all that she believed in. If that meant swallowing my pride and embracing a host of traditions that were alien to me, then perhaps it was a small price to pay. So about a week after Moose and I made up, I went to see Father O'Shea and asked if I could train to be an altar boy. I found him in a small office behind the rectory. The room was painted a pale coffee colour and had brown carpeting that was fraying at the corners. It was lined floor-to-ceiling with dark bookshelves and I couldn't help but notice that the volumes they contained were meticulously ordered by colour and size. On his desk was a single stack of papers in the corner, together with a fountain pen in a holder. Father O'Shea sat with his head lowered, scrutinising an open black ledger in front of him, his fingertips pressed together. His small frame seemed dwarfed by the desk, and on the crown of his head I could see a perfectly round bald patch, surrounded by wiry grey hair. I hesitated for an instant, then knocked tentatively on the frame of the doorway. Without looking up, he waved me into the room. I stepped inside and waited patiently, but it was several seconds before he looked at me.

'Yes?' he asked, indicating with a nod that I should sit.

I sat down in the chair opposite him and told him why I'd come, and as I did his expression became hazy, as if I'd just beamed in from outer space. He took his glasses off and laid them to one side, pausing briefly to pinch his temples. When he raised his head again I saw that his glasses had left a white mark either side of his nose.

'How old are you?' he asked a little dubiously.

'Seventeen.'

He frowned, and I shifted uncomfortably in my chair. A trickle of sweat rolled down my left side. Suddenly I wasn't sure this was such a good idea. The tiny room felt stifling. A shaft of sunlight came slanting through the window and dust motes circled aimlessly in its beam. 'You do realise that most of our boys are considerably younger,' he said then.

'I know that, Father.'

He raised an eyebrow, and the silence in the room seemed to swell. 'Do I know your parents?' he asked.

'I'm not sure,' I replied evasively.

'Were they at Mass on Sunday?'

'I don't think so. They come as often as ... they can.' That was sort of true, I decided. Or it could be.

'And they approve?'

I swallowed. 'They're not opposed,' I said. Which was probably true, though my voice sounded thin and unconvincing. He narrowed his gaze at me, as if he could see straight through my falsehood.

'It's very unusual to take someone on at this point in the liturgical year,' he said finally. 'We began our instruction just after Epiphany, you see, and it's already March.' He looked up at me with a raised eyebrow, as if challenging me to overcome his opposition.

'I'm a fast learner,' I said.

'One would hope.' He allowed his voice to trail off, then picked up a pencil and held it in both hands by its ends, rolling it slowly in his fingers. 'The Church aims to be inclusive in all aspects of its life,' he said. 'So I suppose we might be able to make an exception.'

'Thank you,' I said, even though it wasn't entirely clear to me whether he'd said yes. 'How old are the other boys?' I asked.

'Our youngest is eight. But the average age is nine.'

So I was twice their age, I thought. At least there was a sort of symmetry.

'I'll need to check if we have vestments for your size. How tall are you?'

'Five foot eight.'

'Fortunately not Goliath,' he murmured. He bent down and rummaged around in a drawer of his desk and presented me with a sheet of paper. 'Here is a list of requirements. Perhaps you should cast your eyes over these, before you commit.'

I took the list and quickly scanned it. The requirements included being able to fold my hands together in the proper position, the ability to sit quietly without fidgeting for fifty minutes at a time, the ability to tie and untie my own shoelaces, and the discipline to refrain from playing with my cincture during Mass, whatever that was. I was also to refrain from socialising with girls fifteen minutes before Mass, and afterwards for as long as I was wearing vestments.

'If you still feel that this is something you wish to do ...' Father O'Shea paused and looked up at me, and I nodded.

'Yes, sir.'

'Then so be it. The Lord be with you.'

I didn't say anything to Annemarie. My plan was to complete the training, then appear at Mass in my vestments and surprise both her and Deacon Joe at the same time. But the following day when I walked into the Catechism classroom in the church basement, Deacon Joe was standing behind the desk with his back to me, busy at the chalkboard. I stopped short and watched as he finished writing out a list of the seven sacraments in large block capital letters. All at once I felt nauseous; it honestly hadn't occurred to me that the class would be taught by him. I was about to turn and go when two younger boys came screaming down the corridor into the classroom and slammed straight into me. Deacon Joe turned round with a look of disdain. He picked up a wooden yardstick and smacked it down hard on the desk. Suddenly the room went quiet.

'Deacon Thomas told me you were an unruly bunch,' he said. 'You may have found him to be as soft as warm butter, but I can promise you that I am the human equivalent of cold asphalt. Now stand up straight and tell me your names.'

'Where's Deacon Thomas?' asked the boy on my right.

'Deacon Thomas is in the hospital with a gallstone the size of a grapefruit,' said Deacon Joe. 'So for the foreseeable future, I will be in charge of this class.' The boy glared at him and lifted his chin a little defiantly. Deacon Joe glanced down at a sheet of paper on the desk in front of him. 'What's your name, sonny?'

'Brian,' said the boy.

'Brian what?'

'McCallister.'

'What comes after the Liturgy of the Eucharist in the Order of Service, McCallister?'

Brian flared his nostrils slightly, and I saw his left eye twitch, but he remained silent.

'Cat got your tongue, McCallister?'

'No, sir.'

'Then I guess you're just slow.'

'I'm not that either.'

'Prove it.' He looked at the boy on the other side of me.

'What about you?'

'Isn't it the Holy Communion?' the boy asked cautiously.

'I see someone paid attention last week. What's your name?'

'Eddie Jessup.'

'Mr Jessup, can you tell me why a boy twice your age is in this class?'

Eddie Jessup blinked and turned his head slightly towards me, then shook it quickly from side to side. 'No.'

'Neither can I. Perhaps he'd care to enlighten us?'

'Father O'Shea said that I could join the class,' I said.

'Because?'

'Because I was hoping to become an altar boy.'

Deacon Joe laughed outright. 'Well now, that just takes the biscuit,' he said, smiling. 'Boys, I reckon this class just got a whole lot more fun.'

A lump the size of a fist rose in the back of my throat. At that moment a tiny boy stepped quietly into the room behind me. He was no higher than my waist, and out of the corner of my eye I caught sight of a head of golden curls and near-perfect features, like a skinny human cherub. Deacon Joe craned his neck to get a better look at him. 'Step up, sonny. You're late,' he said. The boy shuffled forward slightly.

'Sorry,' he mumbled.

'Name?'

'Francis.'

'I could have sworn that was a girl's name.'

'I was named after Francis of Assisi,' the boy said quietly. 'He was a boy.'

'I *know* who Francis of Assisi was,' said Deacon Joe. 'And I suppose you too are hoping to become an altar boy?'

'Yes, sir.'

'Well, you look a bit pint-sized to me. But if you can carry a chalice, then I guess you'll do.' He nodded in my direction. 'We'll pair you up with Ethan here. It'll be little and large.'

The boy Francis turned his head to look up at me, and his eyes were shiny and startled, as if he'd somehow landed in the wrong life. I felt bad and gave him an encouraging smile, but he just looked away.

For the next hour Deacon Joe drilled us on the seven sacraments until we could name them backwards and forwards and standing on our heads. Francis learned pretty quickly, and Eddie Jessup could just about manage, but McCallister had the attention span of a newt, and was clearly the sort of kid who got by on wits and bad behaviour and bravado. Halfway through the class he pulled a long rubber band out of his pocket and used it as a slingshot to project spitballs at the back of Francis' head. I expected Francis to do something, but he just sat there frozen, his ears turning redder and redder, until I thought that he would burst. When I couldn't stand it any longer I turned round and snatched the rubber band out of McCallister's hand, giving him my fiercest glare.

'Hey! That's mine!' he hissed. 'Give it back!'

It had been a long time since grade school, but clearly I needed to work on my glare, as he didn't seem the slightest bit intimidated. Deacon Joe turned round from the chalkboard, and his gaze landed squarely on me. 'Is there a problem?' he demanded.

'No, sir,' I said. McCallister scowled.

'As the oldest boy in the class, I trust you will set a shining example to the others,' said Deacon Joe with great emphasis on the word *shining*, as if it was code for *scorching* or *blistering*. Or even worse: *sacrifice*.

'I'll do my best,' I said.

He nodded. 'I'm certain you will.'

He turned back round and McCallister instantly flipped me the finger, mouthing the word: *Sucker!* The kid was bad news, and I didn't want anything more to do with him. But he was also hard to ignore. Somewhat guiltily, I decided that Francis would have to fight his own battles, as I couldn't afford to jeopardise my relationship with Deacon Joe.

The next night I went by Annemarie's house, and as soon as we were alone in her room she smiled and said: 'So can you still recite the seven sacraments?'

'He told you, huh?'

'Did you expect him *not* to?'

'I was hoping to keep it a surprise.'

That silenced her. She frowned thoughtfully, and two little wrinkles appeared on her forehead. 'Am I missing something here, Ethan?'

'What do you mean?'

'Look, I think it's really sweet that you started to come to church and all. But don't you think this is taking the whole religion thing a little too far?'

I hesitated, unsure how to respond. 'But ... *you're* religious.'

'Ethan, from the moment I entered the world, I was raised to be a good Catholic. To believe in God and the Bible and the power of salvation.' She paused for emphasis. 'You weren't.'

'Good Catholics aren't just born, Annemarie,' I said.

'But all the same, isn't it a little like pulling up the shoots to help them grow?' she asked gently. 'Like maybe you're trying too hard?'

Of course she was right. But I couldn't admit it without looking like a fool. 'If coming closer to God is trying too hard, then I guess I'm guilty,' I said stubbornly.

Annemarie paused and tilted her head to one side. She may have been blind, but I swear in that moment she could see right through me. 'So *that's* what you're trying to do? Get closer to God?'

I took a deep breath and looked away. 'Yep,' I said. Blind as she was, I couldn't look her in the eye while I was breaking a commandment.

'And here was I thinking you were just trying to get closer to me,' she said with a smile. She turned away, leaving me speechless, and picked up a hairbrush. I watched helplessly as she began brushing her waist-length hair with even strokes, and I was more in love with her than ever.

The next day at school I told Moose what she'd said. His eyebrows shot up. 'Oh, man. So she saw right through it, huh?'

'Afraid so,' I said ruefully. We were in the back of Study Hall, where Moose spent a large chunk of each day. As an honour student and a star jock to boot, he could weasel out of most of his classes. The teachers loved him. Especially the female ones.

'Dude, I'm really sorry. Now what are you going to do?'

'Become an altar boy,' I said. 'I have no choice!'

'Oh, man. That sucks.'

'You know what else I'm gonna do? Stop taking your advice!'

He shrugged. 'Fair enough. This whole church thing is kind of out of my league.'

'You could have told me that the first time.'

'Dude, I was only trying to help. Besides, it can't be that bad. Maybe Annemarie will like you better in a dress.'

'It's a vestment, not a dress, you moron. And anyway,

she won't see it 'cause she's *blind.*'

'Count your blessings, man. 'Cause I was lying about the dress.'

The next week in class we started our training in earnest. Deacon Joe instructed us on how to walk, sit, kneel, bow, genuflect, and even how to hold our hands correctly in prayer (fingers extended and pointing upwards, thumbs crossed right over left). I reckon he would have taught us the correct way to wipe our butts if we'd asked him. On top of that there was a long list of things that were prohibited. 'You will *not* look round when anyone passes the altar,' he said emphatically. 'You will *not* stand during the Credo, you will *not* put the cruets on the altar without a cloth under them, and you will *not* kiss the chasuble before or after the Elevation. Is that clear, Mr Jessup?'

'Yes, sir,' mumbled Jessup.

'You will take pride in being punctual, you will take pride in personal hygiene, and you will be on your best behaviour at all times. This is a sacred and solemn service. And it is a privilege for you to be a part of it. Isn't that right, McCallister?'

Deacon Joe waited for a response but McCallister said nothing, merely rolling his eyes. 'I am certain that each and every one of you will remind himself of the presence of God and His holy angels, not least when you are in the Sacristy, where you will regulate your conduct at all times, as you are within the precincts of God's house.'

The Sacristy was clearly set apart from the rest of the church, and I had to admit I was curious to get a look inside, as Deacon Joe made it sound like it contained the Holy Grail. I'd seen Father O'Shea emerge from the narrow wooden doorway behind the altar at the beginning of each Mass, and disappear inside it at the end, usually attended by an altar boy who trailed behind him holding the edges of his robes. The next Sunday I tried to crane my neck to get a better look, but all I could see was a faded red velvet curtain that hung just inside the doorway, obscuring everything else from view. I'd never paid much attention to the altar boys during Mass, but now of course they were all I paid attention to. Their duties weren't exactly difficult to master, but I noticed that they screwed up frequently during the service, stumbling on the altar steps, bowing when they were meant to stand straight, or handing the priest items with the wrong hand, whereupon he would glare at them and give the barest shake of his head.

Whenever I tried to imagine myself serving at Mass I got a nasty feeling in my gullet, as if I'd just swallowed a crucifix. Nor could I see McCallister or Jessup behind the altar. But young Francis was clearly desperate to have a go, and at the end of our fifth class he raised his hand and asked when Deacon Joe thought we would be ready. 'When I say so,' said Deacon Joe staunchly. 'And not before. Is that clear?'

Francis nodded and sank down low into his chair.

'Deacon Thomas said we would be done by now,' said Jessup.

'He did, did he? And where is Deacon Thomas this evening?'

'Um ... at home, I guess.'

'Precisely. So his word is no longer gospel.'

'He did say that,' said McCallister sullenly. 'It wasn't meant to take this long.'

'Maybe Deacon Thomas wasn't used to teaching half-wits.'

'Maybe he was just a better teacher,' shot back McCallister.

Deacon Joe's face clouded over. 'Very well,' he said crisply. 'Anyone who thinks you're ready, raise your hand.' There was a split-second pause, then three hands went up in the air. Deacon Joe narrowed his gaze at me. 'Where's your hand, Ethan?'

'Um. It's attached to my arm.'

'Why isn't it in the air?'

I shifted uncomfortably. 'I'm still trying to learn the Order of Service. I haven't quite mastered it yet.'

'Don't be a jackass. You're training to be an altar boy, not a bishop. If they're ready, you're ready.'

'Yes, sir,' I mumbled.

'And I'm counting on you to keep them in line.'

Deacon Joe turned and began to erase his writing from the blackboard, whereupon McCallister swivelled round to face me and winked. I felt the hair rise on the back of my neck, and I knew in that instant I was doomed.

Eva

After my talk with the curate in the churchyard, something inside me settled. I decided that it didn't matter how Annemarie's pregnancy came about: whether she and Ethan had lost their heads in a fit of passion, or her chromosomes had played some kind of fancy game of Russian roulette, or the Virgin Mary had personally dropped the seed into her womb like a stork, the cause was unimportant. What *was* important was the welfare of Annemarie and her unborn baby, and I had a duty to protect them both. I resolved to finish with the doctors in Cleveland and claw back Deacon Joe's overtures towards the diocese. I didn't want my daughter to be the subject of any more scrutiny, religious or medical. I wanted what any good mother would want: for Annemarie and the baby to have a chance at a normal life.

The world of science I reckoned I could handle, but asking Deacon Joe to unravel what he'd initiated with the Church proved more thorny. I'd felt uneasy about it from the start, but Deacon Joe had argued that it was our Christian duty to pursue the truth, and even Ada had said that it would be fraudulent not to inform the diocese if we genuinely suspected a religious miracle. 'Honestly?' she'd said to me at the time. 'What possible harm could come of it? The Church always looks after its own.' But having witnessed the frenzied response to the apparitions, together with the candlelight vigil on our own front lawn, I knew there was a point beyond which the Church no longer had control over its flock. In Jericho we'd reached that point with alarming speed. In little more than a week the sunsets had attracted more than a thousand pilgrims, but the diocese still hadn't sent an official delegation to witness them. Its ponderous approach to dealing with anything out of the ordinary was worryingly slow, and I didn't want Annemarie to fall victim to the process.

So the evening after I'd spoken to the curate, I waited until Annemarie had gone to bed before broaching my concerns with Ada and Joe. I told them that I'd had a change of heart and was no longer prepared to put her through a religious monkey trial. The baby's provenance shouldn't be our first concern, I argued. We should be far more concerned with its welfare. Deacon Joe had been pouring himself a cup of coffee, and he turned around and looked at me with eyes that could have burned the rubber off a tyre.

Ada frowned and quickly stretched a pacifying hand across the table. 'No one's saying that the baby's welfare isn't important, Eva. Of course it is! But this baby deserves to know who its father is, divine or otherwise, don't you think?'

I stared back at her and felt the stirrings of a grudge. I knew Ada meant well, but her words unwittingly gave offence. 'Annemarie never knew her father and as far as I can see that hasn't done her any great harm,' I said coolly. Ada quickly withdrew her hand and shot a glance of alarm at Deacon Joe, who cleared his throat and placed his coffee cup down on the table with a decisive thud.

'The point is: the wheels are already in motion, and it

would be unwise to try to stop them now,' he said.

'Unwise or undesirable?' I asked.

'Both,' he said staunchly, jutting out his lower jaw. 'We appreciate your concern, but if Annemarie's pregnancy turns out to be a genuine miracle then it goes far beyond the scope of our cosy little household here. Even you must see that!'

'And what about clearing her name?' said Ada to me. 'Isn't that still important to you?'

'I'm not so sure,' I said slowly. 'The new curate says that God isn't overly concerned with chastity these days. Maybe we shouldn't be either.'

'The new curate is so wet behind the ears he wouldn't know chastity from charity!' said Deacon Joe angrily. 'That is, if you could *see* his ears! The man has so much hair he looks like Jesus!'

'Joe, his hair is not that long,' said Ada in a pacifying tone. 'And I'm sure he means well. His approach is just different, that's all.'

'We don't want different! We want a priest who looks and sounds like what we're used to! I've already had words with the diocese to say that his appointment here shouldn't be made permanent. Send him out to some hippy parish in Oregon where they grow their own grapes and dip their own candles!'

'Well, I don't agree. I think he's a breath of fresh air,' said Ada. 'And his sermon on Sunday was downright thought-provoking.' I looked at her and thought, *That figures.* No doubt Deacon Joe had already got wind that Ada's interest in the new curate went beyond the spiritual. His rantings smacked of jealousy, through and through.

'The man is deliberately aiming to be provocative! He's trying to stir things up that shouldn't be stirred. And now he's turned Eva's head with all this pregnancy business,' said Deacon Joe.

'He has *not* turned my head,' I said. 'I simply think we should untangle Annemarie and her pregnancy from the apparitions and start planning for the baby's future. Without the help or hindrance of the Church.'

'Annemarie and I are due to meet the Vicar General the day after tomorrow. If we pull out now it'll make me look like a horse's ass,' said Deacon Joe.

'I'm sorry, but that's not my biggest concern,' I replied.

Deacon Joe narrowed his eyes at me, and chewed the inside of his lip. I could see him wondering what he could say that would change my mind.

'Why don't we put it to Annemarie?' he said finally. 'She's old enough to decide for herself.'

'Annemarie is still a child,' I said. 'She isn't ready to take on the Catholic Church, much less the Christian world. And may I remind you that she's blind? Not to mention pregnant! I think that's quite enough for any seventeen-year-old to contend with.'

'I'm not afraid,' said a cautious voice from the doorway. We turned to see Annemarie standing there in her pyjamas, her hair pulled back in a ponytail. For an instant we all froze.

'Afraid of what, honey?' asked Ada tentatively.

'Of the diocese and their investigation. They can interview me if they like.'

'See?' said Deacon Joe, turning to me with a smug glint in his eye. 'She's tougher than you think she is.'

'I'll be fine, Mama,' Annemarie said to me.

'Annemarie, you have no idea what could come of all this,' I said. 'None of us do. It could be the start of something terrible.'

'It's just a meeting,' she said. 'It doesn't have to go any further.'

Deacon Joe broke into a wide grin. 'That's my girl,' he said.

Annemarie

So a few days later, and against Mama's wishes, Deacon Joe took me to Youngstown for an interview with the Vicar General of the Diocese. I'd never heard of a Vicar General, but Deacon Joe said he was like the Bishop's second-in-command. 'Sounds kind of military,' I remarked on the drive over.

'He's just a priest, Annemarie.'

'And a general.'

'That's just a fancy phrase for right-hand man. No one gets to the Bishop without going through the VG first.'

'Does that mean I'm gonna have to meet the Bishop?' I asked with alarm.

'Not today,' said Deacon Joe. I felt the car lurch on to the freeway and my stomach did a little flip. When we arrived I took Deacon Joe's arm and he led me inside. He's about two feet taller than me, and when I gripped his forearm it was like clinging on to a massive wooden banister. As we entered the building I felt like I was climbing the stairway to the Final Judgment.

'What is this place?' I asked.

'Diocese offices.'

'I thought we'd be meeting in a church.'

'Priests don't *live* in churches, Annemarie.'

Once inside he led me down a long corridor to a small, stuffy room that smelled of bad air conditioning. We sat in uncomfortable metal chairs and I could hear the clackety-clack of a lone typewriter in the room next door. Every now and then, the secretary would stop typing and sigh so loud I thought God would hear. Maybe that's what she wanted.

'What colour's this room?' I asked.

'Green.'

'Lime green or forest green or olive green or what?'

'More of a slime green.'

'Figures.'

'Appearances deceive the thoughtless, Annemarie.'

'Well, they can't exactly deceive me. Being blind and all.'

Deacon Joe sucked in air through his nose but said nothing. Just then a buzzer rang next door and I heard the typewriter stop, followed by the creak of a chair and the clatter of high heels across the floor. 'The Vicar General is ready for you now,' the woman said, her voice as sure and steady as a telephone operator's.

'Thank you,' said Deacon Joe, rising to his feet.

'I'll take her in,' she said, in a way that cut him short. 'Here, honey, grab hold of my arm.'

'I think it's best if I come too,' said Deacon Joe.

'That won't be necessary. The Vicar General specifically asked to see her alone.'

For a moment there was a yawning silence. Then Deacon Joe sat down heavily in the metal chair. 'I guess I'll wait here then,' he said.

'That'll be just fine.'

The first thing I noticed about the Vicar General was that he had post-nasal drip. I could hear him clear his throat even before I got inside the room, and he proceeded to do so every ten or fifteen seconds in an almost continuous drum roll that must have been exhausting. Cora Lynn once told me that the average person produces half a gallon of mucus every day, but I swear the VG must have swallowed that much in the first few minutes. I reckoned from his voice that he was in his early fifties and that he made up in width what he lacked in height. His aura, I decided, was wary. Not so much a general's, I thought – more that of a sentry. He explained that he'd been appointed by the Bishop to investigate my case after Deacon Joe had brought it to the attention of the diocese.

'Let me be perfectly clear,' he said. 'The Church receives dozens of requests for validation each year. Normally we wouldn't have considered this one. But your uncle's status within the parish, together with the fact that you live in Jericho, has worked in your favour.'

'Because of Mary?' I asked. He cleared his throat officiously.

'Because of the apparitions, yes. Which have now been authenticated by the Church as genuine.' He sounded grudging.

'Yeah, I heard that,' I said. The news had come earlier in the week via Deacon Joe. The Church had basically acknowledged what we knew already: that the sunsets were supernatural, and worthy of our attention.

'What we're here to establish is whether your ...' He hesitated for a long moment then, as if he couldn't bring himself to say the word out loud. 'Whether your *condition* is somehow linked to the apparitions.'

'Have you seen them?'

'Pardon me?'

'The sunsets. In Jericho?'

Once again, he treated me to a prolonged clearing of his throat. 'No, I have not.'

'But are you planning to?'

'Not at this time.'

'Really? Aren't you curious?'

'The apparitions may have been declared worthy of belief. But belief is not a requirement of the Church.'

'So you don't believe in them.'

The next throat clearing was coupled with an exasperated sigh. 'I didn't say that. Marian apparitions exist to draw attention to the message of the Lord. They are evidence of the Virgin Mother's continuing active presence in the life of the Church. I do not need such evidence. Consequently, my decision not to witness the event.'

'Or maybe you're just afraid,' I said. Actually I didn't mean to say it out loud; it just kind of popped out. I could smell the fear rolling off him in waves by this time. It was dense and inky, and had appeared the moment he began to speak of her.

'Excuse me?' he said.

'Maybe you're frightened that they'll test your faith somehow. Or undermine it.'

There was a long silence, and then a new smell came across the desk: of fear mixed with the faintly acrid taint of anger. 'Fear does not enter into it, I can assure you,' he said. 'I simply have no need.'

'But we all need miracles, don't we?'

'That is where you're wrong. I have no need of miracles to shore up my belief. Belief itself is one of God's miracles, perhaps the greatest of them all.'

'What about the resurrection of Christ?' I said.

'What about it?'

'Well, that's meant to be the greatest miracle. According to the Bible.'

'Yes, of course,' he said dismissively.

'But you said it was belief.'

'They are virtually one and the same.' He cleared his throat with even greater authority at this point, as if to put me in my place once and for all. 'Forgive me, but I think we should continue with the case in hand. Your case.'

'OK.'

'The Church follows a rigorous process of investigation. We use our own medical and theological experts to examine the facts, and always appoint a 'devil's advocate' to put forward the opposing view.'

'Is that you?'

He paused and cleared his throat. 'I'm afraid the process is secret.'

'Oh.'

'With your uncle's permission, we've requested your medical report from the hospital.'

'Don't I have to give you that? My permission?'

'Not when you're a minor. In cases such as these, we always seek to substantiate all the medical and scientific evidence at the earliest opportunity.'

'So you've had others?'

'Other what?'

'You said cases like these. Have there been other unexplained pregnancies like mine?' For the briefest instant I saw myself entering the Home for Unwed Mothers of Messiahs.

'Um ... no,' he said.

Of course not, I thought with disappointment. The Home for Unwed Mothers vanished, just as quickly as it had appeared.

'We employ a variety of criteria in our evaluation of the facts. We scrutinize the degree of moral certainty, we do a character assessment, and we examine carefully the content of any revelations. I understand from your uncle that there may have been revelations, apart from the apparitions?'

'Ethan spoke to her, if that's what you mean.'

'And Ethan is?'

'A friend. Well, he's my boyfriend. Sort of.'

'The Virgin Mary appears to your boyfriend in bodily form?'

'Yeah. At least, he's pretty sure it's her. She's dressed in like ... biblical clothes.'

'And he communicates with her?'

'Well, I don't think he says much. Mostly she speaks to him.'

'What does she say?'

'At first she talked about me. And the baby. But lately she just prays.'

'And what did she say about you?'

'She said that I was blessed. And that the baby was a gift from God.'

For the first time he was completely silent. There was a long pause during which I could hear only the ticking of the clock. Then he sat back in his chair and swallowed. 'Young lady, you do understand that this is a very serious allegation.'

'You make it sound like a crime. Or at the very least a sin.'

'If you're misrepresenting the truth, then it would be.'

'But I'm not.'

He paused again and I felt the weight of his gaze upon me, even if I could not return it. His chair creaked as he leaned right back. 'Deacon Joe has assured me that you are a very devout and faithful member of the congregation,' he said slowly. 'And remarkably well versed in the Holy Scripture.

For someone so young.'

'I guess so.' I shrugged.

'Thy tongue deviseth mischief like a sharp razor.'

'Excuse me?'

'Psalms 52.'

'Yes, I know.'

'He that speaketh lies shall perish.'

'Proverbs,' I replied. 'Somewhere around twenty.'

He cleared his throat. *'Let the lying lips be put to silence,'* he said then.

'This is getting a little repetitive. Don't you want to test me on any other bits? The New Testament maybe?'

'That won't be necessary,' he said briskly, leaning forward in his chair. 'I understand that your religious education has been very thorough. But there's such a thing as a false prophet. One who performs miracles in order to deceive.'

'But I didn't perform a miracle. A miracle happened to me.'

'Perhaps. And perhaps not. That is what I'm here to ascertain. For now, it would be helpful if I could meet your boyfriend.'

Now it was my turn to swallow. I didn't know what Ethan would make of all this. Or whether he'd be willing. 'I'll have to ask him,' I replied.

'I can't give them any proof, Annemarie,' Ethan said later that afternoon. Clearly, he wasn't thrilled at the prospect of being court-martialled by the Major-General. We were sitting on the grass outside his tent. Just then a car drove by and I heard it slow down, and then a male voice shouted out my name. I felt Ethan bristle, and laid a hand on his arm. Ever since the news report I'd been the target of a lot of attention, which I did my best to ignore, though it drove Ethan crazy. After a moment, the car sped away. 'Anyway, there doesn't seem much point,' he added.

'Well, they could ask you questions.'

'About what? The fact that I've never been confirmed, much less gone through First Communion? I'm not exactly a poster boy for Catholicism.'

'You can show them that you're a good Christian at least. That you're honest and kind and caring and helpful.'

'I don't think those things are top of their list.'

'Then they ought to be,' I said grumpily.

'Look, if you want, I'll go talk to them. But I doubt if it will get us anywhere.'

I knew he was right. Especially since I didn't know where I wanted us to be.

The next day Ethan and I drove over to Youngstown on our own. I persuaded Deacon Joe not to come along. He was still fuming over being snubbed by the Major-General on our first visit, so huffily agreed that his presence would be superfluous. When we were finally seated in front of the Major-General, Ethan surprised me by reaching over and slipping his hand into mine. I felt my face flush. 'So you're Ethan,' said the Major-General.

'Yes, sir.'

'Thank you for coming in. It seems you've been at the centre of the media storm over in Jericho.'

'Not by choice.'

'Perhaps not. That's partly what we're here to establish. And you and Annemarie have been going out for how long, exactly?'

Ethan hesitated. I gave his hand a squeeze. 'About a year,' I said.

'I see. And during that time, the two of you have not been tempted to … forgo abstinence?'

'I wouldn't say *that*,' said Ethan slowly. There was a brief pause while the question hung in the air.

'I think what Ethan means is that we've been tempted,' I explained.

'But you've not succumbed?' said the Major-General.

'Yes,' I answered, but at the exact same moment, Ethan said, 'No.'

'Well, which is it?' said the Major-General, a hint of exasperation creeping into his voice.

'We've been chaste,' I said hurriedly.

'Fine,' he said, clearing his throat. 'The doctors appear to agree with you on that point. Nevertheless you are pregnant, so we need to establish how that came about.'

'The doctors have a theory.'

'Yes, I've heard all about it,' he said a little impatiently. 'What I want to hear about today are Ethan's visions.'

For the next hour he grilled Ethan about the Virgin Mary: what she looked like, how she was dressed, what gestures she used, whether she wept or spoke with an accent, whether she remained standing while she prayed, and pretty much anything else he could think of, including whether or not she smelled. 'Smelled like what?' asked Ethan, puzzled.

'Like anything.'

'I don't remember. I wasn't exactly paying attention to her smell.'

'In previous Marian apparitions, there have been instances of the Virgin Mother exhibiting a strong scent of roses,' explained the Major-General. 'And sometimes gardenias,' he added.

'Oh,' said Ethan. 'I don't really know about gardenias. But I don't remember any rose smell. Or any other smell for that matter. But it was hot out, and I was kind of preoccupied. So maybe I just didn't notice.'

'Perhaps you were under the influence of something other than the Holy Spirit,' the Major-General said slowly.

'What do you mean?'

'Ethan's not into drugs, if that's what you're suggesting,' I interjected.

'It wouldn't be the first instance where the effects of a mind-altering substance had been misinterpreted as a religious experience.'

'Well, that's not the case with Ethan,' I said crossly. 'Look, could I just point out to you that we're not asking for your blessing.'

'Pardon me?'

'It doesn't matter to us whether the Church validates Ethan's visions or not.'

'Then why are you here?'

'Because you asked us to come.'

'It was your uncle who requested that we undertake this investigation. In order to ascertain whether your condition was worthy of veneration by the faithful.'

'But I don't want veneration. Yours or anyone else's.'

'Perhaps Mary didn't either,' he replied evenly. 'But she didn't have a choice.'

I had the sudden feeling that maybe Mama had been right, after all.

Ethan

The Sunday after Francis and Jessup complained, Deacon Joe called our bluff and ordered us to turn up ninety minutes early for Mass. This, he said, would give us ample time to iron out any wrinkles in our performance. 'Of which there are bound to be many,' he added. When I got to the church, Francis, Jessup and Deacon Joe were already there, as was Father O'Shea, who was busy preparing himself in the Sacristy. Deacon Joe handed me a clear plastic garment bag labelled 'X-Large'. 'These,' he said pointedly, 'are the biggest we've got. So make do.' The others were already dressed, and poor Francis looked like something out of another century, so swamped was he by his cassock. The hem dragged several inches behind him and the sleeves fell past his hands in a puffy billow.

I pulled on the clothes: a long black gown that buttoned down the front and came to my knees, and a shorter white tunic with bell sleeves that went on top. Until the moment I put them on, I hadn't realised how girly the stuff was – all pleats and puffs and billowing skirts. It struck me as ironic that the Church only allowed boys to be altar servers, but then emasculated them with the uniform.

McCallister arrived just as I finished dressing. He sauntered up the aisle with a smarmy look on his face and when he got to me he raised his fingers in an L sign, looking me up and down. 'Loser,' he said in a low voice as he went by.

'Fuck off,' I replied under my breath.

'You're late,' Deacon Joe called out from across the room. He handed McCallister his own bag of clothes, and I watched as McCallister shrugged them on, somehow managing to make them look cool. It occurred to me that he was going to be one of those kids who waltzed through adolescence effortlessly, and I hated him all the more for it. Deacon Joe disappeared inside the Sacristy and McCallister strutted up and down the central aisle, swinging his cassock and swaying his hips like a stripper, causing Jessup to snigger.

'McCallister!' Deacon Joe suddenly barked from behind the altar. 'Do that one more time and I'll castrate you with it! Is that clear?'

McCallister nodded, but the corners of his mouth twitched with suppressed laughter. Deacon Joe gave each of us something to carry and arranged us in a line formation at the back of the church, with Francis at the front (candles), followed by McCallister (incense), Jessup (bells) and finally me (a large and somewhat unwieldy cross). I'd come to understand that altar service was all about the props – carrying stuff around the place so the priest didn't have to. 'Right,' ordered Deacon Joe, when we were all in position like a chain gang. 'Now walk.'

We set off but before we'd taken three steps he shouted, 'Halt!' For the next half hour we practised that procession a hundred times. We were too fast, too slow, too bunched up, too far apart, too slouched, too bouncy. I nearly lost the will to live, but finally Father O'Shea, who was watching from the altar, pronounced us fit to enter the church. After that we rehearsed our various roles for the Mass. Deacon Joe had appointed me team captain (a move which so dashed the hopes of Francis that I thought he might burst into tears when it was announced) and as such I was to hold the missal for Father O'Shea, and oversee the lighting of the incense, which McCallister was meant to carry in a vessel that hung from a long chain. After Holy Communion, Francis was to pour water into a glass chalice for Father O'Shea to rinse his fingers in. Jessup was in charge of ringing the bells after the Sanctus, whereupon we were all told to fall to our knees *as one*. After the service was finished, it was my responsibility to hang up the priest's vestments in the Sacristy. So the only silver lining to the whole affair was that I would finally get a look inside.

Eventually we finished rehearsing and the congregation started to drift in. I watched for Annemarie and spotted her coming up the aisle. When she got to the front I saw Ada whisper something in her ear. Annemarie looked in my direction and flashed a big smile, and even though she couldn't see my outfit, I still felt my face go red. The service began and we made our entrance from the back of the church without tripping. The first bit went off more or less according to plan, but just before the liturgy, McCallister quietly slipped extra incense into the burner when I wasn't looking. After a few minutes it began to smoke so much that people in the front row started to cough and wipe their eyes, causing Deacon Joe to glower at us from his place behind the altar. McCallister and Jessup could hardly keep a straight face for the rest of the Mass, while Francis went about his duties with an earnest intensity that made me want to puke. I spent most of the time dreaming up reasons for my resignation, which I intended to give at the earliest opportunity, once I could safely say I'd done the job. The list I came up with included: too much homework, band practice on Sunday mornings, an insurmountable tremor, and an undersized bladder. None of which I thought would stand up to Deacon Joe's scrutiny.

After Mass, there were various tasks we'd been assigned. Francis was meant to extinguish all the candles behind the altar using a long metal rod, but as he stretched out the cup towards the last candle, McCallister walked past and gave him a shove from behind. Francis tumbled forwards, upsetting the candle, which sent a spray of hot wax down the front of his cassock. McCallister burst out laughing and danced away, leaving Francis on the verge of tears, staring down at his dirty cassock. I walked over to him. 'Hey. Come on back to the Sacristy and I'll help you clean it off,' I said.

Francis followed me obediently into the Sacristy. Once inside I glanced around and was immediately disappointed. Behind the red velvet curtain was an ordinary room, about seven feet by nine feet, containing a large wooden wardrobe along one wall and a rail for clothing on the other. The room had a louvred window high up on the wall to the right, and at the far end stood a carved wooden statue of the Virgin Mary in a specially formed alcove. Beneath it was a small padded bench for kneeling in prayer. I helped Francis take off his cassock and together we picked at the wax until it was mostly gone, leaving only faint grease stains behind. Father O'Shea entered then, startling us. 'Is everything all right in here?' he asked, frowning.

'We were just hanging up our vestments,' I said quickly. I turned to go, then remembered I was meant to assist him with his own. 'Shall I stay and help you?' I asked.

Father O'Shea looked from me to Francis, who was hovering hopefully behind me. 'Francis can help me, if he wishes,' he said.

Annemarie and I walked home together and once we were alone she turned to me with a teasing smile. 'So,' she said.

'How was it? Have you found your calling?'

I shrugged. 'It's not that bad.'

'Is Deacon Joe a tyrant?'

'Yes.'

'And the other boys?'

'Evil. At least one of them is. The other two are all right.'

'And Father O'Shea? What's he like?'

'He's OK.'

'So you're going to carry on?' There was more than a hint of incredulity in her voice. Suddenly, I felt a surge of pride that I'd defied her expectations.

'Sure,' I said matter-of-factly. 'Why wouldn't I?'

'Beats me.' She shook her head and laughed.

The following Sunday, Deacon Joe scheduled us to serve Mass again and the service went off without incident. Afterwards, when the church had emptied out, Jessup and McCallister raced through their chores and left quickly, but Francis moved slowly around the periphery of the altar extinguishing the candles one by one, his expression taut with concentration. I finished my own duties and went to hang up my vestments in the Sacristy, but Father O'Shea was just emerging. He pulled the door firmly closed, struggling with the lock for a second, then turned and nearly bumped right into me. His startled eyes swept across me, and for an instant he just stared at me, his face ashen. 'I wanted to hang up my vestments,' I said a little awkwardly.

He seemed to come to his senses then, and shook his head. 'Hang them in the closet,' he said hoarsely. I started to turn away, but then he stopped me. 'And Ethan? From now on, you're not to enter the Sacristy. Any of you,' he said. 'Is that clear?' I nodded. 'Where's Francis?' he asked suddenly, scanning the church.

'I don't think he's finished yet. I can help him if you like.'

Father O'Shea shook his head emphatically. 'That won't be necessary,' he said brusquely, making a flicking motion with his hand, as if I was a wasp. I walked back to the closet. Father O'Shea was normally icily composed and I couldn't help but wonder what had rattled him, but I was happy to be free. Once outside I spotted Annemarie and made my way through the dwindling crowd.

'So are you an expert now?' she asked teasingly when I joined her.

'I'm working on it.'

'Surely you must be better at it than the others?'

'I'm pretty good at lighting candles, if that's what you mean.'

'What does Father O'Shea think of you?'

'Father O'Shea doesn't seem particularly interested in any of us. We're sort of like his servants.'

'You don't make it sound very glamorous,' she said with a pout. 'I always thought it was the religious equivalent of being a cheerleader.'

'Not exactly,' I said. Being a cheerleader was way more glamorous than being an altar boy, but I wasn't about to tell her that. We were nearly home when I remembered I'd left my knapsack in the church. I said goodbye to Annemarie and jogged back, slipping inside. As I passed from the vestibule into the nave, I caught a glimpse of Father O'Shea and Francis entering the Sacristy. As they disappeared, Father O'Shea reached a bony arm behind him and pulled the heavy wooden door closed with a thud.

For the next few Sundays I carried on with altar service, and Father O'Shea turned up each week pallid and hollow-eyed. His voice had taken on a brittle edge, and I noticed that his hands shook a little when he lifted the chalice. Even his sermons seemed edgy, their tone laced with anger and righteousness. Each week he kept Francis on afterwards, dismissing the rest of us as soon as our chores were done. It wasn't clear whether it was a privilege or a punishment, but there didn't seem to be any reason why Francis should be singled out for either, so I have to admit it struck me as odd. One evening I mentioned this to Annemarie. 'So he keeps Francis on late ... so what?' she asked with a half-smile.

'It just seems weird. Especially when the rest of us aren't allowed in the Sacristy.'

'Sure you aren't just jealous?' she asked in a teasing voice. Annemarie was right. What did I care, anyway? I'd never wanted to be an altar boy in the first place. On the way home I decided that the sooner I engineered my way out of altar service, the better.

But not before I'd worked out what was going on in the Sacristy. The next Sunday I deliberately hung around after the service, waiting for the crowds to disperse. It was Palm Sunday and people stayed longer than usual, admiring a display of posters made by school kids which was hanging just outside the vestibule, but when everyone had gone I slipped back into the church and made my way back towards the Sacristy. I walked up to the broad oak door and very gently turned the tarnished brass handle, but it wouldn't budge. The door was locked, though I was pretty sure someone was inside. I pressed my ear up to the wood and could just make out the murmur of voices, and sounds of someone moving about the room. I heard the scrape of something heavy being dragged across the floor, then I heard Francis ask a question, and Father O'Shea bark a terse response. I took a deep breath and knocked on the door, quietly at first, then a bit harder. For a moment there was no response. Then I heard footsteps and the sound of the key turning in the lock, before Father O'Shea opened the door a few inches. He peered at me wild-eyed through the gap, his face darkening when he saw who it was. 'Ethan! What is it?' he demanded.

'I dropped my wallet. I thought someone might have turned it in,' I lied.

'Well, they haven't,' he snapped. I hesitated, straining to see past him, but Francis must have been off to the left, hidden out of view. 'If you don't mind, I'm busy,' Father O'Shea said pointedly.

'Sorry,' I mumbled. But he had already shut the door. I heard the key turn again in the lock. I stood there for another moment, then headed home.

I knew Annemarie would just shrug off my suspicions, so that night after dinner I went round to Moose's house. His mom let me in and told me Moose was up in his room doing homework. I found him lying in bed with earphones on, eating his way through a giant box of Cheerios and listening to *The Dark Side of The Moon*. He turned off the stereo and sat up, holding the box out to me, while I related the story of the locked Sacristy door. Moose listened closely, chewing on Cheerios, until I'd finished. 'Dude, I thought you didn't want my advice about church stuff any more,' he said cautiously.

'Yeah, well, I lied.'

'So what are you thinking?'

'I don't know. But something isn't right.'

'I say we have a little talk with Francis.'

The next day we skipped final period and waited in Moose's car outside the elementary school. At five minutes past three we heard the bell ring and watched as a stampede of kids came streaming out on to the playground. There was a gaggle of mothers waiting around to scoop up the younger ones, and the older children headed off down the road in smaller groups of two or three. Among these were a few loners, and somehow I knew Francis would be one of them. He came out a few minutes later, shouldering his backpack, and spoke to no one as he trudged away from the school. We waited until he got to the next block, then Moose slowly pulled up alongside him and I rolled down my window. 'Hey, Francis,' I called over to him. 'You want a ride?'

He froze like a startled rabbit. He blinked a few times, then shook his head. 'I'm OK,' he said. I turned to Moose who rolled his eyes then stopped the car. I jumped out and quickly opened the back door.

'Come on,' I said a little more forcefully. Francis looked from me to Moose, then slowly crossed over and got in the car. I shut the door behind him, then climbed in the front seat, and we pulled back on to the road. 'Good day at school?' I asked innocently.

Francis gave a curt nod. 'It was OK,' he mumbled. 'How do you know where I live?' he asked suspiciously.

'We don't,' I said. 'But you can show us.'

He nodded, his eyes focused straight ahead. 'It's the next left,' he said.

'Okey-dokey,' said Moose cheerfully, and I shot him a glance.

'It's here,' said Francis a few blocks later. We pulled over in front of a modest ranch-style house with a small garage attached. Inside I could see an array of bicycles and hula hoops. As Francis reached for his backpack, I turned around and locked his door. He looked up at me with alarm.

'We need to ask you something,' I said. His eyes clouded over and he pulled his backpack closer to his chest. 'How come Father O'Shea keeps you late each week?' I watched as the colour seeped from his face. Francis gave a brief shake of his head.

'I can't tell you,' he said. 'He made me promise.' His eyes slid uneasily from me to Moose.

'Look, Francis,' I said. 'If something's wrong, maybe we can help. But not if you don't tell us what's going on.' He swallowed, and seemed to be weighing up his options.

'You wouldn't believe me even if I *did* tell you,' he said finally, but there was the barest hint of challenge in his tone.

'Try us,' said Moose. Francis threw me a pleading look, and I swear it was like he wanted us to drag it out of him.

'Come on, Francis,' I said. 'Maybe we can help.'

'You can't! No one can,' he said earnestly. 'No one can stop it. Not even Father O'Shea. He's tried!'

'Stop what?' I asked. Francis hesitated.

'Stop her crying.' His voice wavered unsteadily.

'Stop who crying?'

'The Virgin Mary. She weeps bloody tears. Real ones.'

'What the hell?' Moose said dubiously. He threw me a bemused look.

'You mean the statue?' I asked. 'The one in the Sacristy?'

Francis nodded, his eyes wide.

Moose burst out laughing. 'Oh, man! Who said church was boring?!'

I scowled at him and turned back to Francis. 'Look, just tell us everything. From the beginning.'

Francis took a deep breath. Now that he'd spilled the beans, he seemed calmer and almost eager to shed the burden of secrecy. 'It started that first week we served Mass,' he said. 'After you'd gone, Father O'Shea and I did some more chores in the church and when we went back to the Sacristy to put away his vestments, we found blood running down her cheeks. It was still wet. Father O'Shea thought it was some sort of joke, and he was pretty angry, but I helped him wipe it off and he told me not to say anything. But then the next week he locked the Sacristy up during the service, and it happened again. And it's been happening ever since.'

'Every week?' I asked. 'During Mass?'

He nodded. 'That's how we know it's real. 'Cause no matter what we do, she always cries.'

'Plaster that bleeds,' said Moose, raising a sceptical eyebrow. 'That's right up there with water into wine.'

'The statue's wood,' said Francis, defensively. 'Holy wood,' he added.

'Look, Francis,' I asked. 'If you think the blood is real, then why keep it a secret?'

He shook his head. 'Father O'Shea says that if we tell everyone it'll turn the parish into a circus. He doesn't want a lot of people poking their noses into church business.'

'Why not?' asked Moose.

'He says that people might panic,' said Francis. 'And that the church has a bad track record with hysteria.'

Moose snorted.

'So he hasn't told anyone else?' I asked. Francis shook his head.

'He says that if we ignore it, it'll stop.'

'Ignore *her*,' corrected Moose. 'How devout of him,' he added drily.

'But if it's really a miracle, isn't he supposed to tell someone? The Bishop or something?'

'Father O'Shea says not all miracles can be fathomed.'

'So what do you do when the statue bleeds?'

'We photograph it, then scrub it clean with a brush and some bleach.'

'No wonder she weeps,' said Moose under his breath.

'You take pictures?' I asked. Francis nodded.

'Father O'Shea says it's good to have a record. He says we might need to prove it really happened some day.'

'Either that or he sells them,' offered Moose.

Francis shook his head. 'No. He keeps them locked in the rectory.'

Moose turned to me and raised his massive eyebrows. I could already tell what he was thinking and I started to shake my head.

'Dude!' he said. 'We totally have to get our hands on those photos!'

'They're locked in the rectory. Which part of *locked* do you not understand?'

'So we break in,' he said.

'You can't do that!' said Francis. 'What if you get caught? He'll find out that I told you!'

Moose turned to him. 'We won't get caught,' he said dismissively.

'How can you be sure?' Francis said. Moose dropped a meaty hand on to his shoulder, and poor Francis flinched like he'd been hot-wired.

'Because it's God's will.'

Eva

Annemarie and Ethan survived their meeting with the Vicar General, but in the days that followed I started to wonder if the Catholic Church would prove to be the least of our troubles. Almost overnight Annemarie had become an instant celebrity, with crowds of people hanging about the neighbourhood hoping to catch a glimpse of her. One morning I opened the living room curtains to find a bearded man with bushy eyebrows standing in the flowerbed just outside, his face right up to the window. I screamed and he pulled back, frowning with dismay, as if it was *me* who was intruding. Then I smacked the glass so hard I thought it would shatter, and he grudgingly moved off. Ada came rushing in from the kitchen when she heard the noise. 'What was that?' she asked with alarm.

'The devil,' I replied, still shaken. Ada watched the man go, then frowned at me.

'I'm sure he was harmless, Eva.'

'Well, he can be harmless somewhere else!'

I kept my eye on the window for the rest of the morning, but apart from a gaggle of elderly women clutching rosaries, who eyed the house from the sidewalk, no one else came near.

Later that afternoon I spotted Ethan's mother wrestling with a huge cardboard box, trying to get it out of the back seat of her station wagon. I walked out onto the front steps. 'Do you need some help?' I called over the hedge. She straightened and smiled, brushing a stray lock of hair out of her eyes.

'Well, it's a little unwieldy,' she admitted. I crossed the lawn and together we hoisted the box out and carried it inside, setting it down on the floor in the front hall.

'Where are teenage sons when you need them?' I asked jokingly.

'Camping with the Virgin Mary,' she replied. Our eyes met and she raised her eyebrows, as if to say *holy moly*. 'Would you like that cup of coffee now?' she asked, straightening.

Her coffee was rich and dark and dense, far better than the feeble machine brew we were used to at home. She made it using a fancy glass contraption I'd never seen before, and I couldn't help but wonder what Deacon Joe would say if I brought one home. 'So Ethan's still living in the tent?' I asked, once we were seated at her kitchen table. She smiled.

'It would seem so,' she said.

'And you don't mind?'

She paused, measuring her words. 'Ethan seems to be looking for something these days. Whether he'll find it out by the wayside shrine, I've no idea. But given the circumstances, we've decided that it's best to leave him to it.'

'Has he told you about his visions?'

She looked at me askance. 'Who around here *hasn't* had visions?' she asked.

I held my tongue. If Ethan hadn't told her that he'd spoken to the Virgin Mary, it wasn't my place to do so.

'Anyway, it's not as if he's doing psychedelic drugs out there,' she laughed.

'True,' I admitted. Though that might be preferable, I thought. 'Apparently he led some prayers for the crowd the other day,' I said.

'Well,' she said, pausing to consider this, 'I certainly don't have a problem with prayer. Prayer can be a good thing.'

Her words surprised me. 'Can I ask: do you and your husband belong to any church?' I said tentatively.

She hesitated. 'I think the best way to describe our religious affiliation would be non-committal,' she said.

Ah, I thought. *One of those*. Agnostics were rare birds here in Jericho. But there was something refreshing about the fact that she made no apology for her lack of convictions. I wondered what the curate would make of her.

'I've always thought that beliefs aren't something we can just hand down to our children, like some sort of cherished family heirloom,' she said then. 'We should teach them how to think, not what to think, and let them judge for themselves.' She looked up at me and smiled a little tentatively, as if gauging my response to her words. 'Anyway, I'm pleased that Ethan is exploring his faith,' she said, stirring her coffee. 'All young people should. It's part of their moral development.'

Moral development, I thought. Two words that were starting to stretch and bend like saltwater taffy in my mind. Why was it that it had taken me half a lifetime to examine these two words at close range? 'I guess I've always thought that moral development went hand in hand with spiritual development,' I said. 'At least, that's what the Church teaches.'

'Isn't that one of life's great questions?' Ethan's mother asked, raising her eyebrows. 'Can we be good without God?'

'The Bible says we can't.'

She smiled. 'Well, it *would* say that, wouldn't it?'

I laughed, in spite of myself. Something about this woman's presence altered the world around me, as if I was seeing it through wavy glass. She poured us each a little more coffee from the container, and I couldn't help but think of Daryl. After he'd left, I'd spent some time trying to make sense of our failed marriage. At the suggestion of Father O'Shea, I'd turned to the Bible for comfort, only to discover that the book of *Leviticus* described Daryl's affair with Antonio as an abomination punishable by death. This I couldn't reconcile myself to – whatever else I thought of Daryl's choices, I didn't believe he deserved to die. And if I was prepared to ignore some aspects of the Bible's morality, how was I to judge the rest?

'Personally, I don't think we need the Church to tell us right from wrong. We all have a moral compass deep inside,' Ethan's mother said then. 'Don't misunderstand me – it's not that I don't believe in spirituality,' she said quickly. 'It's just that I don't think we need the framework of the Church to lead good lives. Not unless we choose it,' she added quickly, and I suspected for my benefit.

I pondered her words. In her tidy kitchen, surrounded by the aroma of strong coffee, Ethan's mother made heathenism look almost reasonable. Deacon Joe would surely have a hissy fit if he could hear us, I thought. But who's to say she wasn't right? Maybe the only voice we needed to follow was that of our own conscience. Maybe religion was like gravy – not strictly necessary, but it made everything look and taste better. 'What about the sunsets?' I asked her.

She took a deep breath. 'Honestly? The sunsets make me nervous,' she confessed. 'Not because I'm not prepared to believe in God, but because I feel He's disturbed the natural order of things. God wasn't designed to be down here with us on earth. And we don't respond well when He is.' She

motioned towards the general chaos outside. 'So I guess I'd
have to say that I was happier without the Virgin Mary,' she
sighed. 'And frankly? The sooner she goes, the better.'

Amen, I thought.

Annemarie

A few days after Ethan and I met with the Vicar General, Mama got a call from the doctors up in Cleveland. We were in the kitchen fixing supper when the phone rang. I was peeling a colander full of carrots at the table, while Mama tried to thrash the lumps out of some mashed potatoes on the stove. When she picked up the phone I knew in an instant what it was about, because the air around her started to crackle with anger.

Mama listened for a long minute, breathing hard down the phone, before replying in a curt voice. 'I don't believe that will be necessary. With all due respect, doctor, if this baby wants to be born, it will. Regardless of whether or not you are monitoring every second of its development.'

'Mama,' I hissed.

'Let me handle this,' she whispered back. 'Dr Barratt, my daughter is not some sort of laboratory specimen. She is flesh and blood, just like you and me, and she does not take kindly to the notion of being poked and prodded for the advancement of science.'

'Yes, I do!' I pleaded in a loud whisper.

'Hush!' she said to me. 'We appreciate your concern, but

I think we can handle it ourselves from here.'

And with that she put the phone down.

'What did they say?' I asked.

'They want you to come in for more tests.'

'Why?'

'They said something about some results that came back from the lab.'

'What sort of results?'

'I don't know and I don't care,' she sighed.

'Did it occur to you that I might?' I asked.

'We don't need their tests, Annemarie.'

'How do you know? This whole thing isn't over yet. And we might just need those tests before it is!'

She sighed. 'Annemarie, I don't know how or why you came to be pregnant, but the fact is, you are. No amount of science or medicine is gonna change that.'

'The doctors don't want to change it. They just want to understand what's happening. And so do I!'

'Some things are beyond our comprehension,' she said briskly, picking up the whisk again. 'God did not intend for us to understand everything about the universe, Annemarie. That's why he invented the Bermuda Triangle.'

'But we can try,' I said.

'There's such a thing as trying too hard,' she snapped.

I frowned. When Mama used that tone of voice I knew there was no point in arguing. After another minute she stopped what she was doing and turned to me with a sigh.

'Look, Annemarie, everyone out there wants a piece of you right now. And the way I see it, my job is to protect you.'

'Well, maybe we're *both* trying too hard,' I said.

But I hadn't given up on science, even if Mama had. The next morning I went to find Ethan in his tent. 'The Magi want me back for more tests,' I told him.

'Who?'

'The doctors up in Cleveland.'

'Oh.'

'Mama told them no.'

'Maybe she doesn't want to drive up there again,' he offered.

'That's not why. She said no because she's afraid of the truth. She'd rather be ignorant than enlightened.'

'That's pretty harsh, Annemarie.'

'Well, it's true,' I said crossly. 'But I'm not afraid to find out what's wrong with me.'

'There's nothing wrong with you,' he said. 'In fact, you're sort of perfect,' he mumbled.

'I'm *blind*, Ethan.'

'So?'

'So that's not exactly my idea of perfection. Anyway I intend to do the tests, with or without Mama's blessing.' I waited for him to respond and there was a long moment of silence.

'You want me to drive you up there, don't you?'

I smiled. 'Will you?'

He sighed. 'You know I will. But it'll take us all day. What are you gonna tell your mom?'

I frowned. He was right. I hadn't got that far in my head, but we'd have to have a good excuse. I thought about what sort of thing would appeal to her. 'I know! We'll tell her we're going on a pilgrimage.'

'A pilgrimage? To where?'

'Bethlehem.'

Bethlehem, West Virginia was only a few miles over the state line. It had a Marian shrine that was a popular destination for church tour groups, and I had wanted to go there ever since

I was a little girl – admittedly for the wrong reasons. As a child, I'd always imagined a real-life nativity scene: Mary and Joseph and the baby in a stable full of hay, surrounded by braying donkeys and nuzzling lambs with twitching tails. The reality (according to a girl named Lavinia from my Catechism class) was a six-foot-high plaster statue of Mary in a crumbling grotto, at the edge of a sports field beside the local Catholic high school. Which is why Mama never indulged me. When Ethan and I checked the map, we discovered that Bethlehem was about the same distance to the south-east as Cleveland was to the north-west. So far, so good, I thought. But we'd still have to persuade Mama. I decided to let Ethan do the talking; I was already in enough hot water with her without breaking a commandment.

'Why now?' she demanded when we asked her. 'We've already got the Virgin Mother here. So why would you want to go all the way over there?'

'*She* wants us to,' said Ethan. Mama hesitated, her incredulity so thick I could practically inhale it.

'The Virgin Mother wants you to make a pilgrimage to West Virginia?'

'She wants us to pay our respects at the shrine there,' said Ethan.

Mama took a deep breath and let it out through her nostrils. 'Do you even know how to get to Bethlehem?' she asked finally.

'We have a TripTik!' I said.

We set off early the next morning with our TripTik, heading east out of the driveway and waving goodbye to Mama. We had to circle right round the town to pick up the shunpike heading west, and I didn't breathe easy until we'd crossed the county line. 'What time's the appointment?' asked Ethan,

244

once we were out of town.

'I don't have one.'

'But I thought you told them you were coming.'

'Nope.'

'Then how do you know they'll see you?'

'Oh, they'll see me,' I said confidently. I'd never been more certain of anything in my life.

Of course what I hadn't bargained on was how long it would take to round them all up, once we'd arrived. Fortunately Ethan is a way faster driver than Mama so it was just after ten o'clock when we announced ourselves at the OB/GYN department. The receptionist remembered me straight off, though she seemed a little sceptical when I said I was hoping to see all three doctors without an appointment. But after a few minutes of frantic phoning around, she told us to come back at noon. We got iced coffees from the cafeteria and went outside to sit on a bench. The weather had cooled off enough for the sun to be a boon rather than a furnace and I stretched out my legs to get a bit more of it. After a moment, I could feel Ethan's eyes on me. 'What are you looking at?' I asked.

'Shouldn't you be starting to show or something?' he asked.

'I'm only twelve weeks pregnant. Plus I'm a teenager. Teenage girls can give birth without anyone ever even knowing.'

'How can that be humanly possible?'

'Tight tummies. And baggy clothes. It happens all the time in the *National Enquirer*.'

'Since when do you read the *National Enquirer*?'

'Cora Lynn brings it over every time she comes.'

'Christ. I should have known.'

'Anyway, I thought about it,' I added. It took Ethan a few

moments to work out what I meant.

'You thought about concealing your pregnancy?'

I shrugged. 'Well, yeah. At first.'

'From everyone? Including me?'

'I don't know, Ethan. I decided it was a bad idea in the end, OK?'

'Jesus, Annemarie.'

Ethan seemed really offended, though I wasn't sure why. Actually I'd been wondering lately whether I'd made a big mistake going public about the pregnancy in the first place. All of this could have been avoided, I thought wearily. But the idea of giving birth alone in a bathtub still put me off.

By half-past eleven it was officially hot so we went back inside to wait with all the other pregnant mothers. By then the reception area was heaving with big bellies and women breathing heavily through their noses. I could tell Ethan felt pretty uncomfortable surrounded by so much fecundity. 'Look, you don't have to wait with me,' I told him. 'Why don't you go get some food and come back in an hour or so?'

'You don't want me to come in with you?' he asked tentatively. I knew for a fact that he'd rather be drawn and quartered.

'No, I want to see them on my own.'

'OK.' He sounded incredibly relieved, not to mention grateful. 'I promise I'll be back before one.' Ethan gave my shoulder a quick squeeze and I heard him practically skip out of the room. After he'd gone, the woman next to me placed her hand lightly on my arm and spoke in my ear.

'You did the right thing, honey,' she said in a low voice. 'That boyfriend of yours was looking positively green.'

'Hospitals creep him out,' I replied.

'Men can be such babies!'

'Yeah,' I agreed.

'But I can tell you're gonna be just fine. I had my first at your age. And everybody said I was ruined. But it all turned out good in the end. Now here I am on my ninth.' She sighed and I heard her pat her stomach, which from the sound of it, was enormous.

'Wow,' I said. 'Nine kids. That's pretty amazing.'

'Well, they're not all by the same father, of course,' she said, lowering her voice. 'I have kind of a short attention span when it comes to men, you know?' She laughed. 'And I swear to God, number seven was a miracle, 'cause no man laid a hand on me that time. But the doctors didn't believe me. Said the sperm must've been treading water waiting for the right moment. That's my Jesse. If he isn't an angel of God, I don't know what is. He's a little bit slow, Jesse. But I love him all the more for it.'

'I believe you,' I said suddenly. 'About there being no father,' I added. 'I mean, I think it could be possible.' She paused, and I could feel the weight of her gaze as she took in what I was saying.

'Thank you, honey,' she said in an emotional whisper. 'And God bless.'

It was a relief when I finally came face to face with the Magi, because all that abundance in the waiting room was starting to bring me down. We went through an awkward set of bumbling reintroductions before Dr Barratt spoke tentatively. 'We understood from your mother that you wouldn't be coming back.'

'That's because Mama doesn't know I'm here,' I said. There was a long pause and an anxious shifting about, while I felt them exchange glances.

'Ah,' said Dr Barratt. 'That presents us with something of a dilemma.'

'At seventeen, I'm entitled to seek medical advice without parental permission, isn't that right?'

'Yes,' said Dr Barratt slowly. 'But it's not our preference. If this was a straightforward case of teenage pregnancy ...'

'Which it isn't,' said Dr Marshall.

'Then we might be happy to proceed without your mother's knowledge,' continued Dr Barratt. 'But there are decisions to be made. Possibly difficult decisions. And we feel that you might need ...' He paused.

'A little help,' offered Dr Marshall.

'Or at the very least, some advice,' said Dr Hermann.

'Or maybe even just reassurance,' said Dr Barratt. For a moment I briefly considered, then rejected, the notion of bringing Mama back into the picture.

'What sort of difficult decisions?' I asked.

They'd found something they didn't like. In all the millions of chromosomes they'd analysed, it seemed there were a few wayward ones that didn't look right. And I could tell it troubled them, the way a hairline crack in a slab of marble might trouble a stonemason, or a very slight rasp in a gear might trouble a car mechanic. The long and short of it was they couldn't guarantee the outcome, and they were worried. After listening to their arguments, I agreed to let them do some additional blood tests and a more invasive procedure to draw amniotic fluid from the foetal sac for analysis. We concluded that it would be simplest to gather all the samples right then and there, rather than invent more excuses for Mama, so they ushered me into a treatment room and stuck various needles in me while I supplied them with bodily fluids.

When I finally returned to the waiting room, Ethan was waiting for me nervously. 'You took ages!' he whispered. 'I almost came looking for you!' I had a fleeting image of him fighting his way down the corridor to rescue me from the clutches of mad science.

'I'm fine,' I said with a tired smile. 'But I want to go home.' I didn't tell him much about the appointment on the drive back – only that they wanted to carry on with more tests and with their monitoring of the pregnancy. In fact he didn't press me for details, and I had a strong sense that he didn't want to know. Not because he didn't care, but because the whole thing terrified him. But when I mentioned that the doctors wanted me to return the following week, he panicked. 'We can't go on a pilgrimage every week,' he said. 'Your mom will get suspicious.'

'Don't worry, I'll think of something,' I told him. But in the end I didn't need to, because when we got back home they were all waiting for us. And they were hopping mad.

Ethan

So two days before Easter, Moose and I ended up breaking and entering. Only we didn't have to break into anything, really – we discovered that it was surprisingly easy to commit a felony. We waited until Friday night (*Good Friday*, in fact, the name perversely chosen by the Church to commemorate the death of Jesus) and snuck round to the bushes behind the rectory. Moose had brought along a backpack and as soon as we were situated he pulled out his Walkman, a bag of Oreos, a flashlight, a crowbar, a black balaclava, and a pair of red woollen mittens with kitten faces. When I looked at the mittens he shrugged. 'They're my sister's. I couldn't find anything else.'

'You look like Frosty the Snowman.'

'Fingerprints, dude. We don't want to leave behind incriminating evidence.'

'What's the Walkman for?'

'To juice us up. Thought Aerosmith would do the job.'

'Might be good to hear what's going on, Moose.'

'Good point,' he conceded, stowing the Walkman back in his bag. We settled in to wait while Moose slowly chewed his way through the bag of Oreos. The lights were on when we got there, but just after eleven we saw them go off. We waited another twenty minutes, until our feet were numb, then crept forward to the office, which was at the back of the rectory on the ground floor. It was located in a separate extension and had its own entrance with a narrow hallway. Moose tried the door but it was locked, so we circled round to the back where there was a double sash window. The blinds were drawn so we couldn't see inside, but the room was dark and completely still. Moose took out the crowbar and started to force it beneath one of the sash windows, when I reached over and lifted the other with ease.

'They're not locked, you idiot,' I whispered. I crawled over the sill into the darkened room, pushing aside the venetian blinds. Once inside I listened for a moment, then stuck my head out the window and nodded to him. Moose crawled over the sill and I winced as his legs got tangled in the plastic slats of the blinds, making them clatter.

'Sorry,' he mouthed, standing up. He pulled the flashlight out and shone it around. The room was just as I remembered, with neatly organised bookshelves around the walls, and a wooden desk completely clear of papers. 'Christ, he's a neat freak,' whispered Moose. He wandered over to a filing cabinet and opened the top drawer, shining the flashlight inside. I went over to the desk and began searching the drawers. The papers were arranged in carefully labelled manila folders, and even the pens and pencils were tidily bundled with rubber bands. One by one I went through the drawers but found only legitimate church business. 'I don't see anything,' whispered Moose eventually.

'Me neither.' I closed the last of the drawers and we looked around for a minute. Moose motioned to the door.

'What's on the other side?'

'Just a hallway, I think. One end leads to the house, the other to the outside entrance.' He crept over and quietly opened the door, peering out.

'Come on,' he said, motioning for me to follow.

'We can't go in the house,' I hissed. But Moose had already tiptoed down the hall and was opening the door at the end. I came up behind him and saw him flash his light around a modest sitting room with a sofa and a small round dining table at one end. Through an open doorway we could see the kitchen, and at the opposite end of the room was another corridor that presumably led to the bedroom. Moose tiptoed across to the kitchen and ducked inside, and I reluctantly followed. He went straight to the fridge and opened it, scanning the contents, and I glimpsed a forlorn assortment of condiments. I reached out and shut the fridge, glaring at him, but he was already pointing to a wooden door at the other end of the room.

'Basement?' I mouthed with a shrug. He tiptoed over and opened the door, shining the flashlight down some narrow wooden steps, and before I could stop him he'd disappeared. I waited, but after a minute I heard him hiss loudly.

'Ethan! Get down here!' I crept down the stairs and saw Moose standing in the doorway to a small room, his light flashing eerily around. 'It's a darkroom,' he whispered excitedly over his shoulder. The room was only about four feet by six feet, and along one side was a long, shallow metal sink divided into sections. A series of dark prints hung like dead carrion from a line suspended along the length of the sink. Moose shone his light on one and we saw a close-up of the wooden Virgin Mary: inky drops of fluid trickled from each eye down her wooden cheeks. 'Creepy,' whispered Moose. 'I guess Francis of Assisi wasn't kidding!' One by one he shone the torch on to the black-and-white photos and the bloody wooden statue stared back at us. After a moment Moose reached up and started to unclip the ones closest to us.

'What are you doing?' I hissed.

'Taking some souvenirs,' he said.

'But he'll know!'

'He'll think it's an Act of God.'

Moose stuffed three prints into his backpack and we both turned, just as we saw a light come on in the kitchen up the narrow wooden stairs. Instantly we both froze. Moose turned to me with alarm, and we slipped out of the darkroom, easing the door closed behind us. Just then we heard Father O'Shea open the basement door. In a flash we both ducked under the stairs, crushed against each other. Father O'Shea paused on the top step, then we watched as his slippered feet slowly came down the stairs. When he reached the bottom he went straight into the darkroom, pulling the door closed behind him. After a moment an eerie purple light escaped from a crack at the bottom of the door. Moose turned to me and gave a nod, and in an instant we'd scrambled up the stairs and through the kitchen, back the way we'd come. This time we practically dived through the sash windows, landing in a tangled heap on wet grass.

We didn't stop running until we got home. My mom was in her bathrobe in the kitchen making a cup of tea when we came bursting in through the back door. She turned to us with surprise. 'I thought you were upstairs,' she said suspiciously.

'We went for a run,' I said, out of breath.

'At midnight? With a backpack?' she asked dubiously.

'Weight training,' said Moose. She looked at him, eyebrows arched with doubt.

'Whatever,' she said, shaking her head. 'I'm off to bed.'

When she'd gone, Moose breathed a sigh of relief and

sat down, rummaging in his backpack. He pulled out the photos and spread them across the kitchen table. The Virgin Mary looked back at us in triplicate, bloodied and forlorn. We stared down at her, mystified. There was something strangely tragic about the images, and I had the fleeting thought that she'd gone to all that trouble only to be left dangling in a darkened rectory basement.

'So what do you think?' I asked. 'Is it real or is it some kind of hoax?'

Moose shook his head. I could tell the photos made him uneasy. 'Beats me,' he said, his eyes sliding up to meet mine. 'But either way, it's pretty weird.'

Moose didn't want to keep the photos in his house so I stuffed them under my mattress, and the sorrowful mother lay hidden beneath me while I slept. I almost forgot about them but two days later, when I turned up for Mass, Francis cornered me in the vestibule. 'Did you find them?' he asked uneasily.

'Yeah,' I admitted, looking around.

'What did you think?'

'You're right,' I shrugged. 'It's pretty bizarre. I can't really explain it.'

'So what do we do now?' he asked. I frowned.

'Nothing.'

'But ... shouldn't we do *something*?' Francis blinked a few times, and I thought for a moment he might cry.

'Look, Francis, it's not hurting anybody,' I said. 'Father O'Shea's right. If we leave it, it'll probably just stop.'

Francis looked stricken. 'But maybe *she's* the one who's hurt. Maybe that's why she's crying,' he said earnestly. 'I tried to tell Father O'Shea, but he wouldn't listen!'

I stared down at him. Once again I seriously regretted

becoming an altar boy. 'Look, Francis, if the Virgin Mary wants to bleed, we can't really stop her,' I said.

'But maybe it's a sin to ignore her.'

'You clean her up every time it happens. You're doing everything you can do.'

'If I got you the Sacristy key, you could sneak in when Father O'Shea serves Communion,' he said, his eyes shimmering fervently.

'What? Why?'

'To see it happen!'

I hesitated. I really did not want to see the Virgin Mary weep. 'Look, we sort of know what happens, don't we?' I asked.

Francis looked me in the eye. 'We need to be sure.'

Deacon Joe came looking for us just then, and Francis gave me a pleading look before he turned away. I was anxious to be rid of him, but as soon as I'd changed into my vestments Father O'Shea beckoned me with a malevolent look from the doorway of the Sacristy. *Out of the frying pan*, I thought as I approached him cautiously. 'May I speak with you, Ethan?' he asked coldly, stepping aside for me to enter. I wondered fleetingly about this break from protocol as he closed the door firmly behind me. And then I couldn't help it: my eyes flew straight to the statue in the alcove. The Virgin Mary stood calmly, her hands spread in a gesture of conciliation, her expression benign. No sign of blood, sweat or tears. I turned back to Father O'Shea, who skewered me with his gaze. Only then did it occur to me that he'd wanted me to see her.

'There was an incident at the rectory this week,' he said. 'Something valuable was stolen. I suspect it may have been taken by accident.' His voice trailed off as he raised a querying eyebrow. I felt the blood in my head start to simmer, the heat pounding in my ears. 'I don't suppose you know anything about it?' he asked.

I shook my head, afraid to utter a word in case my voice betrayed me. Father O'Shea waited expectantly. 'No, sir,' I mumbled. I didn't like lying at the best of times, but to a priest, in church, wearing vestments: if hell was real, then I was damned.

'Well, perhaps you'll let me know if you do,' he said. 'It was local teens, I expect, up to pranks.' His voice twisted sharply on this last word. 'But I wouldn't want the object to fall into the wrong hands,' he added.

I stared at him, and all I could think was, *why?* Father O'Shea narrowed his gaze at me, and I swear I might as well have spoken aloud. 'We're a simple parish here, Ethan,' he said. 'We look to scripture and tradition to guide us, and we worship the Father, Son and the Holy Ghost.' He paused and his eyes swept around the room, landing on the Virgin Mary, before turning back to me. 'We have no need for embellishment,' he said. 'Much less interference.' He paused, gauging my reaction.

So the Virgin Mother was *meddling*, I thought. And like an unruly teenager, Father O'Shea was determined to resist her. 'Do you understand?' he asked finally. I nodded. 'Good,' he said, moving to the door. 'Then I trust you'll do everything in your power to assist me.' He held the door open, indicating that I should go.

Once outside Francis caught my eye from the other side of the altar. A few minutes later, when we were assembling for the processional, he brushed past me and thrust something into my hand. 'Don't worry, it's the spare,' he whispered. 'Just give it back to me after the service.' I looked down at the key and thought, *As you sow, so shall you reap.* Because I had definitely brought this on myself.

The Mass seemed to drag on forever. I spent most of it worrying about how I would get in and out of the Sacristy unseen. I didn't have to do it, of course, but a part of me was genuinely curious. And Francis was right: Jessup helped serve Holy Communion, the rest of us sat on a special pew off to one side, and it took about ten minutes to get through the entire congregation. The Sacristy door was directly behind the altar, which was elevated and backed by an elaborate painted screen featuring Christ with the Apostles. It was certainly possible that I could slip behind the curtain during the general chaos of Communion service without being seen. So I waited until both Father O'Shea and Deacon Joe were fully occupied with the congregation, their backs to the altar, and quietly slipped to the rear of the church, ducking beneath the velvet curtain. I fumbled with the key for a moment, my heart hammering inside my chest, then pushed inside, pulling the door shut behind me. At once I turned to face the Virgin Mary in her alcove.

She stood patiently, looking exactly as I'd seen her before Mass, and I almost laughed out loud with relief. I stepped towards her, feeling a little ridiculous, and came to a halt just in front of her. And in that instant a dark drop bloomed in the corner of her eye, followed by another. I stood and watched as the drop swelled and spilled down her cheek, leaving a stark crimson trail. I froze, unable to breathe, and saw the blood gather momentum, moving past her chin and dripping straight on to her gown. And then I fled, scrambling from the Sacristy as fast as I could, the key clutched tightly in my hand.

When I slipped back into my seat, I must have looked pretty shaken because Francis turned to me in alarm. *What happened?* he mouthed. I shook my head, my eyes flicking around the church. They landed squarely on McCallister, who was staring at me intently. He raised one eyebrow and I wondered how long he'd been watching. When the Mass finished, we rose to follow Father O'Shea out of the church. Once in the vestibule Francis cornered me. 'Did you see it?' he whispered.

'I'm not sure,' I said evasively. Francis frowned. I looked over and saw McCallister whisper something in Father O'Shea's ear, then both of them turned to stare at me. Father O'Shea walked over.

'Ethan, were you in the Sacristy during the service?' he demanded.

I froze, my gaze swivelling from Francis to McCallister. How could I have been so stupid? 'Yes, sir.'

'How did you get in?' he asked. I fished in my pocket for the key, then handed it to him. He looked down at the key and took a deep breath, then exhaled. For an instant relief glowed like a halo around him. 'Well,' he said crisply. 'That explains a great deal. If it weren't for McCallister, we'd never have known.' He shook his head. 'Everything is illuminated, Ethan. I thought you'd know that.'

'It's not what you think,' I started to protest. He put up a hand to silence me.

'God can't be mocked, Ethan. And neither can I. I'll accept your resignation immediately. You can hand in your vestments now.' He turned away and I looked over at Francis, expecting him to say something. But Francis just paled and followed Father O'Shea meekly into the church, and I realised that I'd been cast into the wilderness.

Word spread quickly that there'd been an incident at Mass. When I turned up later that afternoon at Annemarie's house, Ada opened the front door with an expression that said *honey-how-could-you?* She shook her head like a referee admonishing a player. 'Ethan, it's really not a good time,' she said in a tone that was equal parts reproach and regret. Just then I heard Deacon Joe holler from the kitchen. She glanced over her shoulder. 'If I were you, I'd steer clear of this house for a few days,' she added in a hushed voice. 'Until all this blows over. Deacon Joe's a little cranky.'

'Cranky is an understatement,' said Deacon Joe loudly. He was standing in the kitchen doorway, his enormous frame filling it like an angry version of the Michelin Man. He took a few steps forward just as Ada took a wary step sideways, as if to distance herself from my transgressions. 'What demon in hell possessed you to do such a thing?' he asked, peering at me.

'It's not how it looks,' I said uneasily.

'It's precisely how it looks. You deliberately set out to ridicule our faith.'

'No. It wasn't me. I swear it.'

'*Lord, confuse the wicked and confound their words,*' he said, walking slowly down the hall until he loomed over me. 'Time for you to go.'

Later that night I went round to Moose's house, and when I told him what had happened, he was gratifyingly indignant. 'Dude, that is so rank!' he practically shouted at me.

'Well, the good news is that I'm through with altar service.' I shrugged.

'Yeah, but what about the statue? You saw it bleed, for Christ's sake!'

'I don't know what I saw, Moose,' I sighed. 'Maybe I imagined it.'

'Don't be a *wuss*! You totally saw it.'

'Yeah, maybe. But who cares? They still think I did it. No one will believe me.'

'Father O'Shea should know the truth, Ethan. You need to tell him face to face.'

'Trust me, he won't listen.'

'You need to *make* him listen.' Moose sat back and crossed his arms.

And then it dawned on me that I had the perfect opportunity to speak to Father O'Shea alone.

I had never been to Confession. Altar boys are meant to go every time they sneeze, but so far I'd managed to avoid it. Having been raised outside the Church, I hadn't been through any of the sacraments, a fact I'd kept from Father O'Shea when I first approached him. I hadn't lied about it. He'd simply assumed I came from a good Catholic family, and I had encouraged this belief. It was a doctrinal point Annemarie had raised with me when I first told her I was training to be an altar boy. 'Ethan,' she'd said in a tone of reproof, 'you've never even made your First Communion.'

'So?'

She frowned. 'Were you even baptised?'

'I'm not sure,' I said evasively.

'So in the eyes of the Church, you're still guilty of Original Sin.'

'Annemarie, do you honestly believe that I'm guilty of other people's sins?'

'Well, the Church does.'

'And what about you?'

She hesitated. 'I don't know,' she said finally. 'But I still think you shouldn't lie to Father O'Shea.'

'I didn't lie to him,' I pointed out. 'I just didn't inform him. There's a difference.'

Annemarie went to Confession every three months, and her visits had prompted some discussion between us about its purpose. I didn't have a problem with forgiveness, but I'd always found the Catholic concept of absolution a little suspect. The idea that priests were somehow invested with the power to pardon people from wrongdoing struck me as both overly ambitious and even a little smug, particularly when they asked only half a dozen Hail Marys in return. Besides, I'd told Annemarie, if we could undo all our bad deeds by way of a few measly prayers, how would that possibly serve as a deterrent? I also suspected that most Catholics stuck firmly to the realm of benign misdemeanour when it came to Confession (what the church called *venial* sin, but I'd come to think of as vanilla sins, such as taking the name of the Lord in vain) and that those who committed chocolate sins (murder, adultery) would not be found within a mile of the confessional box.

The first time we talked about it, I tried to wheedle out of Annemarie what she'd confessed. 'Ethan! I can't tell you that!' she'd exclaimed.

'Sure you can.'

'It doesn't work that way.'

'Why not?'

'Well, my sins are between me and God. And only he can absolve them.'

'What about the priest?'

'He's really just God's agent.

'So how does that work, exactly?' I asked suspiciously.

'Well, you go into the confessional and sit down and the priest pulls back the window and you say: *Bless me, Father, for I have sinned.* Then he asks you to confess your sins, and when you're done he gives you some prayers to recite, and that's about it.'

'A few prayers? That's all it takes to absolve guilt?'

'Yeah. Pretty much.'

'What if you've done something really bad?'

'Well, if you've examined your conscience and are truly

repentant, then God will forgive you.

Huh, I'd thought. It all seemed a little too convenient somehow, like a get-out-of-jail-free card.

I knew from the church bulletin that Confession happened on Saturday afternoons from five to six p.m. I took Ada's advice and avoided Annemarie's house for the rest of the week, and the following Saturday Moose and I hung about outside the church until it was almost six, and then quickly slipped inside. We slid into the pew beside the confessional box and kneeled down next to each other.

The box was a large wooden affair with a carved panel in the centre separating a narrow door on each side. I could hear voices coming from inside. After a few minutes the door on the left opened and a tiny, white-haired woman with plump cheeks and hunched shoulders came out. She carried a small black Bible and a string of wooden rosary beads, and her head was bowed in penitence. I recognised her from church, a childless widow who never missed Mass. Moose and I watched her teeter down the aisle, and the idea that she'd committed sins worthy of Confession seemed unlikely. Moose must have had the same thought, because he turned to me and rolled his eyes, as if to say *spare me*. When she'd gone I heard Father O'Shea clear his throat from inside the confessional, impatient to finish. 'Here I go,' I said.

'May the force be with you,' whispered Moose.

I slid out from behind the pew, opened the narrow wooden door and ducked inside, seating myself on the straight-backed chair and pulling the door closed behind me. Inside it was dark and smelled musty, but pinpricks of light came through the holes in the carved wooden screen. I could see the small square window to my left, and through it the hands of Father O'Shea: long and thin, the knuckles knotted with age, his fingernails cut so blunt the skin bulged around them. I realised he was waiting for me to begin, and for a split-second my mind went blank. '*Bless me, Father, for I have sinned*,' I said finally. He waited a moment, and I wasn't sure what was meant to come next.

'How long has it been since your last Confession?' he asked.

Forever, I thought. 'A long time,' I answered.

'I've been waiting for you, Ethan,' he said. 'I thought you'd come.'

'I'm not really here to confess, Father.'

'The Bible teaches us to look deep within ourselves and seek forgiveness,' he said. 'That is the purpose of the Sacrament of Confession. To look deep within, to repent, and to ask for absolution.'

'But I haven't done anything wrong.'

'You broke into my house.'

Fair point, I thought. 'But I'm not responsible for this,' I said, reaching in to my backpack and removing one of the photos of the Virgin Mary. I held it up to the window. 'It's true that I snuck into the Sacristy last Sunday and saw the statue bleed. But it's been bleeding every Sunday for weeks, without any help from me.'

He deliberated for a moment, and I could hear him breathing through his nose. 'Young Francis has spoken out of turn,' he said.

'That may be, but I've been wrongly accused.'

'Ethan, I've been the priest here for three decades. I'm respected in the community, and I hope to retire soon. When I do, I plan to lead a quiet life of prayer and contemplation.'

I wasn't sure where he was leading. 'What about the statue?'

He hesitated. 'The statue is an inconvenience,' he said.

'Is that all?'

'No one wants miracles, Ethan. Least of all me.'

'So you accused me instead?'

'Until you broke into my house, I had everything under control.'

'Then you're not going to do anything? About the statue?'

'I'm afraid not.'

'What about the truth?'

'God *is* truth, Ethan. And I am his representative here on earth.'

He spoke with almost papal authority, and he didn't need to say the obvious: that the parish would never believe me over him. 'It won't stop, you know,' I said, trying another tack. 'She'll bleed again.'

'We'll manage,' he said.

'What about me?'

'What *about* you?'

'I'd like to clear my name.'

'God listens to the righteous, Ethan. I suggest you pray. Now go in peace,' he added. But it was more like an order.

When I came out of the confessional, Moose was crouched on the ground just beside the screen, and he looked up at me, his eyes wide. He rose to his feet and followed me quickly out of the church. Once outside, he grabbed my arm. 'Jesus,' he said indignantly. 'He doesn't give a shit about the truth!'

'Apparently not.'

'He already knew you didn't do it.'

'Looks that way,' I sighed. Moose shook his head with disdain. We walked down the church steps and I couldn't help but notice that they were starting to crumble at the edges, with tiny cracks running through the marble like capillaries. Moose thrust his hands deep into his jeans pockets, his jaw throbbing with anger.

'It's like they set a trap and you walked straight into it,' he said after a moment.

I stopped and turned to him. This had never occurred to me. 'You mean Francis?' I asked, the thought quickly gaining momentum. Moose shrugged.

We went straight round to Francis's house. His mother opened the door and smiled doubtfully when we asked if he was in. We waited on the step while she disappeared inside, and a moment later Francis came to the door, looking a little pale. He stepped out to join us. 'Hey,' he said uneasily.

'We thought you might come out to play,' said Moose, his tone brittle. Francis looked over his shoulder uneasily.

'Play what?'

'Truth or dare,' said Moose.

'I'm not really in the mood for games,' Francis said. He took a step back and had turned to go when Moose threw an enormous arm around his shoulder.

'Who said it was a game?'

We drove around the block, parking in a cul-de-sac not far from the house. It was past six and the late April sun hovered low on the horizon. A few kids not much younger than Francis were still out, playing kickball in the street. I saw his eyes slide over them, then back to us.

'Francis, did you tell Father O'Shea that we broke into his house?' I asked.

His face tightened, and his eyes flicked from Moose then back to me, as if he didn't know who was more of a threat. In answer, Moose stretched his arms out in front of him, his fingers locked inside out, so that his knuckles popped loudly.

'He asked me if I knew who'd done it,' said Francis slowly. 'I couldn't lie. Not to a priest!' Moose looked at me and raised his massive eyebrows.

'What about the Sacristy key? Did Father O'Shea tell you to give it to me?' I asked.

'I told him it was a bad idea,' Francis half-whispered.

'Jesus,' said Moose, throwing me a look of disgust.

'I'm sorry,' Francis said a little forlornly. 'I didn't mean for you to get the blame.' Suddenly I felt bad for him, for he was truly in over his pious young head.

'It's OK, Francis,' I said.

And I meant it. None of this would have happened if I'd been honest with Annemarie about my faith in the first place. One falsehood had neatly laid the groundwork for the next, and between us all we'd somehow managed to erect an enormous mansion of deceit.

I needed to see her, and I needed to tell her the truth.

Moose dropped me home after we'd seen Francis and I headed straight over to Annemarie's. I rang the bell and wondered what I'd say if Deacon Joe answered, but when the door finally opened it was Annemarie's mom. She frowned when she saw me, then pushed the door open wide, allowing me inside. 'Ada and Joe have gone out,' she cautioned. 'But they're due back within the hour.' She nodded towards the stairs. 'Whatever you've done, go make amends. Annemarie's been in a pit of gloom all week.'

'I'm sorry,' I said.

'It's not me you should apologise to.'

Annemarie opened her bedroom door even before I knocked, as if she could sense me looming guiltily on the stairs. I hadn't seen her in a week and she looked paler than I remembered, and more delicate, and somehow even more beautiful. Gloom suits her, I thought. 'High time you showed up,' she said quietly, and I could tell she was angry.

'Ada told me not to come around for a few days,' I said.

Annemarie raised an eyebrow, as if this was news to her, then stepped aside for me to enter. She closed the door behind me and I turned to face her.

'I'm not sure I believe in God,' I said. 'Or the sacraments. And if I do something wrong, I think that it'll take more than a few prayers to make it right.'

Annemarie frowned. 'Why are you telling me this?' she asked.

'Because I wanted to be like you, but I'm not,' I said. 'And I think you should know.' She considered my words for a moment, then went and sat on the end of her bed, placing a hand on the spot next to her.

'I think you better start from the beginning.'

So I told her everything, except I omitted one tiny detail: I couldn't bring myself to confess that I'd actually seen the statue bleed. I guess a part of me wasn't prepared to admit that, even to myself. Annemarie listened without saying a word, and when I finished, we both sat in silence. It wasn't ominous or angry or loaded, but calm and peaceful in a way that I'd forgotten silence could be. Eventually she laid her hand on top of mine. Her fingers felt warm and slender, and I was grateful for their touch. 'I know you don't believe in absolution,' she said with a half-smile. 'But I forgive you just the same.' She turned to me and I could tell that, in spite of my being a heretic, I'd somehow pleased her. I felt a sudden surge of relief, as if I'd been wandering blindly in the forest and had finally stumbled on to the right path. 'So do you think the statue really bleeds?' she asked. I hesitated, not wanting to lie.

'Who knows?' I said evasively. 'But maybe it doesn't matter.'

'Maybe not,' she agreed.

Later she made me read her a poem by Emily Dickinson,

and while I don't remember all the words, I remember that the point of it was that the truth was something you had to come at gradually, from a slant. Otherwise it might overwhelm you.

But I wasn't out of the darkness yet with Deacon Joe. He still thought I'd broken into the Sacristy, and although he appeared to know nothing about the weeping statue, he was convinced that my motives were somehow diabolical. He tried to persuade Annemarie's mom that I should be barred from visiting the house, but fortunately she didn't agree.

The following Sunday I slept late for the first time in months, and when I came downstairs my parents looked up at me with surprise. 'Hey, Sleeping Beauty,' said Mom. 'We thought you were at church!'

I shrugged. 'Decided to give it a miss today,' I said. 'Might give it a miss permanently,' I added. My father stuck his head out from behind the newspaper, and I saw him briefly raise a quizzical eyebrow at my mother.

'Apparently the priest at St Paul's is doing the same,' he remarked.

'What?' I asked. He held up an inside page of the *Youngstown Vindicator* for me to see. A small photo of Father O'Shea in full vestments stared out at me. 'He's retiring?' I asked.

'Yep. Plans to take up missionary work overseas.'

'Where?' I asked.

'It doesn't say.'

Somewhere far away, I thought. Where he can lead a quiet life of prayer and contemplation, unhindered by the Virgin Mary.

That evening I decided to brave Annemarie's house, even though I wasn't sure I'd be welcome. Ada answered the door and hesitated just long enough for me to know that I was still *persona non grata*. She said a cool hello, then turned away from me rather than bearing down with her customary full-frontal welcome. I should have welcomed the change, but somehow it didn't feel right.

Annemarie smiled a little ruefully when she opened her bedroom door. She pulled me inside and shut the door. 'Have you heard the news about Father O'Shea?' she asked.

'Yeah. We saw it in the *Vindicator*. What did Deacon Joe say?'

'He said that it was a great loss for the parish.'

'That's debatable.'

'I don't understand why Father O'Shea would just run away.'

'Maybe he's afraid.'

'Of what?'

'I don't know. God maybe.'

'Then he's a coward,' she said crossly. 'Not to mention a bully.'

'At the end of the day he's just a man, Annemarie.'

She hesitated. 'I always thought that priests were so much more,' she said slowly. She sat down heavily on her bed, and her disappointment seemed to swell and fill the room.

'I'm sorry.' I sat down next to her. She gave a small shrug.

'Helen Keller wrote that we look so long at a closed door, we don't see the one that's opened for us,' she said philosophically.

'Is that what's happened here? Have we opened a door?'

She paused, drawing a breath. 'Maybe,' she said. 'I'm just not sure where it goes.'

Father O'Shea left Jericho for good in early May, and in the wake of his departure, Annemarie suffered a complete crisis of faith. For the next several weeks she wavered and swerved, changing her mind almost hourly about the nature of her relationship with God in general, and me in particular. I bided my time during this period, busy with end-of-year exams and band concerts, hoping that if I gave her time and space she might eventually decide that love and faith were not mutually exclusive propositions. And we might have gone on like that indefinitely if nearly two months later, on a sweltering day in early July, she hadn't taken my hand and informed me with barely concealed excitement that something strange and miraculous had occurred. When I realised what she was saying, I told her that it was impossible to conceive a baby without sex. But even as I said the words, I knew that when it came to Annemarie, anything was possible. And it struck me in that instant that God had found yet another way to mock me.

'We should have done it months ago,' I told her glumly.

'Don't you see?' she asked breathlessly, placing the palm of my hand on her stomach. 'We weren't meant to. This is why we didn't. *This* is what has kept us apart.'

But I didn't see, all those weeks ago. And I still don't now.

Eva

After we had coffee together, I couldn't stop thinking about Ethan's mother. She was caring and considerate, qualities I'd always appreciated. But she was also open-minded and tolerant – qualities I seemed to have almost sidestepped in my own life. Unlike me, she was at liberty to form her own views, free from the fetters of religion. And she was far less judgmental than many of the folks I rubbed up against within the church community. So it wasn't only that I admired her; I envied her too. I realised with surprise that Annemarie was a lot like her. From a young age, Annemarie had succeeded in blending faith and tolerance and a questioning spirit into an acceptable mix. If my own daughter could do this, then why couldn't I? Somehow over the course of my life I'd managed to paint myself into a corner, like one of those figures trapped forever in a tragic biblical scene.

But if I could raise a daughter like Annemarie, I decided, then maybe I wasn't such a terrible mother after all. And maybe it was time to take the curate's advice to heart and embrace Annemarie's pregnancy. I was gradually coming round to the idea of being a youthful grandmother, and I was even beginning to feel excited about the prospect of diapers, rattles, and baby bottles strewn about the house. Those first few months of Annemarie's life, before Daryl had left, were some of the happiest memories I had. I knew Annemarie was anxious about the prospect of raising a child, and I figured I could help her anticipate its arrival with pleasure rather than fear. So on the day that she and Ethan drove over to Bethlehem, I enlisted Ada's help and we cleared out a small spare room at the end of the upstairs hall. We emptied it completely and spent the morning painting the walls bright yellow. Then we drove over to the mall and bought new curtains, a striped carpet to lay down on the floorboards, and a wooden crib. We even bought a little mobile made of felt elephants to hang over the crib, and persuaded a disgruntled Deacon Joe to put a hook in the ceiling. When he was finished, he turned to me. 'Where is she, anyway?' he asked.

'She's gone to Bethlehem with Ethan.'

'West Virginia! You let her cross the state line with that fanatic?'

'They're on a pilgrimage. Even you can't argue with a pilgrimage.'

'I would not let her go as far as the 7-Eleven with that boy! He's downright unstable. He might even kidnap her!'

'Don't be ridiculous. I am trying to let my daughter live her own life.'

'Her life stopped being hers the day she got pregnant,' he snapped. 'Anyhow, the Vicar General called this morning. They want to know what plans we've made for her confinement.'

'It's a little early to be discussing her confinement, isn't it?' I asked.

'The Church is right to be concerned. We have a moral duty to ensure that baby is born safely.'

'Our only duty is to Annemarie,' I replied. Just then the

phone rang and Ada went to answer it, while Deacon Joe and I glared at each other. When she returned a minute later, she slid into the room uneasily.

'What is it?' I asked.

'That was the hospital up in Cleveland,' she said. 'They wanted to inform us that she has another appointment next week.'

'What do you mean, *another* appointment?' I asked suspiciously.

'Apparently, she and Ethan made a little detour up there this morning,' Ada said. 'The doctors thought we ought to know.'

'She went to Cleveland? Without telling me?' The news truly stunned me. Ada nodded.

'It looks that way. And they want her back next week.'

'You see?' said Deacon Joe, turning to me. 'Annemarie cannot be trusted with this pregnancy! This pregnancy is bigger than she is!'

'Annemarie is perfectly capable of dealing with this pregnancy,' I said flatly. What she is *not* capable of, I thought, is telling the truth. I turned away from Deacon Joe and his righteousness and went to make myself a cup of tea, and by the time Annemarie walked through the front door later that evening, I'd forgotten all about the newly decorated nursery. I was well and truly furious, but it wasn't for the reasons she thought. I knew Annemarie wanted answers about her pregnancy, and that she was determined to get them – and a part of me couldn't argue with that. But once again what angered me most was that she'd chosen to deceive me, rather than face me with the truth.

That night I went outside after dinner and sat on the bench in the churchyard. I don't know if I was willing it to happen, but when the curate came walking across the grass in the dark I said a little thank you prayer to God. The day's events had left me down and I needed someone impartial to talk to. Once he'd finished watering the roses, he sat down next to me with a sigh. 'I was beginning to think you'd given up on us,' he said, nodding towards the roses.

I felt my cheeks redden. 'Sorry. I've been kind of preoccupied,' I said.

He waved a hand. 'I'm only joking. No guilt, remember?' I nodded.

'A priest without guilt.' I smiled. 'What seminary did you say you went to?'

He laughed. We both sat there in the darkness for a minute. 'So,' he said finally. 'Something must have brought you out here tonight.' He turned to me in the dark and I swear he could see straight into my mind.

I breathed in a little nervously. 'I took your advice,' I said. 'But it kind of backfired.'

'Ah,' he said, nodding. 'Then I can only apologise.' He paused for a second. 'Which advice exactly was that?'

I laughed. 'It doesn't matter,' I said. 'It's just ... things don't always bend the way you want them to, do they?'

'You mean people don't always bend the way you want them to?'

'I guess so. Teenagers especially.'

'Well, teenagers aren't the only ones,' he said. 'We all let each other down, from time to time. God doesn't really expect perfection from us. I'm not sure he would want it either. Mistakes are what make us human. And we learn from them.' I thought about this. As usual, he had a point.

'What mistakes have you learned from, Father?' I asked.

'Plenty!' he laughed. Then he added, 'More than I care to remember.' I looked over at him, and got the sudden sense that he was withholding something.

'Before you became a priest?' I asked.

He nodded. 'I had kind of a wayward youth.'

'What happened?'

'Faith happened,' he said simply. 'I met a priest. And he persuaded me that I should devote my energies to something larger than myself.' He paused for a moment. 'Actually,' he added thoughtfully, 'he was a prison chaplain.' He turned to me, and our eyes met in the darkness. For once, he seemed completely serious. I hesitated.

'Are you saying you were in prison?' I asked.

He gave a small, rueful smile. 'Well, I wasn't a guard.'

I swallowed. 'Does anyone else in the parish know?'

He shook his head. 'The seminary knows. And the Bishop knows. But no one here in Jericho.'

'Can I ask why you're telling me?'

'I thought I should be honest with you,' he said. 'Seeing as how we're friends.'

'Oh,' I said. So we're friends, I thought. I wasn't sure what that meant to a priest, but it pleased me nonetheless. I looked at the roses in the moonlight, and they seemed to nod their approval. 'Can I give you a word of advice?' I said. 'Seeing as how we're friends?'

'Of course.'

'Don't tell anyone else.'

He laughed quietly, then looked down at the dirt, scuffing at it with the toe of his shoe. I hoped I hadn't offended him.

'Don't get me wrong,' I added quickly. 'It's just that folks round here tend to make snap judgments. And they can be difficult to ... unsnap.' He looked up at me and smiled.

'Well, I'm glad you're not one of them,' he said.

Later that night I lay in bed and wondered whether he wasn't mistaken. Wasn't I just as critical as the next person? The new curate seemed to see more goodness in the world than was truly there; he certainly saw more goodness in me. In truth I'd been desperate to know why he'd been in prison, but had been too embarrassed to ask. Now my imagination couldn't help but run through the possibilities. I told myself he'd probably committed some sort of white-collar crime, such as writing bad cheques or embezzlement. But a part of me knew that it would be something less ordinary. Because if there was one thing he wasn't, it was boring.

The next evening he was waiting for me, and as I walked across the grass in the darkness I saw that he was holding something in his hands. It was a small rectangular piece of wood, and he was slowly shaving bits of it off with a knife. He looked up as I approached, and smiled. 'So my treacherous past hasn't put you off,' he said. Maybe it was my imagination, but I thought I detected relief in his voice. I sat down next to him.

'No, but the knife might.' I smiled.

He held it up. 'It's only a penknife.'

'And I can see you're very good with it.'

'I'm good with wood,' he corrected me. 'I used to be a cabinetmaker. Before ...' He stopped himself.

'Before God?'

He nodded. 'Before God.'

'Just like Jesus.'

He laughed and shook his head. 'Not exactly.' He shaved a few more pieces from the wood while I watched.

'So how does a cabinetmaker wind up in prison?' I asked. The question had been dogging me all day, and I couldn't stand it any longer. He stopped whittling and fingered the piece of wood in his hands.

'I guess you could say there was an accident,' he said,

276

glancing up at me. 'Between a bottle and someone's skull,' he added.

'Where were you?' I asked.

'On the other end of the bottle.'

'What happened to the skull?'

He grimaced. 'The skull didn't come out of it too well.'

'No one died, did they?'

'No! No. Nothing like that. Just ... some stitches.' He shrugged. 'Quite a lot of stitches, in the end. And a custodial sentence.'

'So you got in a fight.'

'More than one fight, if truth be told. Certainly one fight too many.' He looked up at me and gave a rueful smile. 'I'm afraid it's in the blood. I come from a long line of drinkers and brawlers,' he explained. 'And I excelled at both. Though that's no excuse, of course.' He carried on cutting while I thought about what he'd told me. Last night my mind had conjured all sorts of reasons he might have ended up in prison, but a bar-room brawl wasn't one of them.

'Presumably you've left all that behind now,' I said.

He nodded. 'Far, far behind.'

'Communion wine?' I asked.

He held up two fingers close together. 'Tiny little sips. Just enough to wet the lips. Can't stand the stuff any more.'

'Probably just as well.' He stopped whittling and peered at me in the darkness.

'Any more questions?'

I nodded at the wood. 'What are you whittling?'

He frowned. 'I haven't decided yet,' he said, looking down at it. 'But you'll be the first to know when I do.'

We sat there in silence for a few minutes and he continued shaving bits off the wood, until it looked less like a block and more like an object. 'Who taught you how to whittle?' I said finally.

'My dad. It was about the only useful thing he ever did teach me.'

'Where'd you grow up?'

'Michigan. A logging town up north.'

'Guess that explains the wood,' I said.

He smiled. 'Whittling is a little like meditation,' he said. 'The key is never to rush. You have to listen to the wood, and let it tell you where to cut. Never try to force it to do something it doesn't want to do. And never try to cut against the grain.'

'Sounds like a maxim for living,' I said.

He smiled. 'It might just be.' He stopped and looked at me. 'So how are things with your daughter?'

'We've reached an understanding. For now, at least.'

'I met your sister the other day.'

'Ada?'

He smiled and nodded – a little too knowingly, I thought.

'Let me guess: she came to Confession.'

'That may have been it,' he said discreetly.

Why was I not surprised? Even though it must have been years since Ada had last been to Confession. 'She must have had a lot to talk about.'

He laughed good-naturedly, but again remained silent. I couldn't decide if I admired his restraint, or was disappointed by it.

'Ada's always lived a colourful life,' I said. 'In contrast to mine,' I added.

'Which is?'

I shrugged. 'Monochrome.'

'A single mother raising a blind daughter who may or may not be pregnant through a religious miracle? That doesn't count as monochrome in my book.'

I laughed. 'I guess not. When you put it that way.'

'What happened to Annemarie's father?' he asked, glancing up at me.

I took a deep breath. 'He strayed,' I said. 'Quite far in the end.' No need to go into details, I thought. The whys and wherefores didn't really matter any more.

'When?'

'A long time ago. When Annemarie was just a baby. But we've managed all right on our own,' I added, feeling a little stab of pride. Priest or not, I didn't want this man to see us as unfortunates.

'You seem to be doing just fine,' he said reassuringly. He was working away at the wood, making a series of small but very precise cuts, though I still had no idea what he was carving. 'And you were never tempted to remarry?' he asked after a moment.

I shook my head. 'Once was enough. Plenty, in fact.'

He laughed.

'What about you?' I asked. 'Were you ever married? Before?'

'I'm sorry to say, no,' he said. 'I missed out on that part. Maybe if I hadn't, things might have turned out differently.' He seemed genuinely regretful, and I couldn't help but wonder why.

I laughed a little nervously 'Then I guess we've both embraced a life of celibacy,' I said.

He held up the wood and squinted at it. 'Actually,' he said, pausing thoughtfully for a moment, 'celibacy's never been high on my list. It certainly wasn't why I went into the priesthood.' I glanced over at him and he seemed to be concentrating on the carving, unaware of the potency of his words. 'Don't misunderstand me: I *am* celibate,' he added. 'But I don't regard it as essential to my role. Celibacy is a discipline, not a dogma.'

'Like being teetotal?' I asked.

He nodded. 'Like being teetotal.'

'So,' I said, looking around the churchyard. 'No drinking, no fighting, no sex. What's left?' I asked. 'Apart from God.'

He held up the wood, which had somehow formed itself into a miniature shoe, and smiled.

'Whittling.'

Annemarie

In the end, Mama and I came to a truce about the Magi. She agreed that I could carry on seeing them, as long as I didn't do it behind her back, and I agreed that I wouldn't take any more decisions regarding the pregnancy without her. But Deacon Joe was still pretty irate, and acted like I was dancing with the devil. 'Mark my words, Annemarie, you are playing with fire,' he warned, shaking his head.

'I like fire,' I said. 'And so does God. Remember Moses and the burning bush? Or the children of Israel who followed a pillar of fire to the Promised Land?'

'God did not intend for you to be a guinea pig,' he said. 'Who knows what those doctors will do to you, given half the chance!'

'Joe, I'm sure the doctors won't hurt her,' said Ada.

'She could be jeopardising the pregnancy!'

Would that be such a tragedy? I thought guiltily.

For the next week or so life in Jericho remained stable, if not exactly calm. The Virgin Mary continued to appear hazily on the skyline every evening, though she stopped being the lead item on the nightly news after a man in Knox County chained himself to the local water tower and threatened to blow it up. But while the media appeared to lose interest in the sunsets, the Christian world did not. The town continued to crawl with tourists, and there was a steady stream of traffic to the wayside shrine, especially in the evenings. Local people couldn't be bothered to turn up any more, but religious pilgrims came by the busload from all over the Midwest, with the volume sometimes doubling on weekends. Not surprisingly they brought with them opportunists selling everything from Jesus tacos to 3-D Marian apparition paperweights. Cora Lynn called them entrepreneurs, but Deacon Joe said they were all sharks. The city tried to contain them in a field to the west of the shrine, but they spilled out on to the sidewalk and along the road, unloading display tables and catering equipment out of dusty transit vans and old pickup trucks.

One afternoon Cora Lynn insisted I make a tour of them with her. Mama had warned me about going out on my own after she'd caught a Peeping Tom in front of the house, but Cora Lynn promised to fend off anyone who got overly curious. We wandered around and I stood beside her while she feigned interest to the stall holders, handing me trinkets one by one to feel: rosaries, candles, crucifixes, holy water fonts, apparition magnets, statues and key rings. You name it and they were trying to sell it, apparently. 'Are people actually buying this stuff?' I whispered after a few minutes.

'Hell, yes. Church people are gullible enough to buy anything.'

'They're not gullible, they're just ... devoted.'

'Maybe we should start selling locks of hair.'

'*Whose* hair?' I asked suspiciously.

'Whoever. Wouldn't matter, as long as you told 'em it was holy.'

'You can't just claim anything's holy.'

'Wanna bet?'

'Not with *my* hair.'

'Hey, look at this,' said Cora Lynn. She grabbed my hand and placed something smooth and heavy and round in it, pleasing to the touch.

'What is it?'

'Virgin Mary snow globe.'

'Oh. Nice. Is she smiling?'

'Nah. She looks bored. Probably tired of all that snow,' said Cora Lynn. I gave it a little shake, imagining snowflakes whirling round and round the Virgin Mary's head, then handed it back. 'Thanks,' she said to the stall holder.

'My pleasure,' I heard him reply. We started to move away and suddenly he stopped us. 'Hey,' he called out. 'You're that girl, aren't you? The one from the news broadcast?'

I hesitated uneasily.

'Time to skedaddle,' said Cora Lynn under her breath.

'Wait up,' said the man, coming closer. 'I want to give you something.' He reached for my hand, then folded my fingers around the snow globe, covering them tightly with his own.

'Oh, no, I really can't,' I started to protest.

'Please, take it,' he insisted, cutting me off. 'It's a gift. Anyway, you might need it,' he said, his tone suddenly serious. For a moment I just stood there, the glass heavy in my hand.

'Thank you,' I murmured.

Cora Lynn pulled me away from the stall, my fingers still clutching the snow globe. 'Didn't your mama ever tell you not to take candy from strangers!' she hissed into my ear.

'It's a snow globe! Besides, he was only trying to be kind.' Though I couldn't help wondering what he'd meant.

'He was trying to be creepy,' she said. 'And he succeeded.

But at least you got a snow globe out of it.' We started to walk back, when suddenly I heard a familiar male voice at my elbow.

'Find anything you like, ladies?' It took me a moment to realise it was the new curate, and he was addressing us in a playful tone.

'We found this,' I said, holding up the snow globe. 'Actually someone gave it to us.'

'Ah, yes, I was partial to that myself,' he remarked. Cora Lynn jammed an elbow into my side.

'Sorry,' I said. 'Cora Lynn, this is Father ...' I turned to him with a frown, realising that I didn't even know his name.

'Michael,' he offered quickly.

'Pleased to meet you, Father,' said Cora. 'Though I should probably warn you I'm Baptist,' she added.

Lapsed Baptist, I thought.

'There's room for all faiths here in Jericho,' he said good-naturedly.

'Are you the replacement for that grumpy old guy?' asked Cora Lynn, causing me to wince. ''Cause I hope you don't mind my saying, but you're a vast improvement on him.'

'Um. Thank you.'

'Though you look way too young to be a priest.'

'I promise you I'm old enough.'

'That's good. 'Cause I might just come and hear you preach one day,' she said.

'Please do. You'd be very welcome. Good afternoon, ladies.' Father Michael drifted off and Cora Lynn grabbed my arm.

'Virgin Mary bring him too?' she whispered into my ear.

'Not that I'm aware of.'

''Cause he's a man-size slice of heaven!'

'He's a priest!'

'I'm just sayin'.'

Eventually we got tired of looking at souvenirs and went to sit on the grass by Ethan's tent. Cora Lynn reached over to feel my stomach. 'So how's lil' Princette?'

'Lil' Princette is biding her time.'

'Well, that's just fine with me,' she said, stretching out on the grass. ''Cause things are kinda topsy-turvy 'round here, and I reckon she should just lay low for the time being.'

Amen to that, I thought.

After a few minutes Cora Lynn heaved herself off the ground and said she had to go to work, so I decided to head home. But as I was tapping my way back across the churchyard a male voice stopped me. 'Excuse me, are you Annemarie?' the man asked.

'Yes?' I turned around and something made me instantly wary. His aura seemed too potent somehow, and quietly forceful.

'We're from Sacred Path. Over in Defiance? We're a Christian ministry. You might have heard our radio show on WROK – Sacred Tolling?'

'I don't think so.'

'We're outreach ambassadors. My name's Brendan and this is Lilah.'

'Hello,' a female voice said cheerily.

'I'm afraid I've never heard of Sacred Path,' I said.

'Oh, we're *huge*,' said Lilah. 'We're headquartered in Ohio, but we have fellowships all over the world. We offer guidance on how to understand the Bible, so that our followers can manifest a more abundant life,' she said earnestly. I turned to focus on her. Lilah's aura was definitely less threatening than Brendan's, but there was still something unsettling about it.

'OK,' I said cautiously. 'Guidance can be good,' I added.

I figured I should say something positive, even though it occurred to me that I'd had quite enough guidance of late, and anyway manifesting abundance wasn't exactly high on my list.

'We believe the Bible should be taken literally wherever possible, and we shun those whose practices go against our doctrines,' said Lilah.

'Um ... what *are* your doctrines?'

'That God alone is the father of Jesus. And that it was He who impregnated Mary,' said Lilah. 'Not the Holy Spirit,' she added, just in case I was hazy on that point.

'I always thought that God and the Holy Spirit were sort of the same,' I said, even though that didn't really chime with Catholic teaching.

'Not at all,' said Lilah emphatically. Her aura was just coming into focus, and it was a volatile mix of ardent and impressionable.

'So you can see why we wanted to meet you,' said Brendan, his voice now worryingly purposeful. I turned to him and alarm bells began sacred tolling in my head.

'I'm not sure I understand.'

'It was God who created the sperm that fertilised your pregnancy. You're carrying His seed with you, even now.'

'Actually we think it might have more to do with my chromosomes,' I said uneasily. 'But I appreciate your interest just the same.' I turned away and instantly felt Brendan's presence loom at my side. His hand locked upon my elbow, and he spoke into my ear, his voice low.

'Please. We'd like you to break bread with us.'

'I'm sorry?' I asked, confused.

'We'd be honoured if you'd join us for supper.'

'Now?'

'Yes. Over at our headquarters in Defiance. It's only a

short drive. Brother Carl is anxious to meet you.'

I hesitated. I had no idea who Brother Carl was, but the alarm bells were ringing loudly now. I didn't want to antagonise Brendan, so I forced myself to smile. 'That's a very kind invitation, but I don't think I can,' I said politely. 'Maybe some other time.'

'But we've come all this way,' said Lilah fervently. She was at my other side, and I felt her hand encircle my upper arm.

'We have a car right here,' said Brendan, steering me towards the street. Suddenly I felt as if I'd stepped into a fast current, and might easily slip beneath the seething waters of their abundance.

'I really can't,' I said, pulling away. 'I'm expected at home.' I turned to go and Brendan's hand clamped down harder on my arm, his grip impressively strong.

'Please,' he said urgently into my ear. 'I promise we won't hurt you.'

Now I was definitely frightened. 'Look, I don't know who you are or what you want –' I started to protest. Then I heard a car door open and felt his hand pressing down hard on my shoulder, while Lilah's hand forced the back of my head down. Brendan gave me a shove and I tumbled into the car. Lilah scrambled in after me, pushing me aside as she did so. But before they had a chance to shut the door I heard someone shout from across the road.

'Annemarie!' called a loud voice.

Cassandra! I thought. Maybe God was with me after all.

Brendan and Lilah froze for an instant, then Brendan slammed the car door. 'Let's go,' he said urgently. He ran around and scrambled into the driver's seat, and I heard him start the engine.

'Annemarie, wait!' Cassandra shouted again. I heard

footsteps hurrying towards the car. The engine roared into life and I felt the car lurch forward, then swerve dangerously to the left.

'Cassandra!' I shouted.

'Hush,' said Lilah in my ear.

'Stop!' shouted Cassandra.

But the car sped off, and I heard Cassandra's voice fade.

Ethan

The day Annemarie got kidnapped, Moose and I went swimming over at the quarry. It was a hot day in mid-August and, after more than two weeks of Virgin sunsets, I was starting to get pretty cheesed off with Christian pilgrims. It had got so bad that I'd started going home at sunset every night, only returning to the tent later in the evening, after the tourists had gone. Moose had stopped by the night before, and while he was parked in my driveway, his car had got blocked in by a white Corvette with a bumper sticker that read *Jesus is my Mechanic*. Moose was meant to be going on a date with a girl from Berlin High and he was furious. He grabbed a can of shaving cream from my bathroom and before I could stop him went outside and coated the entire car with mint-green obscenities. When the owner eventually turned up an hour later he was six foot two and built like a refrigerator with a crew cut. His frizzy-haired girlfriend was even scarier: she came stamping up to the front door in shiny metal stilettos, a hot pink tube dress that looked like it had been spray-painted on, and mascara as thick as tar, demanding that we clean the car *or else*.

The next morning I was woken at the crack of dawn by a group of Baptists who'd driven up from Tennessee so they could watch the sun rise with the Virgin Mary. When I stumbled blearily out of my tent, they were seated in a circle on the grass by the church, holding hands and singing 'Abide With Me'. I explained to them through clenched teeth that the Virgin Mary only appeared when the sun *set*, whereupon they insisted that she was right there with them, if only I cared to look. I swear to God if I'd had a gun at that moment I would have shot them, but instead I went home and rolled into my own bed for the first time in weeks, where I slept past noon. By the time I got up the town was already heaving with religious hawkers. I had the day off work so when Moose came by and suggested we go swimming, I was only too happy to escape. The last thing I saw as we drove out of town was Annemarie and Cora Lynn chatting to Father Michael over by one of the stalls.

Moose and I didn't get back until early evening, and when we turned on to Church Road I saw the sheriff's car parked in Annemarie's driveway. I went straight over to her house and when Deacon Joe told me what had happened, I felt like someone had punched me in the gut. He grudgingly invited me inside, then glared at me across the kitchen table as if I was somehow personally responsible for her disappearance. He needn't have bothered – I already felt massively guilty for lounging away the afternoon on air mattresses while Annemarie got spirited away by religious wackos. The Sheriff and his deputy had already conducted house-to-house enquiries throughout the neighbourhood, and apart from Cassandra, no one had seen a thing.

When I finally got home, my mom was waiting for me with a plate of food. She tried to reassure me, but I could tell that she and Dad were just as worried about Annemarie's disappearance as I was. They weren't exactly wild about me camping out that night, but I told them it was more important than ever before for me to be there. I wasn't sure how my presence in the tent would help Annemarie, but if the Virgin Mary *did* appear by the wayside shrine, I wanted to be close by.

Later that night, Moose came by the tent to console me. He sat down heavily in a lawn chair. 'Don't worry, dude, she'll be OK,' he said. 'They probably just wanted to ... bless her or something.'

'It's the something I'm worried about,' I said. I'd already imagined a thousand different somethings, and none of them were good. We sat there as darkness fell and the last of the tourists drifted away. Before that night, the pilgrims who'd flocked to Jericho had mostly seemed harmless to me; now they all looked like potential abductors, and I hated them for it. Moose rummaged in his jacket pocket.

'Here,' he said, pulling out a small flask of whiskey. 'I thought you might need something to take the edge off.' He held it out and I stared at it reluctantly. I wasn't sure I wanted to take the edge off, but he thrust it towards me. 'At the very least, it'll help you sleep,' he said.

'Thanks, man,' I said.

Moose stood up to go. 'They'll find her, Ethan. And when they do, she's gonna be fine.'

I nodded, a lump forming in my throat, and watched him drive away. After he was gone I sat alone in the darkness and listened to the sound of crickets in the grass. It was nearly midnight and the street was finally quiet. I looked around, feeling utterly desolate, not to mention abandoned. Where was the Virgin Mary when we really needed her?

I didn't open the whiskey right away. I tried and failed to sleep, my mind whirling endlessly with feverish scenarios, and eventually decided that taking the edge off might not be such a bad idea after all. The whiskey burned like hell but it felt good, sort of like a punishment for letting Annemarie down. I drank a fair bit – I don't know how much, but after a while I needed to pee. I usually went home to use the bathroom, but it was the middle of the night and I didn't want to alarm my parents, so I went to the bushes behind the rectory.

As I walked back across the churchyard the ground began to see-saw beneath my feet. I passed the Sacristy, recognising the small rectangular window set high in the church wall. It was about eight feet off the ground, hinged at the top, and just large enough for someone thin to squeeze through. I stood beneath it, the ground still swaying, and saw that it was slightly ajar. Father Michael must have left it open because of the heat. Without thinking, I leaped up and grabbed the lower sill and hoisted myself up to peer inside. The alcove with the Virgin Mary in it was off to my right, but I couldn't see the statue clearly in the darkness. With some difficulty, I managed to get the window fully open and pull myself halfway in, where I hung for a minute thinking I might be sick. Finally I scrambled through, scraping one arm badly on the frame, and dropped to the ground, the window banging loudly behind me.

I landed badly, in a heap on my side, and lay with my face against the cool stone floor. After a few seconds, I rolled over onto my back and the room began to spin. I sat up and leaned back against the wall with my eyes closed, trying to make it stop. I must have dozed off for a few minutes, and when I woke the Sacristy was eerily silent. I stood up a little shakily and looked around, remembering the last time I'd been there. I walked over to the alcove and kneeled down on the padded bench, looking up at the wooden statue of the Virgin Mary. Even in the dark I could see there were no tears. I stared up at her, wondering how she could have let something like this happen. Wasn't Annemarie the blessed one? I closed my eyes and bowed my head and pleaded with the Virgin Mary to let Annemarie come home. But she did not appear, nor did she give me a sign that she was listening.

Eventually I gave up. There was a glass cupboard on the opposite wall and I crossed over to it. Inside were folded vestments, various holy books, and all the props used during Mass: the bell and incense holder, the chalice and paten, a pair of crystal cruets, and a squat brass vessel used to sprinkle holy water. I picked up one of the cruets and removed the stopper, sniffing the wine inside. It smelled sickly sweet and my stomach gave another heave. I started to put it back on the shelf when I became aware of something behind me. When I turned around, the statue had begun to glow with a pale yellow light, as if it had been lit from within. I froze, my heart thumping wildly. What in God's name was the Virgin Mary trying to tell me? And why couldn't she just appear to me in person and say it out loud?

I turned and shoved the cruet back onto the shelf, but it came tumbling forward, smashing to the floor with a deafening noise. I looked down at the shattered glass and spilled wine at my feet, and as I did the light behind me faded. Suddenly I wanted to be anywhere but trapped inside the Sacristy with the Virgin Mary. I flew to the door and yanked on the handle, but it was locked from the outside, so I grabbed the room's only chair and dragged it over to the window, hoisting myself back up on to the sill. Once again I pulled myself halfway through the window frame, when suddenly an intense white light blinded me from outside. I stopped and raised my head, squinting at it. Two figures loomed in the darkness.

'Jesus Christ, Ethan! What the hell do you think you're doing?' said Sheriff Dawson.

Eva

The day Annemarie disappeared, we stepped from a storm straight into a hurricane. Thank God her social worker happened to be passing. If not for Cassandra, it might have been several hours before anyone even realised Annemarie was missing. Lord knows I'd had my doubts about Cassandra at the outset, but in a crisis she proved more level-headed than just about anyone else in Jericho. Deacon Joe was especially useless: in those first few hours he blundered around the house wavering between *I told you so* and *The Lord protects the innocent*. (Typically, it transpired that the innocent he was referring to was not Annemarie, but her unborn child.) As soon as Cassandra raised the alarm we called Sheriff Dawson. He turned up twenty minutes later on the doorstep wearing coveralls instead of his usual uniform, and a scraping of fudge across his forehead. 'Sorry about the attire,' he apologised, stepping into the front hall. 'I've been over in Berlin judging a bake-off, and those cupcakes can be the devil's own mess.' He listened carefully to Cassandra's account, then made a string of calls and organised an immediate door-to-door enquiry of the neighbourhood. For a couple of hours, we mistakenly thought the situation was in hand.

But while there'd been dozens of people around that afternoon, no one seemed to remember much about the well-dressed young man and woman who made off with Annemarie in the back of a green Pontiac festooned with Christian bumper stickers. Eyewitnesses saw the car head west out of town towards the Interstate, but though Cassandra had copied down the licence number, it was an Indiana plate and the highway patrol said it might take twenty-four hours to trace. We spent that first evening huddled around the kitchen table waiting for news. At a quarter-past seven the telephone rang and I leaped out of my chair so fast I practically broke my neck answering it. I was overcome with relief when I heard Annemarie's voice, but the call lasted all of six seconds. She told me quickly that she was fine and that she'd be home soon, and when I asked her where she was, the line went dead. I stood there staring at the receiver, my insides turning somersaults.

Sheriff Dawson said the call had been too brief to trace, but he felt certain it was a good sign. He reassured us that if Annemarie was able to make a phone call, she was unlikely to be in any immediate danger, and I suppose I took some comfort from this fact. Also, Cassandra had got close enough to see that both her abductors had worn silver crosses around their necks, so the police were operating on the theory that a local Christian group had got carried away by all the fervour surrounding the sunsets. After Annemarie's call, Sheriff Dawson ordered the phone company to put a tap on our line. He told us to sit tight and wait for her to make contact again. As if we had some kind of choice, I thought. For the next few hours I sat there staring at the telephone, willing it to ring.

A little later Father Michael came by the house. Deacon

Joe answered the doorbell and I could hear them talking briefly, but before I had a chance to get to the front hall, Deacon Joe had dismissed him with a curt *we're-grateful-for-your-concern*. 'Joe, why didn't you ask him in?' demanded Ada after Deacon Joe returned to the kitchen.

'He offered to lead a prayer,' scoffed Deacon Joe. 'As if we were incapable of praying for ourselves!'

'And have you?' I asked, turning to him. He glared at me.

'Have I what?' he demanded.

'Have you prayed for Annemarie?' He hesitated for a split second, just long enough for me to know that he was about to commit a sin.

'Of course I have,' he said. 'And my prayers are worth ten of his!'

For my part I'd spent most of those first few hours frantically appealing to God. But over the course of the evening, my prayers had veered from desperate pleading into something closer to a diatribe. With this latest turn of events He'd pushed me too far, and I was angrier than I'd ever been. All my earlier concerns were instantly banished in the face of this new threat, and the idea that only a few weeks before I'd agonised over Annemarie's chastity seemed utterly ridiculous to me now. Later that night I finally left Ada and Joe to man the phones and walked out into the churchyard. It was a hot, muggy evening and the air smelled of bugs and newly cut grass. When I caught sight of the empty bench in the darkness my heart sank. Deacon Joe may not have needed the new curate, but I did, now more than ever. I sat down heavily on the bench and tried not to think of what was happening to Annemarie at that moment. I had to trust that we would find her, and that when we did she would be fine.

After a few minutes, I heard the noise of flip-flops and Father Michael's shape emerged out of the darkness. 'I was afraid I'd missed you,' I said when he reached the bench. He sat down and turned to me with concern.

'You should have knocked on the rectory door.'

'Thanks for coming by the house. I'm sorry about Deacon Joe.'

'Don't be. I'm sure you're all in shock. Is there any news?' I shook my head, unable to speak.

'They'll find her. Don't lose hope. She's a strong girl.'

'I know. But she's also blind. And she must be terrified.' I was on the verge of tears.

'Then we should pray for her, and we should offer her our strength.' So we sat there in the darkness and we prayed. And after awhile the stars appeared above us like a shimmering carpet of hope. And I knew somehow she'd heard us.

Annemarie

As Brendan picked up speed heading out of town, I was one-part terrified and two-parts flabbergasted. I couldn't help but wonder *what next?* Was being kidnapped by religious zealots part of God's plan, or was it some sort of divine practical joke? On top of that it was hard to know just how scared I should be. Could devout Christians really be that dangerous? I was still clutching the Virgin Mary snow globe tightly in my hand, and the thought occurred to me that it hadn't exactly been much help so far.

After we'd been on the road a few minutes, Brendan and Lilah seemed to relax, and Brendan assured me that I was safe. He apologised for manhandling me into the car, but added that they were under strict orders from Brother Carl not to return without me. Brendan's manner was polite but firm, and I felt vaguely reassured – but the fact remained, I'd still been shoved into the car against my will.

'So is it really just a meal we're going for?' I asked tentatively. They were both silent for a moment.

'Maybe you better ask Brother Carl,' Brendan said.

He explained that Brother Carl was Sacred Path's

founder, and from the tone of reverence they both used when speaking about him, the man was one tiny rung below God. On top of that he clearly didn't tolerate failure. Lilah explained that Brother Carl had only just returned from San Francisco, where he'd spent four weeks establishing a West Coast branch of Sacred Path. He'd also brought two new converts back with him, Noah and Sal, and I gathered that their introduction to the group had caused ripples of dissent. Noah and Sal were married but only in the loosest sense of the word, as both had quickly formed new friendships within the ministry. They were young, blonde and beautiful, and in the space of a few weeks, Brother Carl had elevated them from twigs to branches.

'I'm not even a branch,' said Lilah grumpily. 'And I've been with the fellowship two years.'

'You'll get there,' said Brendan.

'Are you a branch?' I asked him.

'Brendan's way beyond branch,' said Lilah. 'He's nearly a limb. That's one step below a trunk.'

'Sounds pretty hierarchical,' I said. Where did it all end, I wondered, with the Tree of Heaven?

'Actually it simplifies things,' said Lilah. 'It means you can track your spiritual progress through the ministry, so you know exactly where your place is.'

'Does that mean Brendan is in a more spiritual place than you are?'

Lilah hesitated; the question clearly stumped her.

'It means that I'm more spiritually *mature* than she is,' said Brendan carefully.

'Exactly,' said Lilah. Though she still sounded a little unsure.

We drove for an hour on fast roads, then eventually turned on to a gravel surface where we bumped along for a few minutes. Our destination must have been fairly remote, I decided, since anywhere close to civilisation would have been paved. When we arrived at the compound the track got even bumpier, and we had to go through a series of gates. 'How come there are so many gates?' I asked. 'Is it to keep people in or out?'

'Oh, we're free to leave if we wish. We just don't want to,' said Lilah innocently, with no apparent regard for my lack of freedom, but I decided not to push the point. Now that I'd come all this way I have to admit I was curious, so I decided I might as well break bread with Brother Carl. Anyway, I'd skipped lunch and I was starving. We eventually pulled onto grass and the car lurched to a halt.

'Here we are,' said Brendan. 'Welcome to Sacred Path. Brother Carl told us to notify him as soon as we returned.' They helped me out of the car and Brendan steered me across the grass and into a building. 'This is the fellowship barn. We take our meals here, and meet for prayer and Bible study. Have a seat and I'll let Brother Carl know you're here.' Brendan disappeared then, leaving Lilah alone with me. She seemed excited at the prospect of seeing Brother Carl.

'So what's he like?' I asked.

'Brother Carl? He's sort of a father figure, I guess. He's wise and strong and he understands things. Not just everyday things, but how to live and how to think and how to get closer to God.'

'Has Sacred Path brought you closer to God?' I asked.

'Sure,' she said, as if this was self-evident. Brendan returned a minute later with the news that Brother Carl was with a newcomer and would be with us shortly. 'He tries to witness every new convert personally,' said Lilah. 'He's very generous with his time.'

'Did he witness you?' I asked.

'Well, he wasn't here when I arrived. So no, not personally. But I'm sure he would have.'

Brendan went out again, promising to return in a few minutes.

'Do you think I could use your telephone?' I asked. 'To call home? It's just ... they might be worried.'

Lilah hesitated. 'We're not really encouraged to contact our flesh families.'

'Why not?'

'Because it's written.'

'What's written?

'In the New Testament. *Those who forsake their families will inherit everlasting life.*'

'Is that what Brother Carl says?'

'It's what the Bible says.'

It also says *honour thy father and thy mother*, I thought, but maybe that was splitting hairs. Clearly Lilah didn't have the authority to let me make a phone call; I would have to try again with Brendan. After all, he was a branch. I heard voices outside then and Lilah leaned over to me.

'They're coming. Um ... you might want to hide the snow globe,' she said quietly.

'Why?'

'Worshipping the Virgin Mary is a form of idolatry,' she whispered quickly. I stuffed the snow globe into the pocket of my sweatshirt, just as I heard footsteps enter the barn. I wasn't quite sure what was expected of me. Was I meant to kneel, or would Brother Carl be anticipating more of a salute? I was just about to ask Lilah when she whispered, 'He's here. Stand up.' I stood and Lilah moved my chair away slightly.

The footsteps stopped in front of me and I felt a warm, dark presence flood the room. His aura was both powerful and complicated, and the word that sprang to mind was *intoxicating.* He firmly clasped my hand in one of his, and I felt a strange tug of energy. But unlike Cassandra, whose spark seemed to flow right into me, Brother Carl's seemed to have the opposite effect. Somehow I felt the energy drain away.

'Annemarie. We're honoured to have you here with us.' His voice rolled out across the space, and like any good preacher's it was deep and resonant, and acutely conscious of its own power.

'This is Brother Carl, our founder and spiritual leader,' said Brendan.

'Pleased to meet you,' I said cautiously.

'The others failed to do you justice,' said Brother Carl. 'She has angelic looks, does she not, Brother Brendan?'

Brendan hesitated.

'She does,' he said a little uneasily.

'Leave us, please. Both of you.'

I listened as Brendan and Lilah left the room. Brother Carl had not even acknowledged Lilah and her disappointment hung heavily in the air. He still held my hand and now he placed the other on top, so mine was sandwiched in his grasp. 'Please sit down. I've been eager to speak with you,' he said. He released my hand and then pulled a second chair so close that when he sat our knees were practically touching. I found myself edging imperceptibly backwards. 'When did the Lord take your sight?' he asked.

'When I was five.'

'But I sense that he has endowed you with other gifts.'

'You mean the baby?'

'That and other things. Are the rumours true?'

'Well, I'm pregnant, if that's what you mean.'

'And the father?' he asked. I hesitated.

'That's more complicated.'

'So there is no father?'

'Not exactly, no.'

Brother Carl took a deep breath and sat right back in his chair. 'So,' he said. 'A virgin birth. The scriptures told of a second coming. But no one anticipated this.'

'Honestly, it's not like that,' I started to protest. 'It's really more about my chromosomes.' He silenced me by grabbing my hand, and I gave a little yip of surprise.

'Hush now,' he said. 'Those are malign spirits talking, and you must banish them at once. God works in mysterious ways, Annemarie. And now he's brought you here to me.'

Hang on, I thought crossly. *Brendan and Lilah brought me here, on your orders!* But I decided it would be unwise to point this out. 'Can I ask why I'm here?' I said instead.

'We were anxious to meet you. And even more anxious for you to meet us.'

'And when I've done that, will I be free to go?'

'We'd prefer you stay long enough to understand our mission. We hope that over time, with exposure to our doctrines, you might discover they appeal to you.'

'But I already belong to a church.'

'Sacred Path is much more than a church, Annemarie. We're a study fellowship of like-minded souls on a mission blessed by God. You and I are fortunate enough to be living in an age of grace. God designed the universe to support the earth, and the earth to support His children, who love God in return. And that's precisely what we're trying to do here at Sacred Path.'

'So you intend to keep me here?'

'We'd like you to be our guest,' said Brother Carl ambiguously. He rose to his feet then, and I could tell that the discussion was nearly finished.

'Can I at least call my family? And let them know I'm safe?' I asked quickly.

He paused. 'I think that could be arranged.'

So they let me ring Mama. After the meeting with Brother Carl, Brendan escorted me over to the ministry office. He warned me not to divulge any information about Sacred Path or its whereabouts (as if I knew that anyway) and cautioned me that I should only speak long enough to let her know I was OK. When Mama answered the phone, her voice sounded choked with worry, but as soon as she realised it was me, she gave a little cry of relief. I told her I was safe and that I'd be home soon, and just as she was asking where I was, Brendan reached over and hung up.

'Thanks,' I said to him sarcastically. The phone call was better than nothing, but it struck me that it might only serve to worry Mama more. Afterwards we walked back across the grass to the fellowship barn and as we approached I could hear the sounds of others joining us. It was a fine summer evening and the sun on the horizon was still strong enough to feel warm. When we reached the barn it was already beginning to fill. I sat at a table with Brendan and Lilah and several others, including Sal and Noah. 'Doesn't Brother Carl eat with you?' I asked.

'Only on special occasions,' said Lilah. 'He's too busy most of the time.'

'Doing what?'

'Research and writing. Not to mention running the ministry,' said Brendan.

'What do the rest of you do?'

'We study God's Word,' said Lilah. 'And contribute to fellowship life in different ways, by cooking or cleaning or fixing things. Some of us have jobs outside. Those who work outside tithe a portion of their income to the ministry.' Just then, I heard Sal push back her chair.

'Sorry to run, but I promised Brother Carl I'd give him a pedicure tonight. And he told me not to be late.' We sat

304

in silence as she picked up her plate and moved off. After a moment Lilah spoke under her breath.

'*Another* pedicure? How many is that this week?'

Brendan cleared his throat. 'Brother Carl says that what defiles a man is not what goes in, but what comes out of the body,' he said. 'Anyway Sal is very spiritually mature. I'm sure she can handle it.'

Handle what? I thought. His corns? Over the rest of dinner Lilah explained to me that newcomers to Sacred Path were required to do a course in Manifesting the Abundant Life. During the course they absorbed the Word, as interpreted by Brother Carl. Those who adhered to right beliefs would be rewarded with the good life, which meant that they would prosper and be free from sickness.

'So no one here is ever sick?' I asked a little dubiously. Lilah hesitated.

'Not in any way you'd notice,' she said.

'What Lilah means is that we may briefly experience illness,' said Brendan. 'But we're quickly cured by God.'

After dinner we all gathered for Bible study. I discovered that the Old Testament was off limits, as were the Gospels, but that the Word according to Brother Carl could be found in the remaining parts of the New Testament. Brendan led the group but instead of reading aloud from the scriptures, much of what he said seemed to be Brother Carl's interpretation of the passages. We listened as Brendan explained that the soul is the body's life force, but only those who adhere to God's Word are granted what Brother Carl called the 'holy spirit'. Those outside the ministry were like animals without souls; they couldn't be trusted. If followers did not faithfully adhere to His Word, terrible things would befall them. Like being kidnapped? I wanted to ask. For most of an hour we listened to Brendan speak. He was earnest and compelling, if not exactly charismatic, and I was struck by the fact that no one else said a word. No one asked a question, nor did they comment upon his teachings. When we finished, Lilah and I walked back alone to her dormitory and she seemed quieter than before. 'Does anyone else talk at meetings?' I asked.

'We're not encouraged to speak during them,' she said. 'We're told to save our questions until the end. But no one ever has any, because the Word is designed to answer all our questions,' she added.

'Well, Brendan certainly was convincing.'

'God's Word is convincing,' she corrected me. 'But you're right. Brendan explains it better than just about anyone. Until I heard him speak, I wasn't really sure about Sacred Path. But it was Brendan who swayed me in the end.' She went quiet again, and I decided that Lilah's regard for Brendan might go beyond the spiritual, though I wasn't sure it was reciprocated. I hadn't noticed that he'd paid her any particular attention over the course of the evening; if anything, he'd treated her with a sort of cold formality that didn't bode well. When we reached the dormitory Lilah showed me to a tiny bedroom along a corridor with several others. 'Don't worry, I'll be right next door if you need anything,' she said. 'After meetings we usually retire to our rooms for a *duo*. That's the word we use for one-on-one time with God. One of the great things about Sacred Path is that you're never alone,' she added.

Ironically, by the time she left me I was desperate to be on my own. Being shoved into the back of a car had been stressful and frightening, but listening to God's Word all evening had proved utterly exhausting, and the sooner I was *solo* the better. After Lilah had gone I lay down on the bed and tried not to worry about Mama and the others at home. Mama would be beside herself by now, and even though I'd done my best to sound calm and reassuring on the phone, I knew the call would only inflame her worst fears. And Lord only knew what was going through Ethan's head. He'd have imagined me into all sorts of atrocities. I reached into my sweatshirt pocket and my fingers closed upon the snow globe, clutching it tightly. I wasn't sure the Virgin Mary was on my side at this point, but I still found the smooth weight of the glass in my hand reassuring. One way or another, I'd have to find a way to persuade Brother Carl that Sacred Path was not right for me, nor me for it. And if I couldn't do *that*, then I would have to find a way out.

Ethan

Sheriff Dawson and Father Michael helped me down from the window of the Sacristy. In truth, I sort of fell into their arms. 'Jesus Christ, Ethan!' Sheriff Dawson grunted as he struggled to set me upright on the ground. 'You smell like a distillery! Are you drunk?'

'Maybe a little,' I admitted. I looked up at him and he tilted alarmingly. For a moment I thought I was going to be sick.

'What the hell were you doing in the Sacristy?' he demanded. I hesitated, looking from him to Father Michael and back again, their faces blurry with concern. I couldn't very well tell them I'd been watching the Virgin Mary *glow*.

'I was praying,' I said. 'For Annemarie.' Sheriff Dawson gave a sigh and shook his head. I turned to Father Michael. 'I'm sorry, Father. I think I might have broken one of your cruets.'

'Not to worry, Ethan. I'll take care of it,' he said kindly.

'All right, son, let's get you home,' said Sheriff Dawson, taking my arm.

'Do I have to? I mean ... can't I just go back to the tent?' I asked, alarmed at the prospect of facing my parents. Sheriff

Dawson exchanged a look with Father Michael.

'I don't think so, Ethan,' he said, shaking his head. 'Not in your current state.'

'Isn't there somewhere else I could go?' I asked. 'Please?' I really did not want my parents to see me drunk. Sheriff Dawson paused for a moment, then sighed.

'I guess we could scare up an alternative.'

So they let me spend the night in jail. Which sounds like a punishment, but in fact it was more of a kindness. After three weeks in a tent, the jail cell was surprisingly comfortable: cool and dark, with a nice cot and clean bedding. And it was far quieter than the wayside shrine. Sheriff Dawson even left the door unlocked, after making me promise I'd stay put. 'But if we catch any *real* criminals, you'll have to go home,' he warned, shaking his head. This seemed pretty unlikely, as by then it was nearly two in the morning. Sheriff Dawson left me in the care of a deputy and I fell into a deep sleep. But my whisky-fuelled dreams were still tormented with images of Annemarie. In one she came to me dressed as a nun, and when I tried to ask her where she was, she just smiled and shook her head, raising her finger to her lips.

When I woke up in the morning my mouth tasted of sour moss and it felt like someone had taken a mallet to the back of my head. I lay there in the cell, pain zigzagging around my skull, and listened to Sheriff Dawson on the phone in the next room. After a minute I heard him finish the call so I got up and went down the hall, pausing in the doorway to his office. He glanced up at me and shook his head. 'You look like hell, Ethan.'

'I'm sorry for all the trouble,' I said apologetically. He stood up and walked over to a filing cabinet, pulling out a folder.

'Comes with the territory,' he said, shutting the drawer and sitting back down.

'Is there any news about Annemarie?'

'I'm afraid not,' he said. 'But she's out there somewhere. And we'll find her.'

I nodded, my throat tightening.

'I spoke to your folks this morning. Just gave them the bare bones of the story. I suggest you flesh it out for them yourself. When you're up to it.' He flashed me a sympathetic smile.

'OK,' I said. I guess it was too much to expect him not to call them.

'Ethan, did Annemarie ever mention any contact she'd had with other religious groups? Apart from her own Church?'

'No, sir,' I said. 'Not that I can think of.'

He frowned. 'Was she unhappy with the Church in any way?'

I hesitated. Annemarie had definitely experienced a crisis of faith after all that business with Father O'Shea. But I couldn't see how that could be connected to the kidnapping. 'She had her ups and downs,' I said finally. 'But I don't think she would have gone looking for God somewhere else, if that's what you mean.'

He nodded thoughtfully. 'Well, let me know if anything occurs to you,' he said. Another phone call came through just then and he waved me away. I left the police station and walked out into the morning sunshine. The town seemed strangely quiet, as if it was holding its breath, waiting for Annemarie's return. But as I walked home, I wondered whether I'd been completely honest with Sheriff Dawson about her faith. The truth was Annemarie was fully capable of setting out on her own search for God. And who knew *where* it might take her.

When I got home I found my mom and dad at the kitchen table waiting for me, drinking what was probably their hundredth cup of coffee. Mom jumped up and pulled me into a hug, while my dad leaned over and riffled my hair. 'Thank goodness you're OK,' Mom said, releasing me. I looked at her sheepishly.

'I guess you guys spoke with Sheriff Dawson, huh?' I asked.

My dad nodded, raising an eyebrow. 'Sounds like you had a busy night,' he said.

'I'm sorry. I didn't plan it. It just sort of ... happened.'

'Well, it's good to know it wasn't premeditated,' said Mom philosophically.

'We certainly hope you're not planning on a *career* of breaking and entering,' said my dad.

I winced. If they only knew, I thought.

'Ethan, we know you're worried about Annemarie,' said Mom. 'But getting drunk won't bring her back.'

'I know. I know. It was stupid. *I* was stupid.'

My dad laid a hand on my shoulder. 'We all act stupid sometimes, son. If we didn't, the world would be boring.' My mom threw him a funny look and he shrugged. 'What?' he said defensively. 'No one likes perfection.'

'Thanks, Dad.'

'No more alcohol, Ethan,' said Mom, turning back to me and waggling a finger.

'OK.'

'Not until she's found, anyway,' said Dad. 'Then we'll open some champagne. Or at the very least, a six-pack.'

Afterwards I went upstairs and lay on my bed. I felt hollow, as if someone had scooped out my insides and thrown them away. Annemarie had been gone less than twenty-four hours, and already it seemed like an eternity. I stared up at the ceiling and for the first time wondered what would happen if she wasn't found. I realised that my life in Jericho depended almost solely on her presence, on her ability to interpret and explain the world around me. Nothing in Jericho made sense without Annemarie – as if the town itself was some kind of secret code that only she could decipher. I closed my eyes and pleaded with the Virgin Mary one more time. If she could glow, then she could bring Annemarie back to Jericho.

Eva

Once word got out about Annemarie's disappearance, the town rallied round. That first morning we had a steady stream of visitors offering sympathy and foil-wrapped plates, with the result that by late afternoon the fridge was piled high. I knew they meant well, but I still found it exasperating. Anyone who's ever had a child abducted knows that food is not exactly a top priority. 'When all else fails, bake a casserole,' said Ada after the ninth Pyrex dish was dropped off. Deacon Joe was the main beneficiary of all this generosity, working his way through an entire chicken pot pie at lunchtime. 'Joe, how can you eat at a time like this?' said Ada, raising a sceptical eyebrow.

'The Lord would not want all this good food to go to waste,' he said staunchly. 'Besides, how do you expect us to find Annemarie if we are faint with hunger?'

'I don't expect *you* to find her at all,' said Ada.

My own stomach was knotted up like a rubber band. We'd had no more contact since that first phone call, either from Annemarie or her captors, and there'd been only a smattering of information from the house-to-house enquiries, none of which added up to much. Sheriff Dawson turned up late in the afternoon looking exhausted. He came in and sat down at the kitchen table with a sigh, and I got the sudden sense that Annemarie's disappearance might be pushing him beyond his capabilities.

'I'm afraid we've been chasing dead ends most of the day,' he said, shaking his head. 'There was a young woman meeting Annemarie's description spotted on a bus headed for Chicago early this morning, but when the Illinois authorities intercepted it, she turned out to be sighted. We also got word this afternoon that the green Pontiac was registered to an address over near Muncie, but when the local police went to check out the property, it appeared to be abandoned.'

My heart sank when I heard this piece of news. 'So that's a dead end?' I asked.

'Afraid so. Though I may drive over there myself tomorrow, just to double-check. In the meantime, I'd like you all to have a look at this.' He pulled a sheaf of papers out of his briefcase and threw it on the table. I leaned forward to take a look. It was a list of religious cults that included everything from the Moonies to Druids, and it made me feel ill just to look at it. Sheriff Dawson wanted to know if anything on the list looked familiar.

'Familiar how?' asked Deacon Joe doubtfully.

'Maybe Annemarie mentioned one of these groups, or possibly had some contact with them?' Sheriff Dawson suggested.

Deacon Joe harrumphed. 'That is *highly* unlikely,' he pronounced, picking up the list. 'Annemarie is far too level-headed to take up with some cult.'

We sat in silence for a minute, passing the sheets around the table. The list was annotated with brief descriptions of each group and ran to several pages, and it made for sobering reading. One group worshipped comets, another extraterrestrials, and a third believed the Gospels positively encouraged snake-handling in church. An uncomfortably large number had funny ideas about sex, including a group that instructed its followers to imagine they were sleeping with Jesus himself, irrespective of their gender.

'Are these for real?' Deacon Joe asked finally. He was holding the last page at arm's length, like it was some sort of dead vermin.

'I'm afraid so,' said Sheriff Dawson.

'Where did this list come from?' asked Ada cautiously.

'FBI headquarters in Washington. These are just the ones known to be operating in the Midwest. The national list is twice this long.'

'Is the FBI helping you with the search?' I asked. If so, this was news to us. Sheriff Dawson hesitated.

'Not exactly. The FBI is unwilling to get involved at this stage. You have to appreciate that scores of young people run away each week, and many of them hook up with religious groups. I'm afraid they don't regard this as a case of kidnapping. Not yet, at any rate.'

'You mean they think she ran away of her own accord?' I asked.

'They suggested as much.'

'But she was shoved into the back of a Pontiac!'

'A pious seventeen year old heading off in a car with other Christians?' he said. 'Plus the fact that she made contact with you so quickly and easily. All of this puts her disappearance in a different category, at least in their eyes.'

'Annemarie did not run off to join some half-crazed Christian cult!' said Deacon Joe.

'I appreciate that,' said Sheriff Dawson. 'And I promise you we're doing everything within our power to locate her.'

'Well, you're not doing enough or you'd have found her by now!'

'Joe!' said Ada, reaching over to take his hand. She gave it a squeeze of warning and he frowned.

'The FBI also suggested we investigate Annemarie's links to her own Church,' Sheriff Dawson said. For a moment there was an uneasy silence.

'You mean the Catholic Church?' asked Deacon Joe in a stunned tone.

'It's been known to happen,' said Sheriff Dawson with a shrug. 'Sometimes teenagers make contact with fringe elements, either through youth groups, or outreach ministries from other states.'

'Well, that takes us from the sublime to the ridiculous,' said Deacon Joe, slapping the table. 'Fringe elements? There's no such thing within the Catholic Church! We are wasting our time if we are pointing the finger at ourselves! No wonder she's still out there.' He shook his head and Sheriff Dawson shifted awkwardly in his chair. I had to admit I agreed with Deacon Joe on this point. The idea that our own Church had spirited her away seemed pretty far-fetched.

'Nonetheless, I think I better have a word with both your priest and the head of the diocese. Just to cover all the bases,' Sheriff Dawson said.

'Fine,' snapped Deacon Joe. 'You'll find the new curate over in the rectory, though I warn you he's barely out of training wheels. I'll telephone the Vicar General in the morning. I'm sure he'll be only too happy to speak to you,' he added, his eyes flashing. 'But while you're at it you should be talking to those crackpot doctors up in Cleveland! They've got more of a vested interest in Annemarie than just about anyone.'

'Joe, I don't see how they could be involved,' said Ada with a frown.

'Why not? You think doctors don't commit crimes? May I remind you that doctors are scientists, and scientists are completely devoid of scruples!'

'I'm sure the doctors would be willing to cooperate,' I said quickly to Sheriff Dawson. 'If you like, I can give them a call.'

'I'd appreciate that,' he said, flashing me a look of gratitude. 'In fact, I'm inclined to call a town meeting tomorrow afternoon for everyone who had contact with Annemarie over the past few weeks. If we can get everybody in a room together, maybe it'll bring to light some new information. Jog somebody's memory.'

'It's worth a try,' I said half-heartedly. Though I wasn't sure what we'd learn.

After he'd shown Sheriff Dawson out, Deacon Joe stormed back into the kitchen. 'The man's incompetent,' he said, sitting down heavily in a chair. 'He couldn't find his way out of a paper bag!'

'I'm sure he's trying his best,' said Ada.

'That is scant comfort!' Deacon Joe picked up the list of religious cults and shook his head. 'They should exterminate the entire bunch of them,' he said, waving the pages in disgust. 'Looney-tunes, every one!'

'That's a little harsh,' said Ada. 'I'm sure some of these groups are perfectly harmless.'

'They aren't harmless if they claim to speak the truth,' he said.

I turned to him. 'Can *anyone* really claim to speak the truth?' I asked.

Deacon Joe frowned.

'Seriously,' I said. 'Does the Catholic Church have a monopoly on truth?'

'God has a monopoly on truth.'

'And the Catholic Church speaks for God? Always?'

Deacon Joe narrowed his gaze at me. 'What's got into you?' he asked suspiciously. 'You are not yourself.'

'Joe, that's enough!' said Ada, glancing at me a little uneasily.

'Nothing's got into me,' I said flatly. 'I just think it's time we faced the fact that *none* of us has all the answers. Not even the Church.'

Deacon Joe and I glared at each other across the table, squaring off like angry halfbacks, but he held his tongue. 'I need a drink,' said Ada, standing up and reaching into the cupboard.

'Make mine a double,' said Deacon Joe sourly. Ada took out a bottle of bourbon and turned to me, holding it up. I shook my head.

'You should get some rest,' she said with concern. I stood up.

'What I need is fresh air.'

This time I went straight to the rectory door. When Father Michael opened it, his expression creased with sympathy. He opened the door wider to invite me in but I shook my head. 'Can we sit outside?' I asked. I needed the sky and the cool of the evening to calm me down.

'Of course,' he said. We retraced my steps across the grass and parked ourselves on the bench. 'Is there any news?' he asked.

'Not really. Nothing of consequence, at any rate. But I may well murder your deacon before this is all over.'

He laughed out loud and I smiled, in spite of myself. 'His views can be trying,' Father Michael admitted. 'But I suspect his heart is in the right place.'

'Really? I suspect his arteries are clogged with certainty.'

'Well, he's not alone in that respect.'

'No, he is not,' I agreed with a sigh.

'So Annemarie hasn't managed to make contact again?'

I shook my head, suddenly unable to speak. For those few minutes my anger at Deacon Joe had eclipsed my fears for Annemarie, but now they surged up again within me like a dark swell. Father Michael reached over and took my hand. His grip was warm and solid and reassuring, and I clung to it like a lifeline. It did more to comfort me than any words he might have spoken, and once again, I wondered how he knew.

Annemarie

That first morning at Sacred Path, Lilah knocked on my door
while I was still half asleep and asked if I wanted to come
along to target practice. Actually she didn't give me a choice.
'Brendan said to keep you with me today, so hope you like
guns,' she said cheerfully. 'Guess you won't be able to shoot,
but you can still keep me company at the rifle range.' Over
a quick breakfast of pancakes in the fellowship barn, Lilah
explained that she and Brendan and the others were all part
of Sacred Path's Martial Corps. Brother Carl believed in the
discipline and rigour of military training, and any student
who reached the advanced stage of the course was required
to learn survival techniques, as well as how to shoot a gun.

'Why guns?' I asked. 'Who would you need to shoot?'

'Who knows? But better safe than sorry,' she said.

As we walked over to the training grounds I asked Lilah
how she first got involved with Sacred Path. 'I sort of slipped
in sideways,' she explained. 'I was living over in Fort Wayne,
working at a dry cleaner's by day and going to secretarial
college at night, and one day I met a recruiter on campus.
His name was Jason and he was just about the nicest person

I ever came across. He invited me to a home fellowship study group, and before I knew it I had a whole new set of friends. Over the next few months they showered me with love and I was hooked. These days I understand the principle behind it. Sacred Path does that to all its new recruits. We *lovebomb* them until they can't say no.'

'Isn't that a little bit like Hansel and Gretel?'

'I'm not sure I follow.'

'Well, you know, luring people in with the promise of candy and sweets?'

Lilah turned to me and laid a hand on my arm, bringing me to a halt.

'Oh, no,' she said solemnly. 'Sacred Path isn't a false promise. Our love is totally real.'

So was the candy, I thought.

'We're not trying to dupe anybody,' she continued. 'If you join Sacred Path, you'll be surrounded by love and fellowship, and God will look after you until the day you die.'

Or you might get shot, I thought.

When we reached the rifle range Lilah handed me a pair of ear mufflers. 'Guns can make your ears ring like church bells if you don't wear these,' she warned. She was right. For the next hour I stood in the back while she and several others shot at targets. There was an instructor called Travis who moved among them correcting errors in posture and technique, and whenever anybody got a bullseye he'd shout: '*Looks like we got a shooter!*' I spent most of the hour thinking about how I would escape. I'd already learned as much as I cared to about Sacred Path and its doctrines. The crux of their belief system seemed to centre on Jesus, and whether he was an actual representative of God or just a sinless man who was conceived as a result of some kind of divine genetic engineering. According to what I'd gleaned from Lilah, Brother Carl really had it in for Jesus. He'd published a book called *God, Not Jesus*, and maintained that Jesus was crucified on an upright tree rather than a cross. Maybe that explained the tree obsession, I decided, but the whole argument struck me as kind of petty.

After target practice there were chores to do. Lilah worked in the laundry, so we spent a few hours hanging and folding sheets and towels, then walked back to the fellowship barn for lunch. Over lunch I heard Lilah casually ask one of the others where Brendan was, and I could sense her disappointment when she learned that he'd already eaten and gone. She explained to me that afternoons were taken up with classes and individual study, and although I'd been hoping for some *solo* time in my room, Lilah clearly had other ideas. She dragged me along to a two-hour Advanced Abundance class, in which we were exhorted to banish something called the *Spirit of Strife*, a sort of devil-spirit that prevented you from completely absorbing the Word. The class touched on several other devil-spirits, some of which struck me as pretty obvious (jealousy, fear) and some of which just seemed plain bizarre (masochism, cancer). The truth is I dozed off in the end, and only woke when the class applauded the teacher at the finish. As we walked back from class, Lilah informed me that I had another meeting scheduled with Brother Carl. She struggled to keep the envy from her voice, and I decided that she hadn't completely succeeded in banishing her devil-spirits.

On the way over to Brother Carl's caravan we bumped into Brendan. He asked us how the day had gone, but seemed distracted when Lilah tried to answer. His aura was angry, and I wasn't surprised when he cut her off and excused himself. Once again I could taste her dismay. 'Brendan sometimes has issues with Brother Carl,' she said quietly as we carried on walking.

'Really? But he seems so committed to Sacred Path.'

'Oh, he is. It's just that he's not so committed to Brother Carl. I'm not sure what they clash over. But he's usually in a bad mood when he comes back from meetings.' We arrived at Brother Carl's caravan and Lilah knocked on the door. A young woman answered and said that Brother Carl would see me shortly. Lilah and I waited outside for a few minutes until she returned.

'He's ready now,' the woman said. 'You don't need to wait,' she said to Lilah a little dismissively. 'I'll make sure she gets back to the dorm.' Lilah hesitated for an instant.

'Fine,' she said in a clipped voice.

Unlike Brendan, Brother Carl seemed in good spirits. He welcomed me warmly and invited me to sit, then deposited himself next to me on the sofa with a jarring bounce. He asked whether I'd enjoyed my day, and I told him I preferred the smell of clean laundry to that of gunpowder. He guffawed and laid a hand on my knee, leaning in a little too close. 'And this afternoon's class? What did you learn?' he asked. I cast my mind back to the devil-spirits, wondering what, if anything, I'd taken away from the lesson.

'I was interested in the idea of renewing your mind,' I said finally.

'That is vitally important, if you're going to keep within God's Word.'

'The teacher said we shouldn't be afraid to confront those who stray from Sacred Path's doctrines.'

'That is correct. We challenge all errant followers.'

'So there's no dissent within the ministry?'

'None whatsoever,' he said without hesitation. 'We eliminate it at the source.'

'How?'

'Those who stray from our beliefs are asked to leave,' he said simply.

Wouldn't that include me? I thought. But I sensed that my position was a little more complicated. 'I was impressed by Brendan last night,' I said instead.

'Brother Brendan is one of our outstanding young recruits. He'll make a fine minister one day.'

'He seemed a little upset when we bumped into him a few minutes ago, though,' I added. Brother Carl chuckled.

'Brendan's temperamental. And sometimes a little too serious. He needs to loosen up a little, and enjoy the fruit of God's abundance!'

He had a point. Brendan did seem a little stiff. But just then Brother Carl shifted closer to me, and the pressure on my knee increased. Suddenly I felt a little like a ripe melon. 'Would it be all right if I telephoned my family again?' I asked. He pulled back.

'So soon?'

'They're prone to worry.'

'Annemarie, you may not realise it, but we brought you here for a purpose,' he said, his tone suddenly serious.

'Which is?'

'Before you leave us, I need you to understand that while your baby may be divinely conceived, he himself is not divine.'

Oh, Lordie! I thought. So that was it! 'I never said it was,' I said emphatically.

'*You* may not have. But in the months to come, others will. It is vitally important that you, his mother, know and speak out the truth.'

Brother Carl's tone was suddenly as hard as flint, and I got a glimpse of how an apparently ordinary man had managed to corral so many followers. This was all about

Jesus upstaging God, I realised, and Brother Carl wasn't about to let history repeat itself. 'I understand,' I told him.

'Good,' he said.

'Can I go home now?' I asked.

He drew back from me a little.

'Why don't you give Sacred Path a little more time?' he said resolutely.

That evening after supper we all assembled for a concert. For the first half hour we listened to a choir sing a fairly traditional selection of hymns, but then a blues band called Brother Sammy and the Disciples came on, and the mood in the barn suddenly lifted. Brother Sammy's first song was a raucous number called 'Ain't No Blues Within the Word'. The entire crowd erupted over this song, with people whooping and clapping and noisily demanding more. Brother Sammy obliged with another song called 'Red Hot Gospels', and everyone leaped up to dance.

Lilah leaned over and asked whether I minded if she joined in, and I told her to go right ahead. While everyone was dancing I decided to tap my way over to the latrines, whose location I'd pretty well memorised, but once outside I got a little disoriented and ended up over by the office. I was about to retrace my steps when I heard the sound of a door shutting, then a deep male voice about ten feet behind me.

'Not a fan of the blues?' said Brother Carl in a jovial tone. I stopped and turned around to face him.

'No, the blues are just fine,' I said. 'But dancing with a stick's a little awkward.'

'No right-thinking man would let you partner with a stick,' he said, stepping closer. He grabbed my hand and pulled me to him, placing his other hand in the small of my back, and then began to shuffle me around in time to the music that came wafting across the grass. As he did he pulled me right up against him, so that our bodies were touching. I could smell his aftershave, not to mention what he'd eaten for dinner.

'I'm not really much of a dancer,' I said awkwardly, straining to pull away

'Relax,' he breathed into my ear. 'God wants you to enjoy life. He wants you to grab hold of it and revel in it!' Just then I felt his right hand drop down to my bottom and give it a squeeze. I was so astonished that I yelped and Brother Carl responded with a deep, throaty chuckle. He tightened his grip on me and again spoke into my ear. 'The Word separates body and spirit, Annemarie. God doesn't care what we do with our bodies, as long as our minds are pure and our hearts are in fellowship.'

Just then I heard footsteps approaching, and Brother Carl must have heard them too because he stopped dancing and stepped away from me slightly, turning towards the sound. 'Brother Brendan,' he called out. 'Why aren't you enjoying the concert with the others?'

'I've got some work to do on the accounts,' said Brendan crisply.

'You see, Annemarie? God's work is never done,' said Brother Carl. 'By all means, carry on,' he said to Brendan. For an instant no one moved.

'Annemarie, Lilah's looking for you,' said Brendan, his tone cool.

'I should get back to the barn,' I said quickly.

'I'll take you to her,' said Brendan. He stepped forward and took my arm, steering me away from Brother Carl.

'Good night, Annemarie. Keep your head in the Word,' called Brother Carl. He sounded bemused, and completely unfazed by being caught with red-hot hands. Brendan was silent while he frogmarched me back to the barn, but I could tell he was fuming. I didn't know if he was angry with me or Brother Carl or us both. When we got closer to the barn I suddenly heard Lilah's voice.

'There you are!' she said with relief. 'I wondered where you'd got to!'

'You were meant to stay with her,' said Brendan tersely.

'I only left her for a second,' she protested.

'Well, it was a second too long! Take her back to the dorm,' he said, before releasing my arm.

Once he'd gone, Lilah said to me in a low voice, 'Thanks for that.'

'I'm sorry,' I said. 'I only went to find the bathroom.'

'Next time, ask.' We walked back in silence to the dorm. Lilah was sulking, and for my part I was feeling newly alarmed by the prospect of having to fend off Brother Carl's advances. Exposure to Sacred Path's doctrines clearly meant more than I'd realised. I needed to find a way out of here fast, I decided, or soon I might find myself in red-hot fellowship with Brother Carl.

I fell asleep clutching the Virgin Mary snow globe, but I slept badly. I dreamed of Brother Carl's hands, except they weren't human, they were hairy gorilla hands, and there were several pairs, grabbing and revelling in all of me at once. When I woke it was early morning and the dorm was eerily quiet. For a few minutes I considered simply walking down the track we'd driven in on, but without being able to see, I knew I wouldn't get very far. The thought irritated me. I'd lived so long without vision that it rarely presented me with an obstacle, much less an impossibility. But here I was, being held hostage not just by Sacred Path, but by my blindness – and for the first time in ages I felt truly disabled. I lay in bed and considered my options. And then I did the only other thing that I could think of: I prayed.

It wasn't easy. I was no stranger to prayer, but I wasn't in the habit of knocking on God's door for help. Prayer for me had always been more of a meditation than a plea. It was a time when I tried to insert myself into the vastness of the universe, and rid myself of everything that was small-minded and trivial. I didn't ask God *for* things, I asked to be *with* Him, if only for a few moments. For me, prayer was all about escaping the here and now and finding my own quiet corner of grace. I'd always thought that it was blindness that made me both stubbornly independent (and therefore unwilling to beseech God for help) and, at the same time, more receptive to His presence. Blindness taught me how to listen, and how to search between the cracks for transcendence. Had I not lost my sight, I doubt if I would have had the patience for faith – I don't think I could have sat still long enough to hear the whisperings. So I had God to thank for my blindness, and blindness to thank for God. But lying in bed that morning, I realised that I might have to do things a little differently if I was going to escape from Sacred Path. For the first time in ages, I would have to call in a favour. So I swallowed my pride, and I asked God to help me find a way back to Jericho.

When Lilah came to collect me for breakfast, she still seemed upset. We ate apple-cinnamon oatmeal in silence then made our way over to laundry detail. On the way across the parking lot Brendan shouted and ran to catch up with us. Lilah turned to face him hopefully, and I could feel her spirits lift a little. Maybe he was going to apologise for being short with her, I thought. But instead he told us that Brother Carl was sending him to Marysville for the day to deal with a house fellowship that was in crisis. 'Are you coming back this evening?' Lilah asked, a hint of anxiety creeping into her voice.

'I'm not sure yet,' he said evasively.

'But ... what about Annemarie?'

'Just keep her with you. Take her to class this afternoon.'

'Can't she go with you to Marysville?' asked Lilah. Suddenly I felt like an unruly toddler that both parents wanted to offload.

'Look, if it's a problem, I'm really happy to go home,' I said quickly. 'Just drop me off at a bus stop in Defiance.' They both hesitated.

'Just keep her with you, Lilah,' Brendan said with a sigh. 'Don't leave her alone, OK? Not with *anyone*,' he added pointedly. He walked off and I felt my stomach curl with dread. Brendan clearly didn't trust Brother Carl either. While Lilah and I folded sheets, I decided that I wasn't in a position to wait for God to rescue me.

'Brendan can be kind of moody, huh?' I asked.

'You said it,' she said grumpily.

'How well do you know him?'

'As well as anyone.'

'Has he been here a while?'

'Three years.'

'And is he on his own?'

'What do you mean?'

'You know. Does he have a girlfriend?'

She hesitated, then snapped a sheet loudly. 'No.'

'What about you?'

'What *about* me?'

'Well, I thought maybe you and Brendan ... had something going.' Lilah stopped working and I could feel her eyes on me. I heard her swallow.

'We used to. Sort of.'

'What happened?'

'The Word happened,' she said bitterly.

'What do you mean?'

'As soon as Brendan became a branch, he lost interest in everything except God.'

'So does he always treat you like that?'

'Like what?' she asked suspiciously.

'Like he knows you'll do exactly what he says.'

'He's a branch. I'm only a twig. I'm *supposed* to do exactly what he says.'

'So you don't mind?' Once again there was a pause.

'Of course I mind,' she said finally.

'I'm sorry. It's none of my business,' I apologised. I waited, and soon Lilah's confusion was swirling around us like dust motes. She carried on folding towels in silence, but I could sense that I had nudged something deep inside her. After we finished the laundry we walked slowly back across the car park. Lilah seemed like she was on the verge of speaking. Finally, just before we reached the fellowship barn, she stopped.

'Look, I want you to know that Brendan respects me,' she said. 'I know he does. He just doesn't always show it.'

'OK,' I said cautiously. 'I believe you.'

'Why do you think it was *me* he asked to help bring you back from Jericho?' she asked. 'He could have asked a dozen others, but he chose me because he knew that he could trust me.'

'Are you sure that's why?'

'Of course I'm sure.'

'It's just ... I would have said that he chose you because he knew you wouldn't challenge him.'

'What do you mean?'

'You wouldn't question whether kidnapping was right or wrong,' I said.

'We didn't kidnap you!' she said with horror. 'We just ... borrowed you.'

'Lilah, I don't know what Brendan and Brother Carl told

330

you, but I'm not here because I want to be.' She didn't reply, but her doubt was now palpable. 'On top of that, it's a *crime*,' I added.

'Well, I don't know what you expect me to do,' she muttered angrily. She turned and walked off and I followed her into lunch. We sat at a table with Sal and Noah and a few of the others, but Lilah didn't say a word. After we'd got our food, Noah turned to me.

'So, how long are you planning to stay with us, Annemarie?' he asked in a conversational tone. I stopped chewing and felt my face colour. Clearly Lilah wasn't the only one who'd been misled about the nature of my visit. I could sense all of them waiting for my answer.

'I'm not sure,' I said. Suddenly Lilah spoke up.

'Annemarie can stay as long as she likes,' she said. Her voice seemed a little too loud, as if she was broadcasting just to me. 'She's our guest,' she added. I frowned. What exactly did that mean? After lunch was over, I waited until we were alone, then stopped her.

'Lilah, did you mean what you said back there?' I asked. 'About me?'

'Sure,' she said.

'So it's up to me how long I stay?' I asked.

'Annemarie, despite what you think, you're not a prisoner here. You can leave whenever you like.' Her voice wobbled slightly, stretched to almost breaking point by pride and false bravado. I swallowed, my heart skipping a little.

'Can I go now?' I said.

Lilah didn't drive, so I persuaded her to walk me out towards the main road, where I reassured her that I could hitch a ride back towards Jericho. In truth, the prospect of hitchhiking terrified me. Who knew what crazy idiot might come along?

331

On top of that, if Mama found out I'd hitchhiked home, she'd skin me alive. But it was better than spending another night within striking distance of Brother Carl, I decided. We started down the long track, but after a few minutes Lilah grew edgy. 'We better pick up the pace,' she said into my ear, urging me forward so fast I nearly stumbled. After another minute, I heard a car in the distance and Lilah suddenly slowed, drawing a breath. 'Uh-oh,' she said ominously.

'What is it?' I asked. She didn't answer but came to a halt as the car drew near, her hand squeezing my forearm tightly.

'Let me do the talking,' she said under her breath. I heard the car stop just beside us.

'Hey,' called out Brendan from inside. My stomach lurched.

'Hey,' said Lilah uneasily. 'You're back early.'

'Yeah. It was no big deal. Roommate stuff really. Where you guys headed?'

'Just ... out for a walk,' she said a little awkwardly.

'Now?' he asked doubtfully. 'Class starts in ten minutes.'

Lilah hesitated, and my heart skipped a beat. 'Guess we lost track of time,' she said then, her voice deflated.

'Jump in,' said Brendan. 'I'll give you a lift back.' I heard Lilah suck in a deep breath, and for an instant I thought she might defy him.

'Sure,' she said. 'That would be great.'

Ethan

The night after I got caught drunk in the Sacristy, my parents insisted I sleep at home. I guess they'd put up with a lot over the previous few weeks, and were trying to minimise any more surprises. Truthfully, a part of me was grateful. I wasn't sure I could deal with the Virgin Mary any more, even if she *did* choose to appear again by the wayside shrine. I suppose, after all I'd been through, I no longer trusted her. I woke to the sound of pigeons fluttering outside my window, and the realisation that Annemarie was still missing. I lay there, my mind flicking back over the past two years. I thought about the first time we'd met, when she'd teased me in the church basement after Mass, and the first time I'd tutored her in math, when I taught her about perfect numbers. I remembered our terrible date to Wilson Creek Park, and the basketball game against the Longhorns, when she'd practically strangled me with excitement. And for what must have been the trillionth time, I thought about the day I'd kissed her in her bedroom. Even after all these months, I could still feel the heat of her lips on mine, and the soft bend of her waist in my hands. That memory was like a painful wound, torn open again and again.

But so much had happened since then. I realised now that the two people who'd kissed in that room no longer existed. We'd changed, both Annemarie and I. For better or worse, Jericho had altered us for good.

Eventually the smell of frying bacon drove me from my bed. I was scheduled to work at the gas station later that morning, and even though I was exhausted, I was grateful for the distraction. When I got to work, Gabe came out from under a jacked-up Chevy and came over to me, clamping his hands on my shoulders. 'Keep the faith, Ethan,' he said, looking me in the eye. 'Shona sends her prayers, too.' I nodded and we both went to work. Just before noon I heard the gas pumps ring and turned to see a pale blue Ford Escort pull in. I walked out to fill it, and as I did Cassandra climbed out of the driver's seat.

'Feel like taking a little road trip?' she asked pointedly. For an instant I thought she was kidding, but there was a steely look in her eye.

'Right now?' I asked.

'No time like the present.'

'Where to?'

'To find Annemarie.'

I turned and saw Gabe on the phone in the office. I wasn't sure how to explain, so I jumped into the Escort and we sped off.

Cassandra drove the car like it was a Ferrari. As we barrelled down the highway, I found myself clutching the sides of the passenger seat with both hands. 'Do you really know where she is?' I asked.

'I've got a pretty good hunch.' Cassandra explained that she'd been unable to sleep the previous night, and after tossing and turning for several hours, had finally remembered the logo from one of the bumper stickers on the back of the

Pontiac. In the morning she'd driven over to the Youngstown Library where she'd spent two hours in the reference section sifting through pamphlets, until she finally stumbled across one from Sacred Path.

'Did you call Sheriff Dawson?' I asked.

Cassandra pursed her lips. 'We don't want a fight, Ethan. We want Annemarie home safe and sound.' She didn't elaborate, but it was obvious that Cassandra didn't trust Sheriff Dawson with Annemarie's rescue any more than I trusted the Virgin Mary. Still, I wondered whether it was wise for us to attempt it on our own.

'Have you at least told someone where we're going?' I asked.

She shook her head. 'If we did that, they might try and stop us.'

Terrific, I thought. If we disappeared into a religious black hole, folks in Jericho would be none the wiser. 'So what happens when we get there?' I asked.

Cassandra hesitated. 'Honestly? I have no idea.'

When we reached the small town of Defiance, we had to stop four times to ask directions. Everyone we approached seemed a bit hazy on the subject of Sacred Path, as if it was a blot on the town they were only too happy to forget. Finally, an old man sitting outside a diner on Main Street directed us to an unmarked dirt road about three miles south of town. We found it without too much difficulty and drove down the bumpy track, stopping to open a series of gates. Finally we came to a cluster of low buildings laid out in an orderly fashion. The buildings were mostly pre-fab, with corrugated-iron roofs and small square windows, except for a newly painted wooden barn that stood off to one side, and a couple of trailer homes beyond it. The grass was freshly mown and everything looked neat and tidy, if not exactly welcoming. About a quarter of a mile away, across a wide field, we could see what looked like an airplane hangar. We parked the car in a grassy lot alongside several others, and as we got out we heard a series of loud cracks coming from the direction of the airplane hangar.

I turned to Cassandra and her eyes met mine. 'What's that?' I asked uneasily.

'Beats me,' she said. But both of us recognised the sound of gunfire.

Just then a young man came striding purposefully out to meet us. He had short brown hair, a neatly trimmed goatee, and was dressed in white slacks and a polo shirt, like a pool attendant.

'Can I help you?' he asked in a wary tone.

'We're looking for Sacred Path.'

'You've found it. Are you from one of the home fellowships?'

Cassandra nodded. 'We're looking for Brother Carl,' she said.

'Is he expecting you?'

'Not exactly. But I'm an old friend.'

The pool man narrowed his eyes doubtfully.

'Brother Carl's in a meeting just now,' he said. 'He's very busy this afternoon. But you can leave your name and number, and I'll make sure he gets it.'

'We don't mind waiting,' said Cassandra breezily. 'Tell him Heather's here,' she added, flashing him a wide smile. 'He'll remember me.'

The pool man hesitated. 'I'll see what I can do,' he said finally. He turned on his heel and walked towards one of the low-rise buildings, where he disappeared inside. I turned to her.

'Heather?' I asked in a low voice. She shrugged.

'No man can resist a woman called Heather,' she said. 'Now go scout around.'

'Me?' I asked with disbelief. Cassandra nodded.

'If anyone asks, tell them you're looking for the rest rooms.'

I went to the barn first. It looked the most welcoming, with wide-open doors and two wooden barrels outside that had been planted with flowers. I poked my head in and saw a series of benches and tables scattered about, and a blackboard in the corner. At the far end of the room, a man and a woman sat huddled over coffee talking intently. They both raised their heads to look at me, then resumed their conversation. I moved away from the barn, my heart racing. I crossed to one of the pre-fab buildings and peered inside through a window. It looked like some sort of auditorium, with rows of chairs and a lectern at the front. A couple of dozen people were scattered around the seats listening to a serious-looking young man at the front, who held a book in one hand and smacked it repeatedly against the other for emphasis. Every now and then the people in the audience would nod in agreement. I turned away and crossed to another building, but when I tried the door it was locked. I passed the restrooms, and was just about to make a dash across the grass towards a fifth building when I heard a commotion from across the field.

Several people had emerged from the airplane hangar and were now walking towards me. There must have been about a dozen altogether, though they were bunched up so tightly it was difficult to tell. I ducked around a corner so that I could watch them approach, and as they drew near I spotted Annemarie walking beside a short, chubby girl who looked to be only a few years older than me. My insides lurched. They seemed to be deep in conversation, and at one point I saw Annemarie smile. It was disconcerting to see her walking along so easily with a group of strangers, and I had to stifle the urge to call out to her. The group passed by the building where I was sheltering, then headed for the barn, disappearing inside. I ran quickly back to where Cassandra waited by the car. 'Did you see her?' I asked breathlessly.

'She looked OK,' Cassandra said with a frown. 'Actually she looked better than OK.'

'What do you mean?'

'Ethan, is it possible Annemarie came here of her own accord?'

I considered this. When it came to Annemarie, anything was possible. And I had to admit she'd looked pretty content as she walked across the field. 'Annemarie went through a rough patch with the Church this spring,' I said slowly. 'Before she found out she was pregnant.'

'What happened?'

I didn't want to go into details. 'She felt let down,' I said. 'By who?'

'The Church,' I said. 'And maybe God.'

'What did she say to you at the time?' Cassandra asked. I struggled for a moment to remember.

'She said that sometimes we look so long at a closed door, we don't see the one that opens for us.'

Cassandra drew a breath. 'Could Sacred Path be her open door?'

I looked around the car park, feeling a little helpless. Where did that leave me? I wondered. I really did not think Sacred Path was Annemarie's open door, but how could I be sure? 'I don't know,' I said finally, shaking my head.

'Well, I guess we better find out.'

Just then the pool man came striding across the grass

purposefully. 'Brother Carl will be free in twenty minutes,' he informed us grudgingly. 'He suggested that you wait in the fellowship barn.'

'Perfect,' said Cassandra, beaming at him.

The pool man showed us to the barn, and as soon as we entered my eyes flew around the room in search of Annemarie. I spotted her sitting at a table in the far corner, surrounded by several others. A few people glanced in our direction but didn't seem particularly interested, though I thought I saw the chubby girl's gaze linger on Cassandra for a moment. The pool man promised to return with Brother Carl in twenty minutes' time. Once he'd gone Cassandra and I strained to hear the conversation at Annemarie's table, which seemed to be about an upcoming weekend retreat and whether everyone was entitled to go. The conversation sounded pretty bitchy, but even I had to admit it wasn't exactly Charles Manson territory. After five minutes I saw Annemarie whisper something to the chubby girl, who nodded. Then Annemarie stood up and tapped her way out of the barn. Cassandra turned to me wide-eyed, and for an instant we both froze. Then I leaped up to follow Annemarie out the door.

When I got outside I saw her disappear into the ladies' restroom. I looked around and a few people were milling around outside the barn, including the pool guy. I couldn't very well follow her in so I headed for the car park, then circled back behind the buildings until I found the restroom block. There was a series of small ventilation panels down the side of the building, and through them I could just make out the sound of a toilet flushing, followed by running water. At the very back I found a window with opaque glass, cracked open an inch. I bent down and peered through the crack and saw Annemarie drying her hands by the sink.

'Annemarie!' I said in a loud whisper.

She frowned, turning towards the window.

'Annemarie!' I whispered again. 'It's me!'

'Ethan? Where are you?'

'Outside! By the window.'

'What are you doing here?'

'Cassandra's with me. We've come to get you!'

'Thank God!' Annemarie flashed a huge smile and I felt a surge of relief. So Sacred Path wasn't her open door, after all!

'Do they know you're here?' she asked worriedly.

'Not exactly.'

'Then we should hurry,' she said, glancing over her shoulder.

'Can you climb through the window?'

'I'm not sure.' She came closer, then hesitated. 'Ethan, hang on,' she said uncertainly.

'What's wrong?'

'I can't leave without telling Lilah.'

'Are you serious? Annemarie, these people kidnapped you!'

'Yeah, I know, but I can't just disappear. She'll worry!'

'This is a cult, for Christ's sake! They're fanatics! You don't owe them anything!'

'She's also my friend, Ethan. I'll just be a minute, I promise.'

'Annemarie, wait!' I hissed. She disappeared out of view, leaving me practically choking with frustration. Annemarie never ceased to confound me. Of course she'd made friends with her abductors! Wasn't there a name for that? Something to do with Sweden and Patty Hearst? It had only been two days! How long did it take to brainwash someone? I wondered.

I straightened up and looked around. I was at the back of

the building so no one was around, but I was still in sight of the car park, and anyone could come along at any moment. I turned back to the window and tried unsuccessfully to open it. It must have been locked from the inside. An agonising minute later, Annemarie came back into the bathroom.

'OK, we're good,' she said quickly, coming over to the window.

'You didn't tell them you were going, did you?'

'It's complicated, Ethan. I only told Lilah. And frankly, she seemed relieved!'

Yeesh, I thought. This place made Jericho look like Candyland. Annemarie came over to the window and felt for the ledge. 'It's stuck,' I said. 'There must be a bolt or something.' She fiddled with the window for a moment, feeling her way up each side. Just then I saw a male figure appear behind her in the bathroom. I froze.

'I think you'll find that it's latched,' said a gravelly voice from inside. I heard him undo the lock, then suddenly the window opened to reveal a tanned middle-aged man with a silver-blond crew cut and greying temples. He flashed me a knowing smile. 'You must be Heather's friend,' he said.

Annemarie sucked in her breath. 'Ethan, this is Brother Carl,' she said. For an instant we all just stood there.

'Shall we go back to the barn?' said Brother Carl.

Eva

Everybody and his brother turned up to the public meeting held by Sheriff Dawson in the church basement. The room was heaving and unpleasantly hot. Annemarie's nearest and dearest were all there: Ada and Joe and me, Father Michael, Dr Paulson, Cora Lynn and her mom, the piano tutor Mrs Bieber, Kelly from over at the 7-Eleven, Gabe and his wife Shona, Ethan's mom, and Annemarie's friends Moose and Saskia. There were also quite a lot of folks who'd barely said two words to her in her lifetime, including several stray neighbours, kids from her old high-school class, and the Mayor of Jericho. But what really got me riled were the out-of-towners, who were clearly there just to snoop, and the local press, including the smarmy reporter who'd done the story on the six o'clock news. When I caught sight of him, Ada practically had to restrain me, because if it hadn't been for all the news coverage, Annemarie might never have been kidnapped in the first place.

Just as things got going the Vicar General arrived, followed by one of his flunkies from the diocese. Deacon Joe popped up like a jack-in-the-box to greet them and insisted

342

on shifting around the chairs so they could sit right at the front, like they were VIPs. When he returned to his seat he threw me a look. 'I thought you said those doctors were coming,' he said under his breath.

'They promised they'd be here,' I replied. I'd rung Dr Barratt that morning and explained about Annemarie's disappearance. He agreed to shift his late-afternoon appointments and drive over to Jericho to meet with us. He sounded unnerved by the news, and I found myself reassuring him that she was probably fine. When I hung up the phone I wondered whose voice had been speaking, because it surely hadn't been mine. Sheriff Dawson stood up then and called the meeting to order.

'I want to thank you all for coming,' he said. 'The purpose of this meeting is to recap the events surrounding Annemarie's disappearance, and hopefully bring some new information to light.' He paused to clear his throat and Shona called out.

'Sheriff, is this gonna be one of those dramatic reconstructions? Like they do on *Hawaii Five-O*?'

'Not as such, Shona,' he said a little awkwardly. 'I'd like to outline the facts as we know them, and see if they jog anybody's memory.'

Just then the smarmy reporter stood up, notebook in hand. 'Excuse me, Sheriff, but can I ask if the FBI is involved in this investigation?'

Sheriff Dawson scowled at the reporter. 'Let's be clear,' he said curtly. 'I am not here to answer your questions. You are here to answer mine. This is a fact-finding exercise, not a press conference! You can take your questions elsewhere!'

The reporter frowned, obviously disgruntled, then stuck his pencil behind his ear and sat back down, folding his arms.

Sheriff Dawson pulled a piece of paper out of his pocket

and began to read from it. 'At approximately three-ten p.m. on Wednesday afternoon, Annemarie was forced into a car on Church Street by a Caucasian man and woman. Both were in their early-to-mid twenties and both were nicely dressed, wearing religious jewellery.' He paused and looked up at the Vicar General, who was sitting with his arms tightly crossed against his chest. 'That is to say, Christian jewellery,' Sheriff Dawson explained, motioning vaguely to his neck. 'Crosses and such.' The Vicar General frowned and Sheriff Dawson carried on reading.

'The male was described as approximately five foot eight inches, skinny build, with short brown hair, chiselled features and a pointed chin. Good teeth and nice skin. Handsome, by all accounts, according to our only witness.' He paused and looked up at the audience then. 'Where *is* our only witness anyhow?' he asked suddenly, clearly dismayed. Everybody stirred and looked around. 'Anybody know why Cassandra isn't here?' Sheriff Dawson called out. I shook my head, having only just realised she was missing.

'She knew about the meeting,' said Ada. 'We spoke to her on the phone this morning.'

'She and Ethan drove off somewhere at lunchtime,' said Gabe from the back of the room.

Sheriff Dawson frowned at him a moment, then shook his head and looked back down at the paper. 'The male suspect had on khaki trousers and a short-sleeved pale blue button-down shirt. The female was described as five foot five, a little on the chunky side, with a broad forehead and shoulder-length mouse-brown hair pulled back in a ponytail. She wore a navy blue pants suit with a white top underneath. The car they drove was a green Pontiac with Indiana plates, and it was last seen heading west out of town on I-63.

'Excuse me, Sheriff,' called out Gabe again from the

back. 'I saw that car. They stopped at the gas station.'

Sheriff Dawson looked up again, clearly confused. 'Where were you when we were making our enquiries?' he demanded.

Gabe shook his head. 'Sorry, Sheriff. But nobody talked to me.' Sheriff Dawson threw a look of consternation at his deputy, who shrugged.

'Carry on,' said Sheriff Dawson to Gabe.

'They fuelled up, then asked directions to the church.'

'You spoke to them?'

'Yes, sir. I asked them where they were from and they acted a bit cagey and said they were from out-of-town. Then I saw a Bulldogs sticker on the dash and asked if they'd driven over from Defiance. Shona grew up in Turkeyfoot, the next town over.' Gabe motioned to his wife and she nodded emphatically. 'Well, they got a little funny then. The guy said he'd only just bought the car second-hand, so he didn't know anything about the Bulldogs. But I got the feeling he was lying, 'cause the girl kept giving him looks. Anyway that was pretty much it. They paid for the gas with cash and left.'

'Bingo,' said Sheriff Dawson with a gleam in his eye. 'That is precisely what we're looking for.' He turned to his deputy. 'Jeffrey, I want you to get me the names and addresses of every church within a twenty-mile radius of Defiance.'

'Now?'

'Yes, now! And cross-check it with that FBI list too.' He looked back up at the audience. 'That is our first bona fide lead,' he said with satisfaction. 'Now you've all heard the facts as they stand, does anyone else have anything relevant to add?' Several people shook their heads. 'Cora Lynn, you were with Annemarie just before she disappeared. Did she seem normal to you?'

345

Cora Lynn shrugged. 'Normal as she *ever* is. Which isn't exactly very normal.'

'I mean, normal for *her*.'

'Yeah. I guess so.'

'She upset about anything?'

'Nope.'

'You and her talk about anything in particular?'

Cora Lynn hesitated, and I thought I saw her glance quickly in Father Michael's direction. 'Just girl talk. You know. Nothing of consequence.'

'OK. You think of anything else, you let us know.'

Cora Lynn nodded. 'Sure thing, Sheriff.'

'Does anybody else have any other information that might help this investigation?' Sheriff Dawson looked around the room. Several people shook their heads. 'Then I think we'll draw this meeting to a close.'

'That's it?' hissed Deacon Joe into my ear. 'The man is not exactly Sherlock Holmes!'

Just then a bearded man in his forties wearing a Redskins baseball cap stood up. I had never seen him before, but his eyes were small and dark and mean. He crossed his arms belligerently. 'Excuse me, Sheriff. But how do we know this isn't some kind of elaborate hoax?' Sheriff Dawson looked at him askance.

'Which?'

'All of it. The kidnap. The pregnancy. Maybe even the blindness. If this girl is as smart as they say she is, maybe she's faked the whole thing. Start to finish.'

A murmur of dismay rippled across the room.

'What?' I murmured angrily, leaning forward. Ada laid a hand on my arm, and I felt Deacon Joe bristle at my side.

'Maybe she's even behind the sunsets,' the man added, jutting his chin in the air defiantly and looking around the room. Sheriff Dawson gave an irritated sigh.

'And why in God's name would a seventeen-year-old girl fake her own kidnap?' he demanded.

The guy in the cap shrugged. 'Attention? Publicity? Who knows? People do all sorts of crazy things.'

'That is ridiculous!' said Deacon Joe, jumping to his feet and turning to the guy in the cap. 'Who are you anyway?'

'Just a concerned citizen. With every right to be here,' the man retorted, sising him up.

'Well, you can take your concerns and shove them right where they belong!' said Deacon Joe. The room erupted then, and Sheriff Dawson raised both hands like a preacher, struggling to maintain order.

'Quiet, please! Pipe down, everybody!' he shouted. 'Can I respectfully request *everyone* to be seated?' He nodded at Deacon Joe and the man in the cap, who glowered at each other for another second before grudgingly taking their seats. After another moment the room settled. Sheriff Dawson shook his head. 'If nobody else has anything *pertinent* to add,' he said, frowning at the man in the cap, 'then this meeting is adjourned! Thank you all for coming.'

There was a pause, then everybody stood up and started to move towards the door. Deacon Joe turned and glared at the man in the cap, who threw us one last look before he left the room angrily. Ada turned to me with a raised eyebrow, and I could tell she felt as relieved as I did that the meeting was over. Deacon Joe seemed to remember himself, and walked over to the Vicar General. Just then I heard a commotion outside, and I turned to see what all the fuss was about. Suddenly the crowd parted, and Annemarie and Cassandra came walking through the door.

Annemarie

In the end, Cassandra got me out of Sacred Path by pointing out to Brother Carl that second-degree kidnapping in Ohio carried a minimum penalty of ten years' imprisonment. Not surprisingly, he remained completely undaunted when she informed him of this fact. 'Annemarie's not a prisoner here,' Brother Carl insisted in a genial tone. 'She's a much-honoured guest. And it has been our privilege to host her! I only hope she's found her time here as enriching as we have.' There was an awkward silence then, and I could feel all three of them turn to me. I must admit I was pretty speechless at that moment. Brother Carl had a way of twisting the truth so that it wavered right in front of you, like a mirage. I guess that's why so many people were prepared to follow him. I guess he also knew that at the end of the day, it was his word against mine.

Like any good host, Brother Carl insisted on escorting us personally to the car. At the last moment he leaned forward, placing his hand in the small of my back. 'Remember what I said, Annemarie,' he murmured into my ear. 'Keep your head in the Word!'

As we climbed into the car, Ethan leaned in to me. 'What did he mean by that?' he whispered, clearly disconcerted. I knew exactly what Brother Carl had meant, but explaining it to Ethan was another matter.

'It's complicated,' I said again, closing the door. But as we drove down the bumpy track, Ethan's doubt was like a fourth passenger riding along with us.

'Are you sure they didn't try to *convert* you?' he asked suspiciously.

'Yes!'

'It's a fair question, Annemarie,' he said defensively.

'Ethan, in spite of what Brother Carl told you, I wasn't there because I wanted to be! And I promise you, they did not convert me. I'm still the exact same person I was two days ago. *Nothing* has changed.' He sort of grunted then, and for the rest of the ride he was silent.

When we got back to Jericho, Mama practically wept with gratitude. Sheriff Dawson had organised a town meeting in the church basement and half of Jericho seemed to be there, which was a little overwhelming. But after a few minutes everyone went home and Deacon Joe insisted that the Vicar General come back to the house for coffee. As we walked across the churchyard I heard a car pull up and park behind us. 'Uh-oh,' I heard Mama quietly say to Ada. 'The doctors are here.'

'Now?' said Ada.

'Too little, too late,' said Deacon Joe glibly.

'We can't just make them get back in the car,' whispered Mama. 'They've driven all this way.'

'Fine,' snapped Deacon Joe. 'One cup of coffee. And then send them back to where they came from.'

So we all went into the house together. The Magi seemed

hugely relieved that I was home safely, and insisted on taking my vital signs as soon as we got inside. They decided I was none the worse for my ordeal, though Dr Barratt said that I needed rest, which was the understatement of the year. I smiled at him gratefully then excused myself and went upstairs, where I fell into a deep sleep. I only woke later that evening, when Ethan came by to check on me. I think he was more relieved than anyone that I was home safe and sound, but he still seemed a little paranoid about the time I'd spent at Sacred Path.

'Are you sure they didn't do anything weird to you?' he asked anxiously. 'You'd tell me if they had, right?' he added. We were sitting on the carpet in my bedroom, leaning back against the bed.

'No and yes,' I said, feeling for his hand and giving it a reassuring squeeze. He'd already told me about his night of fun in the Sacristy, and I'd made him promise that from now on, whiskey was *verboten*.

'So what were they like?' he asked.

'The people at Sacred Path? Kind of strange. But at the same time, completely ordinary.'

'That's sort of a contradiction, Annemarie.'

'I guess what I'm trying to say is, they were very human.'

'Meaning?'

'Flawed, and endearing, and understandable, at least most of the time. They're just people looking for some kind of truth, really. And hugely relieved that they've found it.'

'And have they?'

'Of course not,' I said. 'But who can blame them for trying?'

'I can blame them!' he said angrily. 'Who knows what would have happened if Cassandra hadn't found that pamphlet?'

'Ethan, they never intended to keep me there,' I said. 'Even Lilah admitted I was starting to become a burden.'

He grunted, and we sat there for a moment. 'Still,' he said. 'We owe a lot to Cassandra. She was there when they took you. And she was there when you escaped.'

I frowned. 'What are you saying?'

'I don't know. It just seems like Cassandra always happens to be nearby when you're in trouble. And maybe it's not just a coincidence.'

'You don't think she had something to do with the kidnapping, do you?'

'No, of course not. I'm just wondering if maybe she isn't some kind of ...' He broke off, reluctant to continue.

'Some kind of what?' I asked.

'Guardian angel,' he said finally. Ethan lapsed into an embarrassed silence then, and I had to stop myself from laughing out loud. Maybe my grandmother had been whispering to him from beyond the grave.

'Don't tell me you believe in angels now,' I said teasingly. Ethan remained quiet, and I suddenly realised that he was serious. I turned to him with a frown. 'You mean like ... an angel of God? Sent to protect me?'

'I don't know. Maybe.'

Huh. The idea had never occurred to me. But the more I thought about it, the more it seemed to make sense. Cassandra did always seem to show up when I most needed her. And she did seem wiser than just about anyone I'd ever met. 'I guess it's possible,' I said.

'Well, maybe you should ask her.'

Eva

After Annemarie excused herself, we gathered in the sitting room with our coffee. As I watched her climb the stairs, even I had to admit that it appeared to have been a relatively benign form of kidnapping. Still, the fact that two people had managed it so easily troubled me. Who's to say it wouldn't happen again? I wondered. I turned to Ada, who was sitting next to me, and said as much. Deacon Joe was on the sofa in close conference with the Vicar General, and looked up when he overheard me.

'That is precisely what we've just been discussing,' he said. 'We think the question of Annemarie's security is too vital to ignore at this point.' The Vicar General nodded in agreement, and I felt my hackles rise. 'The Vicar General has suggested that Annemarie be placed with the novitiates over in Youngstown for the remainder of her pregnancy,' continued Deacon Joe. 'It's a secure facility, and they'll keep her right through her confinement and beyond, if necessary. She can carry on with her studies, and we can visit her at any time.' I looked at him with surprise.

'Placed?' I said.

'Confined. Safely.'

'And what exactly do you mean by *and beyond*?' I asked.

'Who knows what the outcome of this pregnancy will be,' he said, his eyes flicking towards the Vicar General, who once again nodded. I felt a hot geyser of fury rise up inside me.

'This baby is not Church property!' I said. Deacon Joe sucked in his breath, as if he was struggling to contain himself, and I saw Ada give him a brief, curt shake of her head in warning.

The Vicar General cleared his throat officiously, and we all turned to him. 'The Church only wants what is best for Annemarie and her child,' he said. 'The baby must of course remain with its mother, both now and later. But the question of the baby's provenance, together with its destiny, must ultimately reside with God.' As he spoke, the Vicar General let his gaze travel around the room, sermon-like, until eventually it came to rest on me. In that instant, it struck me that I didn't want Annemarie's baby within a mile of God or the Church. This baby was ours, and ours alone. I opened my mouth to say so, but Dr Barratt cut me off.

'Excuse me, but perhaps we might be able to help,' he offered, slicing through the tension in the room. He turned to me. 'You're absolutely right to be worried about Annemarie's safety. My colleagues and I share your concern. We discussed it at some length on the drive here, and we have an alternative suggestion to put forward. The hospital would be only too happy to keep Annemarie as an in-patient on a secure ward for the rest of her confinement. We could carry on monitoring the pregnancy, and ensure both her and the baby's safety. I realise it's a bit further for you to travel, but we may be able to organise on-site accommodation. This is by no means a straightforward pregnancy, and it's vitally important that we keep a close eye on her.'

'Annemarie is not some sort of sacrificial lamb,' declared Deacon Joe, turning to him. 'And we are *not* going to abandon her to the whims of science!'

'Neither are we going to surrender her to the authority of the Church,' I said with equal force.

He leaned towards me and dropped his voice in a feeble attempt at discretion, nodding vaguely towards the other side of the room.

'The Church has far more claim on her than these hare-brained doctors,' he hissed. 'May I remind you that Church is family! *Our* family! And as such, it is entitled to your loyalty!'

'Excuse me, but there's no need to get personal,' replied Dr Barratt evenly. 'My colleagues and I have never once questioned the basis of your beliefs, even though there is not a single shred of evidence to support your claim that the child was divinely conceived.'

Deacon Joe turned to him, his face hot with irritation. 'It isn't your place to question our beliefs! God doesn't answer to science! Science answers to God,' he said staunchly.

Dr Hermann leaned forward, a purple vein pulsing in his forehead. 'May I remind you that the existence of God is a scientific hypothesis like any other,' he said. 'And it has yet to be proven.'

'Hogwash!' said Deacon Joe, with a dismissive flick of his hand. 'You won't find God at the bottom of a test tube!'

Just then the Vicar General cleared his throat loudly, and we all turned to him. 'God dwells beyond the realm of science, and beyond the comprehension of its practitioners,' he said. 'The question of God's existence is one for philosophers and theologians, not scientists.'

'Scientists are better equipped than anyone to examine the evidence for God! And I can promise you that so far it's sorely lacking,' countered Dr Hermann.

'So you're an atheist?' said Deacon Joe, rounding on him. From his tone of voice, Deacon Joe might as well have said *cannibal*. Ada threw me a look that said *here-we-go!*

'Actually I'm agnostic,' said Dr Hermann, drawing himself up.

'Agnostic,' said Deacon Joe, rolling his eyes. 'Then you might as well call yourself a yellow-bellied moron,' he added dismissively. 'Because there's not much difference.'

'Joe, that's enough,' hissed Ada in a quietly forceful tone.

Dr Hermann leaped to his feet. 'I will not sit here and be insulted by someone who believes that the earth was created in less time than it takes for milk to go sour!'

'And I will not have my home invaded by monkey-huggers!' said Deacon Joe.

'Please! Both of you!' Dr Barratt said loudly. Both men turned to him. 'We've strayed from the point,' he said emphatically. He threw an exasperated look at Dr Hermann, who took a deep breath, nodded and sat down again, while Deacon Joe shifted uncomfortably in his seat. For a moment there was silence, but the atmosphere in the room still crackled with hostility. 'The point of this discussion is Annemarie's security, and who is best placed to deliver it,' Dr Barratt said, endeavouring to inject a sense of calm into the debate.

'Well, the answer to that's obvious,' declared Deacon Joe, crossing his arms like an umpire. 'The Church.'

'The hospital,' said Dr Hermann with equal conviction.

'Gentlemen,' said Ada loudly. We all turned to her and she gave a forced smile. 'Who'd like some cherry cheesecake?'

It became clear over coffee and cheesecake that the issue would not be resolved in one sitting, so we agreed to hold another meeting after the weekend, once all the excitement had died down. I had to promise both the doctors and the Vicar General that we would keep Annemarie under lock and key in the meantime. After they'd all gone, Ada and I went back to the kitchen to clear up the dishes. 'Everybody's overwrought,' she said, shaking her head. 'We need to keep a cool head and think this thing through.'

'I've already thought it through. I don't want Annemarie living anywhere but here, under our roof, where we can keep an eye on her.'

'I understand that. But maybe you should ask her what *she* wants.'

'Why would she want to be anywhere else?'

'I know she's a strong girl, but has it occurred to you that maybe she wouldn't mind a little protection at this point? She might well be terrified. And frankly, who could blame her?'

I frowned. Suddenly I realised that I had no idea what Annemarie would want, and the recognition of this sent a ripple of dismay right through me. Ada laid a hand upon my arm. 'Annemarie's nearly eighteen,' she reminded me. 'Blind or not, pretty soon all this won't be up to you. It'll be up to her.'

Later that night I sat on the bench with Father Michael, listening to the rhythmic scrape of his knife as he worked on another carving. I hadn't told him about the argument between the doctors and the Vicar General, but I felt increasingly uneasy about Annemarie's future, as if it was a rope about to slip through my grasp. What I wanted more than anything, I realised, was to turn back the clock. What I *really* wanted was for her not to be pregnant. 'I have a confession to make,' I said finally.

'OK.' He sounded a little hesitant, as if he wasn't used to hearing confessions outside a booth.

'We'd be better off without this baby.'

'Would you?'

'Definitely.'

'How can you be sure?'

'I can't,' I sighed. 'But it's the God's honest truth.'

'Well, it's certainly honest. And to the extent that it reflects your feelings, it's the truth. But as for God, I think we should probably leave him out of it.' He looked over at me and smiled apologetically.

'Fine. I'm just saying that maybe God doesn't always know what's best for us. Isn't that possible?'

The curate hesitated, as if he wasn't exactly sure what he was signing up to. 'That may well be true,' he said carefully. 'But I'm not sure it's relevant.'

He was right, of course. Annemarie was pregnant and there was nothing we could do about it, however much we wanted to. I looked around in the darkness, and couldn't help but feel a vague sense of peril. Maybe Ada was right: maybe we did need protection. Suddenly it all terrified me: the pregnancy, the sunsets, the doctors, even the Diocese. Around us the churchyard was deathly still, as if it was holding its breath, waiting for the worst to happen. And behind us the church itself loomed silently, like an enormous dormant beast that might suddenly rouse and devour us all. 'The truth is, I'm afraid,' I admitted.

'Then you should ask God to give you strength,' he said.

I turned to him in the darkness.

'You don't understand. It's God that I'm afraid of.'

'Ah,' he said. 'I don't think that's what He intended.'

'But isn't that what the Bible tells us: to fear God?'

'God wants us to love and respect Him, and to be in awe of His wisdom. I don't believe that He wants us to cower in terror.'

'So what should I do? And please don't tell me to pray,'

I added quickly. He laughed and held up the wood, gazing at it thoughtfully.

'Honestly? I'm not sure there's anything you *can* do. But I think it was St John who said that perfect love casts out fear.'

'Perfect love,' I repeated, shaking my head. I looked around, as if I might find it lurking beneath a nearby bush. Then I turned back to him. 'Is there any such thing?' I asked.

Annemarie

The morning after I got back to Jericho, I decided to put Cassandra to a little test. I sent a silent appeal to her as soon as I woke up, and then I waited to see what would happen. It was Saturday and Mama and Ada were due to help with a lawn sale the church was organising, and Deacon Joe was working down at the car lot. But Mama didn't want to leave me on my own. 'Why don't you come with us?' she asked anxiously.

'No, thanks.'

'She'll be fine,' said Ada. 'Just don't open the door to anyone you don't know, honey.'

'No chance of that,' I said. Anyway, I thought, I'm waiting on my guardian angel. I said goodbye to them, then went to fix breakfast. But even before I poured the milk on my cereal the doorbell rang. Right on time, I thought. I went to answer it and, sure enough, it was Cassandra.

'Just thought I'd stop by for an iced coffee,' she said brightly, stepping into the hall.

'How did you know I wanted to see you?' I asked suspiciously.

'I didn't. I just wanted some iced coffee.' She followed me back to the kitchen and I fixed us both a glass.

'Look,' I said, as soon as we'd sat down. 'Maybe you should level with me. About why you're here.'

'I wanted to check on you,' she said. 'After all you've been through, I thought you might need to talk.'

'OK. And who exactly sent you?'

'Well, no one, *technically*, since it's a Saturday and I'm not meant to be working. But officially, Shawnee County Social Services. Why?'

'Are you sure?'

'Of course I'm sure. Annemarie, what's all this about?'

'Look, if someone else had sent you, would you tell me?'

'Um. Yes. But just for the sake of argument, someone like who?'

'Someone like God.' There was a pause then.

'You think God sent me here?'

'Ethan does. He thinks you're my guardian angel.'

Cassandra laughed out loud then. 'God bless that boy,' she said.

'Why is that so funny?'

'Annemarie, I was raised Presbyterian. I don't think they even *believe* in guardian angels. And anyway, I haven't been to church in over a year.'

'But what about all those times you showed up when I needed you?' I asked.

'Dumb luck,' she said.

'And the fact that you remembered the Sacred Path logo just like that?'

'Annemarie, I'm fifty-two. My memory isn't what it used to be. I saw the logo on the bumper sticker the day they took you. I just didn't remember I'd seen it until later.'

'Oh.' I couldn't keep the disappointment from my voice.

'I'm afraid I'm just a social worker. Scout's honour. But that doesn't mean I'm not here to help,' she added gently.

'I was hoping for a little more than help,' I said.

'What do you mean?'

'I was hoping you could stop it.'

'Stop what?'

'The baby. The sunsets. *Everything*. It's all a gigantic celestial mistake.'

'What exactly do you mean by mistake?'

I sighed. 'Nothing about this pregnancy makes sense,' I said, shaking my head. 'Not the time, nor the place, nor the people.'

She took a sip of iced coffee, and I heard her swirl the ice in her glass. 'While you're at it, maybe you better define *sense*,' she said.

I hesitated, struggling to find the right words. 'Look, I don't feel the way a pregnant woman ought to feel,' I said.

'How should a pregnant woman feel?'

'Elated. Devoted. Maternal.'

Her chair creaked as she leaned back. 'Yes, one would hope for those things. But trust me, they're not always there. Especially at the outset.'

'And physically,' I continued. 'Most of the time I don't feel pregnant at all.'

'Well, it could be that you've just adjusted to the hormones,' she said. 'You're starting your second trimester now. Women often say they feel completely normal for a time.'

I shook my head. 'That's not it. This baby wasn't meant for me. I know it.'

She hesitated. 'Then *who* was it meant for?'

'I don't know. But she's out there somewhere, and she's waiting for it.'

Ethan

I should have been ecstatic after Annemarie got rescued, but instead I went into a tailspin. When I woke up the next morning I lay in bed and thought about her insistence that nothing had changed. I realised now that this was only too true. Annemarie was safely home in Jericho, and for that I was grateful. But she was still inexplicably pregnant, and we were still stuck in purgatory. Our future had been stolen out from under us, and I was starting to wonder if it wasn't my fault. The Vicar General was right. From the start, I'd been at the centre of the storm here in Jericho, though it was Annemarie who'd borne most of the consequences. I'd been the first person to see the Virgin Mary appear in the sunsets, and the only one to speak to her in bodily form, not to mention the only one who saw the statue in the Sacristy weep and glow. Why had all these things happened to *me*? I wondered. Was it because I'd been dishonest about my faith? Maybe we'd been wrong about Annemarie's pregnancy. Maybe it was a punishment, rather than a blessing.

Once this thought occurred to me, I couldn't get rid of it. I went to work at the garage that day, but on the way home I walked straight round to the church. I'd promised my mom that I would go and see Father Michael to apologise, but really I just needed to speak to him. I knew I'd find him in the confessional booth on a Saturday evening, so I slipped into the back of the church and sat down in a pew to wait for him to finish. The church was empty and eerily quiet, though I occasionally heard a slight movement from inside the confessional box. It looked like it had been a slow day for confessions. A few minutes after I arrived I heard the wooden panel shut, and Father Michael emerged from the booth. He saw me and smiled, then walked over and slid in beside me. 'Good to see you, Ethan,' he said kindly.

'I came to apologise,' I said a little sheepishly. 'I'm sorry about breaking into the Sacristy the other night.' He raised a hand to stop me.

'There's really no need. St James said that we all stumble. Mistakes are what make us human.'

'Still.' I shrugged. 'I'm happy to pay for the cruet,' I offered. He smiled.

'The parish would be pleased to accept any donation you care to make.'

We sat in silence for a minute, and I was reminded how peaceful church could be. In the months before I became an altar boy, I'd come to genuinely enjoy sitting here each week, and now I realised that I'd missed it. 'Can I ask you a question?' I said.

'Of course.'

'Why us?'

He turned to me with a questioning look.

'I mean, why *here*? Why Jericho?' I said.

Father Michael shook his head. 'I'm afraid I can't answer that. But maybe there *is* no reason,' he replied. 'Maybe we are completely ordinary. And maybe that's the point.'

'What do you mean?'

'Faith isn't some sort of weapon that we only deploy during times of crisis, Ethan. The point of faith is that it's meant to underpin our lives every day: during the good times and the bad, the boring and the not-so-boring.'

'So you don't think there's any particular reason why all this has happened here?' I asked. *And to me*, I thought. Though I could not bring myself to say this aloud. He frowned.

'What sort of reason?'

'Like ... maybe we're being punished?' I suggested.

'For what?'

'I don't know,' I said uncomfortably, looking around. I wasn't really prepared to go into specifics. 'Our failings?'

He considered this for a moment. 'I don't believe we're being punished,' he said carefully. 'But it's possible that we're being tested.' He turned to me with an enquiring look, and I felt my face redden a little. I was beating around the bush, and somehow he knew it.

'The statue in the Sacristy,' I said suddenly. 'It weeps bloody tears. And glows. Sometimes.'

He stared at me for a long moment, taking in this information.

'Does it?' he said finally. His tone was calm, as if I'd just informed him of the weather forecast. But I could tell that he believed me.

'I think that's why Father O'Shea left,' I added.

Father Michael nodded thoughtfully. 'That's good to know,' he said. 'Thank you for telling me.'

I exhaled, and felt an enormous burden lift from my shoulders and fly up to the rafters. I hadn't realised how heavy the truth could be. His words were reassuring; perhaps I wasn't to blame after all. And though we might never know the answers to all my questions, it felt good to ask them just the same. Most of all, it felt good to confess.

Father Michael took a deep breath and looked up at the ceiling, as if the solution to all of life's mysteries could be found in its complex geometry. I tilted my head back to do the same. 'It's a beautiful ceiling,' I said after a moment.

'Yes, it is,' he agreed. He took a deep breath and let it out slowly, as if he was preparing himself for whatever came next. Then he turned to me with a look of resignation.

'The one thing I *do* know,' he said then, 'is that life in Jericho is never dull.'

Eva

I'd fully intended to discuss the issue of security with Annemarie over the course of the weekend, but somehow I didn't get round to it. I guess I was afraid she'd be only too happy to scamper off to Cleveland or Youngstown, while I was determined to keep her here with me in Jericho. So when Monday morning came and I still hadn't discussed it with her, Ada tore me off a strip over breakfast. 'Annemarie has a right to know what her options are,' hissed Ada over coffee. We were seated at the breakfast table and Annemarie was still asleep upstairs.

'I know, I know,' I replied.

'And we're due to meet them again soon, in case you've forgotten.'

'I haven't forgotten. Couldn't we just take her somewhere ourselves?'

'Like where?'

'I don't know. Somewhere off the beaten track.'

'You mean go into hiding?' she asked. I shrugged.

'I guess so.' Though the idea of camping out in cheap motels with lumpy mattresses and threadbare sheets held little appeal.

'Who would we be hiding from?' said Annemarie. We looked up to see her standing in the doorway still in her pyjamas, her hair tousled from sleep.

'No one, honey,' said Ada.

'Then why do we have to hide?'

'The doctors and the Vicar General think you need protection, that's all,' I said. 'They've both offered to put you somewhere secure for the rest of the pregnancy.'

'Like where?'

'An in-patient unit at the hospital. Or the novitiate over in Youngstown.'

She frowned. 'You mean a nunnery?'

'Only until the baby comes,' said Ada quickly.

Annemarie turned to me. 'Do you think I need protection?'

'Honestly?' I said. 'I hope not. But I really don't know.'

She stepped forward to the table, felt around for the fruit bowl, broke off a banana, and left the room without a word. I looked at Ada, who raised an eyebrow. 'Well, that went well,' she said sarcastically.

I shrugged. 'I can't force her to do anything, Ada. Even if I did know what was best. Which I don't,' I added. 'And neither do you.'

Later that afternoon, I wandered over to the church. I wasn't sure if I was seeking company or answers, but the building seemed to beckon me from across the field. No one was around but the door was unlocked so I went in and took a seat in a pew at the back. My eyes travelled around the stained-glass windows, as if the saints themselves could tell me what I needed to know. Over time I'd come to regard the figures staring patiently from these windows as old friends. I'd memorized their features and expressions, the clothes they wore and the relics they carried. So much of what I appreciated about St Paul's was visual that I often wondered what Annemarie experienced when she sat here. Perhaps the church's interior had been stamped forever on her five-year-old brain, or perhaps her imagination had painted an entirely new place of even greater beauty. Sitting there, it struck me that I would never see the world my daughter inhabited. But I could scarcely begrudge her that.

I heard a noise and saw Father Michael enter from the back of the church. He was dressed more formally than usual in black trousers and shirt with a white clerical collar, and his shoulder-length hair had been neatly combed back in a ponytail. When he saw me he immediately came and sat beside me in the pew. 'You must have read my mind,' he said. 'I was just about to come see you.'

I smiled, nodding at his clothes. 'And you dressed for the occasion?'

'Not exactly. I was summoned to Youngstown this morning.'

'By who?'

'The Vicar General. He asked if I would lobby you. Actually he did a little more than ask.'

'Let me guess: he wants you to persuade me to send Annemarie to the novitiate.' He put up his hands in a show of innocence.

'Don't blame me. I'm only the messenger.'

'So do you think I should?'

'I don't know,' he said. 'Do you think Annemarie needs safeguarding?'

'Honestly? If God has genuinely gone to all that trouble over my daughter, is He really going to let her come to any harm?'

He nodded. 'Perhaps not.'

'But if God isn't behind the pregnancy, then Annemarie is as vulnerable as the next person.'

'Also true.'

'So I guess I'm undecided,' I said. 'Anyway, I thought priests were supposed to have all the answers.'

He smiled.

'Priests give guidance, not answers. If I thought the priesthood conferred omniscience, I never would have joined.'

'That doesn't exactly make me feel better.'

'Then I can only apologise. And offer you solace.'

'Whatever that is.'

'Technically it means to comfort. From the Latin word *solor*.'

'I knew that. At least the comfort bit.'

'Actually it means more than that. It means to give comfort in sadness, or misfortune.

'Well, *that* I'm an expert on. Me and misfortune go way back.'

'I'm sorry you think so.'

I raised a dubious eyebrow. 'Is that what you call solace? 'Cause I think you might need to work on that,' I said.

He laughed. 'That's why I'm only a curate.'

We both sat quietly for a moment, enjoying the stillness. High up, the saints appeared to be watching over us benevolently. I nodded towards them. 'So do you have a favourite?' I asked. He gazed up at the windows for a moment, swivelling his head around to take them all in.

'That's a tough call. Some days it's Saint Joseph, the patron saint of carpenters.' He looked over at me. 'A little predictable, I know. But I've always felt sorry for him. Not a great position for a guy to be put in: competing with the Holy Spirit over your fiancée.'

'True.'

'But other days it's Saint Francis,' he said, nodding to a window in the corner showing a bearded man in simple brown garb with a bird resting on his open palm. 'He had an unruly youth, by all accounts. Before he relinquished worldly things and turned to God.' He turned to me with a sheepish grin. 'Sound familiar?'

'So it does,' I said.

'What about you?'

'Well, it used to be Saint Thérèse,' I said, nodding to a window that depicted a young woman in a flowing white gown with an arrow piercing her heart. 'But after these past few weeks, I think it might have to be Saint Bernadette.'

'Ah, yes. Our Lady of Lourdes. I should have guessed.'

'I've been reading up on her,' I said. 'A normal girl, by all accounts. Strong-willed. Bit of a temper. But after she ran into the Virgin Mary in a muddy grotto, the townspeople all branded her a liar, a fantasist or a lunatic.' I looked over at him. 'Sound familiar?'

He nodded, eyebrows raised. 'So it does,' he said.

Annemarie

I was pretty freaked out by the idea of a nunnery, and even an in-patient unit sounded kind of creepy. So after I stumbled on to Mama and Ada playing dice with my future, I got dressed and slipped out the front door to go find Ethan. His mom answered the door and said that Ethan was still asleep, so I went up to his room and knocked on the door. 'Ethan, are you up?' I asked. I heard a rustling.

'Annemarie?' His voice sounded sleepy.

'Sorry to wake you. But it's important.' I waited, listening to sounds of movement in the room. I couldn't help but wonder what he'd worn to sleep in. After a moment, the door opened.

'That's OK,' he said with a sigh. 'I had to get up anyway. I have to be at work by eleven. What time is it?'

'Time to talk. Mama and Ada are threatening to send me away.'

'What do you mean?'

'They want to put me under lock and key for the rest of the pregnancy. So they're talking about sending me to a hospital or a nunnery.'

'Are you serious?' Ethan sighed. 'Jesus, this is out of control.'

'Yeah. We have to do something.'

'Like what?'

'I don't know. Can't you talk to her or something?' There was an awkward pause and I heard him take a deep breath.

'Talk to who?'

'You know who.'

'Annemarie, I'm not even sure she's still here,' he said doubtfully.

'Please, Ethan?'

'Look, if she turns up, I can try,' he said. 'But what should I say?'

I hesitated. 'Tell her that I don't want this baby. And that she should give it to someone who does.'

I guess I sort of shocked him, because he went pretty quiet then. I left him to get ready for work and tapped my way home. Mama and Ada were no longer in the kitchen, but Deacon Joe came through the back door just as I was pouring a bowl of Corn Flakes. The screen door banged shut behind him. 'Glad you're up,' he said, sitting down heavily in a chair opposite me. 'Has your mama spoken to you about the novitiate yet?'

'Yep.'

'And what is your feeling?'

'My feeling is not good.'

'Nuns are just people, Annemarie. Think of it as summer camp. With prayers.'

'Except it'll be winter. And it isn't camp.'

'You'll be right down the road. And you'll be safe.'

'I'm safe here.'

'You weren't last week.'

'I was never in any real danger,' I said dismissively.

'How do you know?'

'Anyway, how come you're so anxious to get rid of me?'

'In case you haven't noticed, we are trying to protect you.'

'Well, you're trying too hard,' I said crossly. He shifted in his chair, causing it to creak loudly. I shovelled the Corn Flakes in faster, anxious to be rid of him.

'Is this about being split up from Camper Boy?' he asked after a moment. I swallowed a huge mouthful.

'Why do you always blame everything on Ethan?'

'Because things did not start to unravel around here until he turned up. And that is purely an observation, I might add.'

'Oh my God, Ethan did not cause any of this!'

'I will ask you to refrain from taking the Lord's name in vain!'

'Trust me, it's not in vain. I've been asking for His help,' I said. 'But He sure doesn't seem to be listening!'

'I will thank you not to blaspheme either. God has a plan, and sometimes that plan involves suffering.'

'Well, maybe I don't want God's plan,' I said. 'Or His suffering.' I wolfed down the last of my cereal, dumped the bowl in the sink and left the room.

Once upstairs I decided that I would need a plan of my own. Maybe Ethan and I should run away, I thought. Though where we would go, I had no idea. I thought fleetingly of my father. Perhaps if I could find him, I could persuade him to take us in. But I had no idea where to look. I knew only his name and his birth date, that he had moved to California in 1962, and that he had once had a holiday in Tijuana where he had ridden on a *burro*. Not enough to go on, really. Suddenly I felt like a zoo animal: caged without horizons, and completely at the mercy of those around me.

373

When I was four years old, Mama took me to the Cleveland Zoo for the first and only time in my life. When we got to the bear enclosure, an enormous black bear was pacing back and forth in its cage, swinging its gigantic head like a woolly wrecking ball. I remember staring through the bars with utter dismay and squeezing Mama's hand so tight I thought that it would burst. Suddenly the bear stopped pacing and swung round to face us. His tired eyes locked on to mine, and though I didn't know the word *tormented*, somehow my four-year-old self understood.

I reached under my pillow, searching until my fingers found the snow globe. It may not have done me any favours, but I still found the feel of it soothing. Perhaps that was what the stall holder had intended. I wrapped my fingers tightly around the glass, imagining the Virgin Mary weathering the silent storm inside. Maybe we were both trapped in a maelstrom, and maybe, like her, I just needed to be patient. Suddenly the glass seemed to grow cooler in my hand, until it felt icy cold to the touch. A moment later I felt something almost imperceptibly light land on top of my head. I raised my face to the ceiling, and a single snowflake hit my cheek, melting instantly. I gasped.

'Be not afraid,' said a woman's voice.

I held my breath, my heart beating so hard I thought it might leap out of my chest. The voice seemed to come from all around me, like an echo.

'I am the Immaculata,' she said then. I knew this, of course. I had spent the last few weeks imagining this very scene, though she had no way of knowing. There was so much I wanted to say to her, but my body remained oddly frozen, my voice locked somewhere deep inside.

'You must go to David's city,' she said. 'And there you must pray.'

I nodded, struck dumb by her presence. My own voice seemed to have receded so far within me that I could not find it.

'Pray and seek penance,' she added. 'There you will receive my blessing.'

Ethan

I'd only been at work a few hours when I saw Annemarie standing over by the gas pumps. She looked agitated, as if she'd been waiting for me to notice her. I walked out to where she stood, wiping my hands on a greasy rag. 'Hey. What are you doing here?'

'I saw her,' Annemarie said quickly. I took her arm and walked her a little further away from the pumps, lowering my voice.

'Really? When?'

'Well, I didn't *see* her,' said Annemarie. 'But she was there. I know it. She spoke to me.'

'Where?'

'In my room.'

'What did she say?'

'She told me to go to David's city.'

'David's city?' I asked, bewildered. 'What does that mean?'

'Well, technically it means Jerusalem.'

'Jerusalem? You can't go to Jerusalem!'

'But I think she might have meant Bethlehem,' Annemarie said quickly.

'Why?'

'*For unto you is born this day in the city of David a saviour, which is Christ the Lord,*' Annemarie recited breathlessly. 'It's from the Gospels. It means Jesus's birthplace, which is Bethlehem.'

I hesitated, still puzzled. 'You mean Bethlehem, West Virginia?' I asked. She shrugged.

'I don't know. But I think it's our best shot.' She paused a little uneasily, fingering my sleeve. I realised then what she was asking for.

'Jesus, Annemarie! You want to go to Bethlehem right *now*?'

'That's what she told me to do, Ethan!'

'But I'm working,' I said. 'I can't just ... leave.'

'How long until you get off?'

'I'm supposed to work 'til six.'

'That's too late. Can't you ask Gabe to let you go early?'

'And say what?'

'Tell him it's an emergency.'

'I'm not sure,' I said uneasily. Only three days ago I'd run off with Cassandra during the middle of my shift without a word of goodbye. Gabe had been very understanding that day, but I didn't want to push it. Annemarie seemed to read my doubts, because she reached down and took my hand, giving it a squeeze.

'Because, Ethan?' she said. 'It really is.'

Eva

When I got home from church, I went straight upstairs to Annemarie's room. I intended to tell her that she should do what she thought best, and that I would support her in whatever choice she made. But when I got to her room I found it empty with the door wide open. I searched the house from top to bottom, and there was no sign of her. Ada and Joe were both out so I went to find Ethan in his tent, but it too was deserted. I walked slowly back to the house, trying to quell a sense of vague alarm. That's when I saw Ethan's mother emerge from her front door with a watering can. She waved, then began to water the pots on her front porch. I crossed over to the hedge. 'Have you seen Annemarie?' I called out. She stopped watering the plants and straightened, turning to me.

'Annemarie left with Ethan a little while ago. They borrowed my car.'

'To go where?' I asked.

'They didn't say.'

I stared at her across the yard, and she gave me a funny look, one arm crooked on her hip like a hostess on a game show. Then she set the watering can down and walked across the lawn to the hedge, so that we stood facing each other over the shrubbery. She shook her head. 'I'm sorry,' she said, frowning. 'They told me you knew.'

My stomach took a sour dive. It was hard not to conjure the worst: that, when faced with the prospect of incarceration, Annemarie had taken matters into her own hands and fled. Ethan's mother could sense that something was wrong.

'Did they give you any idea at all where they were headed?'

She shook her head. 'I'm afraid I didn't think to ask. Ethan said they were going for a drive. But I did give him twenty dollars for gas,' she added apologetically.

Twenty dollars! Enough to buy them four hundred miles, I thought with dismay. And who could blame them if they'd gone on the run? I realised now that I hadn't exactly been reassuring over breakfast. Annemarie had asked my opinion about her safety and I'd given it honestly, but what I *hadn't* done was promise her that we would never send her away without her consent. So I had only myself to blame.

I went back inside and sat down at the kitchen table in a daze. I realised that I had no idea where she would go. Annemarie had barely been outside Ohio in her young life – partly because we couldn't afford vacations, and partly because there didn't seem to be much point. We'd taken a few trips over the years to West Virginia to see extended family, and when Annemarie was ten, Ada and I had hired a cabin for a week on Lake Erie, though it had rained the entire time. Annemarie had never dipped her toes in the ocean, nor had she been on a plane, I now thought guiltily. She'd never been to New York City or the Grand Canyon or Disneyworld, all places she'd hankered after. If she and Ethan really had gone on the run, I thought miserably, there was no shortage of destinations they could go. Only money would limit them, but Ethan had been working at the gas station all spring and summer. He must have saved a fair amount by now.

I heard voices outside in the driveway, and after a minute Deacon Joe and Ada came in, their arms laden with groceries. But as soon as Ada set foot in the kitchen, she took one look at me and knew that something was wrong. She dumped the brown bag on the counter and turned to me. 'What's up?' she asked with concern.

'Annemarie and Ethan are missing,' I said.

'Missing? Since when?'

'This afternoon. They took his mom's car.'

'Where were you when they left?' said Deacon Joe accusingly. Ada shot him a glance of disapproval.

I hesitated. I wasn't about to tell Deacon Joe that I'd whiled away half the afternoon with the curate over at the church. 'I was out. They told Ethan's mom they'd spoken to me, and she let them borrow her car.'

'They *lied* to her?' said Ada, wide-eyed. I nodded. 'Did they say where they were going?'

'Out for a drive.' Ada and Deacon Joe exchanged looks of alarm.

'Sweet Jesus in heaven,' said Deacon Joe. 'That boy is a demon in disguise!'

'Joe, don't jump to hasty conclusions,' said Ada quickly.

Deacon Joe shook his head. 'I should have trusted my instincts. I was right about that boy from the start. I'm calling the sheriff.'

'He's not a criminal, Joe! You can't just put out an APB,' said Ada sternly.

'Why not?'

'Because he hasn't done anything wrong! They're just a couple of kids who are scared and confused.' Just then the

380

doorbell rang and Ada went to answer it. I heard voices in the hall and, after a moment, she led Cassandra back to the kitchen. I felt a surge of relief when I saw her.

'I had a feeling something was up,' Cassandra said when we told her Annemarie was missing.

'What do you mean?' asked Deacon Joe suspiciously.

'Well, Annemarie didn't seem at all herself on Saturday.'

'Did she say anything to you?' I asked.

'She said she didn't feel the way a pregnant woman ought to feel,' Cassandra said slowly. Deacon Joe sucked in his breath, and I knew at once what he was thinking.

'I swear if those two kids have done anything at all to harm that pregnancy ...' he said in a menacing tone.

'Joe,' said Ada with a shake of her head.

'Let's not overreact,' said Cassandra. 'Ethan and Annemarie are both sensible kids. They won't do anything rash,' she said in a mollifying tone.

Deacon Joe grunted, and Ada flashed me a look of concern.

I only hoped Cassandra was right.

Annemarie

We stopped en route to buy gas and a burger, and by the time we reached Bethlehem it was almost eight. We followed the signs into the centre and stopped once to ask directions, and eventually found the Catholic high school on the far side of town. Ethan parked in the empty lot. School was still closed for the summer so no one was around. We got out and walked round the back to the football field, where we paused for a moment.

'Do you see anything?' I asked.

'It's nearly dark, Annemarie,' he said with exasperation. 'But there's something over there by the trees.'

'Let's go take a look.' I slipped my arm under his and together we walked the length of the football field. Beneath our feet the grass felt cool and perfectly smooth, and smelled of late summer. After a few minutes the ground became uneven, until eventually Ethan stopped.

'I think we're here,' he said.

'What's it like?' I asked.

'Honestly? What's the opposite of impressive?'

'Unimpressive.'

He didn't reply, so I stepped forward and put out my hands. Ethan gently took hold of my wrists and placed my hands on the base of the statue. I slowly felt my way around the rough stone, starting at the bottom with the folds of her robe and working my way up towards her head, standing on my tiptoes. 'No jokes about feeling her up,' I said over my shoulder.

'I didn't say a word.'

My hands finally reached her face and I slowly felt my way around her features. 'What are her eyes like?' I asked, passing the tips of my fingers over them.

'Kind of open. And staring.'

'Is there a sign?'

'Yeah, at the bottom. It says *Shrine of the Sorrowful Mother*.'

'I never thought of her as sorrowful. But I guess she would be.'

'Maybe her eyes are kind of sad,' he admitted. I lowered my hands and stepped back from her, hoping that we'd come to the right place.

'Now that we're here, what do we do?' Ethan asked uneasily.

'What she told us to.'

He paused. 'Both of us?'

'Well, it wouldn't hurt,' I said.

So we got down on our knees. And we prayed.

We got lost on the way home. It was dark, and Ethan was exhausted, and I wasn't exactly in a position to help navigate. In the end, we didn't pull into his driveway until almost midnight. The lights were on in both our houses, which was a bad sign, but then we weren't really expecting a hero's welcome. Before we'd even got out of the car I heard the screen door on Ethan's house bang shut. 'Uh-oh,' he said quietly. 'Think my mom's on the warpath.' I heard the door slam a second time. 'FYI, so's my dad,' he whispered. I heard footsteps come hurrying towards us.

'Ethan, where have you been?' said his mother. 'We've been worried sick!'

'I told you,' he said. 'We went for a drive.'

'For eight hours?'

'It was a long drive.'

'Well, it was *too* long,' said his father. 'Annemarie's mother was beside herself! You should have known better, after all they've been through.'

'I'm sorry.'

'You better take her home,' his father said.

'I'll be fine,' I said quickly. Just then I heard Mama calling from a distance.

'Annemarie? Is that you?' She must have been watching at the window.

'Yes, Mama. I'm back,' I shouted. I heard voices from inside the house. Clearly they were all awake.

'Is that miscreant with her?' Deacon Joe shouted. ''Cause if he is, he's got some explaining to do!'

I turned to Ethan. 'I gotta go,' I said quickly.

'Do you want me to come with you?' he asked uneasily.

'You better not,' I said.

'OK.' He sounded grateful.

I tapped my way across the lawn and when I got to the front porch they were all there, radiating a mixture of anger and relief. Deacon Joe demanded to know where we'd been, and for a split-second I thought about telling them the truth. But then I realised that not even I understood what the truth was any more. So instead I told them that we'd gone for a drive and a meal, and had got hopelessly lost on the way home, which was certainly part of the truth, if not the whole story. For once Mama was more relieved than mad, and we decided to call it a day. I went to bed and quickly fell into a deep, dreamless sleep.

When I woke the next morning the room was utterly still. I felt as if I was emerging from a cocoon, as if I'd slept for weeks rather than hours. I took a deep breath, stretching my arms as far as they would go, and all at once I knew that something had changed. I sat bolt upright in bed and, in that instant, I realised the baby was gone. I held my breath and counted to ten, just to prove to myself that I wasn't dreaming. Then I laughed out loud, a sound of pure joy and gratitude. The Virgin Mary had listened to my prayers and given me her blessing! I lay back down and gave myself up to relief. For once I felt completely normal – as if a passerby had come along in the night and quietly straightened the crooked frame of my life. The bizarre journey I had taken these past few months had finally come to an end: I would no longer be exceptional, nor would I be asked to single-handedly shoulder the burden of either faith or science. I could be a normal teenage girl like any other. I hadn't realised until that moment how much I wanted to be just that. Ordinary.

But I wasn't sure about the others. I knew Ethan would be relieved, but I couldn't predict how Mama and the others would react, and a part of me dreaded telling them. I could hear sounds of activity in the kitchen, and I knew I'd have to face them sooner or later, so eventually I rose and dressed and went downstairs. But when I walked into the kitchen, it was obvious that news about the baby would have to wait, because all hell had broken loose. Mama and Ada were frantically slinging pots and pans around the room, and Deacon Joe was in the study shouting down the phone.

'What's going on?' I asked, a little bewildered.

'The Archbishop's making a surprise visit,' said Ada excitedly. 'To see the Virgin Mother. He's driving all the way up from Cincinnati to see the sunset.'

'The Archbishop?'

'That's right,' said Mama.

'Is he bigger than the Pope?' I asked. As soon as the words came out, I felt Deacon Joe's presence loom behind me.

'Your sarcasm is not appreciated, young lady,' he said coldly. 'The Archbishop's visit is a tremendous honour for the parish, not to mention the diocese. Your mama and auntie have been busting a gut all morning to get the preparations in order, while you caught up on your beauty sleep.'

I sighed. My revelation would definitely have to wait. 'I'm here now,' I said. 'What do you want me to do?'

Mama placed a metal bowl firmly in my hands. 'Whisk,' she said.

For Mama and Ada, baking was a sign of faith, not to mention respect. For the next few hours we stirred, mixed, whipped, spread, spooned and sliced our way into heaven. I was desperate to speak to Ethan, but there was so much to do that I didn't dare try to slip away. By the end of the afternoon we'd made two different types of angel food cake, a pineapple upside-down cake, three dozen oatmeal raisin cookies, a tray of peanut butter fudge brownies, and a Jell-O mould.

'What about supper?' said Deacon Joe, wandering into the kitchen. 'The man can't just have cake!'

'Diocese said he didn't want supper,' said Ada, pulling a cookie sheet out of the oven. 'Only tea and cake before.'

'Fine, then that's just what he'll get,' said Deacon Joe. 'Tea, cake and a miracle!'

'*Two* miracles,' reminded Ada. I realised she was

speaking of the baby, and I felt my insides curl.

By half-past five everything was ready. Deacon Joe came back into the kitchen and surveyed our efforts. 'Ladies, you've done yourselves proud,' he said appreciatively. Then he turned to me. 'Annemarie, you suppose you could persuade that boyfriend of yours to take down his tent before the Archbishop turns up? Just for the night?'

'It looks a little trashy,' added Ada quickly. 'Right there, next to the shrine?'

'Sure,' I said quickly, desperate for a chance to speak to Ethan. I walked out to the wayside shrine, and as I approached, I could hear someone moving around, and the sound of tent poles clattering to the ground. 'Hey,' I said.

'Hey,' said Ethan.

'What are you doing?'

'Taking down the tent.'

'Oh,' I said with surprise. 'That's funny. 'Cause Deacon Joe sent me out here to ask you to do exactly that. He told me to bribe you if necessary.'

'Yeah, well, tell him it's done.'

'Did you do it because of the Archbishop's visit?'

'Nope. I did it because she's gone.'

He stopped moving and came over to stand beside me. 'Are you sure?' I asked.

He took a deep breath and exhaled. 'When I woke up this morning, I just sort of knew,' he said simply.

'I felt it too,' I said. 'Ethan, that's not the only thing that's gone,' I added.

He turned to me and dropped his voice. 'Annemarie, are you saying what I *think* you're saying?'

I nodded.

'Really?'

'Yep.'

'I can't believe it!' He sounded truly stunned. I reached for his hand.

'Are you OK?' I asked.

He snorted, then laughed. 'Are you kidding? I'm way better than OK,' he said with relief. 'I feel like she's given us our life back!'

I smiled. 'Yeah. Me too.'

'Do the others know?'

'Not yet. But I'll have to tell them soon. They're kind of preoccupied with the Archbishop's visit right now.'

'I guess it's not the best time,' Ethan agreed. He unfolded a chair for me to sit in while he finished taking down the tent.

'Ethan, you don't think she'll show tonight, do you?'

'In the sunset? I wouldn't bet on it,' he said, moving around.

'Shouldn't we warn them or something?'

'Annemarie,' he said, stopping right in front of me. 'Do you honestly think they'd believe us?'

When Ethan had gathered up all the camping stuff and gone home, I walked back to the house and found Deacon Joe in his study. 'The tent's gone,' I informed him.

'That was fast work,' he said suspiciously. 'What did you bribe him with?'

'My chastity.'

'That is *not* humourous, Annemarie.'

'It wasn't meant to be.'

I could feel him scowling but we were both too preoccupied to take it any further. Earlier in the day he'd managed to persuade the police to cordon off the street to keep the crowds away, and now he and Mama and Ada dragged folding card tables outside. While Ada and Mama set up the tables by the wayside shrine, Deacon Joe fetched chairs from the church basement. They covered the tables with white cloths and lace doilies and cake stands, together with pitchers of homemade lemonade and a giant urn for tea. The Archbishop was due to arrive at half-past six, and the sun was due to set just after seven. The weather had been cloudy all day, but as evening loomed the sky suddenly cleared, and I could feel the sun's warmth beating down on me. 'We couldn't have asked for a nicer evening,' said Ada with satisfaction once they'd finished.

I felt a little guilty, but Ethan was right. There was a strange inevitability to the evening as it wore on, as if I was experiencing it for the second time, like a moment of bad déjà vu. At half-past six precisely, a series of cars drove up carrying representatives from both the Cincinnati and Youngstown dioceses. I counted twelve car doors opening and closing, and various men exchanging greetings. I was pretty certain I heard the Vicar General's voice, amongst others. I guess he decided that if the Archbishop needed miracles, then he did too. Or maybe he'd just come for the cake. After shuffling around for a few minutes, they descended on the tables like a pack of starving hounds. I heard Ada and Mama hurriedly pouring cups of tea and lemonade, while Deacon Joe made small talk to one side. 'Yes, sir,' I overheard him say at one point. 'Our little parish has been touched by the hand of God. We are truly not deserving of his grace.'

Just then, Ethan appeared at my side. 'Hey,' he said quietly in my ear. 'Is that the God Squad? There's enough of them. How many people does it take to witness a miracle?'

'Twelve apparently. Just like the Apostles.'

'Which one's the Archbishop?'

'You're asking the wrong person. But my guess would be the one they're all hovering around.'

'Must be the silver-haired guy in the middle. He does look kind of ...'

'Arch?'

'I was gonna say holy.'

'Is Father Michael with them?'

'Yeah, he's there. Loitering in the background. Looks like Ada's flirting with him.'

No surprises there, I thought. 'How come you came back?'

'I wanted to be here. I feel kind of responsible,' Ethan added guiltily.

'For her?'

'For all of it.'

'Ethan, you didn't cause any of this!'

He sighed. 'Yeah, I know. But it still feels a little like the Last Supper.'

We sat down off to one side on the grass. As I felt the warmth of the sun finally disappear, I heard Deacon Joe urge everyone to take a seat, and I got a sinking feeling in the pit of my stomach. Ethan reached over and took my hand.

'Hey,' he whispered. 'What's that thing you're always saying in Italian?'

'*Che sarà sarà?*'

'I think it's time to say it now.'

Ethan

The Archbishop's visit was painful – like watching a slow-motion car crash. Annemarie and I sat on the grass until the sun disappeared, and just as we'd expected, the Virgin Mary failed to show. As the sun went down, the mood among the Archbishop and his disciples slid from pleasant anticipation to sour disappointment. We could hear Deacon Joe making nervous small talk, until eventually even he fell into a morose silence. Finally, after what seemed like ages, the Archbishop cleared his throat and stood up, followed by all the Apostles. Deacon Joe leaped to his feet.

'Your Excellency, I don't know what to say,' he said, shaking his head. 'The Virgin Mother has never disappointed us before. I can only speculate that conditions somehow weren't fitting this evening.'

As much as I disliked Deacon Joe, it was embarrassing to see him spluttering excuses. The Archbishop seemed relieved, however, and only too happy to be making a swift exit. I guess he hadn't really wanted to bear witness to a miracle, after all. We stood off to one side as they climbed into their cars, and after the last one had pulled away, we walked over to the tables. Ada and Annemarie's mom had already begun packing up the food in silence. 'Ada ... Mama?' said Annemarie. 'Virgin or no Virgin, it was a really nice spread.'

'Thanks, honey,' sighed Ada.

'I don't get it,' said Annemarie's mom. 'Why tonight, of all nights?'

'The Lord moves in mysterious ways,' said Deacon Joe philosophically. 'Perhaps we were wrong to call in the Church. Perhaps the Virgin Mother didn't want outsiders.'

'The Archbishop is hardly an outsider!' said Ada.

'But maybe she intended her blessing for us and us alone,' he mused. Annemarie gave me a poke when he said this and I nearly laughed out loud. Only Deacon Joe could turn a PR disaster into a mandate from heaven, I thought.

'The truth is, she's gone,' said Annemarie suddenly, and for an instant they all went quiet. I turned to her with the same creeping sense of dread I felt whenever she took on a battle.

'You mean ... for good?' asked Ada. Annemarie nodded.

'We think so,' she said. Deacon Joe shot me a look of pure malice.

'How can you be sure?' said Annemarie's mom, frowning.

'They can't,' said Deacon Joe irritably. 'And we shouldn't listen to them.' He turned away and started to fold up one of the card tables.

'That's not the only thing that's gone,' Annemarie announced then.

Oh, jeez, I thought. She was gonna do this *now*? They all stopped and looked at her warily. At that precise moment I wanted the earth to swallow me whole.

'The baby's gone too,' she said. Ada and Annemarie's mom threw each other a confused look.

'Annemarie, honey,' said Ada, stepping forward, 'what

exactly are you saying?'

'That I'm not pregnant any more.'

'But ... how can that be?' she asked.

'I don't know how. But it's true. I'm sure of it.'

'What do you mean, you're sure?' said her mom suspiciously. 'Have you been back to the doctors again?'

'No. I just know, that's all. Don't ask me how.'

Deacon Joe stepped towards her menacingly. 'Are you serious? *Don't ask you how?* Annemarie, I swear on the Holy Bible that if you have done anything at all to harm that baby –'

'Joe!' cried Ada, cutting him off. 'She wouldn't do that!'

'Babies don't just disappear, Ada!' he snapped.

'Well, this one did,' said Annemarie quickly. They all turned to her again.

'And you expect us to *believe* that?' asked her mom cautiously. 'After you lied to us about everything else?'

'Mama, I never lied to you. I just withheld the truth.'

'Half a truth is a whole lie, Annemarie,' she said.

'But we didn't really understand how the baby got there in the first place! Why is it so hard to accept that it's gone?' Annemarie argued.

'Because it's too convenient,' said Deacon Joe sharply. 'For you and for him.' He threw me a look of contempt.

'Ethan isn't to blame!'

'On the contrary! Camper Boy manages to be at the centre of just about everything that goes wrong around here,' said Deacon Joe, turning to me. 'I wouldn't be at all surprised to find that he engineered your way out of this pregnancy!'

I shook my head. 'It wasn't like that. I swear.'

'*What* wasn't like that?' he demanded.

Annemarie turned towards her mom. 'Mama, do you really think I would be capable of doing that?' she asked.

Annemarie's mom slowly shook her head. 'Honestly, Annemarie? I don't know *what* you're capable of any more,' she said. Everybody froze for a moment. The air was so thick with rancour you could hardly breathe. Suddenly Ada put a hand to her head.

'Oh, Lordie, I do not feel at all well,' she said uneasily. Deacon Joe frowned and carried a chair over to her, and Ada sort of collapsed on to it.

And then she hurled herself forward, vomiting on to the grass.

Eva

When Annemarie told us she was no longer pregnant, I slid into a dark hollow. I should have been ecstatic, or at the very least relieved, but instead I just felt bad. Lord knows I'd prayed more than once for the Virgin Mary to leave us alone, I told myself. But there was something else I'd prayed for – something I was scarcely able to admit. And I knew I needed to unburden myself, or the guilt would surely kill me. So the following night I took myself out to the bench in the churchyard, and a part of me hoped the curate wouldn't show. The weather was overcast, and it was darker than usual, as if the heavens over Jericho were just as gloomy as I was. I sat in the darkness for more than an hour and was on the verge of giving up, when I heard the sound of footsteps coming across the grass. His form emerged out of the blackness, and he stopped short when he saw me.

'You're here,' he said in a low surprised voice. Clearly he hadn't been expecting me. 'I'm sorry,' he said. 'I had a late meeting. I should have warned you.'

'Don't worry,' I said quickly. 'It's not as if we had a date or anything.' I laughed nervously.

He nodded but didn't reply, and I wondered if I should have opted for the confessional booth. Maybe friendship with a priest was too complicated, I thought – it was certainly tying me up in knots. He stood holding the watering can uneasily. I nodded at the roses. 'You'd better attend to them first,' I said. 'They need you more than I do,' I joked, even though I wasn't sure it was true. He stepped over to the flowerbed and carefully watered each of the roses, then sat down next to me.

'Have you been here long?' he asked.

I hesitated. If I said no, I'd be lying. If I said yes, I'd be pathetic. 'Awhile,' I said finally.

'Did something happen?'

'Annemarie lost the baby.'

'I'm sorry,' he said. 'But perhaps it's for the best.'

I nodded. 'Actually that's not what I came to tell you,' I said. 'I came to tell you that I prayed for it.'

'Prayed for what?' he asked.

'For her to miscarry. Or … something. Not recently, but in the beginning. When we first found out,' I added guiltily.

'And you think God answered your prayer?' he asked.

I shrugged. 'I have no idea.'

'But you feel responsible.'

I nodded. A lump had risen in the back of my throat, and I wasn't sure I could speak. I waited for a minute, and he sat there patiently. 'I feel as if the Virgin Mary has forsaken us,' I said finally. 'Because of what we've done.'

'You know,' he said carefully, 'just because we can't see her any more, doesn't mean she's not here.' We sat in silence for a moment. In truth, this hadn't occurred to me, though I suppose it should have. 'And just because you wished for it to happen,' he continued, 'doesn't mean you were the reason it did.'

I sighed. 'Maybe not,' I admitted. 'But I still feel like a

hypocrite. I was so angry about that baby to begin with. I just wanted to make it disappear from our lives. But then later, after I spoke to you, I started to believe it was a good thing, that it would bring me closer to my daughter, and I pinned all sorts of hopes on it – hopes and dreams and expectations of how things would be. And now I realise that it was all an illusion. Because it was probably never even there in the first place.'

'Hope is never an illusion,' he said. 'And without it, we'd be very poor indeed.' His tone was gentle. He certainly didn't seem to think any worse of me. 'Maybe what you're really feeling is loss,' he added. 'And you'd hardly be human if you didn't.'

For a moment I couldn't speak. I looked at him and his face was shrouded in darkness, his eyes infinite hollows. How was it that an ex-convict-turned-priest understood so much about me? We sat there breathing in the stillness, and gradually I felt a sense of calm return. 'The roses are looking much better,' I said finally.

He smiled. 'It just took a little faith.'

We stayed out later than usual, and when I got home it was past midnight. As I started up the stairs I saw a light in the kitchen, and when I went to the doorway Ada was seated at the table in her bathrobe, staring down at a plastic test tube and a small vial of clear liquid. She didn't seem to notice when I came into the room.

'Ada, are you all right?' I asked.

'Did you know the Egyptians used to pee on barley to see if they were pregnant? Now we use blood cells from a dead sheep.' She spoke without looking up, and for a moment I couldn't reply.

'Are you serious?' I asked, stepping closer.

'Does this look like a joke?' She glanced up at me, and indicated the test tube and vial. I shook my head.

'But ... how?'

'Lord only knows. I swear I have not missed a contraceptive pill since 1967.'

'Are you certain?'

'The test is. Or at least, it claims to be.'

I sat down at the table opposite her, and peered down at the murky fluid in the test tube. How could such an insignificant object hold so much sway over our lives? 'Does Joe know?' I asked.

'No!' she hissed. 'And I do not want him to.' She paused. 'Not until I've decided what to do.'

'Ada!' I said. I raised my eyebrows at her and she glared back at me.

'I am way too old to start being a mother now,' she said in a loud whisper.

'You're only forty-four.'

'I'm not cut out for it.'

'You'll learn. I can help you.'

'Well, maybe I don't want your help,' she snapped. We stared at each other across the kitchen table.

'Is everything all right?'

We turned to see Annemarie standing in the doorway in her nightgown. Ada shot me a warning glance. 'Everything's just fine,' I said. 'You go on back to bed.'

Annemarie hesitated, then nodded and turned to go. We listened to her slowly climb the stairs, and then Ada turned back to me. 'You want to know how this happened?' she whispered. 'Ask that daughter of yours!'

Annemarie

For the next few days I crept around the house, trying to make myself invisible. There was so much tension in the air that I thought we all might spontaneously combust. Ada shut herself in her bedroom and refused to come out, and Ethan said that Mama walked around with a face that looked like someone had moulded it from concrete. The only person who no longer seemed angry was Deacon Joe, and that was because he was completely baffled by Ada's behaviour. She had banished him to a pullout sofa in a spare room down the hall, and once or twice I heard him bleating through the bedroom door, pleading to be let in. But each time she just shouted, 'Joe! Please! I am indisposed!'

I didn't confess to either of them that I'd prayed for it to happen, but I felt guilty nonetheless. Never in my wildest dreams had I imagined that the Virgin Mary's blessing would land on Ada. Ada with a baby was like imagining Moses with a hand grenade: almost too terrifying to contemplate. It wasn't that she wasn't capable enough to be a mother: it was that she didn't have a maternal bone in her body. And I knew she truly did not want a child, which struck me as nothing short of a tragedy. But if the Virgin Mary had made one mistake, I decided, then I suppose it was conceivable she might have made two. We would have to live with the consequences, because she was well and truly gone.

Over the next few days, Mama insisted that I verify the fact that I was no longer pregnant with a medical doctor. She wanted to call Jeremiah Paulson but I insisted on going back to Cleveland to see the Magi. I guess I felt I owed them that much. 'Fine,' said Mama. 'We'll go back to Cleveland.'

'No, Mama. Ethan and I will go to Cleveland,' I corrected her. There was a long silence.

'Well, I guess you'll do what takes your fancy,' she said finally.

'I guess I will.'

Ethan wasn't all that keen, though. 'Do we really have to?' he asked me later. 'That place creeps me out, Annemarie. All those pregnant women.'

'Count your blessings I'm not one of them.'

'I guess so,' he agreed.

'Just one more trip,' I promised. 'Then we'll shut the door on this for good.'

He sighed. 'OK.'

Mama had phoned ahead, so the Magi were waiting for us when we got there. I left Ethan in the waiting room, surrounded by marauding toddlers and a sea of bulging abdomens, and followed the receptionist down the hall to the consultation room. When she showed me in, the Magi popped to their feet like a trio of nervous jack-in-the-boxes. To say they were agitated was an understatement; the air in the room almost quivered around me. I decided to let them speak first, so after I sat down I waited for Dr Barratt to begin. To my left, Dr Hermann shifted uneasily, the fabric of his trousers crackling against the cloth chair seat, while on my right Dr Marshall nervously tapped a pencil against a sheaf of papers. Dr Barratt cleared his throat before he spoke.

'Thank you for coming in, Annemarie. Your mother indicated on the phone that there'd been a change in your condition,' he said cautiously. 'Has something happened since we last met?'

I nodded. 'I think you might want to run your tests again,' I suggested. There was another pause while I felt them exchange glances. All three men shifted uneasily in their seats, and for an instant there was silence. Somewhere on the wall behind me, the hand of a clock moved with a short, precise click.

'Fine,' he said suddenly, rising to his feet. 'That sounds like a good way to proceed.'

So once again I furnished them with various samples, and they scurried off to perform their strange alchemy. I waited alone in the consultation room, and, as with Mama and Deacon Joe, I had no idea how they would react to the news that the baby was gone. On top of that I was tired: tired of knowing things that others did not, and tired of being judged for crimes I hadn't committed. All my life I had been taught that God alone was qualified to judge others, and that I should seek only His approval. But I realised now that I had spent a lifetime seeking the good opinion of those around me: of Mama and Ada and Deacon Joe. And they had bestowed it only grudgingly, and withdrawn it at the earliest opportunity.

I thought about King Solomon, who ascended the throne as a boy of twelve, and prayed to God to grant him an understanding heart so that he could judge good from evil among his subjects. Pleased that Solomon had not asked for riches or a long life, God granted him his wish, and the whole world sought him out to hear the wisdom God had put in his heart. When two women came before Solomon to resolve a quarrel over who was the true mother of a child, he called for a sword, ordering that the child be cut in two and divided evenly between them. Only one woman showed compassion, begging him to spare the child and give it to the other, and Solomon rightly proclaimed her to be the real mother. But over time Solomon's wisdom failed him: he amassed enormous wealth, took hundreds of wives, and turned to false idols, forsaking his covenant with God. In the end he lost his kingdom. When I first heard Solomon's story, I wondered what lessons we were meant to take from it: whether we should strive for perfect understanding, or recognise from the outset that it was somehow beyond us. I thought, too, about the words of Matthew: *For whoever exalts himself will be humbled, and whoever humbles himself will be exalted.* In the past few weeks I had been both exalted and humbled, and I was none the wiser.

In the end, I needn't have worried about the Magi. They were doctors, not family, and their interest in my pregnancy was scientific, rather than spiritual or sentimental. And although they were perplexed by what they found, not to mention disappointed, they didn't feel betrayed or deceived or angry or lied to. When we were all seated again facing each other, Dr Barratt cleared his throat and began.

'It appears that you were right, Annemarie. Your condition has definitely changed.' He paused for a moment and drew a breath. 'I'm afraid you're no longer pregnant,' he said in a slightly bewildered tone. 'Even more strangely, we can't find any trace of the pregnancy. Even your hormone levels seem completely normal.'

'Which is very strange,' added Dr Marshall.

'Annemarie, I don't mean to pry, but I must ask you,' said

Dr Barratt carefully. 'You didn't *interfere* with the pregnancy in any way, did you?'

'No,' I replied adamantly. 'I would never have done that. Not in a million years.' And it was true. But even as I said those words, I felt a vague sense of wrongdoing.

'We thought as much,' said Dr Barratt with a sigh. 'Anyway there's no sign of interference. Such things are generally quite easy to detect. Which means we remain puzzled.'

'You might even say perturbed,' said Dr Hermann darkly. I turned to him. His disappointment hung over him like a cloud.

'I guess we'll never know,' I said. I could live without perfect wisdom. I figured the Magi could too.

When I got back to the waiting room I heard Ethan's voice quietly reciting something in the corner. I made my way slowly across the room, pausing in front of him.

'*I will not eat them in a house, I will not eat them with a mouse, I will not eat them here or there, I will not eat them anywhere,*' he said.

'What won't you eat?'

He paused. 'Green eggs and ham,' he said a little sheepishly.

'You're not reading to yourself, are you?'

'No, I'm reading to Bradley. His mom fell asleep over there in a chair.'

'Pregnancy will do that to you.'

'Apparently.'

'Hey Bradley,' I said in a cheery voice.

There was a long silence, during which I could hear Bradley breathing through his mouth.

'Bradley's not much of a talker,' said Ethan after a moment.

'Guess that'll make it easier to say goodbye.'

We left Bradley in a chair with a stack of Dr Seuss books in his lap, and made our way back to the car. When we got in the front seat, Ethan paused and turned to me. 'So are we done?' he asked.

'Almost,' I said tentatively.

'What now?' I hesitated, afraid to ask. 'Can we go back to Bethlehem?' For a moment he didn't say anything, then I heard him breathe out in a resigned sort of way.

'Have you still got the TripTik?' he asked.

By the time we got to Bethlehem it was late afternoon, but the sun was still warm. We trudged across the grass until we came to a stop in front of the statue.

'Does she look the same?' I asked.

'Pretty much,' he said. 'Did you think there'd be a change?'

'Not really.'

'You're not gonna make us pray again, are you?' He sounded worried. I laughed.

'No. I didn't come here to pray.'

'Then what *did* we come for?'

'To say goodbye I guess. And to thank her.'

'Oh,' he said a little doubtfully.

'I'm starting to think that we can run but we can't hide,' I said.

'Hide from what?'

'I just mean we can't escape from it. Mary. God. The Church.'

'I didn't know you wanted to.'

'For a while I thought I did. After all that business with Father O'Shea, I thought I wanted to be free of it for good. But the thing is: it's here, all around us. Even if we don't want it to be.'

Ethan didn't say anything for a moment. 'I think we'll have to learn to live with it,' he said.

'I think it'll have to learn to live with us.'

He laughed. 'Yeah. Maybe.'

'Because I don't want to follow in her footsteps.'

'What do you mean?'

'That whole virgin birth thing. It was never gonna be me.'

'Yeah, I know,' he said.

'Maybe that's what happened. Maybe she finally realised I was the wrong virgin.'

'Or maybe she just listened to you.'

'Do you think?'

'Well, she's meant to be full of compassion.'

'Let's hope she's full of forgiveness.'

'You haven't done anything wrong, Annemarie.'

'Not yet,' I said tentatively. 'But what about all the bad stuff I'm gonna do?'

'Like what?' He turned to me, genuinely puzzled.

'I don't want to be like Jephthah's daughter, Ethan.'

'Annemarie, I have no idea what you're talking about.'

'When Jephthah's daughter found out that he was going to sacrifice her to God, she asked permission to go into the wilderness to bewail her virginity.'

'I'm still not following you.'

'Don't you see? When Jephthah's daughter was faced with death, the thing she mourned the most, more than the loss of her own life, was that she would never have the chance to lie with a man.'

'But ... what does that have to do with you?'

'I don't want to die a virgin, Ethan.'

'Annemarie, you are not going to die a virgin!'

'You don't know that! Lightning could strike us right here and now. Or we could have a car crash on the way home.'

'I suppose so. But it's not very likely.'

'Well, I'm not taking any chances.'

'Meaning?'

I took his hand. 'Can we just ... go to a motel? Right now?'

'Are you serious?'

I nodded. 'Before the sky falls.'

Ethan

On our second visit to Bethlehem, Annemarie used her strange and compelling logic to convince me that we should not wait another minute. Truthfully, I really didn't need that much persuading by then. We drove back across the state line and headed south along the Ohio River until we came to a place called Shadyside where, just on the outskirts of town, I spotted a motel by the side of the road. It was long and low and looked like a thousand motels in a thousand towns across the Midwest. Most importantly, it looked like something we could afford. I pulled into the parking lot and switched the engine off, turning to her.

'So what's it called?' she asked pensively, biting her lip.

'The Star Lite Motel,' I said. 'Spelled L-I-T-E.'

Annemarie frowned, and for an instant I thought that she might change her mind. Then she smiled.

'Kind of poetic. I think Emily would approve.' She opened her door and climbed out, and it took me another moment to realise that she was waiting for me. She stood patiently beside the car while I went into the office and paid the clerk eighteen dollars for one night's stay. I came back clutching the key and when I opened the door I had a moment of sheer panic when I saw the décor. But then I remembered that the décor didn't matter in the slightest. So I pulled her inside and closed the door. And then I shut my eyes too.

Much later, we lay side-by-side on a lumpy queen-sized mattress in the dark, and I ran my finger down her naked shoulder. 'There'll be hell to pay if we don't go back,' I reminded her. She smiled and shrugged.

'I'll go to Confession.'

'No, you won't.'

She laughed and rolled on to her back, giving a satisfied sigh. 'I reckon God's already forgiven me anyway,' she said then.

'How do you figure that?'

'It's like money in the bank. All those years of good behaviour.'

I leaned in and kissed her, the way I'd wanted to so many times over the past six months, and she responded in a way that made it clear how much she tingled.

'Does that mean we get to do it again?' I asked.

In the end, we did catch hell when we got back to Jericho, but it was worth it. Things might have gone worse for us, but just before we returned, Deacon Joe discovered that Ada was pregnant. To say that he was not best pleased would be an understatement. For a few days, you could almost feel the twin waves of incredulity and resentment rolling out across his immaculately groomed lawn. In their shared opposition to parenthood, it appeared that Deacon Joe and Ada were a perfect match. 'At least you've already got the baby's room ready,' Annemarie offered one day, by way of consolation.

'That is not exactly what I'd call a silver lining,' Deacon Joe replied irritably.

'The Bible says that children are the arrows of the warrior, and blessed is the man who fills his quiver,' she added.

'I never asked for a quiver,' he grumbled. 'Let alone an arrow.'

But there were folks in Jericho who felt differently. Later that month another miracle occurred. One day Gabe came into work and told me that Shona was pregnant with another child. When Annemarie heard the news, she yipped with surprise and practically hurled herself into my arms. I pressed her for an explanation and she confessed that she'd assumed her prayers had backfired, landing squarely and solely on Ada. 'So, who got the Virgin Mary's blessing in the end? Ada or Shona?' I asked, confused.

'Beats me,' she said, shaking her head. 'Maybe neither. Or maybe both. We'll never know.'

'Guess we'll have to dwell in darkness,' I joked, pulling her closer.

'Hey,' she said. 'I already dwell in darkness. And it's not such a bad place to be,' she murmured, raising her lips to mine. I closed my eyes and kissed her deeply. Maybe I was better off in darkness too.

Looking back on it, I realise now that I haven't said much about the sightings. But I guess my part of the story wasn't really about God, or the Virgin Mary, or a miracle birth, or even Father O'Shea. It was about Annemarie – who, in the words of Deacon Joe, really is a rare flower of a girl.

Maybe God picked the right virgin after all.

Acknowledgements

Special thanks to all those who read and commented on early drafts of this manuscript: Clive Bedell, Aurea Carpenter, Kate Leys, Lynn Curtis, Susan Hahn, Ben Twist, Katie Moore, Andy Carl, Susie Tinsley,and Patty Tobin. Big thanks as well to the hardworking team at Accent Press who, under the leadership of the indomitable Hazel Cushion, are rewriting the rules of publishing even as you read this. As always, I remain grateful to my agents for their continued support and sage advice: Felicity Rubinstein and Sarah Lutyens in London, and Kim Witherspoon and David Forrer in New York. Final shout-out goes to Cody Sands for pretty much everything: editorial advice from day one, cover designs for my entire oeuvre, and promotional help in the form of a truly inspired book trailer.

About the Author

Betsy Tobin is a novelist and playwright, born and raised in the American Midwest, now living in the UK. She is the author of five novels: *Bone House*, short-listed for the Commonwealth Prize and winner of a Herodotus Prize in America; *The Bounce*; *Ice Land*; *Crimson China*, a BBC Radio 4 Book At Bedtime and shortlisted for Epic Romantic Novel of the Year; and *Things We Couldn't Explain*. She is a past winner of the London Writers' Competition for her short story, *Joyride*. In between books she also writes for stage and radio. Betsy lives in London and Wales with her husband and four children.

Read more about her work at:
http://www.betsytobin.co.uk

Follow Betsy on Twitter: @betsytobin

Visit her Facebook page:
https://www.facebook.com/BetsyTobinAuthor

On Science, Miracles and Virgin Birth

This story is not as outlandish as it may first appear. Indeed, it is at least partially true: for several weeks during the summer of 1991, the small town of Ellsworth, Ohio was transfixed by a series of strange sunsets in which the Virgin Mary appeared to hover over the skyline. And during that period, a teenage boy did preach to the crowds who assembled there nightly. The similarities to my novel end there, but it is worth noting that sightings of the Virgin Mary have been reported for centuries, and a few have even been authenticated by the Catholic Church as genuine. (Or, at least, they have been deemed genuinely inexplicable...) Similarly, reports of weeping statues are legion.

Even the notion of a virgin birth is not as far-fetched as it seems. In recent years scientists have begun debating the 'implausible possibility' of a world where women could procreate without men. Zoologists have long been aware that some animals are capable of reproducing without males. What they have only recently discovered is that the list of species that can do so is constantly expanding: in recent years female pythons, hammerhead sharks, blacktip sharks, and Komodo dragons have all developed the ability to breed without males. And in the laboratory, scientists can now create healthy, fertile mice with no fathers. (For a good discussion of this phenomenon, see the biologist Aarathi Prasad's book *Like A Virgin*.) It may only be a matter of time – a very long time, admittedly – before men (through no fault of their own) become redundant for the purposes of reproduction.

In the meantime, there will no doubt be plenty more things we couldn't explain. Thank heaven for that.

Also by Betsy Tobin

The Bounce is an extraordinary novel of love, death and lions, set in the glamorous and squalid circus world of London in the 1870's. Nineteen year-old Nathan crosses the Atlantic in search of the mother who abandoned him as a young child. He takes a job in a circus south of the Thames, where he is quickly caught in a complex web of longing. *The Bounce* is gripping, vivid, powerfully evocative: a stunning story of mothers and sons, rejection and belonging, and the treacherous pull of love.

For more information about **Betsy Tobin**
and other **Accent Press** titles
please visit

www.accentpress.co.uk

Also by Betsy Tobin

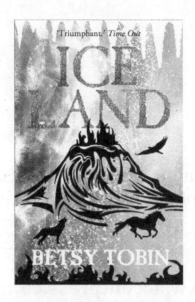

Set in the year 1000 AD, in the shadow of a smouldering volcano, *Ice Land* is an epic tale of forbidden love. Freya knows that her people are doomed. Warned by the fates of an impending catastrophe, she goes in search of a magnificent gold necklace, said to have the power to alter the course of history. But to obtain the necklace, she must pay a terrible price and sell herself to the four brothers who created it. Infused with the rich history and mythology of Iceland, Betsy Tobin's novel is a moving meditation on desire, the nature of belief and the redemptive power of the earth.

Also by Betsy Tobin

Set in seventeenth-century rural England, *Bone House* is the tale of two women. One is large, voluptuous and charismatic – a prostitute to whom many, not just men, are drawn. The other is young, slight and solitary – a servant whose quest to solve the mystery of the prostitute's death leads her to shocking discoveries, unexpected love, and the beginnings of a future.